T0025550

Praise for Book One

Dawn of Fire: Avenging Son

by Guy Haley

'The beginning of an essential new epic: heroic,
cataclysmic and vast in scope. Guy has delivered
exactly what 40K readers crave, and lit the fuse on
the Dark Millennium. This far future's
about to detonate...'

Dan Abnett, author of Horus Rising

'With all the thunderous scope of The Horus Heresy,
a magnificent new saga begins.'

Peter McLean, author of Priest of Bones

'A perfect blending of themes – characters that
are raw, real and wonderfully human, set against
a backdrop of battle and mythology'.

Danie Ware, author of Ecko Rising

THE GATE OF BONES

A DAWN OF FIRE NOVEL

More Warhammer 40,000 from Black Library

• DAWN OF FIRE •
BOOK 1: Avenging Son
Guy Haley
BOOK 2: The Gate of Bones
Andy Clark

INDOMITUS
Gav Thorpe

• DARK IMPERIUM •
Guy Haley
BOOK 1: Dark Imperium
BOOK 2: Plague War

BELISARIUS CAWL: THE GREAT WORK
Guy Haley

• IMPERIAL KNIGHTS •
Andy Clark
BOOK 1: Kingsblade
BOOK 2: Knightsblade

• WATCHERS OF THE THRONE •
Chris Wraight
BOOK 1: The Emperor's Legion
BOOK 2: The Regent's Shadow

RITES OF PASSAGE
Mike Brooks

• VAULTS OF TERRA •
Chris Wraight
BOOK 1: The Carrion Throne
BOOK 2: The Hollow Mountain

MARK OF FAITH
Rachel Harrison

EPHRAEL STERN: THE HERETIC SAINT
David Annandale

THE GATE OF BONES

A DAWN OF FIRE NOVEL

ANDY CLARK

BLACK LIBRARY

A BLACK LIBRARY PUBLICATION

This edition published in Great Britain in 2021 by
Black Library,
Games Workshop Ltd.,
Willow Road,
Nottingham, NG7 2WS, UK.

10 9 8 7 6 5 4 3 2 1

Produced by Games Workshop in Nottingham.
Cover illustration by Johan Grenier.

The Gate of Bones © Copyright Games Workshop Limited 2021.
The Gate of Bones, Dawn of Fire, GW, Games Workshop, Black
Library, The Horus Heresy, The Horus Heresy Eye logo, Space
Marine, 40K, Warhammer, Warhammer 40,000, the 'Aquila'
Double-headed Eagle logo, and all associated logos, illustrations,
images, names, creatures, races, vehicles, locations, weapons,
characters, and the distinctive likenesses thereof, are either ®
or TM, and/or © Games Workshop Limited, variably registered
around the world.
All Rights Reserved.

A CIP record for this book is available from the British Library.

ISBN 13: 978 1 78999 344 8

No part of this publication may be reproduced, stored in a
retrieval system, or transmitted in any form or by any means,
electronic, mechanical, photocopying, recording or otherwise,
without the prior permission of the publishers.

This is a work of fiction. All the characters and events portrayed
in this book are fictional, and any resemblance to real people or
incidents is purely coincidental.

See Black Library on the internet at

blacklibrary.com

Find out more about Games Workshop
and the world of Warhammer 40,000 at

games-workshop.com

Printed and bound by CPI Group (UK) Ltd, Croydon, CR0 4YY

*Thanks to Guy Haley for all his work, guidance
and vision on this book.*

It is the 41st millennium.

Ten thousand years have passed since the Primarch Horus turned
to Chaos and betrayed his father, the Emperor of Mankind,
plunging the galaxy into ruinous civil war.

For one hundred centuries the Imperium has endured xenos invasion,
internal dissent, and the perfidious attentions of the dark gods of
the warp. The Emperor sits immobile upon the Golden Throne of
Terra, a psychic bastion against infernal powers. It is His will alone
that lights the Astronomican, binding together the Imperium, yet
not one word has He uttered in all that time. Without His guidance,
mankind has strayed far from the path of enlightenment.

The bright ideals of the Age of Wonder have withered and died.
To be alive in this time is a terrible fate, where an existence of
grinding servitude is the best that can be hoped for, and a quick
death is seen as the kindest mercy.

As the Imperium continues its inevitable decline, Abaddon, last
true son of the Primarch Horus, and now Warmaster in his stead,
has reached the climax of a plan millennia in the making, tearing
reality open across the width of the galaxy and unleashing forces
unheard of. At last it seems, after centuries of valiant struggle,
mankind's doom is at hand.

Into this darkness a pale shaft of light penetrates. The Primarch
Roboute Guilliman has been wakened from deathly slumber
by alien sorcery and arcane science. Returning to Terra, he has
resolved to set right this dire imbalance, to defeat Chaos once and
for all, and to restart the Emperor's grand plan for humanity.

But first, the Imperium must be saved. The galaxy is split in twain.
On one side, Imperium Sanctus, beleaguered but defiant. On
the other, Imperium Nihilus, thought lost to the night. A mighty
crusade has been called to take back the Imperium and restore its
glory. All mankind stands ready for the greatest conflict of the age.
Failure means extinction, and the path to victory leads only to war.

This is the era Indomitus.

DRAMATIS PERSONAE

INDOMITUS CRUSADE

Fleet Primus

Roboute Guilliman	XIII primarch, the Avenging Son, the Lord Commander, the Imperial Regent
Maldovar Colquan	Stratarchis Tribune Actuarius, Adeptus Custodes
Isaish Khestrin	Primus fleetmaster
Illiyanne Natasé	Farseer, envoy of Eldrad Ulthran
Fabian Guelphrain	Historitor
Viablo	Historitor
Lord Kseyvorn	Groupmaster, Battle Group Orphaeus

The Council Exterra

Geestan	Militant-Apostolic, Adeptus Ministorum
Andiramus	Provost, Adeptus Arbites
Luthian Xhyle	Chiliarch of Rassuneon, Astra Militarum
Lady Filomensya Blaaz	Primaris psyker, Adeptus Astra Telepathica
Arfon Hoiditma	Inquisitor, the Imperial Inquisition
Belisarius Cawl	Archmagos, Adeptus Mechanicus
Dho Gan Mey	Rear admiral, Navis Imperialis

THE RELIEF MISSION

Adeptus Custodes, Emissaries Imperatus Shield Host

Marcus Achallor	Shield-captain
Hastius Vychellan	
Undeyr Amalth-Amat	Vexillor
Pontus Varsillian	
the Many-Gloried	
Menticulous Aswadi	
Ashmeiln	Mistress of Astropaths

Unnumbered Sons of Dorn

Racej Lucerne	Sergeant
Ghorias Kesvus Bheld	
Khastus Omecro	
Sulin	

THE DEFENDERS OF GATHALAMOR

84th Mordian Astra Militarum Regiment

Luthor Dvorgin	General, commander of Gathalamor Imperial Forces
Chedesh	Colour-sergeant, One Platoon
Yenko	Master voxman, One Platoon
Flens	Lieutenant, One Platoon
Dauver	Lieutenant, One Platoon
Vaston	Acting-lieutenant, One Platoon
Stehner	Staff lieutenant
Magda Kesh	Pathfinder sergeant

40th Phyroxian Tankers
Colonel-Chieftain Jurgen

The Order of the Argent Shroud, Gathalamor Preceptory

Imelda Veritas	Canoness
Gracia Emmanuelle	Palatine

THE INVADERS OF GATHALAMOR

Tenebrus	Sorcerer, the Hand of Abaddon

Word Bearers Traitor Legion

Kar-Gatharr	Dark Apostle, minion of Kor Phaeron
Tharador Yheng	Cult leader

Iron Warriors Traitor Legion

Torvann Lokk	Warpsmith
Harvoch	Champion of Chaos
Lorgus	Champion of Chaos
Casipiniax	Warpsmith
Yutil	Warpsmith
Fodov	Grand Battery Master
Jhorgg Klordren	Voidmaster, Iron Warriors void fleet

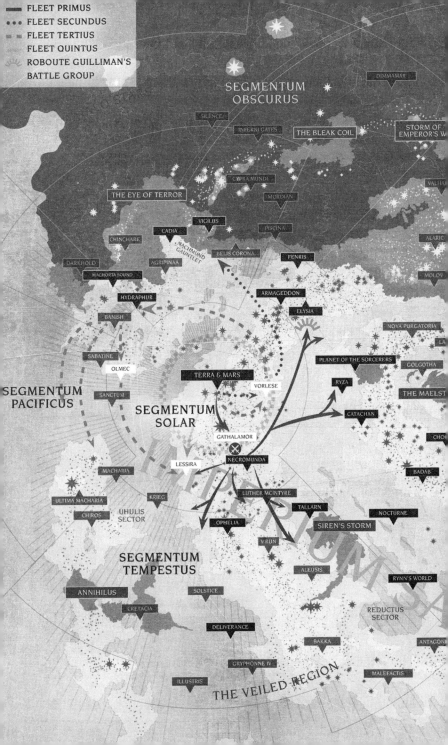

Legend:
- FLEET PRIMUS
- FLEET SECUNDUS
- FLEET TERTIUS
- FLEET QUINTUS
- ROBOUTE GUILLIMAN'S BATTLE GROUP

SEGMENTUM OBSCURUS

DIMMAMAR

SILENCE

INFERNI GATES

THE BLEAK COIL

STORM OF EMPEROR'S W

CYPRA MUNDI

MORDIAN

VALHAL

THE EYE OF TERROR

VIGILUS

PISCINA

CHINCHARE

CADIA

ALARIC

NACHMUND GAUNTLET

BELIS CORONA

FENRIS

MOLOV

DARKHOLD

AGRIPINAA

MACHORTA SOUND

ARMAGEDDON

NOVA PURGATORIA

HYDRAPHUR

ELYSIA

LA

BANISH

PLANET OF THE SORCERERS

GOLGOTHA

SABATINE

RYZA

OLMEC

TERRA & MARS

VORLESE

THE MAELST

SEGMENTUM PACIFICUS

SANCTUM

SEGMENTUM SOLAR

CATACHAN

CHO

GATHALAMOR

NECROMUNDA

LESSIRA

BADAB

MACHARIA

LUTHER MCINTYRE

ULTIMA MACHARIA

KRIEG

TALLARN

NOCTURNE

CHIROS

UHULIS SECTOR

OPHELIA

SIREN'S STORM

V RUN

SEGMENTUM TEMPESTUS

ALEUSIS

RYNN'S WORLD

ANNIHILUS

SOLSTICE

REDUCTUS SECTOR

CRETACIA

DELIVERANCE

BAKKA

ANTAGON

GRYPHONNE IV

MALEFACTIS

ILLUSTRIS

THE VEILED REGION

Chapter One

NEWS FROM THE DARK

GANYMEDE

VIGILUS

Fists beat against the gates. I hear them, feel them, a tumult of impacts, an avalanche of flesh and bone. Insistent. Unceasing. Screams mingle with the thunder of flesh on metal. Cries. Pleas for help. Lamentation. Barking voices demanding orders. Fervent whispers of hope as faith gutters and dies.

Other things, not human.

I stand in the shadow of the gates and upon either side of me waves rise. They are stone and boiling surf. They are madness made real. They rear high and close, only to melt away like mists. The stench of death surrounds me. I gag upon the reek of corpses. I retch smoke. The sky is dark, and all the stars run together like wax and swirl, swirl, swirl into a vortex. I feel its pull and fear impales me. I cry out, though I have no mouth to scream, no eyes to see, no body to turn towards the glimmer of light I feel at my back.

Hope. That light is hope, but it is not for me to look upon. Not now. I must listen to the screams. I must watch the curdled stars.

I must see what I am to be shown.

The gates must burst before the fury that presses from beyond. Chains stretch. Hinges groan. And what then, if I am caught before those sundered gates in the light of poisoned stars?

Terror twists in my chest. I must see. I draw closer.

Closer.

Sound bludgeons me, a roar of amalgamated pain, a chimera of terrors that makes me whine. Charnel stink enfolds. My skin burns. Dismay reaches strangler's hands about my throat.

I draw closer still. I must see.

I see. Each gate bears a brass plaque. They are small. Something like verdigris obscures their words and I know that this is malign and deliberate.

Closer.

The taint churns, becomes thick and dense to obscure all. Yet there is a torch, suddenly, a torch in a sconce set at the very mouth of the gate. I take it up. In its flickering flames I have the knowledge and the weapon that I need. The smoke rises, chokes me. I scour the plaques with fire, and the corruption falls away. It hates me for this. It will punish me. I cannot care.

The plaques are clear and I can see the words engraved. They mean nothing. I commit them to memory, nonetheless. I am the eye that sees, the listening ear, the quill and the parchment page. Others will interpret. Others will understand. I see, and I record.

Sangua-Terra.

Vigilus.

Translocuter First Class Tane hurried along the corridor. He crossed pools of stark illumination thrown by electro-sconces, quickening his step through the patches of shadow, wincing at the ring of his footsteps on the deck.

Lots of whispers about Ganymede, he thought each time he crossed the terminator between light and dark. It wasn't long ago this moon was interdicto extremis. He couldn't forget that.

They said that the moon was safe, cleansed of whatever had haunted its depths. They had been quick to excavate new corridors and chambers beneath the surface, filling them with cogitators and holocasters, the generatoria and datastacks and vox-arrays of the Officio Logisticarum. They had garrisoned Ganymede with regiments of Astra Militarum. There was a veritable army of priests thronging the central corridors, whose numbers rivalled the archivists, lexographers, numeromancers, adepts-materialum, prelates and countless other personnel. They trumpeted Ganymede to be the first of the hub-fortresses that would spring up behind the fleets of the Indomitus Crusade and provide an unbroken chain of support more ambitious than anything the Imperium had achieved before.

Such was Primarch Guilliman's vision, and they would see it realised.

'Well *they* don't have to walk these endless corridors, do they?' Tane muttered, clutching his aquila pendant with one hand and gripping a data-slate with the other.

He spoke to himself because it was better than the quiet, but only just, and the shadows seemed to lean in to listen.

Tane had survived long enough to know that when the Imperium decreed somewhere safe, it only meant acceptably perilous. He'd been on Vorliot during the withdrawal, making it to one of the designated safe-zones for evacuation. In his opinion, 'safe' was not the right word to describe anything that involved that many orks. After his recruitment into the Officio Logisticarum and subsequent assignment to Ganymede, Tane paid more attention to the rumours of malefic phenomena than he had to the moon's threat descriptor of *nil*.

A patrol of Valhallans appeared from nowhere, making him jump. The men and women offered Tane crisp salutes before sweeping past and off down a stairway. He hastened on, following las-etched signs for the Astropathy Transinterpretation

Sanctum. Ganymede was a maze, and even after weeks on station Tane still got lost.

Why so jumpy? he asked himself scathingly. A rhetorical admonition. Truth was, Tane knew what had him on edge. *I shouldn't have read it,* he thought. *Emperor knows I heard half of it from her gibbering anyway, but still...*

Knowledge is a burden, ignorance a blessing. The words had been embossed upon a steel plate a hundred feet high in his scriptorium on Vorliot. The motto had always angered Tane, for he was a curious man. The trait had landed him in trouble several times, almost fatally on one occasion. It eventually led to his induction into the logister corps, so the recruiting adept had told him.

Today, Tane saw the truth in those words. He wished, for once, to be ignorant.

Shouldn't have read it, he told himself again as he passed through a grumbling servo-hatch.

It wasn't as though he understood most of the astropathic communique anyway. He had never heard of Vigilus, nor Sangua-Terra. But images kept coming back to him, as vivid as though he had suffered the visions himself. She was a powerful witch, that one. Insidious, the way she spread her dreams about like that.

Best not to think of it. In that place, no one knew exactly who might be dipping into a man's thoughts. Ganymede was lousy with psykers.

Tane shook off his nerves and hurried onward. The astropath's duty had been to receive her vision, and it had left her slumped in the grip of a coma. Another adept had recorded it and another translated it. They weren't looking too good either. Tane's task, by comparison, was simply to hang about and convey the record of her words to the Transinterpretation Sanctum where it could be properly considered by wiser minds, then disseminated. Or not.

He reached a wider corridor, more brightly lit, but the oppressive feelings didn't leave him. If anything, they felt more intense. Surrounded by people heading to and fro, he retreated into his own private world of fear, and paranoia burgeoned.

He held the slate tighter to his chest.

The archway to the Transinterpretation Sanctum appeared not a moment too soon, and he hurried through it, and over to the immense admissions desk. A stern-looking adept in the green robes of the Adeptus Astra Telepathica gave him a distasteful look from on high. Gimbal-mounted rotary lasguns tracked him as he approached.

'I need to see someone,' he said. 'Someone important.'

'And who would that be, Adept Tane?' said the woman.

'Someone more important than you!' he hissed. He looked about himself as if he might be overheard. He would be, too. He was in one of the most secure places in the Imperium. There were always ears listening.

But secure didn't mean the same as safe. Nowhere was safe.

'I have a message. It's an important one,' he said. 'Someone needs to see it now.'

'Put it in the slot where you put all the rest,' she said, pointing at a lipped marble opening in the front of the desk. 'Get your chit, have it stamped, and go back to your duties.'

He gave her a defiant look.

'No?' she said. 'Maybe I should summon security, and they can explain the proper procedure to you.' She smiled unpleasantly. 'They'll use methods that you won't quickly forget.' Her hand moved towards an unseen button. She didn't like him. He didn't need to be a psyker to know that.

Tane took a deep breath. He wasn't supposed to know what was in the message. He hoped his masters could smooth that over later.

'It's Imperium Nihilus,' he said. He meant to sound firm, but he blurted it like a child with a secret he could no longer hold. 'It's a message from Imperium Nihilus, from a planet on the other side of the Rift. A planet called Vigilus. Don't you see? They're alive. The Imperium is still there. This message has to be heard now, by someone of proper rank.' He shivered. 'The primarch will need to be informed.'

'You are in no position to determine what the Lord Imperial Regent hears, Adept Tane.' The adept stared down her long nose at him for a long time. Then her hand, still poised to press, moved to another unseen button, and descended. There was a click, and the characteristic hiss of an opening vox-channel followed.

'I need to speak to Logister Gunthe,' she said, not taking her eyes off Tane.

Tane didn't hear the reply.

'Yes, I am serious.' She narrowed her eyes. 'Priority Alpha-Red.'

Chapter Two

A WORLD MURDERED

BONE-ROCK

THE MASTER

Gathalamor shook to the blows of its murder. They were shelling the surface again.

Tharador Yheng shut out the muffled explosions. They were unimportant. The conquest of the world's physical form was nothing to the subjugation of its spirit, and that was her business. The smaller noises of picks and spades mattered more, deep underground where her followers dug. Lesser in impact these blows might seem, but it was the working of shovel in bone that would change Gathalamor, and not the hurling of bombs.

Yheng breathed deep. Cool air slipped into her lungs, bearing with it the sweet taint of decay. She held it within her for as long as she could, for surely here, in the desecration of the corpse-god's catacombs, the power of the Great Four stirred.

She tasted it, the coming change. Sacred, to be treasured. She released her breath. The temperature in the catacombs could be predicted with total accuracy, so many degrees warmer for so many feet further down. She hated the certainty of that gradient, but it would change, and she was the catalyst of transformation. The cultists sweating at the dig face were the extension of her will.

Inconstant lumen light lit the dig, one of six primary excavation zones her people currently worked in that sector. From the others the noise of machine tools echoed, but here was only the sound of metal on bone-rock, and the sputtering of salvaged power packs accompanying every dip in the light. Her followers hacked at a tombfall of compressed bone hard as rockcrete. A pair of bored overseers in leather breathing masks watched them, whips coiled.

They had followed the corpse-paths deep into Gathalamor. The world was riddled with this labyrinth, deep into the crust and out under the seas, where the honoured dead of the Imperium were buried head to toe in stone-carved galleries. Near the surface lay newer crypts, their shrines candlelit, their marble floors swept and structures maintained by legions of sanctified servitors, until the invasion came. Below were the older places, the graves of forgotten worthies.

Down there the ways looked the same wherever you went, but Yheng had grown to adulthood on those paths, scavenging a life from the remains of her betters, and she knew each road by its subtle differences. She knew the hidden chapels, the unexpected gaps that opened into gargantuan crypts, where the bones of thousands of faithful were artfully arranged in grim mosaics, places where pillars of skulls gazed upon the tombs of nobles, where finger bones and teeth made up starkly beautiful battle scenes. Generals, heroes, saints, cardinals, great lords and ladies, the nameless dead of thousands of years of Imperial history piled one atop the other, until their sarcophagi cracked, and their remains were crushed flat into ugly strata of bone-rock. Collapsed sections had been dug through again, and fresh catacombs made, so that the dead were nesting within the dead. The surface was always changing to this cycle, as buildings succumbed to subsidence and were drawn down into graves of their own. Gathalamor's geology was given a frantic life by man's obsession with death.

Every corpse, even in the most modest niche, would have been a person of consequence. One would have to be, to find rest on so holy a world. But they were all forgotten eventually, whatever their faith or heroism. Where their names were commemorated by bronze plaques, they were tarnished green to illegibility. Stone rot ate engraved words. Iron signs were reduced to smears the colour of old blood. The air was perpetually moist, wetted by decay, rubbing out each method of commemoration soon after its installation. Tharador Yheng found that deliciously ironic.

The clatter of picks was far louder than the bombs. The planet stood firm. Down there, surface violence was softened to a tremulous beat. Stone shivered. Masonry creaked, but for all the sense of decay, the bone-rock defied the inevitability of change. This was the Imperium, she thought, a dark world of corpses, rotting and crushed by its own immensity, resistant only by dint of mass. Until now.

This would all fail. The catacombs would open to the sky, and endlessly mutable life would take the place of all this death.

All she needed was a little faith.

'The Dark Gods are with us,' she declared, her powerful voice echoing through the crypt. 'Gathalamor yields. Witness it, feel it! Let the Four guide your blows.'

The strokes of her followers faltered, as they clumsily offered her the sign of the octed. There were dozens, men and women, all dirty and tired, all stripped down to their undergarments and glistening from their work. No ventilation meant carbon dioxide built quickly, so their eyes stared from behind the fogged lenses

of industrial rebreathers. They looked upon Yheng with wonder, for by the grace of the Dark Gods she trod the catacombs
with no need for supplemental air, and her skin was dry and
clean. They were bent and ruined. She was perfect. Hundreds
of them had died already. They loved her for her perfection.

Yheng was tall and long-limbed, her skin pallid from life
underground, her eyes a piercing blue whose gaze few could
bear. Her colouring was exaggerated by the night-black robes
she wore. She was, by objective standards, attractive. Years
before there had been a boast amongst her bone-gang that
she had stolen her face from a noble, peeling it from her skull
while she slept. It wasn't true. She had always been that way.
In that kind of world her looks had cost her. Beauty brought
the wrong kind of attention. The wrong kind of worship.

She had responded with a calculated act of change. Finely
cut scarification transformed her elegant face into something
fearsome. Silver rings pierced her brows, the bridge of her nose
and the corners of her eyes. Fine chains secured by further
piercings cascaded from her scalp across her shoulders in a
softly chinking fall. Even Yheng's eyelashes were metal, replaced
with fine implants that rasped each time she blinked.

She looked through needled edges at her labouring followers. Much of the work had to be done by hand, so fragile was
the honeycombed stone. Machines brought down the ceiling. Melta cutters posed a risk from their effusions of scalding
vapour, which in the confines of the tunnels exploded violently.
Hand tools were the only sure way, and yet still they provoked
cave-ins. A dig team had fallen to their deaths when they broke
through a mosaic floor that hid a cathedrum below. Another
had been lost to relic-servitors. The vermin, too, proved a hazard, growing to several feet in length at these depths. Though
eyeless, they could track a human's heartbeat by sound and
strike unerringly.

Yheng didn't care.

These were her people. She had grown with them, resentful in the bitter earth at the beauty of the surface, told by the priests that they should glory in their sacred home. Gathalamor! The faithful travelled decades just to set foot there. Billions wore the corpse-roads as smooth as glass with their passage into the depths, to conclude life-long pilgrimages and leave offerings to favoured saints. Few found the succour they craved, before they were herded, shorn of purpose, back to the planet's surface.

Gathalamor was a lie. It was a prison. Yheng had shown them the truth. They loved her for that, too.

'They look upon you with reverence,' came a bass rumble from behind that Yheng felt as much as heard. Her pulse quickened, for she had not heard her master approach. It was a mark of his power. She shivered with anticipation, and the chains on her head jangled.

'To lead a cult is to be its guiding star,' the voice said, now right behind her. 'It is to be more than those who worship at your feet. It is to be the lens through which the magnificence of the Dark Gods shines.'

Yheng's cultists froze, staring fearfully at the presence she still could not see but which felt like a fist against her spine.

'I have taken power where once I had none,' she said proudly. 'I walk unmasked where they cannot, endure what they cannot. I do so in finery when they knew me in rags. All that I am I have taken for myself, through blood and sacrifice. I was born into stagnation and became change.'

'There is power in such sentiment,' said the voice. 'The Four see you, Tharador Yheng.'

'Thank you, my Lord Kar-Gatharr,' she breathed.

Only then did she feel the heat rolling from his ironclad form, and hear the purr of powerful machinery, and the crunch of stone beneath his heavy tread. What had been a voice became a physical presence. Kar-Gatharr wore the shape of a man, but he was so much more. He burned with a sacred aura that made her knees weak. She yearned to look at him, but would do so only when given permission.

'And they see your delay,' Kar-Gatharr said.

Yheng felt no fear, only anger at her followers. Sympathy, pity, empathy, fear – these were weaknesses. Each member of the Cult of the Blade Unsheathed prevailed on their own merits or was cast aside. If Kar-Gatharr deemed her work unsatisfactory, it was because they had failed her. She wondered whether her followers possessed the presence of mind to cease staring and return to their labours.

They did. The clatter of their tools striking stone rang out once more.

'Look at me,' Kar-Gatharr said.

Slowly, tremblingly, Yheng turned. He dwarfed her. Horns curled from his helm to meet in a twist of bone. The fire-wreathed skull of the Word Bearers screamed from his shoulder. Script ran across his armour plates that resisted reading. A black maul, four feet long, hung from a thong at his belt. His cloak was a shadow that flowed in winds she could not feel.

He was an Astartes legionary, a veteran of Horus' holy war, a Dark Apostle, a priest of the Word Bearers. He was the glory of the Dark Gods made manifest.

'You must work faster. The weapon will soon be ready. Lord Tenebrus lacks only the final piece.'

'Yes, my lord.'

Through glowing green lenses he looked back down the corridor leading from the chamber, towards the other sites the cult worked. 'Why do you spread your efforts so?'

'My lord, the omens are favourable but the maps are ancient and misleading. The way to the tomb is here. Exactly where, I cannot be certain, but I am sure it is here.'

The master made a harsh grunt. 'Dive into the deeper waters of faith. The pantheon will grant you success. Open your heart to them, and they shall provide,' he said.

Yheng heard his fervour. It matched her own, exceeded it. The masters lived for a span that mocked mortal lifetimes. Kar-Gatharr had had aeons to hone his faith.

'The gods have been good to me,' she said.

'Yes,' he said. There was a hint of a smile in his voice. 'I see that. You are favoured, Yheng.' He paused. 'I will guide you,' he said abruptly. 'I feel it calling. We are close.'

'Under your guidance, we will redouble our efforts.'

'I will be present at the moment of revelation. Pray it is soon. Concentrate your efforts here and at sites three and four. Abandon the others. I sense nothing there.'

'Yes, my lord.'

He turned and left her, his long stride crunching down the corridor.

'You heard the master,' she said when he had gone. She nodded to the overseers. 'Jaceth, Voten, speed their efforts.'

Her overseers activated the charge packs on their whips and whirled them overhead, sending hard electric light skittering over the bones and carvings.

'Faster!' she commanded, as the first blow cracked against flesh.

Chapter Three

GREATER FORCES

BROTHER-SERGEANT LUCERNE

DREAMS OF A BETTER TOMORROW

Historitor Fabian Guelphrain lay with his head upon the table. A few inches from his face was a glass of water. The water was a sign of his privilege. Water on board voidships, he'd come to learn, was even more strictly controlled than it had been on Terra. But he wasn't drinking it. He only stared at it. Nearby, his work lay neglected under a listless hand, parchment whose lines finished in a smudge of ink. A corresponding mark stained his fingers.

The *Dawn of Fire* rumbled its secret machine songs. The sound was comforting, soft, like breathing. He supposed it reminded him of his time in utero, on some unfathomable level.

And by the Emperor, he needed comforting.

Nightmares dogged him, though five nights had passed since Fleet Primus had broken its voyage to stop at this nowhere place. Even with Lord Guilliman's demands and Sergeant Hetidor's punishing physical regimen to occupy him, his mind returned often to dark thoughts. He re-experienced the fear that gripped him when the ship's arcane technology split the veil. There was a sense of insignificance too, but that was nowhere near as bad as the feeling of terrible things looking at him and... *hungering*.

Fabian had grown up in a windowless world. Claustrophobia had been an alien concept to him until he had sailed through the warp.

He had found his faith in the Emperor had increased of late. He was praying more.

He had no strength to work, so he lay with his head on the metal, weary to the point of numbness, and watched the water in the glass. Every so often a shudder would run through the ship, and send ripples across the surface. Otherwise the water sat still in the glass, and he saw it as a metaphor for the way his soul sat in his body, as if both luxuriated in the lack of outside disturbance.

Someone coughed at the open doorway. Fabian closed his eyes. Not a soft clearing of the throat, but a loud, wet bark: the efforts of someone who wished for a subtle effect, yet who was poorly equipped with the graces to manage it.

'Resilisu,' said Fabian flatly. His head remained where it was.

'Master, they are looking for you.' Resilisu's cracked voice was permanently on the edge of disdain, though he had a knack for keeping it just servile enough.

'Who is "they", Resilisu?' asked Fabian with a sigh.

'You know, master,' said his servant. 'Them.'

'When you say "them" you mean anybody who is more important than you are. On this ship, that covers around thirty thousand people, I'd say,' said Fabian wearily. 'At a rough guess.'

'Then I'm lucky to serve someone like you, master, who is more important than most.'

Fabian groaned. 'Oh, will you let me be. A moment's peace, please!'

'What are you doing down here, Fabian?' said Resilisu gently.

'There's plenty of space in the librarium. I can serve you better there. Nobody can find you down here.' Resilisu entered the tiny cell and approached his master.

'That's exactly the point,' said Fabian.

'Is it the nightmares?'

'It is the nightmares,' Fabian confirmed.

Resilisu laid a hand on Fabian's back.

'You've done well, master,' he said. 'You are in a position none could have guessed. Your father would have been proud of you.' He paused, and gave Fabian's shoulder a squeeze. 'I am proud of you.'

'Give me a minute. I'm waiting for something. And take your hand off me,' Fabian ordered. Though he did not wish the contact to end, there were standards to maintain.

'Of course, master,' said Resilisu, and pulled back his hand. 'I'm not certain that even a minute is–'

A squeal ran down the length of the ship. It was at times like that Fabian understood how immense the vessel was. It was possible to shut yourself away somewhere small and reduce the *Dawn of Fire* only for so long. When the hull groaned, the illusion vanished.

'It's coming. Wait.' Fabian sat up and looked upwards.

The vessel's engines growled. They and the reactor formed the largest theme in the ship's song. Despite the grav-plating, Fabian felt his humours shift.

'We're passing the moon of this world,' he said. He looked down at the water. 'It's big, almost as big as its mother world. When aligned, their gravity lenses with sufficient force to act upon small amounts of fluid.'

'Master...'

'Just watch,' Fabian said, intent on the glass.

The ship's voice grew deeper. The power systems thumped like a pulse. A constant juddering set into the room, sending its quivers across the water again. But that was not what held Fabian's attention. The water was tilting as a body, gently at first, then more extremely, until it was at a steep angle.

'Though we cannot see them, great forces are at work all around us. They affect us too. Can you feel the pull in your gut?'

'I can, master.'

'It is like history itself, unseen, yet of inestimable influence, and inescapable.'

The water slid around the glass, tracking the position of the celestial bodies. The ship's groaning quietened, and the engine noise dwindled. The water slid back down the glass, and levelled off again.

'And now we are past,' said Fabian. He drank the water.

'We should go now,' said Resilisu. 'The big yellow one is waiting for you.'

'You mean Sergeant Lucerne,' said Fabian. He got up and gathered his materials from the table.

'That's the fellow. The yellow one. He wouldn't come down into the scriptorium. He said he wouldn't fit, and besides, he wished you to be roused gently. I think he guesses why you come here. He's doing the decent thing.'

'Decent thing?' Fabian scowled at him. 'You're not affected by the Space Marines, are you? They don't frighten you.'

Resilisu scratched his head. 'Why should I be frightened of an angel? He's a reasonable sort. I like him.'

'There's no dread in you,' Fabian said wonderingly. 'You don't suffer the nightmares either. You're lucky.'

Resilisu's smirk dropped a moment. 'Oh, I don't mind the angels, but I have nightmares alright, master. I have those aplenty.'

They shared a long look. There was no need for words. They knew each other as only family can. Resilisu had served Fabian's father, his ancestors had served Fabian's ancestors. If either of them ever had children, the tradition would continue – something

Fabian deemed, at that moment, to be highly unlikely. All they had was each other, and a thousand years of shared history welding them together.

Fabian tucked his belongings under his arm and gave his servant a watery smile.

'Then you understand.'

'I never said that, master,' said Resilisu. 'I don't understand the nightmares at all, and I don't want to. It's enough to know that they scare the living shit out of me.'

Brother Racej Lucerne awaited Fabian where the scriptorium corridor opened into a hexagonal way-chapel. There was a score of scribes at work in their own, open cells, all vassals of the ship's quartermasters, but they ignored the angel only yards away. The sight of Space Marines on Roboute Guilliman's flagship was commonplace enough.

Resilisu went straight into the chapel, but Fabian stopped dead beneath the arch some way from the sergeant. During the month of the voyage they had spent much time together, but Fabian had not yet banished the sense of terror the angels provoked, and for all his familiarity that included Lucerne.

When am I going to get over the sight of them? he thought.

Lucerne was frighteningly tall, nearly eight feet, and his limbs were grossly proportioned to match his height. Power armour doubled his mass. Garbed for war, his shoulders were almost as wide as Fabian's outstretched arms. His size threw off the dimensions of the chamber. Fabian felt he could reach out and touch Lucerne though he was ten feet away, as if his brain was failing to process the unbelievable scale of the warrior.

Lucerne's armour hummed constantly, a sound that spoke of imminent action. His backpack gave off a steady heat, and a smell like ozone that mingled with the chapel's sacred oils and the strange, not quite human scent of the warrior himself. His red sergeant's helm was clamped to his thigh. He carried no gun but a blade hung in its sheath to his left, big enough to be a sword for Fabian.

There were tens of thousands of Primaris Space Marines in the fleet, and thousands of others of the older sort, although to Fabian they were virtually indistinguishable. Lucerne wore the shocking yellow of the Unnumbered Sons of Rogal Dorn's line. The pale grey chevron crossing his insignia showed that he had yet to be assigned a Chapter. His livery was so dazzling it made Fabian wince. Tradition maintained that yellow was the colour of cowardice, and yet no man who went into battle in a hue that bright could possibly be called so. Yellow was a colour that announced its wearer's presence, and bade the enemy come test themselves against him.

Lucerne had his head bowed towards the statue in the chapel's votive niche. The Emperor wore His guise as the scholar, in which form He watched over those who worked as scribes, a number of billions galaxy-wide. So represented, He sat enthroned with a quill in His hand, His sheathed sword across His knees, the ledger of account open before Him the greater weapon.

The shelf in front of the effigy was full of burnt-out candles and prayer-scrips sunk into accretions of wax; these were the usual, official sacrifices. However, Fabian noted that more personal offerings were present also, small figurines of plastek and metal, rank pins, drawings, ribbons and sundry scraps of cloth, even small glass pots with fingernail parings or hair inside, presented to the Emperor as pleas for protection.

The enigmatic face of the statue was well above Fabian's eye level. The alabaster had been scrupulously polished, and partly because of the gleam of the stone, His features seemed to shift in the candlelight. His blank eyes were disturbing, and His smile cruel. Fabian looked away.

Brother Lucerne's lips moved in final, silent prayer. He made the sign of the aquila over his heart, lifted up the Templar's cross he wore on a chain around his neck, and kissed it. Only then did he open his eyes. His armour hissed as he shifted position. To look upon Fabian he had to turn a full quarter, or his view would have been blocked by his pauldrons. Even so, his gorget obscured most of his face, though not quite enough to hide the smile in his eyes.

'Fabian!' he said. 'So you found him, friend Resilisu.'

'I did, my lord. He was skulking down here with the scribes again.'

The lines around Lucerne's eyes deepened. Resilisu hadn't said anything funny, in Fabian's view, but Lucerne was rather buoyant, for a Space Marine. 'Skulking, a fine choice of word.'

'What is required of me?' said Fabian.

'That you be present and available, my friend,' Lucerne chided. 'The Emperor's work is never done.'

'I assure you, I was engaged in His service,' Fabian said, and shot Resilisu a warning look.

But Resilisu was emboldened by the Space Marine. 'He was napping,' he said mischievously. 'Or feeling sorry for himself, I am not quite sure which.'

Lucerne put his hand on Fabian's back. His fingers spread across the width of Fabian's shoulders. 'We can't have that. We fight the Emperor's wars. Rejoice, for we do holy work.'

He winked at Fabian. Lucerne baffled him. He was enormously devout, unlike most other Space Marines the historitor had met, and yet he lacked the humourlessness of mortal religious humans. The opposite, in fact; Brother-Sergeant Lucerne had a surfeit of bonhomie. To a man of Fabian's morose character, it was particularly irritating, and made the sergeant all the more terrifying. Violence lurked behind his smiles. Good humour only prettified this engineered murder machine, it could not obscure his purpose.

'Why don't you go and neaten up our quarters?' Fabian said to Resilisu. 'You could use the pulse shower,' he said pointedly. Fabian had changed. He was bigger and stronger than he had ever been. He looked healthy for the first time in his life. He had muscles, and his flab had gone. He was also cleaner, and better groomed. All because of his new, exalted status as historitor to the primarch.

Resilisu had not changed. His personal hygiene remained dubious.

'I don't trust them,' he said. 'Waste of water.'

'How right!' said Lucerne. 'Conservation of resources is an act of service to Him on Terra.'

'But he smells,' said Fabian.

Resilisu scowled. Lucerne chuckled.

'What's so funny?' said Fabian. He showed no respect. Despite his fear and this being's otherworldly origins, irritation lit a strange sort of courage in him.

'Oh, my friend, when you are as blessed with the Emperor's gifts as I have been, you find everyone stinks.'

Resilisu bowed to Lucerne. 'I take my master's hint. I shall go and clean, as bidden. At least I do not hide from my duty,' he said, provoking another laugh from Lucerne.

'I don't understand this warmth you have for him,' Fabian said, as Resilisu left. 'He's only a servant, and not a particularly good one.'

'Are we not all servants of the Emperor?' said Lucerne. He steered Fabian towards the exit of the chapel. The door opened, and they went into a corridor where menials of the Logisticarum went about frenzied as ants. 'What were you doing down here?'

'I needed a little time for meditation, that's all,' said Fabian. He hugged his materials to his chest.

Lucerne glanced at his fidgeting. 'You're looking well, at any rate.'

'Better than when you first saw me on the shuttle to the *Zar Quaesitor*,' said Fabian.

'Indeed. I believe you were vomiting at the time.'

'Belief has nothing to do with it,' said Fabian irritably. 'I simply was.'

Lucerne laughed, and continued to push forward at a pace Fabian found slightly too fast. They reached a shaft where lifters shot upwards and downwards at worrying speeds, and catwalks criss-crossed the open space. A procession of priests walked along one, singing sorrowfully and dipping their icons in blessing at passers-by. Lucerne stopped by a lifter and summoned it, and then examined Fabian more closely.

'That was then. Now you are looking more like a warrior. That is good.'

'Then I suppose Sergeant Hetidor isn't wasting his time.'

'Men of Catachan never waste their time,' said Lucerne.

'He keeps telling me he is. Quite loudly, in fact. He doesn't use those words, either. He's a little more profane, shall we say.'

'A unique motivational style, that is all.'

'I wasn't made to be a warrior.'

'Who is?' said Lucerne. His pauldrons exaggerated his shrug. 'I was going to be a priest before Archmagos Cawl's agents took me from my seminary. We are all soldiers in the Emperor's eternal wars, praise Him!'

'Praise Him,' said Fabian quietly.

The lifter slammed down and the doors clanked open.

'In any case, you are making progress with your blade and pistol work,' said Lucerne, as if he'd had the information passed on in a taverna, and not delivered to him in exactingly detailed reports. He shepherded Fabian into the lifter.

'It wouldn't be my first choice of career.'

'Minding you and the other historitors would not be mine,' said Lucerne.

'Service to Him on Terra?'

'Exactly,' said Lucerne, deliberately ignoring Fabian's sly tone. 'Spinal processional,' he told the machine-spirit. A lens flashed above a bronze vox-grille, scanning the occupants.

'Compliance, Brother-Sergeant Lucerne,' a dead voice responded. The lifter lurched up. The whine of its progress rose to a shriek.

'There is to be a gathering of the council at fourth watch tomorrow,' Lucerne said. 'Lord Guilliman intends to press ahead with the attack on the cardinal world, but first counsel must be sought and given. He has a guest attending.'

'Who?' Fabian asked.

The lifter decelerated rapidly, and Fabian felt himself pressed into the deck. Lucerne was completely unaffected.

'You will see,' said Lucerne.

The lifter stopped, and the doors banged open onto a long mezzanine. The grand upper processional lay below. All the stacked galleries of the way teemed with people. A monorail raced down the centre, loaded with soldiers and bureaucrats.

'You must prepare first. You and Historitor Viablo have been selected to record the proceedings. A pivotal moment in the campaign.'

'Marvellous,' said Fabian.

Lucerne looked back again. 'Come, Fabian, be of better cheer. The darkest hour is before the dawn. Imperium Nihilus yet stands.'

The messages had started to filter out into the fleet a few days before. *Good news, so why do I feel so indifferent?* Fabian thought.

'And you have been given a great honour,' said Lucerne.

'It is an honour,' Fabian admitted. 'I am sorry. I will do better.'

They pushed out into the crowds. The Midway Bell began to toll. A massive thing of bronze the size of a battle tank housed in a cupola halfway down the ship, it rang out the hours deafeningly.

'But I still don't get why you give so much attention to my servant!' Fabian shouted over the din.

'Unlike you, Resilisu and I have in common dreams of a better tomorrow, historitor,' Lucerne replied, his bass voice easily cutting through the bell's noise. 'I find that affirming.'

'Resilisu is an optimist?' said Fabian in surprise.

'Yes.' Lucerne glanced back. 'Have you ever actually asked him what his opinion is?'

Fabian had to admit that he had not.

Chapter Four

THE WAY IN

YOUTH'S FLIGHT

GATHALAMOR'S GLORY

General Luthor Dvorgin of the Mordian 84th squinted into his magnoculars. 'I don't see anything,' he said, which was not so much the fault of the terrain, but of his eyes.

'Wait, sir,' said Pathfinder Sergeant Kesh. She was crouching on a leering gargoyle, dangerously overhanging the drop from the bell tower, but she was fearless. She cradled her las-fusil as if it were a child as she stared into the valley of broken masonry. She didn't need magnoculars. She was the best damn sniper in the regiment, if not the whole brigade. Her eyes were perfect.

'They've hidden it well. The way the land falls disguises the entrance.' She pointed with two fingers at what looked, to him, like a shadow. 'It's down there, I swear it. It's not obvious unless they're coming in or out. They've been at it for a week here, much longer than at the other sites.'

'They better hurry up and show their faces. I have a meeting with the canoness in three hours. It would not do to be tardy.'

'She'll understand, general,' said Colour-Sergeant Chedesh.

'We make a point of punctuality, or we're not Mordian, are we?'

'No, sir,' said Chedesh.

Dvorgin adjusted the magnoculars' focus, annoyed that he needed them to see detail clearly. His twice-broken nose made it difficult to situate them comfortably. The afternoon was wearing on, and precious little light got through the dust thrown up by the morning's bombardments, so Dvorgin could blame the gloom rather than his age. He still felt strong. Self-discipline and the mercy of the God-Emperor had seen him lose little of his vitality. He was, however, getting more irascible with every grey hair he found. Youth didn't last forever, as his eyesight was making him painfully aware.

At least the city was quiet for a moment, blessedly free of the orbital strikes of the Heretic Astartes fleet riding at high anchor.

'I'm sorry, sir. I was hoping they would follow the pattern of the last few days and change work gangs now,' said Kesh. 'I had it all worked out.' She was disappointed. She wanted to impress him.

Dvorgin knew he was a little indulgent with Kesh, but he allowed himself to be. 'I'm sure you did, sergeant. It's too much to expect this rabble to show any discipline. If I didn't trust you, Kesh, I'd not be here at all. The Emperor's spared my strength, praise His mercy, but not my bloody eyesight, that's all. I'm sure you're right.'

'Sir,' said Kesh.

'Master Voxman Yenko,' Dvorgin said, to the fourth and final member of the group crammed into the campanile. 'Have all sections report in. Make sure they keep their eyes open. I shouldn't really be out here. It would be a little inconvenient if I were to be killed.'

'Sir!' Yenko confirmed, and began contacting each unit in the recon group. The rest of One Platoon guarded the bottom of the tower. Others were dug in along their route of return. Coded pulse signals peeped out over the voxmitter. No direct vox. The enemy listened to every broadcast, and from Yenko's headset Dvorgin could hear the damnable drone of the enemy vox-blunt that so hampered their communications. Yenko had the signal amplifier on his master vox cranked up to a strength that would normally get them clear communications over the continent, but which was currently barely sufficient to coordinate troops over a few miles. At that level of broadcast strength, an intercepted signal would doom them all, but so would lack of communication.

'Damned if you do, or if you don't,' growled Dvorgin.

'Sir?' said Kesh.

'Nothing,' said Dvorgin. 'Vox-blunt's annoying me, that's all.'

Unable to spot anything of note in the shadow, Dvorgin switched his gaze to the horizon.

What a horizon it was. Gathalamor Imprezentia marched off into the distance in an interlocking pattern of streets that, from orbit, had reminded him of fretwork screens. There were so many spires. Beyond the drifting dust, the sky was grey with clouds shot with streaks of blue that ran like tributaries between the shrine-tops. On every side angels and saints stared down, wrought in marble, in duratanium, in whitewashed ferrocrete, bronze, gold, silver and exotic, alien stones. Gargoyles peered from crenellated walls. Basilicas and stained-glass prognostoria domes emerged from the stone crowds like breaching sea-beasts.

To the north, the low hills of Ascension Stair blocked out the sea. The space port that covered their flattened summits shimmered behind void shields. West saw the ground crack and plunge into the Canyon of Countless Blessings, which divided Ascension from the western districts, and then further off, the spires of the Temple of the Emperor Exultant, the macro-cathedrum that had been the heart of all worship on this world, now the haunt of the enemy.

When Dvorgin had arrived, Imprezentia had been glorious. The streets were rivers of pilgrims illuminated by flame. The city, the whole planet, was mile upon mile of fortified purity, wreathed in censer smoke. The processionals echoed to plainsong and prayer. He had felt his heart fill with pious joy at the sight.

Then came the Iron Warriors, heresy had reared its head, and that was that.

Dvorgin zoomed in, and the devastation became clear. War had toppled statues to tumbled blocks. There were holes in the skyline where cloudscrapers had slumped to mountains of rubble. Cathedra were fire-blackened shells. Macro-ossuaries had ruptured under bombardment, spilling billions of bones in stark white tangles that made many of the grand processionals all but impassable. Gathalamor was supposed to have been a haven from the madness engulfing the stars. Faith should have kept them safe.

Dvorgin had always trusted his gun as much as he had his faith.

Behind him, the muted bleeping of the vox continued as Yenko contacted the scattered units.

Kesh shifted suddenly. 'I've got eyes on enemy movement, mark the fallen spire. Forty-eight degrees, four hundred yards,' she said quickly.

Dvorgin zoomed in again. Numbers blurred on the focusing gauges. 'I still don't... Wait. Wait, by the Throne... Kesh, you're good. You were right.' Dvorgin pushed his forearm against a chipped block to steady his view. At such an extreme magnification, every pulse of his heart sent the image jumping, but he saw enough: a group of weary, half-naked workers in miner's gear were emerging, as if by sorcery, from the shadow. They came out in a long line, some two hundred strong, guarded by warriors in masks and clothing daubed with cult emblems.

The workers were covered in dust, and came out shielding their eyes, even against the dying afternoon.

'You say they have been doing this all week?'

'Since Firstday, sir,' said Kesh.

'Well,' said Dvorgin. He flicked on the magnoculars' record function and took a few seconds of vid. 'That is intriguing.'

'I can get in there, sir, and scout it out. We might find out what the bastards are up to.'

'Let's not be hasty.' Dvorgin keyed the off rune, and slid his magnoculars back into their case. 'Well done, Kesh. This is a most promising development.'

'Sir, if you gave the order...'

'Not yet,' Dvorgin said. 'We need time to review. That's my final word.' He got up and dusted off his trousers. The blue was filthy again, and it made him *tut*. 'Yenko! Send orders. We're returning to the Sanctum Miraculous.'

Chapter Five

SANCTIFIED MAJESTY

MORDIAN STEEL

JUST IN TIME

Dvorgin rejoined the units at the base of the tower and led the party off. The recon had taken longer than he had anticipated, and night-time outside the cordon was dangerous. When he got back, the canoness was sure to lecture him about this little expedition, but he did what he must. A Mordian always led from the front.

They left the cover of the bell tower and dropped into a drainage channel running along the southern edge of Processional Sanctified Majesty. The angled ferrocrete was strewn with rubble and the remains of the dead, but it was not blocked like the road. Kesh had chosen the route well.

A brisk march of two miles brought them to a small plaza choked with fallen masonry. More processionals radiated from it. Dvorgin rested at the end of the ditch. His well-drilled soldiers spread out to cover their position.

'You can call in platoons three and two, Yenko, make sure they keep low,' the general said, and motioned for Sergeant

Kesh to move up and join him. 'Kesh, take your squad up ahead, four hundred yards, brief sweep, pathfind only, no engagement,' Dvorgin whispered to her.

'Sir.' Kesh removed her peaked cap, rolled it up and put it into a loop on her shoulder, threw up the hood of her camo cloak, then slipped up over the lip of the ditch like a cloud-thrown shadow. Three others followed her.

Dvorgin looked over his soldiers. Their blue uniforms were dirty, torn in places, bloodied in others. Not the image the fiercely neat Mordians liked to give. Several of them bore minor wounds. Not one of them had survived without a few knocks, while weeks of half-rations and sleep deprivation had put hollows in their cheeks and circles under their eyes.

Yet those eyes shine still with good Mordian steel, he thought.

Every soldier's weapon was clean and ready. Their bayonets might be smeared with ash to dull their glint, but they were sharp. Gunners Iloh and Vence had lugged their autocannon all the way from the sanctum, and now they had to carry it all the way back, yet still they looked ready for the fight.

Motioning to his Guardsmen to take a rest, Dvorgin uncapped his canteen and took a deep drink, followed by a bite from a ration block. Around him, the others did the same. He watched, worried his regiment would not last long, that the promised relief would never come. They had been fighting on Gathalamor for months.

Let the Emperor take care of such matters, he told himself, not for the first time. *Attend to the foe at hand before you seek the heretic beyond the horizon.* He leaned back, closing his eyes, and drifted off for a moment, starting awake when Sergeant Kesh slid back into the ditch. Evening had crept up on them and the light was fading. From far away he heard the thump of artillery fire.

Kesh leaned in, her voice a whisper.

'Cult patrols sweeping this area, sir. I'd estimate thirty to fifty heretics in each group, small-arms only. One to our west, moving east. One just south of us but moving away from our line of advance. The problem is in the north, they're blocking Processional Imperial Judgement, and well dug in.'

'That is an issue. Damn heretics,' he spat. Dvorgin had never been an especially forgiving man, but since coming to Gathalamor his attitude had hardened. The number of supposedly loyal subjects who had thrown their lot in with the enemy sickened him.

'They're waiting for us,' she said.

'Were you spotted?'

She gave a small smile. 'No.'

'Right. If they're waiting they know we're out here, but not where. Did you see a way around?'

'I did, sir,' said Kesh. Her usually close-cropped hair had grown shaggy during the campaign and she smoothed her fringe back out of her eyes. 'On the other side of the plaza, there's a partially collapsed shrine complex that we can cut through to Processional Jubilation-in-Obedience. That should take us back to the southern outward pickets of Ascension Stair. The ground past the shrine is more exposed. Bombardment has flattened most structures in a mile radius. The buildings on the other side of the square here look whole, but it's deceptive. Past that, it's rough. There's a smaller group of cultists present, but I don't think they're expecting us to go that way on account of the open terrain. I am sure we can take them, and fight our way through.'

'Can we skirt around the exposed area, and avoid the smaller group altogether?' asked Dvorgin.

'No, sir. The bombed-out zone is bordered to one side by bonespill and to the other by a subsidence of catacombs. It's broken up all the way to the canyon.'

'Then we'd be separated,' Dvorgin said. 'Easy pickings. Can

we risk returning to the campanile and go back the way we came?'

'They'd find us for sure, sir,' said Kesh. 'This is the only route barring a major detour, and with so many cult patrols in the area I wouldn't advise trying to find another. They're waiting to ambush us on the processional, so if we don't show they'll hunt us down instead.'

'At least if we go the way you suggest, they can only reinforce from the north and south. That limits their options. On the other hand, we could be caught with no way out. We'll have to be quick.'

There was a series of muffled clatters and scrapings as members of Two and Three platoons returned from the buildings either side of Processional Sanctified Majesty.

'Is that everyone?' Dvorgin said quietly to Yenko.

The master voxman did a quick tally, and consulted with the group's sergeants, then nodded. There were some eighty men and women of Mordian in the trench now.

'The best way around an ambush is through it,' he said to Kesh. 'Provided you know it's there. Direct route it is then.' He didn't mind that so much. He had never been one for complex manoeuvring. 'The Emperor commends your diligence.'

'Thank you, sir,' said Kesh with a salute. 'Permission to range ahead?'

'Granted,' he said.

Kesh's squad vanished into the urban wreckage. He felt a surge of pride, and a lesser one of concern. He wondered if Kesh knew how much he cared for her. He knew there were rumours, but it wasn't like that.

He couldn't let personal matters get in the way. Kesh was the best trooper for the job. Dvorgin thought for a moment. He weighed his options, then beckoned Lieutenants Flens and Dauver to him, as well as Yenko and Acting-Lieutenant Vaston.

'We've got to take a longer route, and there's a little blockage to clear, nothing we can't handle,' he said, and explained the situation as laid out to him by Kesh. 'We'll move up through the collapsed shrine in two groups, and take them head-on,' he told them. 'Flens, you're beta. Take Yenko. Dauver, you're alpha, with me. Vaston, split your men between the two groups, your discretion, though I want you and your command squad in Flens' group. Alpha takes point, beta forms rearguard, then switch. Two-step, understood? Advance and cover.

'Flens, you don't bring your team up until we signal. I want you to come around and take the traitors in the flank when they think they've got us. We'll give them something to shoot at. When we're advancing, Dauver, we don't move alpha again until beta makes our position. If we're outmatched, rally point is group beta's position, then we form moving-square and press a steady advance out of the open ground. It'll be bloodier than routing them, but we should still make it across, if we can kill enough of them before they draw in reinforcements. Questions?'

'What if the enemy has breached the pickets when we get nearer to home? The northern group Kesh spotted on Imperial Judgement sounds dangerously close to the line. Why haven't they been dealt with by the outward patrols?' asked Flens. There was no anxiety in the lieutenant's voice, only the desire for clarity that was drilled into all Mordians from day one of recruitment.

'Unknown. If we are first to the edge of the line, and no one is there, then we dig in on-site and Yenko will call in backup,' replied Dvorgin.

He didn't elaborate on what might happen if the picket had been pushed back more than a few hundred yards. The enemy had been stepping up their attacks on the space port in recent days, probing Imperial lines in multiple directions for weaknesses. The space port was one of the last sites of Imperial resistance on-world, and he was sure the enemy were preparing for a major push. The pickets were supposed to be fluid. They were the outermost defences, as readily abandoned as defended. Keeping to fixed positions outside of the port void shields was suicide.

'Make no mistake, gentlemen, if the men there have been forced to withdraw a long way, or worse, have been overrun, then things will get desperate. It will not come to that. Your brothers in arms would never abandon their positions, and we've had no signs of major enemy movement while we've been out.' He looked at the dirty officers one after the other. 'There is no reason to expect such difficulties.' No reason, he supposed, except for the numberless foes who hunted the loyalists every time they ventured out into the ruins. No reason except that the heretics were surely winning the campaign for Gathalamor. Who was he to presume that the Emperor hadn't allowed the outer limit of their defences to fold?

Enough of that, Dvorgin told himself.

'Form groups and be ready to advance in one minute exactly,' he said. 'That is all.'

The Mordians divided up with a minimum of fuss. He gave the men and women in the ditch a tight smile.

'One last push, then it's hot meals and bunks for you. You've performed well. Let us make the Emperor proud.'

They all saluted crisply.

Dvorgin gave the order. Group alpha clambered out of the ditch and began their advance. The Mordians jogged low to minimise their silhouettes. They did not crawl, though it may have been safer. Dvorgin knew it pained his soldiers that they could not fight in firing lines, banners flying, but there were limits, and there was no way they were going to behave like Cadians scrambling about in the dirt.

They crossed the plaza at a steady clip. Guided in by Sergeant

Kesh's pathfinders, they took up cover positions amidst the rubble of the shrine complex on the plaza's northern edge. A view up another processional opened to the left. The wreck of a surface-to-orbit macrohauler rested with its prow wedged between fangs of shattered glass. The path to the right was blocked by slopes of broken rockcrete.

Flagstoned pilgrim-walks spread through the buildings on the north side of the plaza, making narrow alleyways. The skeletons of trees rose from bullet-riddled marble planters. Twenty yards to the left, set atop the shell of a shrine, a nest of spikes bore the remains of Phyroxian tank crews. The men and women hung like scarecrows, offerings, Dvorgin presumed, to the heretics' false gods. The sight repulsed him, but he was careful not to let his emotions show.

'Emperor,' breathed one of his troops.

Dvorgin's eyes narrowed. He expected of his men only what he expected of himself.

'Quiet, back there,' he said. 'Mordians do not quail in the face of heresy. We load our lasguns and exact vengeance.'

'Sir, yes, sir,' said the soldier.

'That's more like it,' said Dvorgin. 'Group alpha, provide watch fire. Have beta advance ahead.'

Signalled by pips from Dauver's vox-operator, group beta moved up. A tense moment lapsed as they passed Dvorgin's position and penetrated the ruins. The instant Flens' men and women had taken up cover and sent their own signal, Dvorgin ordered group alpha to press forward into the shadows of the shrine. The wind moaned. Up above, strings of singed prayer banners fluttered. The eyes of every soldier were alive for the slightest movement.

Within the shrine it was cool and gloomy. The last fingers of daylight reached through the shattered stained-glass windows, laying a bouquet of colour upon the grey. Nothing stirred within. They moved past the blackened bodies of pilgrims who had died praying for salvation.

They passed group beta, and Dvorgin called a halt. Again, group beta came up from behind and swept out a little to the right, their footfalls crunching on broken glass. The next time group alpha advanced, they clambered up a fan of rubble through the collapsed rear wall of the shrine and emerged into the failing day.

The bombed-out zone was more open than Dvorgin had expected. It had been hit hard a few weeks before, the enemy unleashing their weapons on the ground near to the Imperial stronghold when they couldn't get through the void shields. Dvorgin had made light of that at the time, calling them lackwits and laughing at their impotence. Now it was a problem. Practically no stone was left atop another. Beyond the blast zone the Ascension Stair hills rose inexorably upwards, the pinnacles of the Sanctum Miraculous on the nearside looking down commandingly over Imprezentia. The sanctum had been the primary outer shrine of the space port, and was currently the Imperial command centre. It was a poor excuse for home, but the glow of the void shields against the darkening sky made it a welcome sight. Unlike anywhere else for miles around, the windows of the District Miraculous still shone with lumen light.

'Nearly back, but that's a long way in the open,' he muttered, eyeing the blasted expanse in front of him. Their position atop the rubble pile was precarious. As Kesh had described, to the right was a plain of human bones fallen from a bombed-out ossuary. To the left, catacombs lay open in shadowy chasms. The destruction zone stretched for some distance, covering over the processional that once bounded the west. On the far side of the rubble field, the Processional Jubilation-in-Obedience stretched south-west to north-east across their line of advance.

Potentially a safe road, but any heretic forces there would surely see his Mordians hastening across the open ground.

Dvorgin fished out his pocket-chron by its chain. It opened with a fussy click, still perfect after all these years.

For the hundred thousandth time, he read the words inscribed across the inside of the cover.

> *Luthor,*
> *Make us always proud, my fierce protector,*
> *Marie.*

'Make us always proud,' Dvorgin muttered to himself. The sun had disappeared over the horizon and it was rapidly getting dark. He had just over an hour before security would be stepped up on the perimeter and the outlying bastions would open fire on anything they detected. Morning was hours away.

He shut the chron and put it carefully away.

This has to be done now, he thought. Dvorgin checked the magazine on his bolt pistol, released the clasp on the sheath of his power sabre, then flashed hand signals to his waiting soldiers.

Group beta took up firing positions along the rubble heap. Gunners Iloh and Vence set up their autocannon with practised economy, so that the long barrel looked over the ground beyond. Dvorgin rose into a crouch and gave another silent order to advance.

Kesh's pathfinders went sliding down the rubble first, raising puffs of mortar dust. At the bottom they made for a cluster of wall remnants. Dvorgin and the rest of group alpha followed. The general moved as quickly as he could, his skin prickling and his heart bumping against his ribs at the expectation of enemy fire.

The open space stretched forever. The sky was wide, the stars coming out spitefully to expose Dvorgin and his soldiers. The Sanctum Miraculous seemed more distant, surely at least a day's march away.

Dvorgin made it into the safety of Kesh's cover and tucked himself behind a wall. There he found himself eye to eye with a grinning skull set in a wall niche that was, miraculously, untouched.

'The Emperor protects, sir,' said Kesh drily.

'On this side of the grave also, let us hope,' Dvorgin replied.

'Yes, sir,' said Kesh, already scanning ahead for signs of movement.

Dauver's voxman sent her signal-pips. Group beta moved up, and swung wide to the left, out of sight of the heretics lurking ahead. They hugged the edge of the shattered catacombs, using it to anchor their flank, and took up station at the corner of a building that stood alone, its broken masonry jabbing at the sky. Dvorgin watched them through his magnoculars. Iloh and Vence broke down their weapon, lugged it into the cover of a wall-stub and set it up again, sighted across the rubble. The rest moved in unhurriedly and, despite their bright uniforms, vanished.

Dvorgin raised a hand and group alpha set out again. Kesh led them at a jog across a forty-yard stretch into the dubious shelter of a raised garden bed.

Group beta moved up afterwards, again hugging the broken ground to the left.

'Halfway, or as near as,' said Dvorgin. He resisted the temptation to take off his cap and dab at the sweat gathering on his scalp. *Emperor, if you have a little of your grace to spare, please shield us now,* he thought.

He got down beside Kesh.

'They're out there, sir,' she breathed. 'Off to the right a little, one hundred yards. They think they've got us.'

'Let's show them otherwise,' he said.

'Lure them out. My team will give covering fire.'

'Don't get left behind, sergeant.'

Kesh's grin flashed in the gloom. 'When did a Mordian path-finder ever fail to find her way home?'

'Very well.' Dvorgin peered ahead, but could see nothing. He gave the signal to advance.

He'd made barely ten strides when shots whipped in from the right. Bullets whined off the rock. Guardsman Hauer took a hit that shattered his shin. As he fell, another took him in the cheek. Lieutenant Dauver dropped onto his face as shots punched into his body. Dvorgin himself felt bullets hiss past. Ricochets sparked from the rubble.

'Down!' he bellowed. 'Return fire!'

Lasguns crackled. Clipped voices barked orders and requests for clarification.

'Enemy positions?' Dvorgin said, daring his vox-bead now they were found.

'Got them,' came Kesh's reply. *'Sighting now. Prepared to give fire on your order.'*

'Scare them out. Group beta, prepare to attack.' He took a deep breath. 'Alpha! Cover-fire, cover-fire! Up-up-up, men and women of Mordian!' he bellowed. 'The Emperor protects!'

Dvorgin felt a sharp sting as a bullet grazed his arm and snatched away a strand of gold braid from his epaulette. Blood sprayed his face as Guardsman Fetzmann was hit in the throat.

Kesh's squad opened up, las-fusil fire burning bright red pin-points into the gloom. He saw the heretics now: shapes rising up to get better angles of fire, then falling as they were taken down by the pathfinders.

'Advance!' he roared. His soldiers ran forward into the teeth of the ambush. Only a handful fell to the enemy's wild fire. More heretics were moving across to the Mordians' left flank, drawn by the snipers, where group beta lay in counter-ambush.

A deep, rhythmic thudding started up as Iloh and Vence raked their autocannon across the enemy's position. Figures in robes and grotesque masks were thrown back as rounds meant to put holes through tank armour blew them apart.

Then Dvorgin was in cover again, and they were nearly across the field.

Sloppy enemy discipline, that's all that saved us, Dvorgin thought as bullets and las-bolts flashed back and forth. *The ambushers are too eager. They should have waited until all our numbers were revealed.*

The autocannon's raucous chugging drowned out everything. The heretics were moving up, shouting out their blasphemies. Dvorgin risked a look. Either they were too stupid to see what peril they were in, or...

He had a sudden realisation.

'Group beta, beware possible rear attack!' he shouted into his vox-bead, giving a silent prayer his message would be heard.

He looked back. Sure enough, he saw movement in the dark: a second heretic warband coming around the foot of the bone-spoil drift. The sight made Dvorgin curse.

'Throne damn it, they've played the same cards as us! Ware, foes rear,' he barked. 'Flens, suppressing fire on the outflankers. Master Voxman Yenko, begin a repeating signal to the sanctum – if anyone is nearby, we need their aid. Platoons, form square on group beta position and prepare to move up on the Jubilation-in-Obedience, on my order, rolling fire.'

Volleys of las-fire flashed out at the heretics attacking the rear, accompanied by the foot-long shells of the autocannon as Iloh and Vence got the gun turned about. More las-bolts flickered across the open ground and felled several heretics attempting to creep up on Dvorgin. The square was formed in double-quick time. Massed volleys forced the first heretic group to drop to the ground.

Realising they had lost the element of surprise, the second enemy group howled and charged. They came in a rush of black cloth and twisted metal masks, clutching crudely stamped autoguns, shotguns with stocks of bone, and clubs made of rebar, wooden planks and femurs wrapped in razorwire. The first group then rose up too, and sprinted straight into the teeth of the Mordians' guns.

The enemy's ranks comprised everything from pilgrims to scriptorium clerics, vendors and labourers and sump-workers to fallen preachers and turncoat people's militia. Formerly subjects of the Emperor, now irredeemable heretics. Dvorgin felt nothing but satisfaction as his men scythed them down.

Dvorgin's men got off several volleys, felling a good two dozen, but the foe did not lack for numbers, and both groups closed on the Mordians simultaneously. Dvorgin intoned the rite of accuracy and fired his bolt pistol. A heretic's head exploded. Bone shrapnel peppered nearby zealots.

In moments they were on the Mordian lines, and the disciplined volleys turned into rippling firecracker pops of individual lasguns. The clash of bayonets against crude weapons joined it, and the hard thump of rifle butts on flesh. They were all shouting, the Mordians bellowing their devotion to the Emperor, the cultists screaming to their false gods. Dvorgin cut down a heretic, his power sabre breaking through the man's club with a flash of blue and cleaving into his body to leave it a smoking shell emptied of its innards. Dvorgin shook his weapon free and engaged a second foe, then a third. They were poor fighters, and he bested them easily.

The heretics' advantage in numbers was beginning to tell, however. The autocannon fell silent. Dvorgin finished his opponent and glanced across to see Vence slumped over the weapon. The outflanking group was nearly done with, but the first lot seemed to have greater numbers than he'd initially guessed. He made a split-second calculation. He didn't like their chances, but to stay here any longer was to be overrun, and he tailored his orders accordingly.

'Now or never!' shouted Dvorgin as another Mordian fell to a shotgun blast. 'Prepare to move square and advance, bayonets forward! For victory, or for death, in all ways for the Emperor!'

'The Emperor!' his warriors shouted.

The square began to inch across the ground, the night strobed ruby by volley fire.

There was a roaring from the sky, and Master Voxman Yenko cried out.

'General! Sir!' He pointed out over the killing ground, and Dvorgin saw five figures clad in power armour dropping from the sky on wings of flame.

'The Adepta Sororitas,' breathed Dvorgin in relief. 'Drive back the enemy! Give the Holy Sisters room!' he shouted. 'Redress lines! Protect the wounded! Gunner Iloh, get that autocannon firing! Stand your ground, sons and daughters of Mordian. Deliverance has come!'

The Seraphim fell into the melee like bolts hurled by the Emperor's own hand. As they plummeted into the foe, they fired twin pistols. Bolt after bolt burst torsos, ruptured skulls and blew off limbs. Death leapt from a hand flamer, catching half a dozen cultists in an expanding cone of fire that sent them screaming. The Sisters reignited their jump packs a moment before hitting the ground and rose up again, soaring on over the battlefield to deliver more of the Emperor's judgement.

To the north, lights slanted up into the sky as an Immolator rose up over a rubble pile, its tracks churning air, then biting into the rocks and bone as it slammed down and barrelled straight towards Dvorgin's beleaguered position.

The general blasted a heretic just before she could fire her

shotgun. A frag grenade bounced at his feet. Dvorgin kicked it
back towards the enemy so that it burst in their midst. He was
shielded by their bodies from the shrapnel, but the blast was
close enough that it threw him and several others into the rubble with bruising force.

Dvorgin's vision see-sawed, his eyes full of smoke and blood
and his ears ringing. He got an arm over a block and pulled
himself up in time to see a huge cultist rear out of the smoke,
his torn robes revealing a chest covered with scales and spikes
of bone. The mutant roared, and swung a length of metal down
on Guardsman Vyko's head. Guardsman Jurn cried out in anger
and raised her lasgun, only to take the backswing of the cultist's
club to the jaw. Her head snapped back, and she fell.

Dvorgin fired his bolt pistol, hitting the cultist in the gut.
The shell exploded, eviscerating the heretic. Still he came on,
screaming from behind a blackened mask, blood gushing from
wounds that should have killed him thrice over, club raised to
strike. Dvorgin raised his sword to block the cultist's blow, but
before it could connect, a sheet of flame leapt out to engulf the
giant from head to foot. His roars turned to porcine squeals and
he toppled, writhing, blazing, and was still. Heretics recoiled
from the flames, and suddenly the armoured flank of the Adepta
Sororitas tank was between Dvorgin and the enemy. The burning mutant burst under its tracks. The rear ramp and side doors
slammed open and a squad of Battle Sisters ran out.

'General Dvorgin, praise be that the Emperor brought us to
you – and just in time, it appears.'

Dvorgin looked up dazedly to see the Immolator's gunner
staring down at him. The firelight shining through the stained
armaglass of her turret-shield made her look like an image from
a shrine.

'Just in time,' he agreed. Bolter fire and explosions boomed
beyond the tank. His soldiers were exploiting the shock of the

Sisters' arrival to reorganise themselves into lines, and were shooting down the enemy. Black smoke boiled up into the night, along with the heretics' screams.

'General,' said the turret gunner, recapturing his attention. Dvorgin shook his head and tried to focus. 'Canoness Imelda Veritas requests you pull your remaining forces back to the sanctum. We will eliminate the heretics. She is waiting for you.'

'My thanks, Sister,' said Dvorgin, straightening his back and giving her a proper salute.

'All walk the paths upon which the Emperor sets them,' replied the gunner. 'If you wish to give thanks, give thanks to Him.' The tank ground forward, and the air sang as the Immolator vomited sheets of fire at the fleeing heretics.

The Mordians had done enough. Dvorgin pushed himself to his feet.

'Cease fire!' he called. 'Cease fire!' The order was taken up by his subordinates. 'Designate corpse-men, gather the dead and aid the wounded,' ordered Dvorgin as the sounds of gunfire diminished. 'I am now unconscionably late, and that will not do. Where's Kesh? Call in the pathfinders.'

There were a few moments of confusion as his men collected themselves. The dead were piled together, and would be burned. There was no time for proper shrouding rights, and they could not carry them back, but Dvorgin would not leave their comrades to be defiled. Minutes passed, and Dvorgin's worry for Kesh grew. It was fulfilled as his men were setting magnesium flares to light the dead.

'Sir!' One of Kesh's pathfinders came running to him, his camo cloak soaked in blood, face starkly shadowed in the bright white light of the flares. 'It's the sergeant, sir, she's been hit.'

Chapter Six

CHAMBER ASTARTES

A PRIMARCH'S THRONE

HISTORY MADE

Fabian was getting used to associating with the lords of humanity, and he viewed the coming meeting with more curiosity than fear. He and Viablo were installed in their scribing booth, in the raised gallery over the gate, before the great and good were admitted. The menials who had been rushing about to finish preparations left in twos and threes, and for a short while the historitors were alone in the Chamber Astartes.

The Chamber Astartes was a large cupola atop the superstructure of the *Dawn of Fire*. From his position, Fabian was able to look across the room and into the void beyond. Tall gothic arches of plasteel filled with armaglass made up the walls. The pointed roof was also transparent. The floor was inset with zodiacal designs describing the superiority of humanity. Three-quarters of the chamber's circuit housed stepped benches, one-third part of those oversized to accommodate transhuman attendees.

At the leading edge of the dome was a giant throne: the

primarch's seat, awkward-seeming, for its great size had been designed to accommodate the Armour of Fate. A raised stall held ten more thrones suited for humans; these were for the Council Exterra, representatives of the High Lords in Fleet Primus. Another seat, also large, was close at Guilliman's left hand – this for Stratarchis Tribune Actuarius Maldovar Colquan of the Adeptus Custodes. Finally, a third, human-sized throne was provided for Primus Fleetmaster Isaish Khestrin, this one raised up so that the top of it was level with Colquan's, and only a little lower than Guilliman's.

There was a fourth station at the front – though this was not a throne, but a series of sockets chased in gold – for Archmagos Belisarius Cawl.

All was as yet quiet. Viablo was busy cross-checking his notes, a preparatory habit Fabian did not share. Most of the last night, by the ship's reckoning, Fabian had been learning all he could about the cardinal and shrine world of Gathalamor. Such a big Imperium, he was discovering; such a depth of history. In his old role at the Departmento he had thought he knew far more than most, and had looked down on the masses ignorant of the past.

He knew better now.

Looking out of the windows at the majesty of Fleet Primus unmanned him. Twenty-six battle groups were arrayed in great formations against the velvet void. There was the world they orbited, a nameless ice giant about a pale sun, whose swollen moon followed it closely. Cracks were visible on the ice covering the world's seas. The potential for life beneath in the water; the power of the world's sun, feeble as it was; the thousands of ships, the endless night and billions of stars... The size of reality was overwhelming.

Names on scrolls were all Fabian had ever seen in the past. He had known nothing, he was nothing. His hand strayed to the amulet around his neck. *Forgive me, oh Emperor,* he thought.

The sheer scale of things dismayed him. The numbers involved. Gathalamor was only one of a million human worlds. It was settled over ten thousand years ago; it had hundreds of gargantuan cathedra, a population in the billions. On the main pilgrimage route to Terra from the galactic south, it had become an important place to the Imperial Cult, a world where countless of His holy servants were interred in vast necropolises whose catacombs totalled hundreds of thousands of miles in length. Trillions of pilgrims visited the world. Untold wealth was generated there.

Gathalamor performed a crucial role in the structure of the Adeptus Ministorum, being the seat of a cardinal responsible for the spiritual welfare of dozens of subsidiary systems. Old, rich and strategically important, there was nevertheless a stain upon its history. The renegade Cardinal Bucharis had come into power there, unleashing the so-called Plague of Unbelief upon the galaxy. The details were scant, as much had been suppressed, and it had been thousands of years ago. More deranging numbers. More history on top of history. And the story itself was frightful.

'Does it not disturb you?' Fabian said to Viablo suddenly.

'What?' The voidborn looked up from his notebook irritably. His neck was so thin inside its brace, Fabian feared it might break.

'The history of this place we are going to.'

'You mean Cardinal Bucharis?' Viablo frowned. 'I suppose so. It is a horrific tale.'

'You suppose so? He enslaved hundreds of worlds to feed his own vainglory. His faith turned to greed!' Fabian shuddered. 'Do you not think he is worse than most of the monsters in this galaxy because of that?'

'How so?' asked Viablo, though he made it clear Fabian was disturbing him.

'He used belief against the Emperor,' said Fabian. 'I know he was only a man, but the fact that he was not something more powerful makes it more shocking somehow.'

'Perhaps,' said Viablo. 'But men do not have to be able to bend steel in their bare hands to do great harm. I have found that evil wears whatever guise it deems best, Fabian. Xenos, daemon, or deluded mortal, it doesn't matter.' His pen scratched loudly. 'The story is never simple. Look beyond the tale. Think about the consequences.'

'What do you mean, Viablo? Bucharis was a bad man.'

'I mean,' said Viablo, 'what is good and what is evil is subjective. It is decided by the victor.'

'You're not condoning him, are you?'

'Absolutely not, but consider that before the cardinal made his great folly, Gathalamor was a poor backwater. Without the macro-cathedrum he built, and the shrine to Confessor Dolan, who helped overthrow Bucharis, Gathalamor would have remained insignificant. Now the faithful flock there. It is one of the richest planets in the southern Segmentum Solar, and a great bastion of the Imperial faith. History is rarely simple. You could argue that evil was the making of that world, and therefore evil leads to good, sometimes.'

'Then the corollary is that good can lead to evil,' said Fabian.

'Unfortunately, yes,' said Viablo. He went back to his work.

Fabian shook his head. 'I was so ignorant,' he said.

The scratching of Viablo's pen stopped again. 'Perhaps you should prepare for this meeting?' he said tersely. 'We do have a function to fulfil here.'

'You and I are different, Viablo,' said Fabian. 'I need to order my thoughts in my own manner.'

'By interrupting mine? Each to their own, I say, but I wish you could do it quietly.'

Fabian let him be, and sat back down. He grimaced. The gallery was fine to look at, but painful to occupy. There was not enough room to sit with his legs out in front of him, and his knees rubbed on the back of the box panelling. As this was heavily carved inside as well as out, it was highly uncomfortable.

A low, mournful blast sounded from the horns mounted beneath the gallery, making the wooden structure shake. A babble of voices followed, and men and women began to stream into the chamber.

'It's beginning,' said Fabian. He reached for his writing materials.

'Then look sharp, historitor,' said Viablo. He closed his notebook. 'History is about to be made, and we are the ones to record it.'

Chapter Seven

LORDS OF FLEET PRIMUS

XENOS

A WARNING

They came in then, the great and powerful of Fleet Primus, the groupmasters, generals, bureaucrats, captains, magi, admirals and all the others in their braided pomp. The purr of power armour insinuated itself into the babble of voices as Space Marines clanked in and took their places. Lucerne had said that while on campaign, Space Marines performed all their duties in their battleplate, in case the need for action arose. Occasionally Fabian would see them in robes, but they were hardly less daunting unarmoured.

The Space Marines arrived en masse, and took up their over-sized benches together. Armour of clashing liveries made a lurid display, more so as each one of the giants was bedecked with honours. Collectively, these men had millennia of fighting experience, for they were veterans of long standing, and there were only a few of the Primaris type among them. For the time being, the Space Marines of Cawl's Gift were firmly under the command of the older sort.

Fabian noted all this down in shorthand on parchment. His data-slate read his hand movements and recorded it in its simple mind. The slate read the words and passed commands to a small drone fashioned in the shape of a hound's skull, and this hovered amidst the flock of cyber-constructs growing under the dome, recording audex and taking picts to supplement the historitor's work. Viablo had a skull of his own, and their unique paths revealed the preferences of their masters.

The chamber was almost full when a hush fell. It was so pronounced that Fabian half rose to peer over the edge of the gallery to see why, and found himself looking directly onto the head of Stratarchis Tribune Maldovar Colquan. This being, striding now towards his throne, his auramite armour casting scintillations across the stars, had stood in the presence of the Emperor Himself. He had seen Him with his own eyes. Fabian felt nauseous at the thought. He fell back into his seat, shivering, and was gratified to see the tribune's arrival had had a similar effect on Viablo, who sat, pen motionless, as Colquan took his throne.

Cawl clattered in next, accompanied by his own swarm of servo-skulls and sundry other devices. He stopped and exchanged words with others coming into the room, like an old man in a district market and not one of the most powerful beings in the Imperium.

Colquan took off his conical helm and rested it on his knee, revealing a face so judgemental Fabian couldn't look at it. When he tried to sketch it his trembling fingers refused. Cawl slithered to his input dock, and pressed his bewildering array of limbs into the sockets.

When the rest of the audience had filled the benches, trumpets sounded, and the chanting of priests welled up from the corridor outside the chamber. In came a solemn procession, shrouded in clouds of incense vomited by skull-faced cherubim.

Behind the priests went nine of the lords of the Council Exterra. Swathed in clouds of scented smoke, they took their places in their stand.

Militant-Apostolic Geestan, a truly ancient creature who represented the Adeptus Ministorum, creaked to his feet and began a lengthy blessing. Fabian tasked his cyberdrone with recording it while he watched the reactions of the people gathered there. They ranged from boredom to rapture. Colquan stared ahead stonily. Cawl seemed occupied with some business of his own, though he performed it with respectful quiet. Most of the mortals in the room bowed their heads. The Space Marines waited, their engineered faces blank.

Eventually, Geestan sat back down. The priests left, and Guilliman came in.

The primarch arrived with only two Ultramarines of his Victrix Guard. He strode with the purpose of an efficient man who finds himself unusually busy. The guards peeled off either side of his throne where they stood to attention, boltguns across their chests. Guilliman turned about, gathered up his cloak, and sat down. He was enormous, but his presence outdid his physical size, his soul pushing at them all, as if there were not room enough in the chamber to contain him.

'My lords and ladies,' Roboute Guilliman said without preamble, as Fabian had come to expect. 'We find ourselves delayed. Some of you are aware of the reasons why. For those of you who are not, I shall now explain.

'Shortly after leaving Vorlese, our psykers reported a building disquiet about the coming battle for Gathalamor. These ranged from visions interrupting astropathic communication to repeated, identical spreads of the Emperor's Tarot observed by the fleet cartomancers. Those who know me well know I do not put much stock in such scryings, but they have been consistent enough that we must assume something is amiss. We have had no message from the holding force I deployed upon the world. There is, according to our seers, a rising disturbance in the warp occurring around the system that is barring communication. Our prognostications were dire, but imprecise, so I sent for aid. That is why we came out of the warp. The herald of the one I petitioned has arrived.'

He looked around the room.

'The nature of this herald will appal some of you. You will not voice this opinion. You may feel the need to show your loyalty to the Emperor by displaying aggression. You will not. You will receive this emissary with cordiality, and you will listen to what he has to say with respect. He and his people are not to be harmed while they are here. Any man or woman who takes it upon themselves to act against our guests will be found out, and they will answer to me.'

He asked for no understanding, but looked around the room again, silently conveying the sincerity of his threat.

'Provost Andiramus, please bring our guest into the Chamber Astartes.'

The sound of a single set of marching feet approached, though two figures emerged into Fabian's view. The first was a high-ranking judge of the Adeptus Arbites resplendent in white armour. The second Fabian took for a man, though only for an instant.

It had a humanoid shape, two arms, legs and a head. Its body was proportioned similarly to a human being's, but not the same. It was too thin, too elegant – but beyond its form, its manner of movement gave it away. No man or woman walked so precisely. It moved soundlessly despite its trailing robes and the dozens of angular charms hanging from cords all about its armour. Then there was the smell: spicy and sweet, faint and not unpleasant, but the revelation it brought made Fabian recoil.

'Xenos,' he said. His hand stopped moving across the page.
He was not the only one to voice the word.

Xenos. It whispered around the chamber. Colquan tensed, even he unable to disguise his shock.

He didn't know, thought Fabian.

The alien's gear was outlandish. A tall helm with a curved, forward-pointed crest, huge eye-lenses of deep green reminiscent of an insect or a deep-dwelling fish. It wore a dull gem upon its front as big as Fabian's fist, carried a tall staff topped with a geometric symbol inset with another gem, this one shifting with a treacherous light. At its waist was a bizarre gun with a flaring back and a fluted snout, and a slender power sword.

Fabian looked on in horror. It carried weapons in front of the son of the Emperor! All his life he had been told to loathe the alien; here was one in front of him, and it was armed. Hatred was his automatic response.

Whispers hissed around the gathering.

'You will be silent!' Guilliman said, and the voices dropped, though the tension remained thick.

The arbitrator went to his place among the other lords of the council. The xenos approached the front of the room. Guilliman did not move. Fabian felt a sick panic. This thing could strike at any time, and yet Guilliman did not move!

The xenos stopped before the throne and performed a complex series of gestures with its hands. Black robes rustled but still its charms did not rattle. It bowed, and then, to gasps all around, it dared make the holy sign of the aquila. It reached up and unclasped the front of its strange helm. Its gorget shrank back into the high collar of its robes. Fabian could not see its face yet, but had an impression of a long skull, pointed ears of near-translucent flesh, and a high topknot of black hair fine as silk.

'My greetings to you, Lord Guilliman, son of the Anathema,

humanity's hope. My people's hope. Our ally, our friend.' It spoke Gothic flawlessly, but with a musicality that made the words seem vile. 'Eldrad Ulthran sends his greetings to you, his old and valued friend.' It got down on one knee. This was done stiffly, unlike all its other movements, as if the alien had to force itself to kneel.

Viablo recovered his wits first. 'Write!' he hissed from behind Fabian. 'Write down what it says! This is important!'

'You are well received, farseer,' said Guilliman to the alien, then he addressed his generals. 'Lest any one of you believe that this noble guest of ours interferes in the affairs of humanity without cause, let it be said again that I called upon his master, and that he comes here knowing of the danger it represents to him. If you cannot look past his heritage, then at least acknowledge his courage, and hear his message.'

Guilliman rose from his throne. The alien was tiny compared to the majesty of the armoured primarch, yet weirdly he seemed apart from him, as if they did not occupy the same frame in time and space, and in that he appeared even more dangerous.

'Rise,' said Guilliman. The xenos stood, and turned around. For the first time in his life, Fabian looked a member of another intelligent species in the face.

It appeared to be male, though its features were androgynous, pinched, with a sharp chin like a child's and a blade of a nose. Its eyes were too big for its face, and almost completely black, with only a hint of white in the corners. It was a caricature of a human being, drawn by someone trying to accentuate human beauty, and failing, making it ugly and hateful instead.

'We welcome you, Illiyanne Natasé of Craftworld Ulthwé,' Guilliman said. He pronounced the name strangely, speaking like the alien did, and that struck Fabian as grotesque.

'Lords and ladies of the Imperium, I greet you in return,' said Natasé.

palpable, yet the aeldari stood firm in front of it.

'This news I bring you I saved for your ears. Even your primarch, Lord Guilliman, has not yet heard all that has come to pass. Firstly, I tell you that your empire persists on the other side of the Rift.'

A murmur went around the room.

'My kind are at war there, as are yours. This–'

A commodore of the Navy shot to his feet. The aeldari turned his disturbing face towards him.

'Lord Guilliman has already confirmed that Imperium Nihilus stands.'

The alien cocked his head. 'Is this true?' he asked the primarch.

Guilliman inclined his head. 'We learned not a few weeks past.'

An unreadable expression flickered across Natasé's face. 'Then that is ill news. The skein suggested you did not know.'

'Not only do we know,' said the commodore, 'after the first news, we received many messages from the far side of the Rift, some of which detail military actions by your people against ours!'

Uproar broke out in the chamber.

'And I do not speak of just any faction of your perfidious kind, but the black-clad warriors of Ulthwé!' shouted the officer over the tumult.

'Murderer!'

'Xenos scum!'

'They cannot be trusted. We have never trusted the aeldari!'

'Not only a xenos, but a xenos witch!'

'Silence!' boomed Guilliman. His voice was a weapon that slew all complaint. Quiet fell instantly. 'I told you to hear him out,' said Guilliman. 'Without his master, I would still be trapped in stasis. Do not forget this.' He turned to Natasé. 'Perhaps we are not so helpless as your people sometimes believe,' Guilliman said. His words fell into the silence like dropped iron bars.

'Perhaps,' said Natasé blankly. Fabian could still not read his expression. He was cold, lacking human emotion. 'Though our seers are more skilled than yours. For this reason, you should listen to me,' he said.

'Why should we?' said a voice from the Council Exterra. Luthian Xhyle, Chiliarch of Rassuneon, and designated representative of the Lord Commander Militant of the Astra Militarum.

Guilliman turned towards him. 'Because I say you should. Would you defy my command, Lord Xhyle?'

'But my lord, we cannot trust them!' protested Xhyle. 'I accept full responsibility for saying this, but someone must speak out.' Sweat trickled down from beneath Xhyle's shako. He shook with the effort of looking the primarch in the face. 'Many of us here have fought the aeldari. I admit that they have been our allies at times in the past, but only when it suited them.'

'Then you are saying that they brought me back because it suited them?' said Guilliman neutrally. His words covered a dangerous gulf. Xhyle bravely stepped into it.

'Yes,' he said.

Cawl chuckled to himself, as if he were amused by a private joke, or communicating with someone else and not paying attention to what went on in the chamber.

'It was the Emperor's will that you return,' said Xhyle. 'He used them as His instrument, but the aeldari are not selfless. They did not do it for the sake of humanity. They are cruel, and cold, and regard us as little better than animals. I know. I have faced them on the battlefield. I have spoken with their leaders. This is the greatest military force the galaxy has seen since the Emperor left Terra and retook the stars. Why do we need them now?'

'You are right,' said Guilliman, and though he continued

speaking as if he addressed his fellow humans, his words were meant for the aeldari. 'I have known Eldrad Ulthran since the days of the Great Crusade. He and I have made common cause more than once, but I do not trust him. I do not trust one of them. We fight to save our species, they fight to save theirs. It is an evolutionary struggle, and in that there can be no true friends. I know that if their prognostications demanded it, they would do all they could to wipe us all out without a second thought. I suspect some members of some of their nations have tried.'

He looked at the farseer.

'Know, Natasé, that although I extend to you full hospitality, and I swear you shall not be harmed while you are here, and that I have great respect for Eldrad Ulthran, I know your kind. Choose your words carefully. Speak truth, if you can.' He loomed over the farseer. 'Know that although the Lady Yvraine and Farseer Ulthran were instrumental in bringing me back, I will not be manipulated by any of you. Xhyle is correct. The wrath of humanity is roused like at no other time. We could crush your species root and branch if it pleased us.'

He looked around the room.

'But it does not please us to do so. For too long the foes of Chaos have been foes to each other, when they should have been allies. Both human and aeldari stand on the precipice of extinction. The galaxy teeters on the brink of annihilation. Now, more than ever, our goals are in accord. That is why these people brought me back. Because the aeldari know they cannot win without us. Without mankind, they are doomed, while we need all the aid we can find. Some have likened we primarchs to weapons,' he said. 'And it may be that the cabal of sorcerers who rule their peoples thought to employ me as one. But be aware, aeldari, if I am a weapon, I was not one made by your kind. I have a will of my own.'

He turned around and went back to his throne. There he sat again, and raised his hand.

'Now tell us what you came to tell us.'

Natasé waited as if all this talk were the jabbering of ill-behaved children. He cast his alien gaze about to see if any more disobedience was coming, then spoke.

'You risk disaster at the Gate of Bones,' he said. 'The skein reveals a confluence of dire events. A psychic storm brews at the world you call Gathalamor.'

'Could this be an attempt to extend the Rift, as we saw at the Machorta Sound and elsewhere?' Primaris Psyker Lady Filomensya Blaaz spoke now, the representative of the Adeptus Astra Telepathica, an old woman whose spare frame hid immense power. She addressed the aeldari directly, and earnestly.

Natasé cocked his head at her. 'You have seen this?'

'I have seen something,' she said.

'You are strong in the warp, but your skills are poorly refined. My species had been using the sea of souls for tens of millions of Terran years before your ancestors had even evolved. It was our undoing, and because of that we know its currents better than you. This is not an attempt to tear time and space and let out the waters from the othersea. We have witnessed a great outpouring of horror emanating from a point in time exactly twenty-six days from now. The way I can describe it to you, in your limited tongue, is of a stirring of souls, and a betrayal of faith.'

'Souls living or dead?' said Blaaz.

'Your division is superfluous to our eyes, but you would call it a disturbance of the dead,' said Natasé.

'This is preposterous,' said the Inquisitorial deputy, Arfon Hoiditma. He was small, dark-skinned, with yellow eyes of ferocious intensity.

'Is it?' said Blaaz. 'Are the holy powers of the Emperor a joke to you too, or the vile sorceries of the Archenemy? This being may be a creature of dubious truths, but he is powerful.' She turned watery eyes onto Natasé. 'I can feel it.'

'He is a witch and a xenos, and though you are only a witch,' Hoiditma said, 'you are still a witch.'

'In a certain sense, our astropaths are witches, our Navigators, many of the people we rely on to maintain the Emperor's most holy realm,' said Geestan. He smiled, his face wrinkling further. 'They are touched by the God-Emperor in order to be ordained fit for their purpose. Lady Blaaz has stood in His presence and withstood His power. Can you say the same, Inquisitor Hoiditma?'

The inquisitor looked away, muttering.

'This is difficult for you to understand,' said Guilliman, 'even though many of you have faced the agents of the Ruinous Powers in the past. But I must make it clear that we are not fighting armies alone. We are fighting gods. It took my brothers and I far too long to understand this in the last great war, and it almost cost us everything. I do not make the same mistake twice.' He paused. 'Xhyle, inform us of the current military strength present upon Gathalamor.'

Cawl seemed to find interest in the conversation finally.

'If I may?' he said pleasantly. A limb unfolded from his back. Eyelid shutters clicked open over a lens, and a hololithic display of the Gathalamor System spread below the dome. Cawl frowned at the large number of cyber-constructs floating through his image, and let out a binharic screech that scattered them.

'Much better,' he said.

'My thanks, archmagos dominus,' said Xhyle. 'I–'

'Not at all,' said Cawl.

Xhyle nodded. 'Then we shall take a look at the last reported strategic–'

'I am happy to be useful,' Cawl said.

'Belisarius,' warned Guilliman.

'Of course,' said Cawl. 'I shall be quiet now.'

'Continue, Chiliarch Xhyle,' said Guilliman. 'And speak freely in front of Farseer Natasé. Let him see the power of the forces at our disposal, as a token of trust.'

'My lord,' said Xhyle. 'I cannot–'

'Freely and openly, chiliarch,' said Guilliman.

'As you will,' Xhyle said reluctantly.

The system of Gathalamor floating above the gathering was a number of worlds around a healthy, orange star.

'As we are all aware, Gathalamor is one of the key warp nexuses that have come into being since the Great Rift opened,' said Xhyle. 'Most of the principal warp routes employed for the last ten millennia have been greatly disrupted, and new, strategically vital confluences of fast currents have come to rest beneath different planetary systems. Of the eight proximate to Terra, seven are currently in the hands of the enemy – all, in fact, except Vorlese. Olmec was supposed to be taken by Fleet Tertius before it was diverted to the Machorta Sound, though Tertius should now be en route to that world and we expect news of its taking soon. Fleet Quintus was designated to fall upon Lessira, but was delayed. Indeed, with our layover here, the crusade as a whole finds itself in an overall state of delay.'

He paused.

'Gathalamor is home to one of these nexuses, and the key to Fleet Primus' breakout from Sol. The plan was to take it, then divide Fleet Primus into battle groups, enacting simultaneous strikes in conjunction with Quintus and Tertius across multiple theatres in this segmentum and the Segmentum Pacificus while Fleet Secundus took the slow road to the Eye of Terror. Problems with Quintus and the diversion of Tertius mean that plan hangs by a thread. If we are successful here, then it may be the initial strikes of Tertius and Primus may still be somewhat coordinated. Having secured these relatively peaceful parts of Imperium Sanctus, then the crusade would have been able to accelerate territorial reacquisition.' He paused for effect. 'If we do not take Gathalamor, that plan will fail. Furthermore, by revealing our assets piece by piece, we will have given the enemy time to reorganise his disposition, making any new plan hard to formulate and enact.'

Xhyle gestured at the cartograph. 'Please magnify Gathalamor Prime, archmagos,' he said.

Cawl obliged. Gathalamor grew. Its sister worlds sped away out of focus.

'There were only small military presences on the planets of the Gathalamor System when the enemy attacked,' the chiliarch said, 'it being distant from all warfronts before the Great Rift opened. At the giving of the Lord Guilliman's order, all assets were redeployed to the primary world. Other forces were redirected from nearby warzones. These include a division of the Astra Militarum from Mordian, principally the complete Eighty-Fourth Regiment, supported by numerous smaller elements from the same world, and the Phyrox Fortieth Armoured Regiment, a force of over two thousand fighting vehicles, taking total estimated Astra Militarum forces there to double brigade level. The other primary fighting forces present are multiple preceptories of the Sisters of the Argent Shroud, some of whom make Gathalamor their home, along with a number of other smaller formations, most notable of which is five full lances of House Kamidar Questor Imperialis, and their sundry support elements.'

Xhyle continued, reeling all the figures off from memory. 'That gives us two hundred and fifty thousand infantry, three thousand tanks, and a few dozen war engines of medius scale and above, give or take.'

'Can you not be more precise?' asked a groupmaster.

'He cannot, sir.' An adept of the Departmento Munitorum turned around in his seat and replied for Xhyle.

'There are no Adeptus Astartes present?'

'None,' said Xhyle. 'None were close enough. Our best outcome was that this force hold the world until Fleet Primus arrived. Obviously, we are present in such overwhelming strength that any conflict for the system will be short. However, as directing our efforts from a ruined world would be difficult, the orders to the holding force were to preserve it at all costs. But we are late, and the enemy committed to the campaign with greater numbers than anticipated. Reports give a Grand Battalion of the Iron Warriors Traitor Legion in-system, including fleet assets, and allies.'

Those who did not know the situation on Gathalamor began to speak among themselves, and Xhyle had to raise his voice.

'That is not the worst of it,' he said. 'The last astrotelepathic communication is sorry reading. The Iron Warriors' arrival was accompanied by mass cult uprisings on Gathalamor itself. Our forces were taken by surprise by traitors from within, and at the time of the last communication had lost over two-thirds of the planet's surface to the enemy.'

More conversation flared up.

'What about fleet support?' asked another groupmaster. 'Could we bring in more reinforcements? Could we drive off the Heretic Astartes' voidships and strand them there?'

Dho Gan Mey, rear admiral of the Navis Imperialis and Exterra Council representative, got to her feet. 'Fleet elements have been withdrawn. The remnants of Battlefleet Gathal were insufficient to oppose the enemy. They were ordered to withdraw and regroup at Necromunda. It was deemed better to save them than lose them.'

'Then they're fighting with no void support,' said another.

Guilliman spoke again. 'I do not ask that men and women give up their lives lightly, my lords, but the purpose of this force is simply to buy time. To save a world humanity might live upon still, and keep the enemy's eyes away from the stars and our approach. When we arrive, we will destroy them, no matter their strength. It is the portents that give me concern. Eldrad Ulthran's warning only makes what we have seen in our own scryings more worrying. If the enemy were to destroy the balance between materium and immaterium, or deploy some other manner of sorcerous weapon, then our attack could end in disaster. Our greatest strength is our weakness here. Fleet Primus will crush any mortal foe, but that is not all we face, and if there exists a means to oppose us, then the whole of Fleet Primus may be in danger.

'For the time being, we can assume our movements remain obscured from Abaddon's sorcerers. Wherever forces of the crusade have struck, they appear to have been unanticipated. With Fleet Secundus moving on the Eye of Terror, the War-master's attentions will be elsewhere. We must also assume that we cannot rely on this situation persisting. Gathalamor must be taken. We cannot afford to tarry, and so I hereby amend our plans thusly. We shall send ahead a small party in a fast ship to determine the situation and report back. They will also have my leave to intervene should the need arise. This force will leave tomorrow. We shall depart a day behind them. Depending on the vagaries of the warp, they should have between two and six days before the remainder of the fleet arrives.'

He turned to Colquan.

'Tribune Colquan, this effort will be led by the Adeptus Custodes and supported by the Adeptus Astartes. Select your warriors now. We cannot delay. Come what may, Fleet Primus must take Gathalamor before the month is out, intact. The Emperor demands it, and time is fleeing before us.'

Chapter Eight

SAFE HAVEN

SANCTUM MIRACULOUS

CANONESS IMELDA VERITAS

Dvorgin's party reached the outer pickets with minutes to spare. Whistles shrilled from glassless windows. Yenko replied with the day's coded responses. Once past the sentries they picked up pace. The city was less damaged closer to the void port, and the going became easier.

Mordians called out to their general from foxholes. Dvorgin made a point to salute all who saw him before their officers ordered them back to silent watch. Every so often they passed heavy weapons teams occupying scratch bunkers ringed with sandbags. The bunkers were laboriously broken down every day, the bone dust in the bags tipped out, and the positions moved. Attack from the void or the air was unlikely so close to the port's defences, but sometimes Heretic Astartes patrolled the ruins in place of cultist rabble, and the Imperial forces had little to counter them.

The void port and its district occupied a range of low hills bounded by the Canyon of Countless Blessings to the west, and the ocean to the north. The eastern approach was a tangle of steep, narrow streets climbing carved cliffs: the 'stair' that gave the area its name. Only the south presented an easy way in, and there the Imperial defences were the most complex. Even though the gradient was shallower than on the other three sides of the hills, it was only relatively so. Mordians moved double-time when they could, the men trying to smooth out their gait so as not to jar the wounded they carried. Dvorgin feared for all his injured men, but Kesh most of all, and at the checkpoints on the first and second trench lines he nearly lost his temper. Nowhere was there medicae support to be had. They would have to get back to base for that.

Within the inner lines, signs of loyal civilians became apparent. Scattered bone fires in broken buildings at first, where the survivors burned the remains of the sacred dead to survive, then whole, ragged encampments thousands strong. Those remaining on the surface were truly desperate. Most had taken to the relative safety of the catacombs. All were under suspicion and watched closely by the troops in case insurgents hid among them, drawing more men away from the front.

Bombardments struck up in unpredictable patterns. The echoes produced by Gathalamor Imprezentia's streets made judging the direction difficult, but Dvorgin was certain they were pounding the western approach again, at Saint Claytor's Span.

They took a raised expressway that led directly to the Ascension Stair's main landing mounds. These grew on the horizon once Dvorgin's group gained the plateau, beehive lumps illuminated by the flash of artillery firing from the landing fields. Nothing attacked the voids that night, so they were spared the nightmare displays of displacement discharge, but as midnight approached, Dvorgin's party had to pass through the sickening barrier themselves. Dvorgin took a deep breath before stepping through. Cold fingers teased out the stuff of his soul. Some of his men rushed off to vomit once they were past. It took an effort of will for the general not to follow suit.

Only when he had the warp barrier to his back did Dvorgin allow himself to relax. The void port was as safe as anywhere on the planet. Ahead the Sanctum Miraculous rose up, six hundred feet tall, guarding the route to the port's heart.

There was a roadblock across the highway. Helm lenses glinted in the dark.

'General.' A voxmitter spoke from the shadows. 'We offer our praise to the suffering Emperor that you are returned safe to us.'

A trio of Battle Sisters manned the barrier. All three wore the gunmetal armour and white robes of the Order of the Argent Shroud. Their leader had the hood of a flakweave habit pulled up over her helmet.

'Palatine Gracia Emmanuelle, is that you?' Dvorgin asked. 'What are you doing on guard duty?'

'You think this too lowly a task for the canoness' second?' she asked. 'We all must serve.' She looked over the wounded. 'I will escort you,' she said, indicating that her Sisters should remain.

'I can find the way,' Dvorgin said.

'Of course, general,' said Emmanuelle. 'But allow me to give what little aid I can. Your soldiers are tired. I can clear the way for you, and summon help. I know you are proud, and you should be so, but embrace humility for a short space, so that you might have the succour you require more rapidly, and so return to the Emperor's war refreshed.'

'Praise Him,' said Dvorgin, abashed. Technically, he outranked this woman by many degrees. That didn't stop her being right. He bowed his head. 'And forgive me.'

'You need no forgiveness. Praise for Him is all we require,' said the Sister. 'Come.'

She turned and led them down off the expressway by way of a cast ferrocrete stair, adjusting her pace so that the wounded

Imperial Guardsmen could keep up. At the bottom they entered the sanctum via a large arch that led into an entrance vestibule. A thick gate at the back barred the way inside.

Dvorgin waited while the Sister proceeded with the necessary security. Her helm vox clicked as she communicated with her fellow Sororitas within, and occasionally she spoke aloud to the machine-spirit guarding the gate.

Dvorgin wasn't familiar with this entrance, but he could have gained access himself, as could his officers. He was in command, after all, but he was grateful of the rest, and the opportunity to go to his injured warriors it brought.

Many were fading. Such were the sacrifices the Emperor demanded, and those who had died had done so with honour and courage. He could ask no more than that. Dvorgin's own wounds bothered him, but he paid them little mind as he went to offer quiet words. He would have a medicae attend to him only after they had seen to his Guardsmen.

He made himself leave Kesh until last, for he thought he might spend all his time with her if he did not.

'You look pale, Guardsman Kesh,' he said. He tried not to stare at the bloody bandage at her side.

'We're all pale, sir,' she replied, her voice a hoarse croak. 'We're Mordians. Night world, sir. We're supposed to be pale.'

Dvorgin couldn't suppress his bark of laughter. Still, he could see that Kesh was growing weaker, despite her bravado. If they didn't reach a medicae soon...

The last check was passed. The door gave out a brief trumpet blast, and it sank agonisingly slowly into the ground. 'We go within,' said Emmanuelle. She was serene in all she said and did, and though armoured in heavy gear she made it seem as if it weighed nothing at all. 'Your soldiers require medicae attention, rations, resupply and rest. I will see to it.'

'Thank you,' said Dvorgin.

'I mean you too, general. You must also be seen to,' said the Sister.

'Every wound is a test of faith. The devout endure,' said Dvorgin. 'I can wait. I must meet with the canoness.'

'Does He not say, better to heal the sick and bid the wounded walk, so that they might serve me again?' countered the Sister. 'Follow,' she said, and led them down a sloping passageway.

They clattered down long runs of marble stairs into the stone corridors of the upper catacombs. There were many chambers there, most occupied by dead-eyed civilians huddled around braziers. Other spaces contained caches of arms, stacks of crates under oiled tarps, or stockpiles of rations and clean water. One chamber had been repurposed from a shrine into a church, where armoured Adepta Sororitas knelt in prayer alongside the ragged people. Another was a morgue, with shrouded forms stacked one atop the other along its walls. The Sisters were present in some numbers ministering to the faithful, and guarded the major junctions in ones and twos.

A thick plascrete wall barred the way, a small door set into it. They had reached the reinforced foundations of the inner sanctum, beyond which was the domain of the military alone. The checks proceeded more quickly, now they were inside.

The door opened. On the other side there were many people, mostly administrative staff of the planetary government. Dvorgin heard the familiar strains of a cask-organ ahead. Only the folk of his world played those compact instruments. Only Mordians knew the words to *I carry Him with me in Shadows and Light*. He'd not been this far down before, but he recognised the room layout from the plans. This area was given over to the Second Battalion as barracks.

'Your men have a field hospital that way.' The Sister pointed down the corridor. 'I will see to it that Sisters Hospitaller attend also. Come with me.'

'Later,' said Dvorgin.

'I cannot convince you?'

Dvorgin gave a tired smile. 'Duty first.'

'If you insist. The Hospitallers will be waiting to see to you.'

'I thank you, Palatine Emmanuelle, I will mention you in my prayers tonight.' He went to his party, and gathered his officers. 'See to it that everyone is treated,' he told them. 'Inform the quartermasters that all from the recon group are to be issued double rations, by my command, and that the machine-spirits of your weapons should be honoured. Return to your own barracks if you are able. I'll expect a full situational appraisal and personnel roll call by the morning. Pass on your recommendations as to who should be entered into the book of Mortis Honoria to Colour-Sergeant Chedesh.'

The lieutenants saluted, clicking their heels together smartly, and herded the exhausted Mordians away. Dvorgin heard the cask-organ stop abruptly, voices raised in greeting and calls for the medicae.

His cuts stung. His body ached. He wanted nothing more than to follow Emmanuelle's advice, join his soldiers' reunion before sinking into his bunk for a few hours' sleep.

But that was not command.

Dvorgin pushed exhaustion aside. He took a flight of steps. By then he had a good idea of where he was; life in Mordian's labyrinthine hive cities gave all born there an unerring sense of direction, and he headed upwards out of the underworld to the sanctum's high command chamber.

A chapel near the pinnacle of the sanctum served as the command centre. A dome of stained armaglass made up the ceiling. When daylight spilled through the glass, the dome shone with luminous angels, but at night it was if a shroud had been cast over the Emperor's light, and the chapel was lit only by flickering electro flambeaux.

Staff officers saluted as Dvorgin entered. An altar dominated one curving wall, and that was still hung with prayer scrolls and fuming censers. The rest of the room had been given over to war. Incense coiled across orbital picts affixed to the stonework with brass nails. Banks of cogitators and datalooms crowded the floor. Power cables wormed out of the chamber through a hole knocked through the wall. There were maps and parchments unfurled across the lids of sarcophagi, and the faces of revered cardinals were uplit by the hololithic glow of chart tables.

Members of all the forces on Gathalamor were represented: Mordians, Sister-sages, Colonel-Chieftain Jurgen's Phyroxian staff with their stiff sashes of grox leather, higher ranks of the remaining planetary defence units who were bowed by the shame of their comrades' betrayals, the strategos-castellans of Knightly House Kamidar in rich purple, and a smattering of others. Gun-servitors watched over the whole with uncomprehending eyes, and in one corner kneeling priests chanted quietly, their eyes blindfolded so they would not be distracted from their devotions. Adepts in the robes of the Gathalamorian Administratum hastened about, busy with pleas on behalf of the remaining civilians.

Dvorgin's adjutant, Lieutenant Stehner, came over as soon as he saw the general. His uniform was immaculate, though Dvorgin wished he'd shave off the pencil moustache he'd taken to wearing. It looked ridiculous.

'Good to see you, sir,' said Stehner.

'Likewise, Stehner. Where's Veritas?' said Dvorgin. His eyes were good enough to shoot straight, but in the dim light of the instruments faces were blurry.

'She's over there, sir,' said Stehner, gently pointing the general towards the main tactica displays. 'Shall I fetch your spectacles, sir?'

Dvorgin scowled. 'Yes,' he said. 'Please.'

'Right away, sir.'

Stehner returned a moment later. Dvorgin put his spectacles on, and the room became clear in a way he found alarming. He stepped forward, then found himself pausing and smoothing his rumpled uniform down before he approached the canoness. Stehner produced a stiff brush from somewhere and dusted him off. Dvorgin wished he had time to press his uniform. Throne, even to wash it! Foolish, he knew, at the height of a war like that, but the canoness had that effect on him.

He approached Veritas from behind and cleared his throat respectfully. 'Canoness,' he said.

'General Dvorgin,' she replied without looking at him. She was examining a light-weave cartolith of Gathalamor Secundus, armoured fingers at her chin. The continent was rendered as a high-veracity relief map, with enemy movements around the remaining Imperial enclaves painted in bright reds. Their own forces were rendered in a variety of colours: blue runes denoted Mordians, the grey the Sisters and the crimson the Phyroxian tankers. These were more or less accurately placed, but the enemy positions were guesswork, pieced together from on-the-ground reports.

They had no recent orbital view. Gathalamor's satellite network had been smashed, and there had been no contact with any Imperial void craft for weeks. The last messages told that all warp-capable craft had been ordered to withdraw. Whether there were any of the in-system monitors left, he did not know. Nobody did. Messages from the other worlds in the system were rare. Even communication on Gathalamor itself was hit and miss. The vox-blunt choked off technological communication, while growing warp turmoil stymied their astropaths. Partly because of this, the Imperial forces had fragmented.

Veritas finally turned to look at Dvorgin. She was stocky, thick-necked, with mid-brown skin that carried enough lines to give her age away. A hard white fleur-de-lys was tattooed on her throat. Eyes the colour of steel stared from wide-set sockets; a scar ran close to the edge of the right. Her face was framed by bobbed grey hair. Her armour was more ornate than that of her Sisters, its gorget studded with a trio of blood-red rubies, and her white robes were embroidered with thread-of-gold prayer-script.

'Back from our little adventure, are we?'

Dvorgin cleared his throat again and dropped his eyes. There was more than a little of the scholam mistress to the canoness, and that took Dvorgin back to his education.

He had not been a model student.

'I had to see for myself,' Dvorgin said. 'I'm not going to throw the lives of my men away without seeing what they're getting into.'

'You know,' she said drily, 'in my experience, most senior officers of the Astra Militarum take a step back from front-line combat operations, to stop themselves getting killed. It's not my place to say so, but might I recommend you do the same? Losing you would be a blow to our efforts.'

She gave him a disapproving look. Dvorgin harrumphed with embarrassment.

'To remain watchful is to remain faithful,' Dvorgin quoted.

'Excepting only that one beware watchfulness not become inaction.' The canoness finished the homily and favoured the general with a thin smile. 'Well chosen. Quoting scriptures at a canoness to cover your own rashness is bold, but you know I'm right. You are supposed to be in command here, Luthor, we cannot lose you.'

'Yes, well,' he said. 'I apologise, Imelda. But my men have found something.'

'Do you think?' she said. 'The enemy have been digging for months. What makes this site so special?'

Dvorgin scratched under his hat. His head was itchy with

rock dust. 'I'm not sure. Call it a feeling. You remember the initial strikes, how senseless some of them seemed, and how quickly they started excavations? Whatever they are looking for is important to them. It should be important to us. This site has been in use for more than two weeks, longer than any other we've yet seen. They're not guarding it overtly, I think to avoid drawing attention to what they're up to. I believe they've found what they're looking for, or they are close.'

Veritas turned back to the hololithic map. Its soft light stained her face, so she looked like one of the saints in the glass above.

'It's flimsy intelligence to risk lives upon, but there are other recent developments that support your concern.'

Veritas keyed additional information onto the display.

'Deep auspex today registered movement through the mid-depth catacombs from sector eleven through to sector eighteen, close to your dig site. I took it for them repositioning themselves away from the Phyroxians' artillery.' Veritas gestured to a string of runes beneath the map's nominal surface. 'Maybe not.'

Dvorgin looked over the information. 'It looks like they are moving in more men, which suggests I am right.' He glanced up at the canoness. 'But what are they doing? The mystery gnaws at me,' said Dvorgin.

'The Emperor moves His servants in mysterious ways, and always the path to which He guides us ends in victory, yet the Dark Gods have designs of their own to disrupt His holy plan,' said Veritas.

'Sorcery. Magic. Insanity,' Dvorgin grunted. His exhaustion was dragging at him, and being reminded of the bizarre things he'd witnessed since the Rift wasn't helping.

'On the other hand, you and I can both see we do not possess the forces to investigate the traitors' activities in the catacombs properly and still hold Ascension Stair,' said Veritas. 'Maybe we should let those who come here later deal with it.'

'And what if it is a threat to them?' said Dvorgin. 'What if we are bait?' The general moved in closer. 'You and I have both seen too much of the powers they can call upon. This could be crucial to our survival here. It must be investigated.'

'Our orders were to await relief,' she said. 'Matters are at a stalemate. I believe we will keep this port until the appointed hour. It would be a poor reflection on our devotion to Him if there is nothing left to relieve.'

'Is relief coming?' he said unguardedly. 'I pray daily that it is, but...'

She frowned at him. 'Keep the faith, general. Gathalamor is a precious shrine world. Guilliman himself commanded us to come here. Do you believe that the Emperor will not despatch His servants to reclaim that which is His? If this port falls, the retaking of Gathalamor will take months, if it is ever accomplished. Think of the deaths. Think of the shame. If one position is to remain in loyal hands on this world, it must be this space port.'

'Of course.'

'Therefore, we cannot afford to waste our troops by sending them underground.'

A messenger came in with a dispatch pouch, passing it on to the captain in charge of intelligence. Veritas walked around the floating chart as Mordian officers input new data. The light weave shimmered. Arrows and runic signifiers denoting force dispositions and supply corridors shifted. Friendly lines around Fort Bastabus out to the north-west notably shrank.

Dvorgin followed the canoness, clasping his hands behind his back to stop himself swaying with tiredness.

'We are losing the fight for Gathalamor, Luthor,' said Imelda Veritas. 'A world that for thousands of years has been a beacon of faith. Not since the evils of Bucharis has this planet known the touch of heresy.'

'Would that we had realised how many traitors we sheltered here,' he said. 'If it hadn't been for the cult uprisings, the Iron Warriors would never have prevailed against us.'

'Even surrounded by the most tangible evidence of His divinity, millions turned from Him,' Veritas said sadly.

'Was it fear, weakness of spirit, madness, even?' Dvorgin said. Having seen what he'd seen, he could not credit that any sane person would abandon the Emperor for the Archenemy.

'Imperial citizens are but animals before the wolf. It is not the fault of the innocent that evil comes to call,' said Veritas.

'I don't blame them entirely,' said Dvorgin. 'I blame their rulers. The cardinals here lived like kings.'

'If the rod of government is applied either too laxly or too harshly disaster awaits. Livestock will roam if neglected, and turn on their handlers if ill-treated,' she said. 'If we survive this, we must learn to do better, by His will.'

'His will,' Dvorgin echoed. 'And so here we are.'

'And so here we are,' Veritas echoed. She sighed.

She had slept as little as he, he thought, but her will was greater and she showed her tiredness less. She smiled, infinitely patient.

'Your soldiers are being seen to?'

'They are,' replied Dvorgin. 'I lost a dozen on the reconnaissance. Cult presence beyond the pickets is getting thicker. The Heretic Astartes are shelling the districts around the bridge again. They're going to make a move soon. The canyon is the hardest barrier to breach but if they can take that bridge they'll be into the heart of our position in hours. It's what I would do.'

Veritas laid her hand on the edge of the chart desk. 'The noose tightens.'

'For all that, we remain in reasonable shape,' Dvorgin said. 'Our defences are holding around Ascension Stair. House Kamidar sweeps aside any foray against us from the south. The northern cliffs are impregnable and the Stair warrens keep them

port still,' he said, pointing at various positions both of them
had come to know intimately. 'We have all three primary generatoria in this sector, all but two of the Munitorum supply
depots. The defence batteries and void shields over the port
remain operational, keeping the enemy fleet below the horizon
and out of direct fire lines, which keep our voids up. Beyond
Imprezentia, General Marsdeen's battalion has the Bastion Fam-
ulous. Fort Bastabus remains in the hands of the Lodovians.' He
glanced at the updated display. 'Though perhaps not for long.'

'Whereas two of my preceptories hold the Petitioners' Palace
and the Altocathedrum in Essenia,' Veritas added.

'Then at the moment, we're stopping them getting a strangle-
hold upon this part of the world,' said Dvorgin. 'No news today
from Gathalamor Primus and Gathalamor Tertius?'

'We keep trying, but the vox-blunt confounds us. If the Emperor
knows the fates of the other continents, He has not seen fit to share
a revelation,' said Veritas. 'We must assume that He now places
His trust only in we faithful few, general. I fear we have to accept
that the time of coordinated planetwide resistance is over. We are
in the last days. We must simply endure.'

Dvorgin ran a palm over his face as if he could rub exhaustion away.

He looked again at the map. The markers of House Kamidar, Ascension Stair's most potent military asset, were absent.

'Where is the princess?' he asked.

'Do not fear, the runes of her lances are absent because I do
not know where she is, not because she has fallen.'

'I see we lost more tankers, though,' he said.

'The Phyroxians and their war engines bore the brunt of
the first engagements,' Imelda Veritas replied. 'Colonel Jurgen
reports that the remains of his regiment are still being hunted
by the Iron Warriors mechanised company.'

'It makes sense for the enemy to eliminate them,' said Dvorgin. 'They'll take out our armour, then go after the Knights. With no tanks or war engines supporting us, they will feel confident enough to roll in here and mop up the surviving infantry. They won't need orbital support for that. That bridge is looking more vulnerable by the minute.'

'I concur,' Veritas said.

The runes swam. Dvorgin cursed inwardly. He was going to need stronger lenses on his glasses. 'A number of units have relocated beyond the third line since I left,' he said, following the troop movement with a finger. 'This was on your orders?'

'Hidden outside the main defence line, so we can continue to resist with hit-and-run attacks,' Veritas said. She looked as though she were attempting to discover some deeper pattern within the tangle of sigils.

Seeking the hand of the divine, perhaps, thought Dvorgin. The canoness had been busy, establishing covert supply lines, carefully building rally points, bringing in units of beleaguered soldiers and swapping them for fresh ones.

He pressed a few rune keys and zoomed in the cartolith to the edge of the defences.

'You're preparing for the lines to fall. This is a resistance pattern.'

'If you had been here on time for our meeting this evening, then I would have shown you all this already. We should be ready. If the void port falls, we may continue to fight for a while. I pray I have done you no offence by moving some of your men and supplies.'

'Not at all,' he said. 'It is good work.' Dvorgin took off his cap and rubbed at his head. 'I'm sorry, I'm exhausted,' he admitted.

'Do you agree with these new dispositions?'

'It's done, isn't it?'

She nodded.

'Then I agree,' he said.

'Thank you,' she said.

Dvorgin shot a last, uneasy glance at the catacombs stretching east to west under Imprezentia, between the Petitioners' Palace, under the void port, on to the Temple of the Emperor Exultant and all the way out under the ocean. Not for the first time, and despite the heresy of the sentiment, Dvorgin found himself wishing that he knew the minds of his traitorous enemies. What he wouldn't give to know what they might do next.

'Well then,' he said. 'Our first priority is to prepare for an attack over the bridge. I'm going to form a detail to get into the catacombs.' He held up his hands before Veritas could object. 'It'll be a limited mission to find us a prisoner, handful of men. A reconnaissance in force would be a disaster anyway. My best pathfinder is down, that makes it more difficult. I'll probably wait until she's back on her feet.' He stifled a yawn. His eyes felt like they were made of sand.

'Very well,' she said. 'That seems sensible.'

'Can you spare some servo-skulls, to map it out before they go in?'

'I can find a few,' Veritas said.

'Then I'll start work on the defences at the canyon.'

'You should,' Veritas said gently. She put an armoured hand on his arm. 'But you're tired, Luthor, and you are injured. So first you must get some sleep.'

Chapter Nine

SHIELD-CAPTAIN ACHALLOR

COLQUAN'S JUDGEMENT

A TRUE SON

Shield-Captain Marcus Achallor was called to attend upon the tribune at the thirtieth centile of the second thousandth of the day. He arrived at the tribune's door exactly as the chron in his helm display chimed. Machines that dwelled in the walls sampled his presence, and opened the gate for him.

Security aboard a Custodian vessel would have seemed lax to an observer, if they could have watched the Emperor's guardians go about their business. There were no checkpoints or roving servo-skulls. The doors opened automatically to the golden giants, for everything aboard the ship was tuned to the physiology of the Adeptus Custodes. The same observer would find themselves trapped, the doors barred to them, and the machine-spirits uncommunicative.

Colquan's quarters were spartan, similar in look and feel to the personal chambers of every Custodian. On Terra their cells were often bare stone. On the ship the naked metal of the hull took the place of that. A huge cot was built into the wall, rarely used. There was a desk, shelves with perfectly aligned books and data crystals, and a small reader for the latter. A cogitator screen was set over the desk, its runeboard folded away. A door to the left led off into Colquan's personal armoury. Achallor glimpsed neat workbenches and the tribune's enormous armoured suit displayed in a case. His face was reflected perfectly back at him in the crystal panes: tan skin, broad cheeks, and the epicanthic eyelids of the ancient Pan-Asiatic peoples. His hair was trimmed to a bristly fuzz over his scalp. Custodians were all perfect beings, but there was something particularly fine about Achallor. He was a handsome man, beautiful even.

He did not register this. It was not important to him.

Colquan's quarters were in every respect exactly like Achallor's own accommodation. Seeing that the tribune was neither in the main living area nor in the workroom, Achallor went through the door in the right-hand wall into Colquan's final room, and this alone had any sign of luxury or adornment. Colquan differed to Achallor in that respect – the shield-captain's rooms were austere throughout – but whether it was because the stratarchis tribune must receive visitors more often or from personal taste, Achallor did not know. Despite their common, manufactured natures, Custodians had their own quirks, and Achallor did not know Maldovar Colquan well at all.

There was a loom in one corner bearing a half-finished carpet of fantastically complicated design, a variety of musical instruments made to suit a Custodian's stature, and a stack of papers on a carved table. All were perfectly made, all almost certainly by Colquan himself. There were several chairs in the room, pushed up against the wall, a couple of which were made for standard humans and therefore seemed ridiculously tiny.

Colquan sat cross-legged upon a rug, his hands turned palm up on his knees, his back straight and eyes closed. Achallor stopped on the metal, not wishing to intrude upon the field of cloth, and waited. He did not announce himself. Even if Colquan were lost in meditation, he would know Achallor was there; not least he could have relied on Achallor's timing. Like most of his kind, Achallor was punctilious about punctuality.

The tribune took three deep breaths, then three short, loud ones, a pattern Achallor recognised from the yothagna techniques. He raised his arms high over his head, opened them. Only then did he acknowledge his visitor.

'Captain Achallor,' Colquan said. He got to his feet. 'I thank you for your attendance.'

'You summoned me, I obey, tribune,' Achallor said. He saluted his superior.

Colquan went to the side table and poured a measure of liquid into two goblets and handed one to the shield-captain. Achallor lifted it to his nose and inhaled.

'Verven flowers?' he asked.

Colquan nodded. 'I have developed a taste for them,' he said. 'Funny.' He drank the flavoured water down.

Colquan had a bullet-shaped head that rose without the inconvenience of a neck from hugely muscled shoulders. Achallor watched him, this man elevated suddenly to the highest rank. There were only two tribunes, and they answered directly to Captain-General Trajann Valoris. As stratarchis tribune, Colquan was responsible for all off-Terra operations of the Adeptus Custodes. In Fleet Primus, he was the will of the captain-general.

Colquan finished his drink and put it down. He moved with the supreme control common to all their kind, but it had an edge of abruptness to it that sheared it of grace. He was of the Dread Host, a great warrior. *This is a violent man for violent times,* thought Achallor. He doubted Trajann Valoris would have chosen Colquan otherwise. Even so, in Achallor's opinion, excellence in the Blood Games was not sufficient justification for such power.

Achallor swallowed a mouthful of his drink. 'Pleasant,' he said.

Colquan nodded, sharp as the chop of a blade, as if Achallor could not possibly have offered another opinion.

'I will sit,' said the tribune. Achallor was fully armoured, and so remained standing. His auramite would have shattered the furniture had he attempted to use it, not that he thought Colquan would have invited him to do so. He was beginning to get a sense of this tribune.

'The primarch is sending a reconnaissance force to Gathalamor ahead of the main fleet,' said Colquan.

'I had heard,' said Achallor.

'Do not interrupt me,' said Colquan flatly. 'I have selected the Emissaries Imperatus Shield Host to have the honour of performing the duty. Your kind is well suited to this sort of mission. I have chosen you to lead. Your current orders are rescinded.'

'Thank you, tribune,' said Achallor. 'If I may, I had anticipated that you might order this to be so, and have taken the liberty of drawing up a plan of action.'

'You were the logical choice, so you were not presumptuous,' said Colquan, 'but I do not wish to hear your plans. You are here to receive orders. Listen to me.'

'Yes, tribune, as you command.'

'You will select four of your brothers from among your host, no more.'

Achallor frowned. 'I had thought to request thirty.'

'Thirty is enough to take a world,' said Colquan.

'My reasoning,' said Achallor. 'We do not know what we will face.'

Colquan stared at him. He seemed used to anger. Achallor wondered if he had access to the rest of the suite of human emotions, or if only fury resided where compassion and empathy should also dwell. They varied in that way.

'For all our numbers in this fleet, we are precious few among millions. We cannot spend ourselves carelessly. If Gathalamor has fallen, you are not to attempt to retake it. You are to perform reconnaissance. You are to report back. These are the primarch's orders. If Imperial forces are still active upon the planet, and you believe your presence might swing the balance in their favour, or if you can neutralise the threat this vile xenos warns of, only then are you permitted to act. In all other circumstances you are to return to Fleet Primus. I will not have a single one of the Ten Thousand throw his life away. Do you understand?'

'Perfectly, tribune.'

The tribune rested his arm upon the table and looked at his hand as if it were alien to his body, twitching the fingers one at a time. It was the action of someone who yearned for battle. 'You will take with you an astropath of ability, I have selected her for you already.'

'Astropath Qu'lim is well suited for–'

'I have chosen you a younger, stronger example,' said Colquan. 'You will leave your usual servant here. Empyrical circumstances dictate the choice.'

'What of my ship?' said Achallor. He was a phlegmatic man, but Colquan's brusqueness was galling. '*Radiance* is assigned to the thirteenth torchbearer expedition. I was due to leave for Paragon with Primaris technology for the Emperor's Hands Space Marine Chapter.'

'You will keep your ship. The Emperor's Hands will have to wait. This mission supersedes all other considerations.'

'If I may, tribune, five Custodians are ample for a torchbearer mission, but surely a greater force would be more flexible under these circumstances?'

'It would,' said Colquan. 'Which is why I am not giving it to you. I am taking temptation away. I know of you, Achallor. You are a careful warrior, but you err too far on the side of heroics.

By restricting your entourage, I restrict your options. You will, however, be accompanied by thirty Space Marines. Primaris warriors, of Dorn's line. They are led by a warrior of the primarch's choosing. This is Lord Guilliman's will.'

'Unnumbered Sons?' said Achallor.

'All of them,' said Colquan. 'Further, this Brother-Sergeant Lucerne the lord primarch has chosen to lead them is a religious warrior, unusually. There are a number of them among Cawl's get, and that causes me some concern. There is a reason why the Space Marines are discouraged from venerating the Emperor as a god.'

'I understand that Cawl's hypno-training was avowedly non-religious.'

'So the archmagos says, but these men were taken and made in ways that do not follow the norm,' said Colquan. 'They have had no spiritual guidance. No illumination according to the tenets of any Chapter cult. No exposure to the truth of the Emperor's nature. It could be useful, I suppose, having a believer among them, and no doubt this is the primarch's reasoning. There is a large contingent of Adepta Sororitas on Gathalamor. All this is unimportant to me. You are to watch the Primaris Marines, Achallor. Your secondary objective is to report on the effectiveness of them in combat and the way they behave. I have insufficient information about them.'

'I have heard, tribune, that you do not trust these new warriors.'

Colquan looked at him dolefully. 'So you pay heed to rumours? Even among our own?'

'I am an emissary. It is my duty to listen to rumour,' he said.

'Well, you heard right,' Colquan said. 'We were supposed to be the last legion, Achallor. The Space Marines and their primarchs nearly destroyed everything the Emperor planned, and now Roboute Guilliman has the largest number of Adeptus Astartes under arms since the Great Heresy War, all of them the product of unproven, bastardised sciences wielded by a magos who is little more than a renegade. I don't trust them, Cawl, or the primarch.'

'The Emperor has sanctioned Lord Guilliman's command.'

Colquan raised an eyebrow. 'Has He? We have only his word for that.'

'And the word of Lord Valoris,' Achallor corrected.

Colquan snarled and pushed himself to his feet.

'I have heard and discounted all the arguments of your emissary brethren, Achallor. I know the prevailing opinion among your host, and I disagree. Guilliman is one of the primarchs, the Emperor's gravest errors! Now he is at the head of legions he himself banned. He is a new warmaster of the Imperium in all but name. I believe completely that the returned Thirteenth thinks himself to be acting in humanity's best interests, but only because he was made to think that way. He is a pragmatist of the most ruthless sort. When there were twenty, there was a balance built into their combined abilities and propensities. Alone, he is unchecked, so we must be the check.'

'We do not have the right,' said Achallor.

'We have the only right!' said Colquan. 'What if he decides that it is in all our best interests that he replaces his father? What if he grows impatient with the machineries of state? He is a creature of logic. One day, he will reach the conclusion that the Imperium might be better if he took it all over himself, and what then? Do we fight him? Do we support him? Do we betray our most sacred trust?'

Achallor had no answer.

'Our fraternity says it will not be so,' said Achallor.

'You emissaries are so credulous,' Colquan said. He looked away on the verge of fury, breathed, and calmed himself. 'I hope you are correct. It is your opinion that currently holds sway. Should the day come when I must say that you were wrong and

I was right, I will regret it. We can both agree that our single role is to serve the Emperor, and while our interests currently overlap with those of the primarch, they will not always. Be wary. Watch his new Space Marines. Do not throw your lives away to achieve his goals. These are my commands to you.'

'Even if it means Gathalamor falls?' Achallor asked.

'Even if it means Gathalamor falls. Every one of the Ten Thousand that dies on this crusade is one less to defend our true master, and He is the Master of Mankind. Never forget that.'

Achallor had a sudden, chilling insight into why Valoris had chosen Colquan. He was there to watch the primarch.

'I say that you fear too much, and that Roboute Guilliman is a true son of the Emperor,' said Achallor.

Colquan glared him. 'So was Horus. You and your ilk forget that to the peril of us all.'

Achallor dipped his head. 'I shall depart today, for the Emperor.'

'For the Emperor,' Colquan responded.

Chapter Ten

ALTAR OF WAR

KNIGHTS IMPERIALIS

HOUSE KAMIDAR WALKS

Jessivayne Y'Kamidar watched her household from the observation balcony of the drop keep *Altar of War*. She was a tall woman, wiry beneath her white-and-gold flak tabard, but though strong, her legs were atrophied, so she was supported by servo-callipers. People underestimated her because of her disability, until they looked into her eyes. She was the heir to the Ironhold, and only the slow-witted failed to see the steel running through her soul.

Beside her stood her cousin on her father's side, First Blade Sheane Y'Kamidar. Rangy like her, he was sandy-haired to her black, skin weathered and scarred to her youthful smoothness, old enough to have laughter lines at the corners of his eyes. To her other side was Baron Gerent Y'Kamidar. The younger brother of Jessivayne's mother, he was not much older than the First Blade. Stocky, hearty, and known for the truth of his speech. 'As sure as Gerent's word,' they said on Kamidar.

The nobles wore hand-and-a-half blades upon their backs, the traditional *oighen* of their homeworld. The weapons were ornately worked, with disruption-field generators concealed in their hilts.

All had seen plentiful action.

About the nobles spread the ironclad vastness of the *Altar of War*'s command centre. A hundred feet up and to their rear, a choir raised their voices in vox-amplified hymns that stirred Jessivayne's heart. The light of sanctified electro-braziers painted everything in fiery hues. Kamidari cyber-canids prowled the deck.

Standing behind his holo-lectern in the command apse, Captain Daithi Cochlain directed his crew with a booming voice and occasional cracks of an electro-lash. There were more than a hundred of them, including the smattering of servitors, and they laboured at their datapews in terror of the giant captain.

Through the command centre's colossal oculus, flanked by stained glass and grotesque iron gargoyles, the sun crawled up over the spires of Gathalamor.

'Another day, another sally,' said Jessivayne. 'A fine day.'

'Aye, this world our Great Grandsire Laughlen swore to defend,' replied Sheane. 'We defend it still, to the last.'

'To the last,' Jessivayne agreed. Laughlen's list of victories rose unbidden in her mind. Though long, it was but one small part of the house's history she had been required to memorise. 'The Emperor commands we fight and die for this most holy of worlds,' she said. Sunrise over Gathalamor, even ruined, suffused her with holy fervour.

'Let us not forget the rich rewards Grandsire Laughlen received here for his service,' Sheane added. He was in jovial mood. All of them felt light on campaign, when the tedious rituals their family must adhere to were put to one side, and battle filled the hours.

'We are not here for reward, cousin,' said the princess. 'We are here because mother is sworn to uphold those same oaths, and I shall see them upheld or die trying.'

'Emperor's grace there will be no need for that, now, eh?'

said Baron Gerent. 'Fifty-two days we've fought here, and only one engine lost.'

'He wills our victory,' she replied. The callipers on her legs hissed as she stood tall, better to feel the sunlight washing through the command centre.

'He wills it. Our lances are full of faith and fury, princess. They would follow you into the warp and carve out the Dark Gods' rancid hearts if you commanded,' said Gerent.

She smiled. 'You are prone to hyperbole, uncle, but I thank you for the sentiment. I cannot promise them such an honour, but we shall slay the Dark Gods' worshippers again, by His will. Do you have targets for today, First Blade?'

'As always. I think you'll find them particularly pleasing.' Sheane crooked a finger at one of the strategos, and a tactical hololith ignited, showing the environs to the south-west, before the canyon split the earth and divided the Ascension Stair hills from the plains. Swarms of red dots moved around the periphery. 'An Iron Warriors armoured column, advancing from the south.'

'A fine hunt.' She scrutinised the target area. 'We will be far out, at risk from the enemy fleet.'

'The enemy ships are cautious, my lady,' Gerent said. 'They will not be able to draw direct line, though we will be at risk of guided munitions.'

'That makes this battle all the more thrilling, and the honour greater, don't you think?' Jessivayne smiled. 'Is there any sign of the alpha target?'

'Yes, my cousin,' Sheane said. 'I took the liberty of liaising with Colonel-Chieftain Jurgen, and he was only too glad to oblige, as he has his own score to settle there. The alpha target is being distracted. Two squadrons of Phyroxians have laid the trail and the bait. With luck, they may fell him themselves, meanwhile we can winnow the numbers of this column more easily with him absent.'

She frowned solemnly. 'To hunt the alpha predator, first diminish his pack.'

'My thoughts precisely, princess.'

'Let us give our hopes to the Emperor that the Phyroxians survive, but let us not wish them too much good fortune, for I would kill the alpha myself.'

Sheane grinned. 'It would be only right.'

'To battle then,' she said.

'To battle,' Sheane and Gerent echoed.

Princess Jessivayne sighed as her neural jacks connected with the ports in her spine and the Throne Mechanicum lowered itself gently from the arming room. There was no rush today, no need for the bone-jarring slam of hasty interface, and she entered her steed sedately. Control panels and vid-screens rose up to meet her. The throne mated with its sockets in the cockpit, the hatch closed softly, and she was within her Knight, *Incendor*. It was quiet before the reactor lit. The instruments were silent. The baroque metal throne cradled her. She was at peace. She could have fallen asleep, she thought.

The cockpit vox let out a rasp.

'*Connection secure,*' one of her sacristans droned. Jessivayne struggled to tell the monastic tech-adepts apart. Their machine-modified voices were identical. '*Reactor ignition in three, two, one.*'

Incendor shook. Ready lights flickered on all around her. Screens lit. The cockpit filled with the whine of electronics and mechanisms at work, and under that was the constant, terrible hum of the Knight's plasma reactor. When it was active, the whole construct trembled, as if with restrained rage.

'*Plasma reactor active, all praise the Omnissiah. Initiating MIU link.*'

Jessivayne grinned, partly in pain, partly in joy, when the

cable connecting her to *Incendor* pulsed. As the white leather saviour straps of the throne held her physical self, so the mind link held her soul. A tension passed over her head, back to front, and she bit back a cry as her mind expanded to join with a cool, dark space. Presences shifted in that gloom, fluttering around her soft as moths' wings, offering sensations of fealty, pride and piety that transcended words.

'My ancestors, Emperor's grace be upon you,' she whispered as the mind link settled. *Incendor*'s cogitation units came online and screeds of data overlaid her field of vision. 'Rejoice, for this day we go to battle again, to fulfil our oaths and to deliver a benighted world back unto the light of the Master of Mankind.'

Thoughts from other souls passed eagerly through her. Phantom hands grasped her wrists in the echoes of warriors' handshakes. The ghosts of her ancestors settled behind her eyes. She was *Incendor*'s pilot, she was its master and the one who led the household, yet her ancestors would be there to aid her.

Behind them, Jessivayne felt another presence; huge, brooding and monstrous: the machine-spirit of *Incendor*. The Knight's reactor rumbled its welcome, and she replied with a wordless rush of joy.

Jessivayne was heiress of a ruling noble house, a pious servant of the God-Emperor. She was the girl who had never allowed anything to hold her back, the woman who followed in her mother's cinder-strewn footsteps. For all that, when she went to war she became so much more.

Here, within *Incendor*, she was the Knight of Thorns.

She opened *Incendor*'s marvellous eyes, remaining half aware of the whirring, glowing cockpit her mortal form occupied. Laid over it, and far more arresting, were the flashing amber lumens of the entombing chamber. She looked down and saw the gleaming white ceramite of her war-limbs. She turned *Incendor*'s head, and saw the other Knights awakening as their pilots established their neural links. One by one the war engines straightened, raising up their humped backs, their heads jerking and looking about as their engine stacks snorted plumes of exhaust.

Jessivayne reached out with her mind as her hands flickered across familiar controls, activating the rest of *Incendor*'s systems and bringing his weaponry to life. She chanted the cross-check litany as she did so.

'Thunderstrike gauntlet roused.'

'So mote it be,' her sacristan echoed.

'Ion shield set.'

'Let His light be your guardian and your guide.'

'Motive actuators aligned.'

'From the power of the machine cometh the victory of the righteous.'

'Conflagration cannon roused.'

'Oh, glory, glory, give unto Him who dwells upon the Throne, He who hath sacrificed himself for mankind, the living body of the Machine-God, who liveth among us, the guardians of His Great Work.'

This last armament was traditionally a weapon reserved for the immense Dominus class, but *Incendor* was one of a kind, an engine fashioned by the tech-magi of Forge World Ferrovarum as a gift to mark Jessivayne's Becoming. It carried a relic plasma core, while its chassis was reinforced the better to bear the conflagration cannon and the thrice-armoured promethium tanks that fed it, modifications that gave *Incendor* an asymmetrical build that set it apart from other Questoris Knights.

'Plasma core at optimal output.'

'Where there was cold steel, let there be life.'

The Knight came fully online, thrilling with the urge to move. By the power of thought alone, Jessivayne directed it towards the great armoured gate of the drop keep. Servo-actuators whined. Plasmic energy flowed hot through mechanical arteries.

Incendor took one long stride, then another, ironclad feet booming on the decking. Around Jessivayne the other nobles were moving forward, coming into a line behind her.

Sacristans thronged their feet, ringing gongs and pounding drums, singing praise to the Emperor and the Omnissiah while cyber-cherubim swooped amongst them wielding aspergillums. Sacred oils spattered on the upturned faces of the rapturous priests and anointed the pristine armour of the war engines.

'Knights of House Kamidar, are you ready to serve your queen and your Emperor?' asked Jessivayne over the vox. Her heart was pounding in time with *Incendor*'s reactor, and her soul sang.

'*We are ready, praise the Golden Throne!*' her nobles cried in response.

The last word from Captain Cochlain had been that the enemy fleet was on the other side of the world. Taking into account time to detection and requests for support getting through, once combat began House Kamidar had maybe an hour, two at most, before the enemy would be in a position to target them from orbit. The ships were the greatest threat to House Kamidar, forcing them to operate close to the protection of the void port defence lasers. Otherwise, the enemy had little that could touch the Knights.

Oh Emperor, she thought, *we shall serve you well.*

'Nobles of Ironhold!' she cried. 'Let your mortal selves burn away in the blessed fires of your reactors. May you be born again into plasteel and ceramite to wreak terror upon our enemies!'

'*Kamidar! Ironhold! Victory!*' they roared.

Klaxons blared. The armoured gates of the drop keep opened onto the landing pad it occupied. A few miles away, the void shields made the air sparkle. Beyond that was the enemy.

'Forward!' she cried. 'Forward for Kamidar! Forward for the Emperor! For the Imperium! For humanity!'

The Knights let out a lowing chorus from their war-horns.

With Jessivayne at their head, they broke into a loping run, a mixture of Armigers, Questoris and two towering Dominus, spreading out as they left the drop keep, and raced towards the city.

Chapter Eleven

DRACOKRAVGI

A TOKEN OF YESTERDAY

SHADE

Torvann Lokk drove across a glittering field of shattered glass. His tank was a Vindicator Laser Destroyer of the Deimos pattern, dating from before Lokk had followed his lords into rebellion. Then, it had been commanded by Captain Ossark Kayth, and the brotherhood Lokk fought with had been known as the Sundering Fist.

They had fought the Emperor, they had lost. The Legion splintered. Lokk killed Kayth, and took his tank and his warband both. The former, *Dracokravgi*, he claimed as his own. The latter he had renamed the Beasts of Steel. He had led them ever since, never once wavering in his commitment to the Long War, until now.

It had been many years since Lokk had relished life. He dimly remembered a time when the fires of vengeance burned within him. The centuries saw them dwindle to ashes, yet still he fought on.

The gods demanded it.

Lokk was hunting, and that gave passable relief to his boredom. His quarry was a handful of Imperial tanks that had crept out from the void port the day before. He yearned to pit himself against the Knights who struck and struck against his brothers, yet there were always other orders, always for less worthy targets.

Tenebrus was to blame for that. All because of his damned holes in the ground.

And yet these tanks still needed to die, and he was mollified that there was, as yet, no sign of the Knights.

'Duty is duty, and foes are foes,' he muttered to himself. 'Duty must be done, foes exterminated.'

At least this hunting ground was interesting. Sprawling across forty square miles at the edge of Imprezentia, it had been the primary transportation hub for Gathalamor Secundus, the glittering heart of a web of maglev lines and highways, covered over with roofs of stained glass. No doubt the corpse-worshippers had gloried in the immense images of saints and primarchs, but they had proven no protection.

A flimsy shield of make-believe, Lokk thought contemptuously. The structure had been visible from space as a scintillating lake of glass. Lokk had personally seen that it was bombed during the first hours of the invasion. He had done this only partly to cripple the continental infrastructure. In truth, he had more enjoyed the notion of cowering Imperial vermin looking up to see their protectors smashed and cast down in razored falls to slaughter them.

The image was almost enough to make Lokk smile.

The treads of his tanks ground through fields of glass. In places it had melted in the heat of the bombardment, trapping burned corpses and sections of machinery like insects in amber. In others it formed colourful drifts many feet deep, comprising a billion jagged shards. Human remains could be

seen amidst them, flensed limbs reaching out like the hands of
drowning men.

How many millions did we purge in the fire? Lokk wondered.
The noise of breaking glass gave pleasing musical accompaniment to his thoughts. *How many corpse-worshippers have died
since in these lethal fields?*

Lokk drove by neural linkage. In Legion days the tank had
required a crew of three. Now, he alone was sufficient to man it
and fire its weapon. The malevolent spirit that dwelled in *Dracokravgi*'s systems, a gift from the gods for his devotion, helped
with other tasks. The laser destroyer never failed. Its power
couplings never needed replacing. *Dracokravgi* was loyal and
fierce. He thanked Kar-Gatharr for that.

Lokk's hand strayed to the metal disc around his neck, another
gift, from an earlier era, pierced at the top for a leather thong
he'd replaced a thousand times. The disc was worn paper-thin
by millennia of handling, the design on it long gone, though
Lokk remembered it clearly: a three-headed serpent, the badge
of a warrior lodge long disbanded.

It remained the symbol of his brotherhood with Kar-Gatharr,
and so he had made it the symbol of the Beasts of Steel.

Lokk remembered asking Kar-Gatharr about his own medallion, long ago, when the Word Bearer had been assigned to
his Grand Battalion to foster bonds between the Legions. Kar-
Gatharr had grinned broadly, and covered his medallion with
his hand in a mock display of secrecy.

'I cannot say,' he had said.

Lokk received his invitation to join the lodge the next day.
He and Kar-Gatharr had been friends ever since.

A token of yesterday that still held resonance. So few did,
any more.

He grunted. Drool slipped from the corner of his mouth
and pooled in his respirator mask. His armour was twisted, its

plates rough with excrescences of bone and scaled metal, its lines warped like they had part melted and reset poorly, and beneath his flesh had bonded extensively to the ceramite so that he could no longer remove it completely. The same was happening with *Dracokravgi*. Lokk went long periods without leaving the driver's compartment, and when he did he had to break the interface spikes. They were always repaired, *regrown*, when he returned, ready to plunge into him anew. The tank was his body. *Dracokravgi*'s sinister spirit the counterpoint to his soul. Let other Iron Warriors fret about mutation and cut their bodies. Lokk sank into his changes gratefully. They were the gifts of the gods and were a balm to him, a reward for thousands of years of unrelenting war, and, he hoped privately, would one day prove a release.

The character of the glass desert was changing. The bomb-blackened shells of structures emerged from the jagged drifts. The immense metal frames that had held up the roof were tangled here, curling overhead like the ribs of some carrion carcass, softened by the heat of that first bombardment so that they had buckled, and fallen down like talons to drive deep into the earth.

Dracokravgi passed beneath one of these spars then into the shadow of a mag-train hanging off an elevated track, where the mummified driver lay, shrivelling face glued to the cockpit glass by a pool of tarry blood.

Torvann Lokk looked up at the corpse without feeling, and returned his attention to his tank's auto-senses.

'*My lord, grid-sector eighty-one is bare of prey,*' came the rasping voice of Harvoch through Lokk's helm vox.

'Proceed to eighty-two,' Lokk responded. Harvoch was his first lieutenant, and but one of the ten tank commanders spread in a loose net to Lokk's right and left. He could see the signifier runes pulsing dully on his strategic overlay, along with other sigils proclaiming possible power sources, potential movement and other factors pertinent to his hunt.

'All vehicles, increase pace,' Lokk voxed. 'These weaklings have already stolen much of our time.'

He rounded the support that held up the maglev engine. Ahead, Lokk saw a smattering of burnt-out relay towers, each several storeys high. Between them the glass was deeper, and here his quarry's trail was revealed at last. Something big had shouldered its way through the glass, ploughing a deep furrow.

'How do they think to hide from us in this?' muttered Lokk in disgust. 'I have a trail, grid-sector eighty-eight,' he reported. The lords of other Traitor Legions might have kept such news to themselves until they had secured the glory of the kill. The Iron Warriors still did things properly.

Confirmation runes winked in his helmplate. The hunting pattern shifted, tightening and moving with purpose to enfold any potential foes near to his location. He heard the soft growl of other tanks approaching. He might not like any of the warriors that he led to battle, for Torvann Lokk had grown to hate almost every living being in the entire, miserable galaxy, but he still respected their abilities in war, and they were still *his* warriors.

Lokk followed the trail between broken buildings. *Dracokravgi* was deep in glass now, fording a river of deadly colour. If not for his indomitable tank, even Lokk would have struggled to make headway without injury, yet the glass yielded to *Dracokravgi*'s passage, as all things surely must.

As these damned corpse-worshippers should, he thought. They had to know they were beaten. Did they not comprehend what events they stood in the way of? The Great Rift had opened! The warp churned as Lokk had never seen. And now, within the very bounds of the Segmentum Solar itself, no less than Abaddon the Despoiler had commanded Torvann Lokk and his fellows to claim Gathalamor in his name.

'This is artful destruction,' Lokk grunted, scanning his tactical read-out.

He had said as much to Kar-Gatharr days before, as they had stood on the walls above the despoiled Saint's Gate and stared out over the blasted city. They watched the ongoing battle, listened to the crackle of las-fire, the chatter of autoguns, the thumping of bolters and the roars of the warp-born terrors they had unleashed. Lokk smelled brimstone, blood and smoke. Once, that would have raised real passion. He had felt nothing.

'This is the Despoiler reaching out,' Kar-Gatharr had said. 'He is preparing the way for the end. It is the Warmaster, the *true* Warmaster, readying himself to do what the pretender Horus failed to achieve. And we, war-brother, are instrumental in it.'

'Yes,' said Lokk. 'Soon it will be finally over, and we will have played our part, for what little that will contribute.' He spoke not triumphantly, but wearily. He shifted his weight. His right ankle, boot and greave had fused, giving him a lumbering cripple's walk. Standing for any time was uncomfortable. He had wanted to see Kar-Gatharr, craved contact with the one being he still held any love for, but his mood had soured, and he had the urge to retreat back to *Dracokravgi* to brood.

'You are right to be humble,' said Kar-Gatharr. 'We are but the tools of the powers. We are blades to be drawn against the Carrion-Emperor as the Dark Gods see fit. Never set yourself above the gods. As these mortals are nothing to us, we are nothing in the great struggle. We are proud weapons, but weapons are all we are.'

'Our purpose is at hand,' said Lokk, and he could not hide the yearning in his voice.

'Patience, brother. You are touched by dark majesty. You are on the cusp of glory. Think not of death, but of eternity.'

Lokk smiled his crooked smile, felt the sting of lips tearing from the decayed interior of his helm.

'I think of nothing else,' he said.

Kar-Gatharr was the only one who could see Lokk's desperation: the need, the mania even, for the Long War to finally be at an end.

'Stand firm,' Kar-Gatharr said, 'and remain steadfast. I know you wish for release, but the end is not at hand. Your reward is.'

A massive impact shook Lokk back to the present.

The battle cannon shell was preceded by a sudden surge of power readings across Lokk's auto-senses, and yet he had no time to react. The shot would have blasted open a ferrocrete bunker. Against *Dracokravgi*'s armour, it barely made a dent, glancing off the glacis and caroming upwards into a twisted spar. The shell blew, fire billowed over him. *Dracokravgi*'s systems wailed, and the daemon in the machine whined like a cur. Lokk's head rang. He saw his attacker half buried in glass and plascrete rubble. His lassitude was swept away by a sudden, powerful anger. To be caught unawares by mere humans, and in a damned Leman Russ battle tank no less. Hardly a sleek ambush hunter.

They must have powered everything down and sighted the shot manually, he thought with grudging respect. As the smoke cleared, he got a look at the tank. Its hull was painted off-white and banded with geometric blocks of brown; urban camouflage chipped by weeks of warfare. Lokk noted the streaks of fresh blood on the hull and turret, and the bloodied entrenching tools lashed to one track guard. His respect increased. The crew had disembarked into the glass to fill in their trail and hide their machine.

Yet the tankers had revealed themselves now. All they had suffered up to this point would be for naught.

'Contact in my grid-sector,' said Lokk across the vox, pre-empting the questions of his warriors. 'Ambush attack. Single armour unit. Probable distraction, adopt beater-pattern four.

Lorgus,' he called to his second lieutenant. 'Be ready for flushed quarry and potential ambush.'

'*Yes, my lord,*' Lorgus' phlegm-thick voice oozed over the vox, but Lokk wasn't really listening. Through supernaturally heightened senses he could hear the frantic movements within the Leman Russ tank as its crew exchanged muffled shouts and scrambled to chamber another shell, and the gunners roused the spirits of their heavy bolters. He could smell their blood. His mouth watered.

The prey's claws were out. At least that would make the kill more interesting.

Lokk spun the tracks of *Dracokravgi* in opposite directions, bringing the long snout of the laser destroyer to bear. The Leman Russ shuddered as its power plant awoke. At the same time the heavy bolters in its sponsons and prow mount roared to life, spitting shells at him with commendable accuracy, their impacts shuddering through *Dracokravgi*'s armour and washing out the aural feeds.

He powered the main weapon with a thought, driving forward to kill at point-blank range.

The Leman Russ turret gun spoke again, but in their haste the enemy crew hadn't depressed the barrel enough. Their shot whipped over *Dracokravgi*'s roof and detonated behind him, sending a storm of glass shards in all directions. Still Lokk advanced, and as he did, he incited the machine-spirit of the laser destroyer to fire.

The mind-impulse link was still of technological derivation, but had been corrupted by its union with the daemon, and Lokk felt the weapon's half-formed excitement as it fired. He aimed for the right track. A blink of coherent light slammed through the armoured cowling, blasting the metal cover to pieces and part fusing the links beneath. Stung into action, the Imperial driver tried to move the Leman Russ out of its hiding place. It lurched, and the left track spun helplessly, making the tank shift to the side a little, but no more. Black smoke boiled from its exhausts. Glass sprayed everywhere. The gears ground horribly. The right track's drive wheels blurred around, caught, and snapped the damaged track, which spooled off the wheels like a long, lascivious tongue.

Lokk lined up for the killing shot. The Leman Russ was doomed. A single shot would core the thing through and slaughter the crew. The laser destroyer was charged and humming impatiently, but Lokk paused.

I'll finish this personally, he thought. The fight had shaken a little of his lethargy off, and made him feel like getting his hands dirty again.

Two enemy signifiers appeared on his tactical display as the rest of the Phyroxian squadron sprang their ambush. By the time his warriors reacted, the enemy were moving, feigning flight from the more numerous Iron Warriors. Lokk had seen the pattern a hundred times before; this was a layered ambush, a nest of traps.

'Squadrons, pursue with caution,' he said. 'Beware secondary assaults.'

'*Confirmed,*' Lorgus said. He was always so eager to gain Lokk's favour. Sickening lickspittle.

Meanwhile, his own quarry wasn't going anywhere.

He opened the door at the rear of the driver's compartment, and hauled his twisted frame through the cramped innards of the tank, pulling on his power claw, Cruelty, and taking up his meltagun, Dragon's Maw. Then he put down the rear ramp, plugged in his weapons' power feeds to his armour ports, and stepped out and around the hull into the panic-fire of the heavy bolters. Gunfire of that magnitude would have hurt him once, or even killed him. Now he hardly felt it. He shrugged it off, limping forward with bolt explosions flashing from his armour. Where the rounds left dents in his ceramite, they bled.

He took his time to reach his enemy, so eager to feel anything that he lingered to enjoy the hot pain of the bolt-rounds. He stepped outside the prow gun's traversal, into the dead spot between it and the sponsons, and the sensation ceased. His body throbbed as it began to heal. A slash of his claw took the muzzle from the prow gun, prompting a series of dull rattles from inside as the bolt in the breech exploded and set off the magazine. One of the sponson guns fell silent also. The other carried on firing, though the bolts passed by harmlessly. Crack, crack, crack, one after the other their rocket motors ignited, speeding them on. Smoke drifted lazily from the tank's ventilators. Moans of pain sounded from within.

'*Prey moving, my lord,*' came Harvoch's growl over the vox. '*Two armour units disabled, closing for the finish. Three more detected outside the inner net.*'

'*Outer net secure, prepping to kill,*' gurgled Lorgus.

'Execute,' Lokk said. He had his own kill to enjoy.

'*Warpsmith,*' Lorgus called him. '*I have notification from the Ferric Brotherhood. They are under attack by House Kamidar.*'

'Position?' Lokk replied. He eyed the tank as he spoke. He would peel it open like a mollusc and give the tankers inside the honour of a slow death.

'*Five miles south-west of the bridge. They are at the limit of their safe operational range, so will probably withdraw soon.*'

'Advisory?' Lokk said.

'*If we abandon this hunt now, we could catch them.*'

'*Those were not Lord Tenebrus' orders,*' Harvoch interjected. His guns were firing, and his voice broken.

'I am in command here,' Lokk replied. 'I will decide.'

On his tactical display he could see that the slaughter was all but over. His warriors were converging on the last tanks and butchering those that had not made their escape. With a bitter sigh, Lokk tuned Dragon's Maw's focal length to the absolute

minimum and placed its muzzle on the hull. The corpse-dogs
would die quickly, after all.

'To Khorne, to Nurgle, to Tzeentch and to Slaanesh, I dedicate this kill,' he growled, and fired. Praying voices turned suddenly to screams as superheated metal vapour boiled within, searing out the crew's lungs and cooking them alive. He let Dragon's Maw scrape over the hull and drop to his side. 'We go.'

'We should remain and finish these Phyroxians,' Harvoch said. *'Four tanks are escaping. Lord Tenebrus–'*

'Curse Tenebrus,' Lokk spat. 'I am not his slave. All units,' he voxed, limping back to *Dracokravgi* as quickly as his deformed leg would allow. The Imperial tank coughed. Its engine block exploded, and the hulk burned behind him. 'Abandon pursuit and re-form at point bellepheron. The princess is abroad.'

Chapter Twelve

THE PRIDE OF KAMIDAR

THE ALPHA TARGET

A MEETING PROMISED

Jessivayne sent *Incendor* into a charge at the Predator tank, pitching the Knight forward. The fingers of her thunderstrike gauntlet ripped up trails of lightning from the rockcrete. The Predator waited to fire until her ion shield had passed over its hull, but the shells only clanged off her armour. Her fingers touched ceramite, and she flipped the tank off the ground. She pivoted back, firing her inferno cannon into the tank's exposed underside. Pressurised fuel blasted the Predator away from her. Flame peeled paint from its hull, its ammo cooked off and it crashed down ablaze, then she was past it, heavy stubber gunning after the retreating Heretic Astartes infantry.

'*A spectacular kill,*' Sheane voxed her. Heavy footsteps overlaid his voice. Battle cannon shells streaked past Jessivayne in paired bursts from her lance mates, detonating amid a squad of enemy heavy weapons troopers. Cultists ran in terror from the rampaging Knights. They were well into the vanguard of the traitor force, scattering the infantry supporting the column.

'The house strategos are advising withdrawal. In twenty minutes the traitor fleet will be over the horizon...' He paused. His words were replaced by the rising howl of his meltacannon and the roaring of its discharge. *'...There are targets moving in from the south. Enemy armour. What are your commands?'*

Jessivayne was aware of both. Her strategos-ultra had been bleating at her to fall back. *Coward*, she thought, even when he was safe in the sanctum and not out on the field. 'The alpha target,' she said.

'Perhaps,' said Sheane, *'but we are in no position to engage.'* There was a vox-click as Sheane opened a second channel. *'Baron Gerent Y'Kamidar, could you please speak with your niece? She's not listening to me.'*

The beginning of Gerent's response was lost to the racket of his Avenger gatling cannon. *'...two ways about it,'* he said. *'The First Blade is right, we must withdraw.'*

Jessivayne played her promethium stream over a crowd of cultists. There were only a few Heretic Astartes; most were mortal scum who had abandoned the light of the Emperor, and they came in crowds. She slew them gladly. Those that were not blasted to ash scattered like rats into the ruins of cathedrals they had helped destroy. Such faith carelessly abandoned. Such beauty smashed. How she wanted to chase them all down and show them a hotter light than that of faith, to burn them from their holes, to...

'Princess,' said Sheane.

'I'm going to withdraw my lance, niece,' said Gerent. *'It would be better for us all if you gave the order. The Emperor would prefer we follow the proper hierarchy, but I won't let it stop me if you won't.'*

Her eyes strayed to the display showing the closing enemy force. It was bigger than the one they'd smashed their way through, comprised entirely of battle tanks, alert to their presence, and would soon crest the brow of a low ridge south-wards. They would get good sighting down the processional leading to the summit, and there was plenty of cover among the ruined chapels there. The fleet was a series of ominous red blobs on another display, approaching a shallow curve denoting the horizon. It was ten miles back to the safety of defence laser coverage, thirty back to base. A good run.

In the other direction she could see the macro-cathedrum clearly, blotting out the western sky with its marching pinnacles. So close.

She snarled in frustration.

'House Kamidar!' she widecast. 'The enemy flee and the battle is done. Turn about and return to the void port. We fight another time.'

She swerved her Knight angrily, putting it into a tight turn that threatened to topple it. Her squires raced ahead in their lighter Armiger Knights, but as she came around she looked to the south-west, down the processional, where she saw a single tank emerge over the brow of the ridge, light winking from its periscopes. She raised her mechanical fist and clenched it, sending out a crackle of energy. She knew it was him; in her bones, she knew it.

She disengaged her vox-cyphers and broadcast in plain, uncoded Gothic.

'We will meet, you and I,' she said. 'And I will strike you down, for the God-Emperor.'

Incendor's swift stride took her across the processional and into the cover of the buildings on the other side, stealing her foe away.

'There will be other days and other battles,' her uncle assured her. *'Praise be to Him on Terra that we live to fight again.'*

'Praise be,' she said through gritted teeth.

* * *

Lokk watched the Knights cross the processional. The old schema of lines and distance indicators still worked down one side of *Dracokravgi*'s ranging display. The other was patterned with branching veins that pulsed distractingly. The ridge was a low prominence, but Gathalamor Imprezentia was largely built on coastal plains, and being away from the great knot of land that heaved up under the space port, the ridge's elevation seemed considerable, so he had a fine view of the Imperial war machines withdrawing at a sprint, another of their hit-and-run missions accomplished. They were so heavy they made the ground shake even so far away.

His targeting sensors bleeped, and circled the engine of Princess Jessivayne in rotating reticules. He knew her name – she was hardly shy about who she was – but though she did not know his, she had marked him out, and she saw him then. Her ion shield swung to cover the quarter facing Lokk's tank. As she raised her fist in challenge, he itched to discharge the laser destroyer; it was ready, its spirit light shone bright and tempting green. He refrained. The shot was distant, there was plenty of dust in the air. The energy of the beam would be substantially reduced by photon scatter, and then the ion shield of the Knight would turn the last aside.

All I will be doing is showing my impotence, he thought, and the firing light's hope remained unfulfilled.

His vox crackled. A message on Imperial frequencies. He brought it to the fore with a thought.

'*We will meet, you and I, and I will strike you down, for the God-Emperor.*'

'We shall see whose gods are greatest,' he said to himself, 'when we clash machine to machine.'

'*We are advancing obliquely across their path, my lord,*' Lorgus voxed. '*We could catch them before they reach the canyon, cut off their route of escape, and allow you to assail them from the rear.*'

Lokk looked to the east, where the ground rose to the space port. There was a break in the spires that marked the line of the canyon. The tall piers of Saint Claytor's Span were visible over the rooftops. As the land dropped further to the north, he could see the sea shining diamonds. It was beautiful, and reminded him of days when his Legion aspired to be builders, not destroyers. Weariness tugged at him.

Harvoch answered before Lokk could. *'Don't be a fool, they'll kill all of you, cut right through you, slag you iron within and iron without. There's more pus than mettle in that brain of yours.'*

'My lord?' Lorgus gurgled.

'Let them go,' Lokk replied. 'We will hunt them another day, and dedicate their deaths to the Four in the warp. They are worthy offerings. Our hunt must be done with proper reverence, so our gift is most beneficially received.'

'Yes, lord!' Lorgus gave a roll of phlegmy laughter.

Harvoch made a noise of disgust, for he had no truck with the worship of the powers. Lokk couldn't understand. Had Perturabo not taken the power of Chaos into himself, and ascended to daemonic glory? There were forms of strength greater than iron. For not seeing it, Harvoch was as big a fool as Lorgus, in his own fashion.

Lokk caressed his medallion, the corroded tips of his gauntlet scraping the metal thinner, molecule by molecule, as he watched the last of the Knights depart, leaving nothing but dust hanging in the air, columns of smoke rising, and the ocean in the distance, untroubled by war.

Chapter Thirteen

A SHORT TRIP TO OLD HELLS

THE SLEEPER

SHADOW IN SHADOWS

Kesh peered up the street, and winced. Her side hurt still, a week after being hit, even after being given rapid healing gels and the best care. She still didn't think she deserved that; normally a soldier would have been off active duty for a month with so serious a wound. Needs must in the Emperor's wars, she thought. Dvorgin was insistent she lead the recon mission into the catacombs. At least, that was his excuse for getting her such favoured treatment.

'When do we make our move?' Emmanuelle asked.

'No offence, Holy Sister, but I think it is better if we go ahead alone here,' Kesh said. Her pathfinders pointed their las-fusils down the street. With cameleoline cloaks wrapped about them, they were virtually invisible, though Kesh was keen to move on. A single patrol of Heretic Astartes or a unit of turncoat Guardsmen with decent auspex gear would be enough to spot them.

'Canoness Veritas ordered us to protect you,' said Palatine Emmanuelle.

'You move well in that armour, Sister,' said Kesh, 'but it's not stealth gear. In the tunnels the quieter we are, and the quicker, the better.'

'Very well,' said Emmanuelle. Her swift agreement relieved Kesh. Her armour power plant was humming noisily, so she couldn't disagree.

'Thank you, Sister.'

'This is your choice of ingress?' Emmanuelle inclined her helmed head towards the gaping, doorless portal of a bombed-out penitent processing centre.

'Yeah,' said Kesh. 'Ricard there has been tracking a lot of coming and going that way.' Having both her hands occupied with her fusil, she pointed Ricard out with her elbow. 'It's a minor entry into the workings, little enough that we can get in unobserved, but not so underused that we won't find any prisoners to take. It's not far from where we took the general.'

'Which is?'

Ricard answered reverentially. 'Four processionals over, that way, blessed one.'

'We shall cover the entrance then,' said Emmanuelle, noting the direction. Her voice was rendered husky by her helm voxmitter.

'Just don't do anything... heroic,' said Kesh. She felt awkward. Emmanuelle and her companion were battered by the months-long war: dust and blood had collected in the cracks of their silver armour, and the plates sported more than a few dents, while their robes were as ragged and filthy as the Mordians' uniforms, but they projected an air of serenity that made Kesh feel inadequate. They were so holy, so pure, just talking to them was awkward. 'This is my kind of war, alright?'

'I am surprised Mordians employ such tactics. You are not renowned for your stealth.'

'Yes, well, we pathfinders are not greatly celebrated. You won't find us in the edification pamphlets,' Kesh said. She came

down, put aside her fusil, then checked over her bayonet, pistol,
respirator and the small auspex unit the general had found her.

'But most people on Mordian grow up sneaking around in the
dark, and every army needs someone to gather intelligence.
Marching about in brightly coloured uniforms and shouting
hosannas at the enemy only gets you so far.'

'It gets us quite a long way,' said Palatine Emmanuelle mildly.

Kesh frowned. Was that a joke?

'Get ready,' she said to her men. 'Ricard and Dion, you're
coming with me. Galatka, stay here, cover the entrance from
this side. Change position every twelve minutes.'

'Got it,' said Galatka.

'Where are you going to put yourselves?' Kesh asked Emmanuelle, privately hoping it was going to be some way from
Galatka.

'Fear not, we will find a place. The Emperor will conceal us.'

'Praise Him for His mercies,' murmured Dion.

'Do you know the way?' asked Emmanuelle. 'The maps are
incomplete.'

'Yes,' said Kesh. 'We know enough. Don't worry about us.'

'It is my duty to worry about all of Terra's faithful children,'
said the Palatine. 'Be careful. We lost several servo-skulls map-
ping this area, and the amount of time they were operative
diminished with each one sent. Something was waiting for
them, in the end. It might be waiting for you.'

'Thank you, Sister,' said Kesh.

'Are you sure you do not want us with you?'

'Stealth and thunder? Bad mix.' She rapped a knuckle on the
Sister's thigh plate, and instantly regretted her over-familiarity.
'Too noisy,' she mumbled.

There were muted sounds as Ricard and Dion divested themselves of their fusils. They would have no use for sniper rifles

down in the dark. All of them snapped stablights to the tops of their pistols, then they touched up the nightblack on each other's faces. Dion folded up his cap and stowed it. Ricard and Kesh had put theirs away earlier, Kesh rolling hers up and tucking it into her epaulette, as was her custom.

'Could you bless us, Sister?' asked Ricard.

Emmanuelle looked to Kesh.

'Please,' Kesh said.

Galatka kept watch as the three of them knelt before Emmanuelle, crossed their arms in the aquila and bowed their heads. Kesh's eyes fixed on the head of the flanged power mace dangling by Emmanuelle's calf.

Emmanuelle gave them a quick blessing, commending their souls to the Emperor in case they should fall. It was the usual mantra of service to mankind and its master, but coming from Sister Emmanuelle it felt more potent somehow than when Preacher Scavukus had recited the words.

He was dead now, of course, like so many others.

'For Him on Terra,' Emmanuelle finished.

'For Him on Terra,' said the Mordian scouts.

Kesh looked to Dion and Ricard. Bright white eyes shone out of sooty faces. 'Are you ready?' she said.

They nodded. Galatka lifted her right hand up and made a circle of affirmation with her thumb and forefinger, though she kept her rifle trained on the street.

'Then move out.'

They swept across the street, sticking close to cover. Ricard and Dion went into the building first, their laspistols drawn. Kesh risked a glance back. She couldn't see either Galatka or the Battle Sisters, but she gave a quick salute before going after. The auspex slapped uncomfortably against her leg.

A path had been cleared through the detritus. Dotted about were signs of people, scraps of cloth and discarded ration packs in the main, but Kesh paused over a patch of blood soaked black into the dust. They moved on, footfalls barely audible, towards a stairway at the back. The building had suffered a fire, and the rooms within were scorched, making it dark. Ricard held up his hand, drew his gun and peered down the steps, laspistol steady in both hands.

Clear, he signed, and they pushed on into the first sub-level. Another set of stairs, then another, and in a pillared cellar they reached the entrance to the workings.

It looked like the door giving access to Gathalamor's endless underworld had been removed and the portal hacked into a wide, round maw studded with rebar teeth. There were piles of bones beneath the dripping bricks of the cellar vaulting. They'd been sorted from the rubble meticulously, which made Kesh uneasy. Emperor alone knew why. Though she was down there to find out things like that, part of her had hoped she wouldn't.

'Scout, observe, then withdraw,' she said to her men. They all had their guns out now. Dion took out his bayonet, swapping his laspistol to his left hand so he could hold his blade in his right. Ricard left his bayonet sheathed. He favoured a two-handed grip on his gun.

Dion covered the cellar entrance. Ricard knelt by the hole in the wall, peering into the darkness of the catacombs. There was no illumination, so they were going to need their stablights, a situation Kesh had wanted to avoid.

She took out the auspex and activated it. Its tones were switched off and screen muted to combat glow, but still the light it gave out made her uneasy. Fearing its emanations might be detected, she selected a short scan pulse.

Nothing living appeared on the cartograph. Orange lines in some corridors were power feeds, lumens were splotches. Air currents played as ethereal patterns. But no life, no movement.

'Go, go,' she said. 'Light on, Ricard. We'll follow your lead.'

Ricard's lumen beam stabbed into the dark, lighting a cone of the tunnel starkly. He moved off at a steady walk, sweeping his light back and forth.

The catacombs went on forever, as far as Kesh could tell. Each one had its own character. *Throne*, she thought, each level of each catacomb had its own character, and yet they somehow contrived to seem all the same. Here the dead were stood upright, lining each side of the corridor, facing forward, in a macabre recreation of a parade. The air was dry and the corpses were desiccated, so that most of them were held together with rock-hard sinew beneath their fragile costumes. She'd have expected the heads to fall free at least, but as Ricard's light swept over them she glimpsed rusty wires holding limbs in place, and once seen, she noticed more. Someone had been down there repairing the dead. Judging by the thick layer of dust around the corpses, that had been centuries ago.

They came to a junction. Ricard stopped. Again Kesh pulsed the auspex. Its dim screen seemed dazzling in the dark.

'Clear,' she said. 'No life signs.'

They went on, stopping at every junction, ears straining, as Kesh ran a scan. The unit had a good part of the catacombs there preloaded, enough for them to head with confidence towards the dig site she'd shown Dvorgin last week, but the edges led off into unknown tunnels the skulls had failed to map.

Emmanuelle's words came back to her.

'It might be waiting for you.'

'Nothing,' Kesh said over and over again, until: 'Wait. I have something.'

Ricard snapped off his light and looked about. Mordian eyes were sharp in the dark, and there were a few lumens strung down that particular tunnel, giving them enough to see by.

'How many?'

'One. Weak life sign.'

Kesh tuned the auspex to a sharper reading.

'No,' she said. 'Sleeping.'

'Wake up, traitor scum,' said Ricard. He poked the sleeper in the ribs with his gun and stepped back quickly from the niche she occupied. The skeleton that had lain there was in pieces on the floor, its bones replaced by a warm body.

She looked like a bundle of rags, until she turned over, and the Mordians saw she was a woman, not old but prematurely aged by a brutal life. Few teeth, dirt caked into every line on her face, eyes red with corpse dust. She held up her hands.

'Nottodon!' she said. She was wild, blinded by the stablights, and afraid. 'Lone sleptet! Ni-ni mortan, bekinde!' She scrambled out of the niche, scattering bones. She threw herself onto the floor and pressed her face into the dirt. 'Besta I digern, harderly andan. More fro-me worku! Bekinde!' She fell into an incomprehensible jabber. What words they could pick out were jumbled and heavily accented. 'Yesto four great onis, all resterly andan! Forgivernit I, begern I! Notto betaten, notto killaten andan!'

'Gathalect,' said Kesh in disgust. They'd heard it plenty, mostly among the traitors. Always it was the poor who heard the call of Chaos loudest.

'You are lucky,' said Ricard slowly to her. 'We're not you're masters.'

He hauled her up, wrinkling his nose at her smell. The woman stank of something worse than poor hygiene.

She was weak. Dion had no trouble grabbing her wrists and binding her hands behind her back with plastek detention bracelets.

'Gag her, before she works out what's going on,' said Kesh. The woman's struggles were easily dealt with. Dion stuffed a rag into her mouth and tied it in place. They had no muzzles with them. Supplies of everything at base were low. They'd been lucky to get the cuffs.

'Stablight,' said Kesh.

Ricard shone his into the face of the woman, which had the benefit, from Kesh's point of view, of levelling his pistol at her eye.

'Listen to me,' Kesh said slowly. The higher classes of Gathalamor spoke standard Low Gothic, and most of the population understood it. 'We will not hurt you if you come quietly. If you don't, you'll wish your masters had found you sleeping.'

The woman seemed to take a moment to process Kesh's words, then she nodded frantically and moaned. Tears streaked her dusty face. She was trying to speak through the cloth.

'Quiet!' Kesh nodded to her men. She looked about uneasily. They should go deeper, but something wasn't right. The woman wasn't much of a prisoner, but she was all the excuse Kesh needed to leave.

'We're leaving,' Kesh said.

'Right then, back up we go,' said Ricard, shoving the woman forward.

'We should be quick. Finding this is a stroke of luck. Luck never holds,' said Dion, and spat in the dirt.

Kesh used the auspex again. Seeing nothing, she followed her men.

From a dark spot close to the edge where the map ran out, Kesh watched the tunnel with growing worry. Quiet when they entered, now a work gang was coming down from the surface in double files. Overseers in cured leather masks watched, electro-whips coiled in their hands. Small teams were setting up arc lumens.

'Shit,' said Kesh. She slipped away, back into the junction.

'I told you luck never holds,' said Dion glumly.

'What about that way?' said Ricard. He nodded down the main tunnel, away from the work gang.

'No. It's not mapped, and it smells deep,' said Kesh. It did; a draught carried chill, musty air up to them.

'It's away from the enemy. We could find another way out once we've got a bit of space between us and them,' argued Ricard.

Kesh shook her head. 'We stick to the mapped area. If we get lost down here, we'll never get out. These tunnels add up to thousands of miles.'

The noise of the work gang covered their voices. Ricard had their prisoner face down, his pistol pressed into the nape of her neck. Dion watched the side tunnel entrance.

'Maybe they'll move on by,' said Kesh. 'Then we can slip past and get back out the way we came in.'

Dion leaned forward. 'I don't think so.'

'What makes you–'

'Shhh!' Dion said. 'Listen.' The clatter of tools came to them. 'They've started digging here!'

Ricard cocked his head. 'Those aren't tools. Too hollow-sounding.' He looked at his comrades. 'Bones?' he said as he craned his neck to see. 'They're throwing the corpses onto the floor, and picking up the bones.'

Kesh glanced back down the side tunnel. 'We'll take this one instead. It looks like it runs parallel to the basements on this street.'

'Not mapped either, though,' said Ricard.

'No, it's not mapped either,' said Kesh harshly. 'But that's the way we're going.'

Ricard hauled the prisoner to her feet.

They vanished into the shadows.

Within twenty minutes they were hopelessly lost.

* * *

'We're going down,' Dion said. 'The air's getting warmer.'

Kesh checked the auspex thermo-register. It was possible to gauge their depth by temperature. It was cool underground to begin with, then as one got deeper, the temperature climbed until it became unbearably hot. She couldn't tell exactly how far underground they were, but Dion was right; they were descending.

'We're not too far down,' she said truthfully. 'It's not that warm. We should be out soon.' That was a lie. She had no idea where they were.

They stopped at a junction, as they had at all the others. She let out an auspex pulse. The return came quickly, sketching in the three-dimensional maze of catacombs and adding it to the machine's store of data. Where the pulse gave out, all ended in blackness, so Kesh twisted a knob and moved the display back to the areas mapped by the Battle Sisters' servo-skulls. There was a gap of several hundred feet between their current position and the nearest known area. Not too far at all, and there were no signs of life or of movement between.

'I think we've got a way out,' she said. She pointed down a black tunnel. 'That way.'

Dion and Ricard went ahead, Dion in the lead with his stablight on, Ricard with the prisoner behind. The darkness seemed particularly thick, the light of the lumen a hard circle that trapped the bones in the walls.

Dion suddenly stopped. 'Did you hear that?'

They listened. Kesh heard nothing, but felt a stirring of air move across her. Hairs on her neck prickled.

'There was nothing on the auspex?' Dion asked.

'I'm going to check again,' she said. She let out a pulse. Energetic particles soaked their surroundings, their delayed return giving the data. Half a second passed, and the screen filled with information, the same tunnels, the same distance to known halls, and no...

'Wait,' she said.

A red mark flared in a position on the map behind them.

'I've got something.' She looked up. Dion, Ricard and the prisoner were chiaroscuro studies; they could have been oils from the umbral school on Mordian. She glanced back down. The dot, and the map, was fading out. She put the auspex to constant scan, a power-hungry and easily detectable setting. The catacomb walls filled in more firmly. The red dot reappeared in another corridor beneath them. She slapped the auspex with her hand.

'That's impossible,' she said.

'What?' said Ricard.

'It's like it just sank through the floor.'

'Maybe there's a hole?' said Dion.

There were no holes. 'Get moving, quickly now,' said Kesh.

They began to jog. A hiss sounded in the darkness, far too well formed to be anything but a voice. She looked at the screen. Its light shone over the tunnel walls and the bones inside their niches, lending them an eerie glow. The red dot vanished and reappeared in a passage on their left now, and was closing.

'Faster!' she said. 'Take the next right.'

Ricard swore at the prisoner as he forced her to move. She was weeping around her gag. Dion snapped his stablight around, getting nervy.

The pounding of their footsteps changed as they went into a large chamber. Dion's stablight danced over crumbling angels and faceless saints. Long frills of calcium leached from the buildings of the city engulfed tombs and carved screens.

'Which way?' he said.

He panned the light around, passing it over a wall where a thousand skulls stared out of circular holes. The beam glared suddenly as it crossed a spur foundation of a building driven thoughtlessly through the chapel. Three exits greeted them on the other side of that.

Kesh looked at the screen. The dot had vanished.

'Which way, sergeant?' Dion said. He half turned, shifting his light.

'That way. The middle one,' she said, trying to stop her voice shaking. 'It should go up. It's not far.'

'Thank the Throne for that,' said Dion. 'This place is seriously giving me the fear.' He turned again. His stablight caught something floating right in front of him.

Kesh only got a glimpse. She had an impression of a collection of heaving rags in vaguely man-shaped form, like a phantom with a skull for a face, its eyes covered over with a collection of brass-bound lenses.

Something moved out from the rags. Dion's head flew free of his shoulders. A jet of hot blood washed over Kesh's face as he fell. His stablight hit the ground and went out. The prisoner screamed.

'Run!' shouted Kesh. Ricard let out an oath no Emperor-fearing Mordian should ever voice. Kesh felt something move past her, and ducked. A blade hissed close by her face.

Ricard's light came on. She chanced her own. Two shafts of brilliance lanced the gloom. The shape darted through both, daring them to fire. Ricard did, the crack of his laspistol loud in the chapel. A flick of blue light stamped a glowing hole into the stone, but the shape weaved by, swift as a fish in the water.

It veered around them, and vanished behind. The auspex clicked frantically. The device was still locked into stealth mode, and the sounds were ever so small, but they were so many that they needled Kesh's hearing as they grew closer together, warning of growing proximity.

They reached the exit, fearing a blade in the back every step of the way. She'd have preferred a tighter tunnel, one where the thing couldn't get past, but it was tall, and wide, a major thoroughfare once, perhaps, though it had been truncated by a

There was a gap in the bottom, a human-sized version of the
holes used by house vermin.

That's what we are, she thought, *vermin in the tombs of saints.*

'Get ahead, sir, get her out!' Ricard said. Kesh hooked the
prisoner under the elbow and dragged her on. Ricard stood his
ground, his gun up. Kesh shoved the moaning woman towards
the hole in the wall. The prisoner sprawled, unable to get
through. Kesh was cursing and taking out her knife to cut her
hands free when she heard Ricard open fire.

She looked back. Blue flashes and the cone of his stablight
chased the shadow around the tunnel, but it looped and dived,
screeching a perverse mix of animal howls and binharic. Was
it some kind of servitor?

Ricard hit it precisely never. Glowing impact marks shone all
over the tunnel. The thing had vanished, and Ricard was chasing
shadows with his beam. The prisoner was whining something.
Kesh shoved the woman out of the way and bent down, shining
her stablight into the hole.

There was another layer of blocks behind the first, these whole.
They were trapped.

She stood, gun out. The auspex was silent.

'Has it gone?' She shouted now. With all the crackle of gunfire and the thing's wailing, anybody nearby would have heard.
The alert would be going up. If that thing didn't get them first,
something else would.

'I don't know,' said Ricard. 'Stay back, sir.' He sounded scared.
Ricard was never scared.

The thing hadn't gone. It was as if it was waiting for Ricard to
show his fear before it dropped down from the ceiling, maybe
through the ceiling, and engulfed him.

Flapping strands of shiny cloth wrapped about his head, and
constricted. Whipping metal tentacles, each tipped with a cruel

blade, flashed in Kesh's lumen light. The thing's head turned around to regard her, even while Ricard tore at the rags, his screams muffled.

Soulless lenses glared in the dark. The rags twitched hard, snapping Ricard's neck. Blades sliced down, ripping his arms from his body.

By then, Kesh was firing.

The shadow-shape unwound itself in the strobe of las-fire. Kesh was sure she had it lined dead in her sights, but every shot seemed to go wide. It rose up, seeming to grow. One shot punched a hole in the rags, but it was closed by more pulsing shadow, and it rushed at her, fleshless jaw open in a howl.

Kesh howled back.

The thunder of boltgun fire had her diving for the floor. Rocket flare lit up the tunnel. The shadow was caught in a crossfire between two weapons either side of the entrance. These did not miss. The bolts were swallowed by the shadowy mass, and many did not detonate, but enough were tripped to end the thing. It was torn apart in a flurry of micro-explosions, and fell to the floor with a wet slap.

It hissed slowly, though it had no mouth nor any mechanical apparatus of speech to make so human a sound. The skull lay still at the head of the rag pile, a metallic spine poking through cloth. Like that, it seemed no menace, a thing of little mass too light to hurt anyone. The eye-lenses were out. Sparks puttered from a whirring mechanism. It was clearly dead, but Kesh kept her laspistol pointed at its head just the same. Her side throbbed. In her exertions she'd torn her stitches.

Palatine Emmanuelle and the other Battle Sister approached. Kesh had been right about one thing: power armour made a racket in those confined spaces.

'How did you find us?' Kesh asked.

'The Emperor is our guide,' said the palatine. She toed the thing.

'What is it? A servitor?'

'Mechanismus diabolus,' said Emmanuelle. 'A daemon machine. I have never seen one so small, but that is what it is. A creature of the warp, clad in technology and stolen flesh.'

Kesh had heard the stories of warp xenos. They all had, since the Rift opened. She felt like vomiting just being near the thing.

'Are there more?'

'Perhaps,' said Palatine Emmanuelle. She looked past Kesh. 'You have a prisoner. Then your mission is a success.'

Kesh looked at the dead thing again. Noisome vapours were beginning to spew from the mouth. Her desire to vomit grew.

'The animus is leaving its shell,' said Emmanuelle. 'I suggest we exit quickly, before it tries to make a home in us.'

Chapter Fourteen

THE APOSTATE'S TOMB

SARCOPHAGUS

A CARDINAL'S LEGACY

Tharador Yheng had chosen a grand portico as the place to greet her master. The saints clustered around the top of the columns had been ritually desecrated for him. She herself had chiselled off the first barred Imperial 'I' before letting her minions loose on it with their tools. They had been thorough, and imaginative. Real severed heads replaced those of decapitated statues. A fresh tableau made of the tormented dead had been set up near the entrance, the bodies arranged on wire armatures and, where necessary, stitched together to create a rotting glory, where craven Imperial priests gave praise to the true gods. Other holy displays were arrayed about the square entrance, and the road beyond was lined with soldiers impaled upon metal spikes and pierced with shards of glass.

The marble paving cracked into powder under the weight of Kar-Gatharr's ancient Rhino. It was black and maroon, the colour of the masters – the true masters, they who spoke with the voices of the gods, not the dour unbelievers of Perturabo.

Its hull crawled with holy scriptures, making its surface seethe. She wished she could read it, but she could not – it was the language of the warp, beyond her ability to decipher, and it hurt her to try. The day would come when the scales would fall from her eyes, and the words would read clear. She had been promised as much by the whispers in the night. Her discovery would bring that gift, she was sure, and she smiled.

Her followers grovelled in a half-circle, arms outstretched and faces to the floor. They whimpered where bits of debris cut at them, but none dared move. Their pain was agreeable to her.

She herself was dressed to impress the master. She wore a clinging black gown that plunged to her navel, showing off new links forced through her flesh down the centre of her chest. The piercings had been painful, but she took it as a sign of the gods' favour that the flesh had closed up immediately. Barely a drop of blood spilled, she marvelled. In her hand she carried a staff, whose forked top gave out a constant blue fire.

The night the power had come to her had been terrifying, yet ecstatic. A whisper on the breeze, a breath on her face, and new understanding bloomed in her. It was only a few days ago, but she clung to the memory for fear it would fade. The fire gave off a cool heat, but she could, she thought, immolate one of her servants with it if she wished. She was tempted to try.

The Rhino came to a clanking halt in front of her, its engine growling like a monster set free from ancient hells. The side door opened, and Kar-Gatharr stepped out in curls of scented smoke, his cloak of shadows writhing around him.

He looked around the square and grunted, unimpressed, but when he looked at Yheng, his eyes lingered on her flaming staff.

'Your powers grow,' he said. 'Such sweet puissance you display. So... charming.'

'A gift for my discovery,' she said.

'Careful, now. You might have found it.' The flame's reflection danced in his eye-lenses. 'Or you might only believe you have.'

'I have, for I have already been rewarded.' The cold fires flared higher.

Kar-Gatharr's chuckle came out of his fanged helm as a growl.

'You know very little still. The gods may be testing you. They enjoy tripping the prideful.'

She dared be bold then. 'You believe it too, or else you would not have come.' When no word of killing magic or gunshot came in answer to her insolence, she gestured at the portico, and the bronze doors ruptured onto blackness. 'If you will follow, my lord, I will show you the way.'

'We will see if you are right about this,' said Kar-Gatharr. 'I enjoy my acolytes' failures as much as I like their successes.'

'The Dark Gods willing, my lord, you will have the latter pleasure,' she said with a tilt of her head. It was here. She had found it, she knew it. Sending for Kar-Gatharr would have been suicidal otherwise. 'It is not too far, a little way, but it is deep.'

'Then lead on, Tharador Yheng,' he said.

Tharador went under the portico to the doors. Bright metal shone through verdigris where her servants had cut and bashed them in. She passed into a cool gloom, the master's heavy tread at her heels. Kar-Gatharr's armour sighed as if with pleasure as he stepped underground.

They proceeded a hundred yards down a well-kept corridor, then took a side door. These upper levels had been in use until the invasion. Further in, there were tangles of bodies where pilgrims had died, but the way they were going went much farther under the earth. Behind the door a set of rough-hewn steps led relentlessly downwards.

Kar-Gatharr sniffed the air. His voxmitter amplified the sound into something animalistic.

'I smell damp, and rot. Salt,' he said.

'The sea is close,' said Yheng. 'These tunnels go out underneath it, eventually. Somewhere they have been breached, and the ocean has intruded under the city.'

As they descended, the witch-light of her staff danced from the walls.

'Do we venture past the boundary of earth and water?' Kar-Gatharr answered.

'The tomb is at the edge,' she said. 'Stone and salt, water and earth. Always the greatest power is concentrated in liminal places.'

'It is so,' he replied approvingly.

The stairs were dead straight and narrow, and the stone damp. Kar-Gatharr's pauldrons scraped a pattering of sand from the walls. His feet crushed steps into dirt.

'The deeper one ventures into the catacombs the more ancient they become,' she said. 'Some have been places of pilgrimage for thousands of years, but deep enough and the catacombs become a place of slow forgetting and decay. No saint lasts forever. Even the most beloved martyr falls out of favour. I have seen the most glorious monuments down here, buried in the filth of ages, the saints they celebrated anonymous. Another illusion of the Imperium's permanence.'

'Our gods are eternal,' said Kar-Gatharr. 'To be their servant is to never be forgotten. To die in their name is to join them in the warp. Serve them, and see how the faithful are rewarded!' His voice boomed. The dark and the echoes gave the sense that the steps went down forever. 'Or fail,' he added, 'and know damnation. It is all the same to them.'

'I will not fail,' Yheng said, and led him onward.

She was proud that she and her followers had been sent deepest of all, down through collapsed stairwells and compacted layers of bone. Day after day they had toiled with machines, hand tools and, when they had to, bloodied fingers. Down they had dug through grottos of marble and iron where discarded offerings to discarded saints lay in mouldering heaps. They had dug through layers of glass many feet deep, the glare of their arc lights creating unsettling motion in the depths. Faces swam there. The eyes of figures peered from vitrified purgatory.

They had dug through stone, and sand, and death.

Through all the hardships Tharador had driven her followers on, allowing the weak to perish and the strong to prevail. Her own gifts had grown as she drew closer to their prize. This place had been the making of her; now she would become its mistress.

She led the master off the steps into a broad tunnel roofed with weeping rock and floored with earth. She had ordered all work to cease out of respect for him, and they passed dig teams who knelt silently in the shadows. Handcarts waited to be pushed upwards, loaded with carefully selected bones dragged from their repose.

You are eager, she thought of Kar-Gatharr. *Lord Tenebrus bade you hasten us.* She would not have dared to voice the thought; she did not want to die, she knew Kar-Gatharr did not like to acknowledge Tenebrus' seniority, and took pains to conceal it in front of their cult minions. Yheng was not fooled. She had spent her entire life embroiled in the politics of one violent hierarchy after another. She saw the signs of resentment.

They walked a long way north. Miles under the ground, past workings where bones were sorted, howling ventilation shafts, idling machines, always going towards the sea.

At last they came to a sloping tunnel that clung to hints of fineness. The scent of corruption was sweet there, mingling with brine, as of dead things rotting on the seashore. Harsh light spilled up the tunnel from the arch at its far end, accompanied by the snort of a portable generatorum. More of her followers waited, respirators wheezing.

Kar-Gatharr stopped.

'I sense something here,' he said.

'That is glad news, my lord,' she said, and allowed herself a private smile.

They passed a buzzing arc light, and went back into shadow, going through an antechamber, then into a wide, perfectly cubical room, lit from every angle. A pair of huge adamantium blast doors faced them, half open, their locking mechanisms bored out. Their black faces were heavily worked with hexagrammatic wards that drew a growl of disgust from the master.

'It cannot have been easy to open this gate,' he said.

'It was not, my lord,' she replied. 'We were obliged to bring fusion beams to melt the locks. It took four days and cost the lives of ten of my people.' She led the way into the high-ceilinged chamber beyond. Yheng had grasped immediately that this was not a place of repose, but a prison. Adamantium reinforcing bars ran through the structure. Thick black columns of gheist-iron inscribed with further runes held up the ceiling. Every surface was covered in warding marks. Despite the heavy construction of the chamber, it had not been strong enough to protect against time, and half of the chamber's ceiling had collapsed.

Yheng gestured at the end of a black sarcophagus jutting from beneath the rubble.

'What they hide in shame and fear, we embrace in the gods' names,' said Yheng. She flourished her staff, lighting up High Gothic letters picked out in theldrite across a beam. Much of the inscription was lost, but there was enough to see it for a warning. At the end was a complete word, a name written in blood in every book of history it graced, and all those were forbidden.

Bucharis.

'Behold,' she said simply. 'The cardinal's tomb.'

Kar-Gatharr nodded. 'Are you sure it is the genuine resting place, and not another decoy?'

She smiled openly now.

'Bucharis!' she shouted.

A draught rose to a low moan, her fire danced, and the sickly smell of rot swelled. Despite her new-gained power, Yheng found herself afraid. A sense of brooding menace pervaded the crypt, something that lurked in its far edges and rushed in to fill the shadows every time a lumen spirit failed, or a figure moved in front of the lights. There was a malevolence here. Calling it into the open tested her nerve.

'He is present,' said Kar-Gatharr, with a tone approaching delight. 'How fascinating.' He glanced over the wards. 'These kept his soul in here, I suspect. Oh, how piquant his suffering. Thousands of years trapped in the earth.' He laughed.

The moan returned, louder now, and Kar-Gatharr's uncanny cloak fluttered in the force of its anger.

'It hates us for our intrusion,' she said quickly. 'It will hurt us if it can. The presence was weak at first, but the more we dug out the sarcophagus, the stronger it became.'

'Do not fear this shade,' said Kar-Gatharr dismissively. He looked at Yheng. 'We serve masters more powerful than he. Uncover the sarcophagus,' he commanded. 'We shall have what we came for.'

Yheng's followers moved to obey, dozens of them, working at the immense weight of rubble that still covered the sarcophagus and adding to the heaps of spoil growing in the corners. They were brave to do so. Bucharis' hungering presence haunted them all. Many had died. All knew fear. They pressed on, showing their devotion to the gods with every pick stroke.

Yheng and Kar-Gatharr watched for an hour as another foot of the sarcophagus' length was cleared. It was featureless, smooth basalt. No carving of its occupant adorned its lid. There was no inscription. After another hour they had cleared the top, so that it might be worked free.

'There,' said Kar-Gatharr. 'Our prize is revealed.' Many of the cultists glanced back at the sound of his voice, but they had the sense to keep labouring.

'Yes, my lord,' she replied. 'It ought to be but a matter of hours before the base is cleared and the rockfall made safe–'

'Open it now,' he commanded. His words reverberated through the watchful gloom. The shadows thickened. The workers stopped. Yheng felt a swell of panic.

Bucharis is powerless, she berated herself. *Focus.*

'My lord, if we open the sarcophagus prematurely, without the proper bracing in place or the cult's witches present–'

'Open it now,' he cut her off again. Yheng fought her fear. Her cultists looked to her for direction and in that moment, she hated them for it.

'My lord–' she tried again, but her voice faltered as his heavy hand fell upon her shoulder.

'Look upon me, Tharador Yheng,' said the master. Silver chains jingling quietly together, she did as he bade. 'You are a magus of the gods,' he said. 'You are favoured in their eyes. There is nothing here but an echo of old hates. Are you afraid of something so pitiful?'

'No, my lord,' she lied.

'Then open the sarcophagus.'

Yheng turned back to the diggers. In the depths of the chamber something scraped against stone.

'Do as the master says,' she commanded, her tone iron-hard despite her nerves.

To their credit, the cultists did not hesitate. The dig team moved back from the sarcophagus and laid down their tools. Half a dozen of them took up pry bars, and attempted to jam them into the fine join between lid and base. The steel would not bite, and skidded from the stone. One got the crow's foot of the bar inside, but when he wrenched down on the metal, it broke as if it were made of ice, and he fell. They looked to Yheng, and she ordered them back.

'Drills,' she commanded.

Three cultists chosen from the largest and strongest hefted drills with long bits. Backpack power sources were awakened with whispered rituals, and the men raised the whining tools.

'Begin,' she said.

The men applied the drills to the black stone of the sarcophagus. Yheng pushed her will outwards, feeling for the metal, strengthening it, helping it find weakness. She marvelled at her new powers, even as the touch of otherworldly malice chilled her soul.

Sparks flew. The lumens flickered, died, lit, flickered again.

An angry growl rose upon the very edge of hearing, more felt than heard. It caused Yheng's scalp to tighten. Towards the back of the group of cultists, someone cried out in terror, then their courage failed and most scattered from the chamber. The shadows were coming alive, black as tar, reaching for the living.

The lumens strobed.

'Courage! No weakness before the gods! Keep working!'

The drills screamed as they bit deeper into the black sarcophagus and the lights flashed madly. Several lumen bulbs exploded. Yheng knew a moment of horror as she imagined what might happen if they all went out.

One of the drillers screamed, and she saw a flash of his terrified face before he was dragged through the floor as if it were water, his drill clanging on the surface, its power cable embedded in the stone. The remaining two faltered, and stepped back. She unsheathed her ritual dagger and dropped into an old gangers' fighting stance.

'Enough,' Kar-Gatharr said. He stepped forward, pushing her out of the way, unhooked his mace and held it high over his head. 'Abjurum nulifactum absolutis!' roared Kar-Gatharr. His voice rolled like thunder. A deathly light danced about the head of his weapon, black in its own way, yet possessing a strange luminance that pushed back at the shadows. 'Thing of hate, I deny you! Wasted spirit, I command you! Turn aside in the name of Khorne the mighty, Slaanesh the bountiful, Nurgle the life-giver and Tzeentch the wise! I am an agent of the pantheon's will, I bear the fire of Lorgar's truth in my hearts and you shall obey me!'

A halo of black lightning blazed from his mace's head, piercing the darkness with shadows darker yet. A piercing shriek echoed from some distant place. Yheng fell to the floor, her hands over her ears. There was a sense of rushing wind, anger, pain. All faded.

The lumens fizzed weakly.

'Yheng,' said Kar-Gatharr. 'Rise.'

Yheng uncurled and stood.

A few of her cultists remained. Several were dead, bloody messes embedded in the solid rock. The survivors had drawn close to Kar-Gatharr. Their fear of the master was evidently less than their terror of the spirit.

'You will find no more resistance,' Kar-Gatharr said. 'Continue.'

The drillers stepped over their comrade's half-entombed tool, and applied the bits to the stone again. The tips hammered in and out as they drilled, and this time, the sarcophagus yielded.

There came a sudden crack and crumbling of stone, and a portion fell away. The two cultists stepped back, quieting their drills. Yheng stared into the broken sarcophagus. Absolute darkness lay within, cold and ravenous as the void of space.

She must go forward first. She must take it. If she did not and Kar-Gatharr removed the relic, he would discard her.

This was her moment. This was her success, or her failure. It was her choice.

Sick with terror, Tharador Yheng advanced across the chamber, away from the protective aegis of the Dark Apostle and towards the source of the terrible thing haunting this chamber. Within was a force of evil greater than anything she had ever encountered.

Still, she had a duty. The gods rewarded only those who *earned* it.

Muttering prayers to the pantheon, she knelt in the sharp rubble at the sarcophagus' side. She steeled herself, then thrust her arm into the icy dark, aware of Kar-Gatharr's eyes on her. With every thudding heartbeat she expected something dreadful. She imagined a clawed hand snatching her wrist and dragging her into the black. She imagined the shadows flowing forth to asphyxiate her, or some ghastly thing crawling from the gloom and into her soul.

Instead her fingers found ash, dust, then, to her surprise, something hard and smooth.

A skull? she wondered. *Do I hold the very skull of Bucharis in my hand?* But it felt wrong. Ceramic, she thought, *or metal.* Throat tight, flesh taut with terror, Yheng closed her hand around her prize and drew it from the shadows.

It was an urn, little larger than her hand, fashioned from night-dark pottery across which sigils crawled profusely, and sealed with black wax that still seemed fresh.

Her heart almost stopped as something loomed over her. Yheng looked up to see Kar-Gatharr, and not some monstrous phantasm. The Dark Apostle reached down and opened his free hand, the massive weight of his crozius mace hanging easily at his side in the other.

'Give it to me, Tharador Yheng,' he said.

She obeyed.

Kar-Gatharr gave a rumble of satisfaction as he raised the urn up to the glowing eye-lenses of his helm. Yheng walked away from the sarcophagus with what dignity she could muster, rejoining her remaining cultists and hoping against hope that the Dark Apostle would give them the command to depart. She didn't trust the last few lumens. She could still feel the cardinal's malice pressing in upon them from the shadows. Yet

Kar-Gatharr stood without concern, holding the urn before himself and admiring it.

At last he turned back towards them and gestured at the chamber's huge doors.

'It is time to return to the surface,' he said, and Yheng heard the satisfaction in her master's voice. 'Gathalamor has yielded its prize at last.'

She bowed her head. The silver chains clinked. She could feel Kar-Gatharr looking at her for a long time. Her heart pounded when he spoke again.

'You will accompany me,' he said measuredly. 'You have done well, and so you shall present the relic to Lord Tenebrus yourself.'

Yheng felt a surge of triumph.

'Thank you, my lord,' she said.

Chapter Fifteen

A PRAYER FOR REDEMPTION

MAKE US PROUD

THE SISTERS' MERCY

The bombardments that day were particularly intense. Dull explosions started at dawn and were still going in the evening when Dvorgin took his prayers.

In the morning he prayed with the men, as he should, and he sat at the front of every regimental service, even when he was not required to address the troops himself. He believed sincerely in the will of the Emperor. It was his duty to share worship with those he commanded.

Eventide prayers were for him alone. He gave orders that he was not to be disturbed, closed the door to his room quietly and removed his boots, cap and gun belt. He arranged them neatly on a chair, then got down on complaining knees before his portable shrine. Beneath the figure of the Emperor were mementoes of friends he'd lost, and at the front, a small plastek figurine of a woman.

Marie.

He lit the candles. He made the sign of the aquila over his

heart, and kissed the icon he wore about his neck. With gentle hands he took out his pocket chron and opened it.

> *Luthor,*
> *Make us always proud, my fierce protector,*
> *Marie.*

He read it again, and touched the words with his fingers. They trembled, the only time they did that. Then he laid the chron next to the figure, as he did every night, situating the inscription so that it caught the candlelight. The sanctum trembled to the beat of the enemy guns. They were targeting the southern reaches, and bringing down whole sections of the city that still stood outside the void shields. Nevertheless, he found the noise soothing. After so many years of war, quiet made him nervous.

He bent his head and let his thoughts wander. Meditation was supposed to be the voiding of the mind, so as to let the grace of the Emperor replace the burden of individual will, but Dvorgin had never had the knack of such absolute devotion, and instead he used these few moments of peace to think without command pressing on him. He called to mind Marie, as she was the night before he left, when precious energy was burned to push back the ceaseless Mordian night.

Only one thing frightened Dvorgin, and that was that he would forget the face of his wife. He had no pict of her. He had lost all those early on. He remembered with painful clarity the shells coming down out of the sky onto the camp on Drossian, wiping out his tent and all his personal belongings with it. At no point since had he felt more despair. His men had had to hold him back from rushing into the fire.

He now remembered that event better than her face. All he had left was the pocket chron, and the inscription.

Make us always proud.

Would she be proud? he wondered. Some might call him a hero, he supposed. He didn't feel like one. Some of things he'd done shamed him.

'The Emperor expects,' he said obediently. 'Duty is paramount, whether distasteful or a joy.' He tried to bring the Emperor's grace to the forefront of his mind. He tried to beg for redemption for his one, little lapse.

As usual, he failed.

It had gone like this. His last night with Marie. They had stolen some time away from the raising celebration. The bands' music filled the city and the people cheered their departing heroes, fresh in their uniforms of Mordian blue, more grist to the mill of the Emperor's ambition.

'They know they may die,' said Dvorgin, looking down from a high balcony on the soldiers marching through the street. 'Yet they go anyway.'

Marie nestled into his side. She was sad and she was content, for though her heart was to depart with Dvorgin, she was proud that he was to go.

'You are not afraid, Luthor,' she said.

'Never,' he said proudly. 'I am Mordian born. To serve the Emperor off-world is the highest of honours, and the gravest of responsibilities. I accept it gladly.'

He turned from the parade and the shouts in the street. The dark of Mordian's skies arced overhead; the false day only stretched so far. The streets were rivers of light cutting between squat, pyramidal hives.

'I leave you sadly,' he said. He brushed a stray strand of hair from her face.

She looked at him fiercely, though tears gathered in the corners of her eyes. 'I will die happy knowing I married a hero.'

He smiled. 'I'm no hero yet, my love.' He looked at the pocket chron she'd given him only half an hour before. Then it was new, and its weight unfamiliar. He depressed the catch for only the third time, and read the inscription that he already knew by heart. 'But I'll try to make you proud.'

The marching bands swelled. Flights of void fighters streaked overhead, fireworks bursting between them. He looked down into her face. In his memory she was shifting, changing. The harder he tried to hold the vision, the more uncertain her face became.

'I love you, Luthor,' she said. She kissed him, and laughed as the braid on his uniform tickled her face, though there were tears mixed in.

He remembered her words perfectly, but her face was fading

She laid her hands on his chest and pushed back a little. 'Luthor,' she said. She bit her lip and looked down, unsure. 'I want to ask you something, and I want you to say yes.'

This was the one time. It was coming. He forced himself to relive it as he did every day. His penance for his failure.

'Anything, my dear,' he said.

The only time his faith had failed him. The one time he had refused her, and Him.

She smiled and looked up at him. 'I want you to leave me with a child.'

His own smile froze on his face, for his first and overwhelming reaction was to say no. He wanted to say: why would I bring a child into this universe? Why would I want a child only so they too could grow in the dark, then join a regiment to go off and die on some faraway world? There is only pain in life, and service that leads to death, he wanted to say. He served gladly, but to force that on someone else... He could not doom another to his fate. He could not doom one who did not ask for it. Though he knew it must be done, he knew also what awaited him in the stars. Glory was a poor reward for horror.

She looked up at him, expectant, waiting for an answer. 'Luthor?' she said. Her smile faltered at his silence.

'I...' he began. He could not finish. How could he tell her what he felt? How could he say no?

'Luthor?'

He turned away. In the streets, the music played on.

He couldn't bring himself to remember any more. This was the failure of his faith, his greatest sin: an unwillingness to give the Emperor His due and honour Him with children to fight His eternal wars.

'Forgive me, my Emperor,' he whispered. 'Forgive me, Marie.'

A sharp rap on the door broke his reminiscence. His cheeks were wet and he wiped them hurriedly.

'I gave orders that I was not to be disturbed!' he shouted angrily.

Stehner's muffled voice came through the wood. 'My apologies, general, it is most urgent.'

Dvorgin swore and got to his feet, wiping at his face some more, until he was sure it was dry.

'Enter!' he said.

The door opened. Stehner took in Dvorgin's blotchy face and red eyes and looked hurriedly away.

'Forgive me, general, sir, but I have been asked to inform you that Pathfinder Sergeant Kesh has returned to the port.'

'Was she hurt?' Dvorgin asked. He turned on the pretext of pouring some wine to hide his face.

'No, sir, but two of the others who went out with her were killed.'

'Who?' Dvorgin asked.

The messenger consulted a note. 'Pathfinder Troopers Ricard and Dion, sir. Trooper Galatka returned with Pathfinder Sergeant Kesh.'

Dvorgin pulled a face. More dead, and Ricard and Dion were

especially good men. 'Inform the regimental priests to add their names to evening prayers. Special prominence. Get Colour-Sergeant Chedesh to begin appraisal of their deeds for inclusion in the book.'

'Yes, sir.'

'Did Kesh return with prisoners?'

'One, I believe, sir,' said the messenger. 'The Sisters have her and have begun interrogation.'

'What?' said Dvorgin. That was not what he and Veritas had agreed. 'Where?' he said sharply.

'Tower twelve, sir.'

Dvorgin pulled on his cap and buckled his weapon belt about his waist.

'Hand me my boots, Stehner, then go ahead to tell the canoness I am attending.'

Stehner saluted. 'Right away, sir.'

Tower twelve was one of many subsidiary turrets of the Sanctum Miraculous, but though sizeable, its contribution to the great bulk of the building amounted to little more than an architectural flourish. The outside creaked under the weight of religious sculpture. Internally it was a series of stacked rooms, hollow circles less than thirty yards across, with a spiral staircase running up the centre. The topmost floor was larger, as the tower broadened significantly there beneath its conical roof, where the central stairwell ended on a small landing. There was a Battle Sister standing at guard by the door. Nearby, Dvorgin found Kesh sitting with her back to the wall and her las-fusil across her knees.

Kesh began to scramble up when Dvorgin appeared. The Sister did not react.

'At ease, sergeant, no need to get up for me.' She relaxed and he crouched down beside her. 'What's going on?' he asked quietly.

Kesh's teeth flashed white in her dirty face. There was grave dust in her hair, and the remnants of nightblack clinging to her skin.

'They've got my prisoner. They won't let me in on the interrogation but I wasn't about to leave before you got here, sir.'

'What happened out there?'

She hesitated before answering.

'We were lucky, and then we weren't. We found the prisoner sleeping, looks like she gave her work detail the slip. She was more scared of her own than of us.'

'That's the luck, where's the misfortune?'

'She's not a high-value catch. I'm sorry, sir, but that place is bad. We had to get out. We didn't go further, then we took a wrong turn trying to avoid the enemy, sir. I know it sounds like cowardice, sir, but I was right to order us to leave. We ran into something. Something evil. Palatine Emmanuelle saved us, saved me anyway.' She paused uncertainly. 'She said it was a daemon machine,' she whispered.

Dvorgin frowned. That Palatine Emmanuelle openly spoke of such things with someone like Kesh was significant, even after the Great Rift.

'Don't worry. I'm sure this woman will give us something.'

'Ricard and Dion are dead. It got them.' She looked at him, a need for forgiveness writ across her features. 'I couldn't hit it.'

'It's dark down there,' he reassured her.

'No,' she said, shaking her head. 'You don't understand, sir. I tried. You know how good a shot I am. It was like it didn't want me to hit it.' She shook her head again. 'So I couldn't.'

He squeezed her wrist. He often thought if he'd had a child with Marie, they'd be about Kesh's age now. She was like a daughter to him, and he couldn't help but favour her. Another failing. 'I believe you, sergeant.' He stood up. 'Your vigil is done. Return to barracks.'

Kesh pushed herself up, using her gun as a crutch. She winced, and put her hand to her side.

'Your wound, has it opened again?' asked Dvorgin with concern. 'You'd better get to the medicae.'

'Nothing I can't handle,' she said, though she was gritting her teeth. 'Save the space for someone worse hurt.'

'I shouldn't have sent you on this mission.'

'What, and let someone else down there to do my job? I might have been scared, but with respect, sir, not a chance.'

'Well, get it seen to,' he said. 'That's an order. Then pray for an easier tomorrow, and get some rest.'

She nodded. Now she was upright, her face was more visible under the sole lumen illuminating the little landing. She was drawn. Pain had etched lines into what should have been a youthful face.

'Yes, sir,' she said. 'Sir?'

'Yes, sergeant?' he said.

'I could have done better. Dion and Ricard should have got out. I'm sorry.'

'We can all always do better, sergeant,' he said, and Marie's spurned request bubbled up to bother him again. 'You served. You fulfilled your mission. No soldier can do more than that. I am sure what they bought with their deaths will be valuable.'

She nodded her thanks, and left.

'Sister,' said Dvorgin to the sentry. 'Open the door.'

She said nothing to him, but he heard the muffled click of vox-communications, and the hint of words exchanged. *They are playing this close to their chests,* he thought. *They might not let me in.*

But they did.

'You may enter,' she said, and the door opened onto a world soaked in blood.

Dvorgin found himself in a wide room lined with unglazed, arched windows looking out over the city and the void port. It was open to the rafters, where avians stared with beady eyes. Fire burned in the night in numerous quarters, and the sky flashed periodically with the duelling of big guns. The rumble of the artillery was loud there, the thumping of detonations elevated to true explosions that crashed like cymbals. Cool wind scented with smoke blew in, pushing the smell of blood around.

The prisoner was bound to a penitent's chair and surrounded by Sisters of Battle, who watched her with their bolters ready. Canoness Veritas stared at her impassively. For the moment, little was happening. A confessor hooded in black stood ready at the woman's side; a second Sister in plain white robes waited at attention at the other side, singing soft songs of mercy to keep evil at bay, though she bore a tray of cruel instruments. Close by a robed member of the Sisters Dialogus waited. Nobody spoke. They had already been busy with their tools.

The captive was dressed in a plain smock soaked with sweat and blood. Her bare arms had new, fresh brands of Imperial eagles burned over cult tattoos. Her back was forced into a stress position by movable sections in the chair. She squirmed against her bonds and the blocks of wood. A brazier sprouting a spinney of irons burned uncomfortably close to her.

Dvorgin looked on with distaste. 'Veritas, why wasn't I informed that this interrogation was taking place?'

'I wished to save you the spectacle of this bloodshed,' she said mildly. 'What we are about here is unpleasant.'

'I should have been told,' said Dvorgin, though the smell in the room had him half thinking the canoness was right to spare him. He went to the canoness' side. 'What have you learned?'

'I have learned pity,' said Veritas calmly. 'For she is a daughter of Terra, and fallen far from His grace. This woman is a victim of the lies of the Archenemy. Poor child,' she said. 'She was a whittler. They made a living scrimshawing bones and selling them on as saint's relics to the pilgrims. Who knows, some of them might have been holy. Illegal, but tolerated. Theirs was a mean existence, but so it was ordained by the Emperor, and it is not our place to question His plans for us.' She stared at the prisoner. 'What she did to escape her life was neither moral nor excusable.'

The woman whimpered. She spoke the local debased version of Gothic, and Dvorgin couldn't follow it at all, but the dialogan translated her pained words in a near monotone.

'Please,' the dialogan relayed. 'I had no water, I had no food. My children starved and died, then the masters came and promised to make it better, to give us the fine palaces in the light where the fat priests lived. I did not know, I did not know.'

'You did not know it would be worse,' said Veritas.

The dialogan translated the words to the prisoner, and her response.

'No, no, I was tricked!' she said. 'I had little and I lost it all. We were, and we remain, slaves.'

'What are you digging for?' said Dvorgin. He made to go forward, but Veritas stopped him with a hand on his chest.

'Not too close,' Veritas said. 'She looks weak, but the enemy is powerful, and may work through her.'

Dvorgin nodded. 'What are you digging for?' he repeated. 'Tell us and this will be over.'

'No, no, no, no,' the woman moaned. 'The shades will come and devour my spirit! I cannot say, I cannot say.' She lapsed into babbling prayers, a mix of entreaties to the Emperor and the dark lords of the warp. The Sister abruptly stopped her translation as the prisoner went into open blasphemy, took out a silver flask from under her robes, drank from it, swilled out her mouth, and spat scented spirits on the floor.

'We will learn nothing from her,' said Dvorgin.

'We shall,' said Veritas. She nodded at the confessor. The woman leaned closer to the prisoner.

'Confess,' she hissed. 'Tell us what your lying masters were doing in the catacombs, and we shall release you so that you may face the Emperor's judgement, and be free of ours.'

The prisoner dropped her head and wept.

'Confess!' said the confessor, and motioned to the Sister in white. The tray was brought forward. The confessor picked up a hooked knife. 'Confess and know no more pain. Confess. The Emperor is more merciful than we are.'

Dvorgin turned away. Veritas kept watching as the prisoner's tears turned to screams.

'I knew I was right,' said Veritas to Dvorgin. 'You are a soldier, but we do the Emperor's holy work here. It is not for the faint of heart, though I know you loathe these heretics. I understand. It is hard when evil wears a human face.'

'I do loathe them,' Dvorgin said. 'But torture sickens me.'

'Be strong. Her pain will avail us of the answers we seek.'

The screams subsided. The instrument was placed back on the tray with a click. The confessor began to whisper into the woman's ear. There was no need to translate her intent. In moments, the prisoner was moaning for death.

'She is a dupe,' said Dvorgin.

'Yet she chose to follow Chaos, when she could have chosen death, and for that she cannot be forgiven. Mercy is in the Emperor's power to give, if she accepts His love again, but it is not for we, His servants, to make that choice for Him.' Veritas turned to look at him. 'Leave, if you wish. I will inform you of what we learn.'

'I will stay,' said Dvorgin, though he dearly wanted to walk out of the door. Pride, a desire not to be seen as weak, and a deep need to confront the evil that must be done in order to achieve good drove him to remain. There was the small matter of his lapse in faith too, and Marie. He had never removed that stain from his soul. He never would.

He was punishing himself.

He swallowed to lubricate his dry throat. Despite the cold wind blowing through the arches, the heat from the brazier was intolerable. 'Proceed,' he said.

He made himself watch until the end.

Chapter Sixteen

EMPEROR EXULTANT

THE HAND

GOD-KILLER

The Temple of the Emperor Exultant was the wonder of the segmentum, the macro-cathedrum of Asclomaedas the Builder, and it towered over the city. Upon first seeing it, Kar-Gatharr had thought that if a volcano had vomited the contents of Gathalamor's catacombs in flows down its own heaving flanks, it might have looked like this. It was a hideous structure, over-ornamented in clashing styles, a hundred towers reaching up, all covered in angels raising their hands so that when Sol passed overhead on Midsummer's Eve, it was followed by a forest of beseeching fingers.

Now Tenebrus had it for his lair.

Tharador Yheng went at his side when they went to see Tenebrus, escorted by Kar-Gatharr's honour guard, the Chosen Sons. Each warrior's armour was painted with runes of fresh blood. The lead pair carried censers trailing perfumed smoke. The two behind them carried braziers on brass poles. The following two bore a portable altar bearing a velvet cushion. Upon it was an iron reliquary, and inside that was the urn that Yheng had recovered from Bucharis' tomb. Ten more warriors bore banners of sacred design, the rest carried weapons.

They climbed a hill of steps and went across the miles-wide plaza that surrounded the cathedrum. Kar-Gatharr took the procession under the giant northern arch, its saints now daubed with gory sigils, down the colossal nave and into the first of the outer prayer halls. The space had been sanctified to the true gods. Spiked chains wrapped marble columns, binding in place Ecclesiarchical preachers who still moaned weakly for mercy. More chains had been anchored in the high, vaulted ceiling, puncturing the faces of the angels painted there; from them cages swayed in the cold breeze, each containing a Battle Sister, viciously cut with runes of the true gods and left to slowly starve. Braziers belched thick incense, crimson-hued and rippling with shadowy half-shapes. Immense banners depicting the glories of Warmaster Abaddon hung between the pillars. Servo-skulls thrummed through the air, trailing brass thuribles that spattered blessed blood. Where once an Imperial congregation of thousands had gathered, the pews held Chaos worshippers screaming their praises to the warp. Word Bearers of Kar-Gatharr's band stood around the edges, weapons sheathed, helms removed as they offered their own prayers.

'So much pain. So much despair,' said Yheng approvingly. 'I remember when this was a place of hypocrisy. It is pure now.'

'This is but one chamber amongst many,' replied Kar-Gatharr. Yheng visibly swelled with pride that he deigned to speak to her, and he indulged her further. 'My brothers have been tireless reconsecrating this fool's paradise to better gods. You are a part of that.'

They passed into another prayer hall boasting a sacrificial circle made from a thousand corpses, down cloisters around burned gardens where iron octeds thrust at the heavens. They

crossed a bridge between buttressed spires where hanged Impe- 177
rial adepts dangled, rotting in razor wire nooses like spoiled
fruit. Howling wind dragged at the banners the Chosen Sons
carried. The distant rattle of gunfire and the thump of explosions sounded from somewhere away in the city-sprawl far
below. Kar-Gatharr wondered where Lokk was right now.

THE GATE OF BONES

Hunting, more fortune to him, he thought, and he wished that
he could join his comrade in the slaughter.

They reached the antechamber to Tenebrus' lair, a room
dominated by a statue depicting the Emperor, complete with
lumen-lit halo and raised, blazing blade. The stained-glass windows surrounding Him had been desecrated, each in differing
ways. Kar-Gatharr himself had anointed the statue with thrice-
cursed blood, had carved the runes of desecration into the face
of the corpse-god, then impaled Gathalamor's cardinal upon
the raised stone sword.

That had been an effort. The blade was not sharp.

Passing the decomposing cardinal, they ascended a final flight
of steps to Tenebrus' throne room. Towering doors of plasteel
swung open at their approach.

'Remain without,' he commanded his bodyguard. 'Yheng,
take the relic.'

Tharador Yheng took the casket, shivering when she touched
it, but he noted again her mastery of fear.

'Come,' he said to her.

An opulent chamber was remade in darkness. The clear dome
and the arched windows were covered by slabs of iron, so that
now the only light slanted through gaps in the metal, or was
cast by a scattering of candles. These illuminated the black banners that hung about the chamber, each bearing the staring eye
of Horus. Under the dome was a half-seen squirming: Tenebrus' shades, fusions of flesh, technology and the daemonic,
fashioned for the sorcerer by the Mechanicum Lord Xyrax.

At the sanctum's heart was a font with daemonic faces worked around its rim. Over this, staring into oily liquid, was the sorcerer.

As Kar-Gatharr advanced into the chamber the shades rustled, and he caught the faint glint of bone and the gleam of red eyes from the slithering on the underside of the dome.

'Master...' said Yheng unsurely.

'They are shades, cybernetic constructs possessed by the lesser powers, the servants of Lord Tenebrus,' said Kar-Gatharr quietly. 'Remember who Tenebrus speaks for. He is the Hand of Abaddon. Show him your awe. Disrespect him, and even I will not be able to protect you.'

Kar-Gatharr halted several steps from the font and bowed deeply. Yheng kneeled, her silver chains tinkling.

Tenebrus looked up from his scrying. His shades hissed.

He wore a simple black robe belted with a golden sash with the hood up, leaving visible only his serpent's smile and eyes like twin pools of blackness. Maggot-white, taloned fingers poked from his sleeves, overly long and many-jointed. Tenebrus was slender. Kar-Gatharr could have picked him up by the throat with one hand and snapped his neck like a dry branch. Yet a sense of power rolled off him. The heat of it swallowed all the air in the chamber, pressing outwards until Kar-Gatharr was sure the doors must shatter.

'Apostle, you answered my summons!' said Tenebrus, and his voice was soft, rich and cultured. He sounded genuinely pleased, even touched that Kar-Gatharr attended him. To hear such sentiment from that needle-fanged mouth made the Dark Apostle's skin crawl.

'Of course, Lord Tenebrus,' Kar-Gatharr replied. He rose, reached up and removed his horned helm, exposing a handsome face covered in lines of golden script.

'And... have you brought me an offering?' asked Tenebrus, walking slowly around Kar-Gatharr and peering towards Yheng.

'No, Lord Tenebrus, that is my acolyte,' said Kar-Gatharr, ensuring his tone remained respectful even as it carried a note of warning.

Remember who I am, he thought. *Remember that you are not the only champion of the gods here.*

Tenebrus' fingers twitched.

'A shame, for I have been divining. I do not mind telling you that it gives me *quite* an appetite,' he said, still staring at the cult leader. His eyes glinted like beetles' backs. 'And there is something about this one...' He reached up and wiped a strand of drool from his mouth onto his sleeve.

'There is plentiful sustenance in this place, Lord Tenebrus,' said Kar-Gatharr, moving to stand between the creature and his acolyte. 'Allow me to send for a more suitable meal.'

'Kind of you, but no,' sighed Tenebrus. 'If I may not eat it, then please send it away, Apostle. One cannot think clearly when one's appetite is so aroused, no?'

'Then you must control yourself, for I will not dismiss her,' said Kar-Gatharr. 'She has something for you. A different sort of offering.'

'Yet not her soul or her flesh?' Tenebrus smiled his predator's smile. 'Oh, how fascinating. You must show me!'

'Rise, Tharador Yheng, Mistress of the Blade Unsheathed.'

Yheng got to her feet and presented the casket, her head bowed.

'I gave Yheng the honour of this audience, for it was she who found that which we sought. The Apostate Bucharis' bequest,' said Kar-Gatharr. He summoned a column of black light with a gesture, and placed his helm upon it, then he opened the reliquary and lifted out the contents.

Reverently, Kar-Gatharr raised the ward-engraved urn in one fist, his other hand cupped below it. Then he squeezed.

Millennia-old ceramic gave beneath his fingers. Warding runes flared like embers then died. A terrible wail rolled through the prayer hall. Every candle blew out. Shadows crawled long and hungry across the chamber and a sawing tremor ran through everything, as though the world itself vibrated with malice. Kar-Gatharr felt ancient malevolence directed against him as ash blew through his fingers, and something small and metal clinked into his armoured palm. The runes painted onto his flesh glowed with heat as they held Bucharis' maddened soul at bay.

'Unto you I present Bucharis' Gift,' intoned Kar-Gatharr, clenching his fist around the small object that had fallen from the urn. 'Unto you I present the weapon of the Dark Gods, the opener of the gates, the maker of the path, the breaker of faith, that which was prophesied!'

Spectral winds howled about the Dark Apostle and Yheng cried out, though whether in exultation or terror he couldn't tell. Shadows and ghostlight passed wildly through the open space.

Nearby a bell tolled.

'And I accept it,' said Tenebrus, and his calm, oily voice cut through the madness and stilled it with shocking suddenness. He reached out one pale hand and plucked the treasure from Kar-Gatharr's smouldering gauntlet.

'The Ring of Bucharis,' he crooned. His treasure glinted, a signet ring as black as marble set with a blood-red stone. 'Now,' he said in exultation. 'Now they will know our vengeance.'

Tenebrus slipped the ring onto a finger.

He admired it a moment, then said to Yheng, 'Well done, well done! Kar-Gatharr was right not to let me eat you.' He wagged a finger at her as if this were amusing. 'We have everything we need to end this foolish crusade of the corpse-god's son, yes?'

'Magos Xyrax's weapon is ready, then?' said Kar-Gatharr.

'Nearly, nearly,' chuckled Tenebrus. He peered at Yheng. 'You are a native of this world, yes?'

'Yes, my lord.'

'Tell me then, what do you know of the apostate Cardinal Bucharis?'

'Little, my lord,' said Yheng. 'I only know that he is important to the gods' plans, that he was a famous figure in the past, which is why I humbly set myself to seeking out his tomb.'

'Ah! So you know nothing. To be expected, because that is what they intended,' said Tenebrus. 'The suppression of true knowledge, you see?' he said to Kar-Gatharr, smiling again. 'Ever the corpse-god's modus operandi.' He walked around Yheng, looking her up and down hungrily. 'Bucharis, young lady, was a cardinal of this world, its ruler some four thousand years ago. You will not find his name on the Cardinal's Column, nor will you find it in any but the most secret of histories. Tell me,' he said. 'You must surely know who built this delightful building?'

Yheng looked to Kar-Gatharr in confusion. The Dark Apostle inclined his head.

'My lord knows that this building was the project of Cardinal Asclomaedas,' said Yheng unsurely.

'No, no!' Tenebrus said, raising an admonitory talon. 'That is what they tell you. No, this cathedral was built by Bucharis. It was the cause of his rise to power.' His too-wide smile grew wider still. 'And the cause of his downfall. Despite its importance as a cardinal's seat, Gathalamor was once a very poor world. Though it has always possessed a favourable siting on the currents of the soul-sea, it was largely overlooked in favour of other, more developed places. Cardinal Bucharis decided to change that by attracting the attention of his selfish god. So he constructed this temple, the largest cathedrum for hundreds of light years in any direction. Sadly, for the people he ruled, he needed labour, and he needed money. They gave their lives in providing both. He worked a remarkable number of labourers to death to ensure its completion. He was quite the orator, and they died for their god willingly. Those that wouldn't were burned, or fled. I believe that the catacomb gangs, the ones the locals call bone-whittlers, your people, yes? They originated from that... trying time.'

Tenebrus lifted his hands and spread them. 'But still the cathedrum was not finished. His plans grew more grandiose. He needed more materials, more bodies and more coin. When he could gather no more from the neighbouring worlds by diplomatic means, he merely took them by force. Then he took more, and more, until, before the rotten bureaucracies of Terra had noticed, he had carved himself out an empire. What an empire it was, little acolyte! The faith of the corpse-worshippers harnessed, and turned against their god for the benefit of one man, Cardinal Bucharis.'

He waved a hand, and scenes of battle appeared wavering on the air. Imperial soldiers killing each other, both under banners of faith, their faces twisted in hatred.

'It could not last, of course. Terra is slow to react, but it reacts. Bucharis was caught and slain, and Asclomaedas succeeded him. He was a man as vain as he was fearful, and corpulent,' Tenebrus said with a short bark of laughter. 'In fact, the cardinal rather resembled this building. What could he do? Asclomaedas couldn't destroy this place, for it was a monument to the Emperor. But it could not be left in the name of Bucharis the Apostate, oh no, so it was altered, and reconsecrated. Asclomaedas' name was attached to it. More men and women died to remake it. More worlds were beggared, though not Gathalamor, and this time at the Imperium's behest.

'As Bucharis originally intended, the pilgrims did come, and by their billions. They enriched this place.' He gave a half-feline growl. 'Foundations laid upon a strata of exploited workers, watered with blood and seeded with bitterness,' said Tenebrus, savouring the notion. 'It is perfect, is it not, little acolyte? Perfect. Always the corpse-worshippers erect their own gallows and willingly jump, and the pantheon smile to see them dance upon the rope. Delicious. You see, Bucharis had nothing but a desire to exult his god, yet by trying he favoured ours.' He paused. 'And tell me, do you know what became of Bucharis, after he died?'

'No, my lord,' said Yheng. She did not enjoy Tenebrus' attention. She tried to hide her fear, but Kar-Gatharr could see from the movement of her chains that she was trembling.

'Asclomaedas was chosen for his level head, yet the new cardinal became obsessed with the idea that the spirit of Bucharis haunted this world. He feared his diocese would be tainted by Bucharis' incorporeal presence. He was advised to shoot Bucharis' mauled remains into the sun, but he feared that would set the apostate's spirit free. Perhaps he was right, for Bucharis was a wilful man in life. Instead, Asclomaedas chose to bury Bucharis and the Gathalamorian ring of office far underground. *This* ring.' He held up the jewel. 'Asclomaedas refused to wear it, you see. You have seen the decoy tombs? The ancient constructs left to prowl the deeps? The warding spells put about Bucharis' resting place?'

Yheng nodded; she had seen all those things. 'Yes, my lord.'

'All that was the work of Asclomaedas. By the time he died, he was mad with paranoia, but it is thanks to him we have this weapon.'

Tenebrus held his curled fist up and greedily looked at his prize. In response, the ruby on the ring flashed with hidden fire.

'How is it a weapon, my lord?' Yheng asked.

Both Kar-Gatharr and Tenebrus looked at her.

'The little acolyte speaks without prompting! Bold, bold!'

Tenebrus crept forward, reached out his spidery fingers and gripped Yheng's face. She flinched, but did not move as he turned her head about, examining her. A thin tongue flicked over his lips as he tasted her scent.

'How is it a weapon, little acolyte? The answer is... it is not.' He sniggered. 'Bucharis' spirit still clings to this jewel, but what is that? One man's soul. Nothing. The ring really is little more than a gewgaw. In one respect.' He let Yheng go. 'But in another respect it is a symbol, and symbols are important when harnessing the energies of the warp. It is a symbol of how one man followed his faith as far as one can go, and faith, no matter the kind, always leads to the warp. It is a symbol of how belief in a false god can be turned to the service of the true gods. Sorcery, young lady, needs symbols, and this is one of the greatest you will find.'

Tenebrus waved his hands about airily. 'Human beings are crude and weak, but it is within our power to remake ourselves into something greater. That is the power the Emperor denies His grovelling subjects. He keeps the power of the warp to Himself, for He is a jealous god.' His eyes glittered more intensely. 'The Emperor would have all humanity be slaves, to deny us choice as He crawls closer towards His apotheosis. He wants men to be like servitors, yes? Or orks. One sees it in the ork, this singular purpose. But we are not orks, are we? We can rise above the limits others place upon us. We who follow the Four are truly blessed, for we have seen the light.' He smirked again. Needle teeth flashed in his cowl.

'This is a symbol I will build our weapon around.' He raised his hand high over his head, so that the ring caught a stray shaft of daylight. His sleeve fell back to reveal a skinny arm covered in tumours. 'A weapon that could slay a god!' he shouted.

His words reverberated around the dome. The shades were sent into a rustling frenzy. Tenebrus' power blasted through Kar-Gatharr, overwhelming his own. The pillar of darkness vanished and his helm crashed to the floor. Yheng was flung back.

A gale rose out of nowhere, and Tenebrus' laughter filled the world. Kar-Gatharr's cloak of shadows streamed away to nothing, and he was forced to set himself into the psychic storm, and harness his own power, so meagre and impotent, to keep to his feet.

The wind stopped.

Tenebrus lowered his arm and pulled down his sleeve, covering his disfigurements, his hand and the ring. His shades settled into rustling disquiet.

'Do you know, Apostle,' he said, his voice quiet and genial again. 'I believe I will take you up on that meal after all. Have them send someone up on your way out, yes?'

'Of course... Lord Tenebrus...' said Kar-Gatharr. He stood up. His cloak returned, shyly at first, like a frightened animal. His throat was dry. His mind numb. All around him the shades rattled. It was getting dangerous. Tenebrus was fickle, and might slay them on a whim. He retrieved his helm, took Yheng by the arm and dragged her away.

'And, Apostle,' Tenebrus called after him as he reached the doors. 'Make it someone *hearty*, yes? I find myself famished...'

The doors clanged shut behind them. Kar-Gatharr hauled Yheng to her feet.

'No more will his power cow me,' he said to his acolyte. 'Gather your sorcerers, my faithful witch. I have business with the gods.'

Chapter Seventeen

ARRIVAL AT GATHALAMOR

EBELE SANGAR

RADIANCE

'Navigator Teshwan has sent the first signal. Prepare for translation.'

Hard and resonant as blade striking blade, Shipmistress Ebele Sangar's voice carried over the noise of the command deck.

Achallor watched her from his observation platform. The shipmistress was impressive, so much confidence and purpose contained in her frail, mortal body. In appearance, she was short and heavily built. Her face had the permanent scowl of a Terran-bred aristocrat, a look intensified by the augmetic that replaced her right eye. Around her throat was a vox-unit in the shape of a golden torc. She was both the terror and beloved talisman of her crew. Achallor, too, had an amount of affection for her.

Her command throne swept over the deck in its gyrosphere cradle. 'Dim lumens. Geller fields to full. Begin translation hymns,' the shipmistress commanded.

Golden light turned red. A choir began to sing. Klaxons blared a harsh tune to compete with them.

'Check locks on oculus shuttering. Power off non-essential mechanisms. Brace all sections. Void shield control, prepare for emergency activation. Stealth control, ready obfuscation fields. Stand by enginarium for reactor output increase and realspace drive ignition.'

The commands were always the same, drawn from ancient Naval checklists. Achallor knew them well. He and the *Radiance* had a long association, but though the commands had changed little in the centuries he had used the vessel, they had changed, subtlety by subtlety.

And so what was becomes what will be, he thought. *Not even the Imperium can arrest change completely.*

The ship rode over some roughness in the warp and Achallor's companion gasped. Mistress of Astropaths Ashmeiln was easy to miss, being slight beside his armoured bulk, and he himself had almost forgotten she was there.

'Be ready,' she said. Where Achallor stood easily, riding every jump of the ship with a mariner's ease, she gripped the railing of the platform with white-knuckled hands. 'This will not be a pleasant experience.' She was saying it for her own benefit rather than his. He pitied her. Transition to and from the warp was painful for psykers, especially in the benighted times.

'You should take your seat, mistress astropath,' Achallor said.

'Not likely,' she replied grimly. She hunched further over the railing. 'I feel safer next to you, shield-captain.'

Ashmeiln was young. Though she was blind, like most of her kind, she wore a sight-visor wired into her temples, so she saw well enough. The augmetic was broad and mirror-faced, almost big enough to cover the pink spiderwebs of scarring around her eye sockets. She was healthier looking than most astropaths, something that spoke to a certain indomitability of spirit, for all but the hardiest souls were eroded by exposure to the warp, and she was powerful enough to warrant an Eta grading on the

Imperial assignment scale. Even a little higher and Ashmeiln would have found herself serving the Emperor in a different capacity. It was rare to encounter an astropath of such potency.

Unfortunately, Achallor had discovered Ashmeiln's talent came with a tendency to speak her mind.

'Stay close then, and try to keep to your feet,' he said.

'Easy for you to say,' she responded sharply. 'You are ten feet tall and have magnetic boots.'

The ship listed hard to port. Ashmeiln stumbled to the side and stifled a cry.

Achallor didn't activate his maglocks. He didn't need to. No amount of turbulence would upset his balance, but he did not comment. Unlike Ashmeiln, he felt no need to have the last word.

He instead watched the crew, finding their collective efforts fascinating. He had never lost his interest in humanity, and that had recommended him for service in the Emissaries Imperatus Shield Host. He felt at one with humans, but apart from them, a feeling that gave him cause for sadness, on occasion.

The *Radiance* was of cruiser mass, though being an Adeptus Custodes vessel no standard class designation could be applied to it. The bridge was a comparatively small, hollow sphere busy with walkways and platforms. Its instruments were fashioned from burnished brass and a wood so hard that Achallor had originally taken it for stone. A hundred deck officers and tech-magi worked at its consoles. Armsmen stood sentry at the back. All the ship's crew, Imperial and Mechanicus alike, wore black-and-bronze armour and robes in place of the typical Naval attire, and they looked impressive for it. It was noisy. Commands competed with the clatter of bone ordinator keys, the whirr of cogitators, the howling of klaxons and the choir of priests. Clades of servitors mumbling their way through repetitive tasks filled out the racket.

Another roil of turbulence shook the vessel. Ashmeiln gave out an involuntary moan. The crew began strapping themselves into seats and restraint alcoves.

'Maybe you should sit?' said Achallor.

'I said no!' she snapped.

'Increase warp engine output! Begin translation!' Sangar commanded, and the activity on the bridge intensified. Hazard lumens strobed, transforming familiar bulkheads into shadowed lairs for unclean things. Achallor shifted as he felt spiritual resonance build, thickening the air with false pressure.

Translation was the most perilous time aboard a ship. It was the moment at which the door between materium and immaterium was forced widest. It was when the ship's Geller fields were most stressed. It was the time that the malefic might creep in.

Achallor's hand twitched, thinking of his sword, Prosektis, maglocked to his back. Anything daring to manifest aboard a Custodian vessel would suffer for its foolishness.

The warp engines screamed. Gossamer touches trailed across Achallor's skin beneath the auramite of his armour. There were many deed names engraved across the inner surfaces of the plates. He loathed the idea of some unclean entity touching them, tasting and knowing them, but the thought never surfaced on his face.

A searing heat washed over him, followed by intense cold. The human crew cried out, and many of them shouted prayers, but Marcus Achallor was Adeptus Custodes, the product of potent alchemy. He was one of the Ten Thousand, beings fashioned by the Emperor to stand at His side. The unholy touch of the warp found little purchase upon such a one as he, and he stood impassive as a rock in a storm while the mortals on the bridge suffered.

A woman manning an augury station slumped forward, blood streaming from her eyes. A member of the helm section unstrapped himself from his restraints and ran full tilt into an iron pillar, knocking himself out. The ship yawed violently. Only exceptional individuals could serve the Adeptus Custodes, and yet the violence of the warp in that new era taxed even them, and Achallor was witness to a scene of controlled pandemonium.

The ship's motions became more extreme.

'Warp engines primed for empyrean egress!' a crewman shouted.

Achallor felt his armoured weight lighten as the *Radiance* went into a dive and the grav-plating laboured to compensate. Shudders raced through the decking. A pipe burst near the back of the bridge, sending out a plume of gas.

'We will not survive much more of this, shipmistress!' the master of integrity shouted. They were all shouting, for a fearsome roar had built. The shaking increased, blurring Achallor's sight, doubling images, quadrupling them, then again, until every person trailed a rainbow smear behind them, and the ship's architecture was a confused mess of vibrating colour.

'Await my command!' The shipmistress' eyes were fixed on a run of glass spheres set into her throne arm: the navigatorial signal lumens. All but one now shone red; the last remained dark.

Something hit the ship hard in the side, and it slewed around. Alarms blared at the Geller control platform. One of the consoles exploded, showering the officer manning it with hot sparks that made her scream. A servitor moved from its alcove to attend to the damage, but the next jolt of the ship saw it flung across the deck into a cogitator bank. Ashmeiln shrieked, and Achallor put a protective arm around her.

'Shipmistress!' the master of integrity relayed. 'Geller field down to sixty-three per cent. Integrity fields failing on decks fourteen through seventeen. We have to translate now!'

'Wait!' Sangar commanded.

The turbulence increased with every moment. Achallor rode out each new roll, Ashmeiln hugged into his side.

'I can feel them,' she whimpered. 'I can feel them trying to get inside!'

The final bulb on the arm of Sangar's throne shone out red with a soft *plink* that Achallor's enhanced hearing caught even through the tumult.

'Now!' Sangar screamed. 'Warp engines to maximum! Geller command, pierce the veil! All hands prepare for immediate translation!'

Wailing trumpets blared from every quarter, and the unbearable caresses wormed their way insistently across Achallor's flesh.

There was a flash of bright light, and the noise abruptly ceased. The unnatural sensations faded with the swiftness of a dream forgotten. The turbulence was done.

A numb silence prevailed.

'Translation successful, all stations report in,' said Sangar.

One by one, the various divisions of the ship's officers gave their reports.

'Throne alive,' said Ashmeiln. She wriggled out of Achallor's grip, turned, bent over and vomited copiously upon the floor. She was not the only one.

'Are you alright, mistress astropath?' Achallor said.

Ashmeiln wiped her mouth on the back of a shaking hand.

'Of course I'm not... Oh, Throne.' She vomited again.

At last the klaxons ceased their wailing and the lumens returned to their usual golden glow. A soft chime issued from Achallor's vox, followed by the gruff voice of Hastius Vychellan.

'What did I miss, Marcus?'

'The usual performance.'

'I felt it. A bad translation. The seers were right, there is something amiss in this system. What does the astropath say?'

Achallor looked down at Ashmeiln. She was bent double, back heaving as she struggled to keep her stomach climbing out of her mouth.

'Nothing. She is inconvenienced at this time.'

There was a soft rumble as the realspace engines ignited.

'What of the Primaris Marines?' Achallor asked.

Vychellan grunted. *'I've not seen anything to worry me. They're Adeptus Astartes through and through. They barely stopped drilling for the translation. They're off to start again now.'*

'Nothing unusual?'

'Nothing.'

There was a hollow boom from somewhere above.

'You hear that?' asked Vychellan.

'Physical impact,' said Achallor.

'I'm coming up to you,' said Vychellan. *'The Space Marines can look after themselves for a while.'*

'Shipmistress Sangar, what is the nature of the strike we experienced?' Achallor asked.

'Debris, my lord,' Sangar called down from her throne orb, where she was poring over her instruments. The throne cradle shifted on its gimbal, swinging across the bridge to be closer to the augury consoles. 'A field of some size. Determining now.'

A hololith came on, displaying near space as a graphical datasplay alive with swarms of red dots. Those pieces of debris nearest were rapidly scanned, and accurate volumetric light sculptures popped into being, appended with tags of data, until a real-view holo was established showing the *Radiance* in a cloud of metal.

'Battle's aftermath,' said Achallor. 'Someone was fighting here. A large engagement.'

'Indeed, my lord,' Sangar said. Further impacts rattled off the vessel, all minor, but according to the displays there were large elements moving erratically close to their position. 'Get the void shields up, please, Magos Kzarch, nobody will spot us among this unless they are on top of us. And get me the oculus open. I've had enough of sailing blind.'

Instruments sang. The shutters across the grand window at the front of the deck clanked back, revealing a voidscape thick with spinning metal chunks. The command deck was mounted far back on the spine of the superstructure, and Achallor could see particular debris hitting the ship's narrow length forward. Space flexed, the voids initiated, sparks lit upon the energy skin as the debris was shunted into the warp, and the rain was largely stymied.

'Mister Osmor, have you determined the extent of this debris field?' Sangar asked.

'Auspexes indicate a forty-thousand-mile dispersal, my lady.'

'A compact but fierce fight, then,' said Achallor.

'Helm adepts, report,' Sangar commanded.

'Wreckage dense and mobile, my lady, but the *Radiance* is agile. We'll be out of this in minutes, the Emperor's my witness.'

'Thank you, Miss Pheng. Carry on. Magos Kzarch, how are my shields?'

'Fully roused and formidable, Shipmistress Sangar. The obfuscation engines are ready. We may invert voids and engage shrouding at your command. Advisory – the rituals of awakening were completed only seven point nine seconds previous. Resultant – impact damage to hull sections quartus, sextus, septimus. Extent of damage currently unknown.'

'Understood, Magos Kzarch. Report to me the moment you have initial damage reports.'

'Confirmatory, Shipmistress Sangar.'

A choral chime accompanied the opening of the bridge blast doors, and Hastius Vychellan entered.

Vychellan was huge, even for a Custodian, and wore his bulky plate as comfortably as a lesser man would a robe. He wore his hair tied back in a neat queue; it was as white as snow and had been since his earliest days, as was his close-cropped beard. Eyes of a piercing blue looked out from beneath an aquila marking his forehead.

'Marcus,' said Vychellan as he joined Achallor.

'Hastius,' said Achallor.

Vychellan looked down at Ashmeiln and grinned. 'Mistress astropath,' he said.

'Custodian,' said Ashmeiln weakly. She took Vychellan's arrival as the cue to rally herself, and got up.

'This was not a small fight,' said Vychellan, running expert eyes over the hololithic displays and the view outside.

'Indeed,' said Achallor. Debris winked in the sun as far as they could see.

'Miss ChoKvell,' Sangar was asking, 'do you have anything for me on the nature of the wreckage?'

'Pict analysis suggests–'

A klaxon blared, sudden and loud, overriding the buzz of conversation. An instant later the void shields blazed, and the *Radiance* shook. On nearby gelscreens, Achallor saw grainy shapes, tumbling huge and ragged through the void. The *Radiance* had ploughed into one of these and shouldered it aside.

'Helm adepts, what in Throne's name was that?' barked Shipmistress Sangar. 'How did you miss something that big?'

'Apologies, shipmistress, it was the lesser of two evils,' came the shaken voice of Helm Officer Pheng. 'A larger fragment is bearing in from the forward arc, three hundred degrees vertical, shielded by fleck swarms. Moving slow enough to avoid displacement response from the voids. Evasive action was required.'

'Debris field exit reduced by four point four minutes, my lady,' added her fellow officer, O'Casver.

'Very good,' replied Sangar. 'But if you put any more dents in my *Radiance*, I'll have you both out there in hardsuits smoothing them out by hand, clear?'

'As Corphian crystal, my lady,' replied Pheng.

'Miss ChoKvell, in your own time,' prompted Sangar. The

adept-analyticus continued her report as though nothing had occurred.

'Initial auguries suggest that a number of ships were destroyed during whatever conflict took place here. There is also a residual warp trace. Several ships entered the empyrean here.' She listed a number of vessels whose warp engine signatures possibly matched.

'And their enemies?' Sangar asked.

'Hereticus Diabolus Extremis, my lady,' replied ChoKvell.

'Mandeville battle,' said Achallor to Vychellan, as ChoKvell delivered her report. 'The ships falling back to Necromunda took to the point, with the non-warp system ships to cover their retreat. Brave. How many got out? That is a question Lord Guilliman would want to know.'

'It does not seem long ago,' said Vychellan.

'Holding action maybe, or perhaps they delayed to perform hit-and-run actions, wearing the enemy down for a few weeks before they were finally forced to flee,' said Achallor. 'Or it could be the Rift. Time is all ravelled, they could have fled the moment the enemy arrived, and we translated only days later according to local time.'

'Then we need to get an idea of *when* we are,' said Vychellan.

'I concur.'

'Shipmistress Sangar,' Vychellan said. 'Please provide us with a chronological estimate.'

A date was given. Vychellan frowned.

'Twenty days after our departure. We're cutting this close.'

'We were in the warp longer than anticipated,' said Achallor. 'Fleet Primus will soon be here.'

Sangar's throne turned around, and moved on its mechanical arm towards the Custodians until she was level with the observation gallery. Many of the Emperor's servants were entirely undone by the presence of a Custodian, their senses oppressed by their aura of power. But Ebele Sangar had spent most of her adult life serving the Emissaries Imperatus Shield Host, and she didn't avert her gaze.

'As you appreciate, my lords, sailing the empyrean at this time is an imprecise endeavour,' Sangar said.

'Have we been noticed?' said Achallor to Sangar.

'Probably not,' said Sangar. 'This battle has come and gone. We tread its ashes.'

'Keep it that way,' said Achallor. 'How many days out from the target are we?'

'At full speed I can have you at extreme teleportation range in three days,' she said.

'We should not rush in,' said Vychellan.

'And yet we cannot afford to tarry,' said Achallor. 'Have the *Radiance* linger within the bounds of this debris field for a few hours. Let us be just another wreck. I want a full system scan and anything you can gather from the vox. Ashmeiln, see if you can contact the planetary astropaths. We need a clear picture of what is going on here. Once we have more intelligence, or by the second watch, make full speed for Gathalamor. Whichever comes soonest.'

Sangar offered him another salute and ascended to the centre of the deck, where her orders rang out like bolt shells.

'Fleet Primus is likely but days behind us,' commented Vychellan.

'Battle groups Praxis, Orphaeus and Styxx at least,' said Achallor.

'And Lord Guilliman and Tribune Colquan not far behind,' added Vychellan.

The words were redundant, of course; both Custodians knew the stakes of this mission, yet the custom was an old one between Achallor and Vychellan. Reiterate the basic facts aloud, the better to process the plethora of details racing through their minds.

'If there is a threat here, as the xenos witch predicted, the crusade could be decapitated.'

'Consider Scorathio,' suggested Achallor, naming a military philosopher from the thirty-seventh millennium. Both of them had read his treatises, and had meditated at length upon them.

'"The foe who considers themselves victorious courts only their own defeat,"' quoted Vychellan. 'I always liked that one. Pithy, but I found him far too optimistic, shield-captain. That quote, here applied, assumes the foe now sits indolent upon the spoils. What if they are instead present in great number and alert to retaliatory incursion? I confess, my brother, I will happily kill them all, but still...'

The ship gave a shudder as though to underline Vychellan's caution. It slowly changed course, ascending relative to the debris.

'Taghitus the Unorthodox,' replied Achallor, his eyes flicking across viewscreens.

'"The greater the enemy's number, the greater honour shall I do unto the Emperor by their slaughter,"' said Vychellan. 'Choleric, my friend. I think I like that one better.'

Achallor saw the ghost of a smile hovering about Vychellan's mouth. Vychellan was as intellectual as every one of the Ten Thousand, but he had a powerful love of fighting.

'We are five Custodians beneath one vexillum, Hastius,' said Achallor. 'Whatever foes we may meet in this place, we shall know victory over them.'

'I am buoyed as always by your resolute spirit,' Vychellan replied.

The two warriors fell silent. By Achallor's count a further two hours, twenty-three minutes, seven seconds passed before they spoke again. Early on, Ashmeiln left for the astropathicum. Achallor allowed himself to fall into a trance, absorbing each new nugget of information as the ship's augurs quested out into the system. Vychellan processed as much of the battle data as was available.

The Navigator confirmed the empyrean at Gathalamor was

as navigable as anything he had seen since the opening of the Cicatrix Maledictum. Getting out would be far easier than getting in. The currents were as strong as predicted.

Contrary to that, after a short trance, Master of Astropaths Ashmeiln described teleprayer conditions in-system as being entirely obscured, so that she could make no contact with any of the Gathalamorian worlds, and cautioned that the cause was a strange resonance emanating from Gathalamor itself. She informed Achallor she would commence a reading of the Emperor's Tarot for guidance.

Less esoteric readings were returned. The augury arrays showed a substantial traitor presence, their vox and immaterial communications centred upon Gathalamor but coming also from around the worlds of Rhanda and Chyrosius' Rest. Imperial signals were faint and infrequent, and to begin with the ship's crew feared that no servant of the Emperor remained active on the shrine world. Yet as the minutes ticked by it became clear that there were still loyalist forces present. They were, however, making efforts to mask their presence.

Little by little, a strategic picture emerged of the situation. A cartolith of Gathalamor was presented over the main hololithic pit. Shining seas, green forests and great cities with interlinked streets as fine as the branchings of coral. Though much was scorched and fires burned all over the planet, it was as yet not lost. Over this, enemy and Imperial positions were laid.

'That's quite a fleet the enemy have, but Imperial forces are holding out,' said Vychellan, after a while scrutinising the augur returns. 'The largest concentration is on Gathalamor Secundus in the city of Imprezentia. It is there we should go, if we are to make landfall. Are we to proceed, or withdraw?'

'Everything the augur soak has so far detected suggests that the enemy do not possess sufficient strength in this system to hold against the crusade fleet,' said Achallor.

'However…?' said Vychellan.

'However,' said Achallor, 'conventional military theory cannot be applied to the followers of Chaos. It is our duty to assume that there is a greater threat here, and that Guilliman's advisors were correct.'

'What about Colquan's orders?' said Vychellan. 'A cautious man would withdraw.'

'Are you a cautious man, Vychellan?' asked Achallor, already knowing the answer.

'Throne, no,' he laughed. 'I would like a fight.'

'Then you shall have one, my friend. Time presses us,' Achallor said to Sangar. 'The battle groups draw closer by the hour. We can learn nothing more here. Move us into the inner system. I like not Ashmeiln's talk of emanations from the shrine world, nor the effect they have upon communications. The company shall deploy via the veilbreaker teleportarium to the surface of Gathalamor, shipmistress.'

'Of course, my lord,' replied Sangar. 'The obfuscation engines are roused – no foe shall see us, and none shall detect your descent upon this world. I swear it by the Golden Throne.'

The Emissaries Imperatus Shield Host went openly for the most part, as ambassadors of the Throne, but they had other roles that were not well known, for they specialised also in covert strikes. They were the subtle blade in the Emperor's arsenal; where words failed, swords prevailed. Much powerful techno-arcana had been placed at their disposal. The obfuscation engines were one such gift, an adaptation of ancient Heresy-era technology that inverted the void shields, rendering the *Radiance* an invisible blank to even the most powerful augurs.

Achallor had always thought the *Radiance* was ironically named.

The veilbreaker teleportarium was another ancient treasure,

with a vast operational range and remarkable precision. This device alone was more precious to the Adeptus Custodes than the warship into which it had been installed.

'Spend the approach gathering additional intelligence, shipmistress,' Achallor commanded. 'Concentrate scans on the area around Imprezentia. Find us the best place to intervene.'

'And once you are planetside?' asked Sangar.

'No non-essential contact. We shall meet with the surviving forces and manage the situation there,' replied Achallor. 'You will take the *Radiance* and do what you can to rally any surviving Navis Imperialis assets that may still be in system. Though you are not to expose yourself if possible.'

'Yes, my lord,' said Sangar. 'May the Emperor walk with you.'

'It is we who walk with Him, shipmistress,' corrected Achallor.

He and Vychellan strode from the bridge.

'This could all be a trap, you realise that?' said Vychellan as they exited through the blast doors. 'The enemy know the significance of this world. Their forces here are enough to deal with local planetary defence, but not what is coming. The Warmaster is no fool. He dangles the bait.'

'Absolutely he does,' replied Achallor. 'But I pity he who springs the jaws of a trap on us.'

'Splendid,' growled Vychellan. 'I knew I would enjoy this mission.' He smiled broadly as they set off down the corridor towards their barracks. There they would prepare themselves, and rouse the Adeptus Astartes to battle.

And then, thought Achallor, *we shall secure Gathalamor, in the Emperor's name.*

Chapter Eighteen

SAINT'S GIFT

ARCHANGELS

MARTYRS

Shanni Saintsgift ran.

Her breath rasped. Each exhalation filled her mouth with the acid taste of bile, each inhalation was a bloom of fire in her chest. She ran though her leg muscles had turned to water.

It felt like the nightmares Shanni had endured as a child, aboard the *Mendicant*, the hauler aboard which she and her family had completed their pilgrimage to Gathalamor. In her dreams she'd fled the rats that lived in the bilges, the ones that had made her flesh crawl with their every scratch in the ducts. In her dreams, her legs had refused to work and her throat had refused to produce a scream. All she had been able to manage was a reedy wheeze. The dream always ended with Shanni waking just before the tide of rats engulfed her.

There would be no such luck this time. She panted out a prayer, begging for mercy.

But what did the Emperor know of mercy? Shanni's father had died in a crowd-surge the day they put down upon Gathalamor, before they even made it as far as the shrine of Saint Tremande. They laid his cane as an offering at the saint's shrine, weeks later, praying for his soul to the marble statue he had striven his entire life to see.

Her older brother, Jhara, had fallen in with the bone-whittlers once it became apparent they weren't getting out of the slums. An enforcer's shotgun had sent him to join their father.

Still she and her mother had remained faithful. They made offerings of what little they had to atone for the wrongs they must have done to suffer so.

And then the stars tore, and the invasion came, and they all found out how worthless the Emperor's mercy really was.

She was exhausted to delirium. She had been running forever. She shouldn't have come out. She shouldn't have left the catacombs. *Oh Emperor, forgive,* she thought, *oh Emperor, save me. What choice did I have?* another part of her snarled back. *There is no food down there, nothing but statues with pious faces. The Emperor protects no one.*

Shanni fled between towering macro-mausolea. The morning coated the flanks of the buildings with molten gold. It rendered everything it touched blinding, wrought everything it didn't into hard black shapes. Stone cherubim stared down at her, heads haloed by the dawn, uncaring of her fate.

They know what is coming for me, she thought desperately, *and they do nothing.*

A burst of gunfire crackled across the ruins. Close behind her, something heavy dislodged a spill of rubble. There was a howl, a sound so unnatural that it froze Shanni's blood.

She looked back, knowing even as she did so that it was a mistake, compelled by instincts she couldn't fight to do it all the same. She saw them, five huge and twisted shapes turned to living fire by the glory of the sunrise.

She let out a breathless cry, and tried to go faster, but her foot found a gap between two chunks of masonry, stuck fast, and the ground rushed up to meet her. Her hands hit sharp gravel and glass as they sought to break her fall. Something in her leg bent too far and cracked, then her face was bouncing off the ground and she tasted blood. She lay there for a stunned, stupid moment.

Groggy, Shanni rolled over. Broken bones ground in her ankle and she screamed, a cry of despair and agony and anger. Anger at the things that had hunted her. Anger at the Emperor who had allowed all this to happen to her, to her family.

To her poor mother.

Gasping, shaking, drenched with sweat, Shanni looked for any hope of escape but there was nothing. They were coming closer, monsters from the darkest scripture, things her mind all but refused to accept as real. They were tall, so tall and... armour like old blood and knife-blades. *Oh God-Emperor, the talons and the fangs and the eyes...*

Despite it all, despite all He had taken from her, Shanni found herself pleading.

'Oh God-Emperor almighty, oh lord of angelic hosts and provider of succour.'

Can't do anything for yourself so you beg the Emperor for help, a treacherous part of her said.

'Please, I beg you, hear your faithful servant's prayer.'

Like He heard when father died screaming? Like when they took Jhara? Like...

'See now my peril, oh God-Emperor, and in your divine beneficence give sanctuary to this unworthy soul.'

Not that He ever has before, not that He ever will, the voice inside her said. *There are other gods, and they are better.*

The creatures loomed over her, drool running from fangs that grew right out of their twisted helms, obscene claws and talons gleaming in the dawn light. Were they machine, or flesh, or something of both? There was hunger in their glowing yellow eyes, and she prayed they would make her death swift.

He won't even offer you that mercy, the voice in her mind said. *You are nothing. He does not care for you at all.*

The glow of the dawn grew hazy as the things leaned in. One caressed her with the tip of a cruel talon, then wrapped an outsized hand around her waist and hauled her off the ground. She whimpered as her broken foot came free.

They will take their time over you, and you will beg for death long before they are finished, and then you will face the blackness, alone, for there is nothing, there is no mercy, there is no kindness. The Emperor hates you, said the voice in her head.

A fanged maw approached her face. It seemed that the helm opened, but it was at the same time part of the face, a mix of armour and man. A long, thick tongue slipped out. Shanni closed her eyes and prepared to die.

A bolt of golden lightning arced up from the ground and sent one of the monstrous figures reeling. A piercing whine filled the air. The golden light of dawn was outshone by a coruscating vortex that caught up stone and shards of stained glass and spun them round. The things that had been hunting her were driven back, howling words she didn't understand. Shanni was dropped like a sack of bones. She was numb with fear, and could not move, but her heart soared. After everything, the Emperor had answered her prayers.

'The Emperor...' she breathed. 'The Emperor protects!' She found her strength, and scrambled back, her broken leg dragging agonisingly over the rough ground.

The creatures were in uproar, slashing at the light. A volley of thundercracks sounded from all around her. Suddenly giants appeared, their red-and-gold armour steaming ghostly shapes into the dawn.

'Angels. The angels of our lord, the Master of Mankind,' croaked

iours. The fierce light of the sunrise kindled along its wingtips
and reflected from the gem that formed its single eye, and she
understood.

Thank you, she thought, and in that moment Shanni Saintsgift
felt as though the blazing sunlight was falling into her, filling her
up with a faith stronger than anything she had felt in her life.

'Contact front, Traitor Astartes, daemonically possessed,' barked
Shield-Captain Achallor. He raised Prosektis before the teleport
flare died and squeezed the trigger built into the hilt. Unerringly
aimed bolt-rounds thumped into the flesh-metal of a traitor and
detonated so fiercely his horned head was thrown into the sky.

Ichor sprayed in a fountain, but those who had given their
mortal forms over to daemons were not easily slain. Though
open like a bloody flower, the headless Traitor Marine was still
on his feet, pincer limbs snipping the air as a hissing nest of tentacles and eyes boiled up from its ragged neck.

The storm of bolt-fire that erupted from Achallor's comrades'
guns engulfed the possessed. Armour ruptured, unholy flesh
burst, and the befouled Chaos Space Marines were driven back.

Hastius Vychellan went forward to Achallor's right. Vexillor
Undeyr Amalth-Amat had Achallor's left. Pontus Varsillian the
Many Gloried and Menticulous Aswadi made up the five, and
they moved out to the flanks, sentinel blades locked onto the
tops of their shields, gunfire blazing over the rims.

The Custodians blasted the possessed to a bloody pulp. It was
a catastrophic, overwhelming application of force, an engagement more akin to a firing squad than a fight. Only once the
last of the daemon-tainted traitors had stopped twitching did
Achallor look down at the mortal woman lying in the rubble
near his feet. Her face bore a beatific smile.

'Emperor,' she said. 'Emperor be praised.'

'She's gone into shock,' said Achallor. 'Varsillian, attend to her.'

'Shield-captain,' Varsillian acknowledged. He set his weapons aside and knelt to tend the woman, his massive armoured hands moving over her injuries expertly.

'Distance to target, Hastius?'

Vychellan consulted his armour's systems. 'We've come down several miles off course, outside the port's perimeter, due to the empyric interference from whatever is going on here, I'd say. Poor fortune for us, good fortune for her that we did so,' he said, gesturing at the wounded civilian.

'Even the *Radiance* cannot achieve a wholly traceless teleportation, especially from such range. We will have been noticed, and we need to relocate swiftly,' said Achallor. 'That was a louder and messier arrival than I would have preferred.'

'Blades would have taken longer,' said Vychellan, still looking down at the wounded woman.

'Come, get her up. We're moving out,' said Achallor.

Varsillian locked his shield to the back of his armour and gathered up the woman, speaking soothing words as she cried at the pain. He bent to retrieve his sword.

'We could consider leaving her,' said Vychellan quietly.

'Then what would we be?' Achallor said. 'Look at this place.' He swept his gaze around the ruins of Gathalamor Imprezentia. 'How many people like her have died here, and for what? They are slaughtered before the images of their protector, no doubt crying out His name to the end. Imagine the power that gives our foes. Imagine how they must *feel*. I say no. We can save her with minimal inconvenience, and we shall. Varsillian will fight almost as well carrying her as he will unburdened.' He looked to the blue morning sky. 'No sign of the enemy fleet, but we will go under cover where we can.'

Vychellan snorted. 'Aye, my friend, no point travelling all

the way from Terra just to be evaporated by a lance strike.' He pointed to where the spires rose up in toothed ranks almost as steeply as the walls of the Outer Palace, They crowned a range of low hills, and behind the spires were the silhouettes of buildings common to void ports the galaxy over. 'It's that way,' he said.

The Custodians made speed through the ruins, their genhanced frames pushing them over uneven ground that would have caused a mortal group to founder. In less than an hour they were approaching the outer bounds of the Ascension Stair district. They approached from the east, where the ground leapt up in steep cliffs, and the city climbed by switchbacked streets, ascending several hundred feet before the ground levelled again. They climbed this deserted stair until they saw the port ahead once more. Weapons boomed not far away, and they saw void discharge soiling the atmosphere to the west.

'That is the centre of their resistance – all intercepted communications emanate from that tower,' said Vychellan, pointing.

Achallor followed. The tower looked to be to the south of the port's heart, purely religious in design, for although it was of sufficient height to serve as minor traffic control or a comms hub, it was lacking the arrays to perform either role.

'A good site for a command centre. We are close,' said Achallor.

There came a chime from the auspexes in their helms.

'Shield-captain, movement. Two hundred yards out, closing,' voxed Amalth-Amat. 'Power armour signatures.'

'Guard stance,' Achallor ordered.

'You have this habit of speaking too soon,' said Vychellan. All of them were ready, blades up, shields presented in a ring of auramite, Varsillian in the middle with the woman, but Vychellan set his blade on his shoulder.

'You have signum keys,' said Aswadi, letting his guard down.

'I do,' said Vychellan.

Armoured figures emerged from the archways of an Administratum building. Their gunmetal armour shimmered in the sunrise.

'Adepta Sororitas, Order of the Argent Shroud,' Vychellan said. 'Here is a more hospitable welcome.'

Twelve Battle Sisters came out onto the street. They were all battle-worn. They went helmed until they approached, when their leader revealed her face and Achallor saw that her eyes shone with something close to rapture. Then they all removed their helmets, as if they wished to drink in the sight of the Custodians without the intervention of their auto-senses.

As one, the Battle Sisters knelt and bowed their heads with deep reverence.

'Praise be!' they proclaimed. 'Praise be!'

Their leader stood. 'Praise the Emperor for your arrival. I did not think to see so glorious a sight as you, most holy lords, in my lifetime. I give thanks that I have borne witness to your glory, and stand in the presence of those who have stood in the presence of Him on Terra! Praise! Praise! Praise!' she shouted.

'Sister, hail and well met,' said Achallor. 'We go to meet with your leaders. Our presence upon Gathalamor is not yet known to the enemy, so we must go with some haste.' Over the squad vox, he heard Vychellan chuckle. Most Custodians respected the faith of the Adepta Sororitas, but Vychellan had never been able to take the religion of the Adeptus Ministorum seriously.

'Of course, of course!' said the Battle Sister. 'You bring hope to us all, and it should be shared. In my selfishness, I seek to enjoy this moment for my own pleasure.'

'She'll be at the scourging bench later for that,' Vychellan said via private channel. Achallor held up a finger to silence his friend.

'What is your name?' Achallor asked.

'Forgive me, I am Palatine Gracia Emmanuelle of the Order

the Sanctum Miraculous.' She pointed to the tower. 'If you will
accompany us, my lord, I will gladly take you to our canoness.'

'That would do well,' said Achallor. 'The sooner I am able to
coordinate with the surviving Imperial leadership on this world
the better. Is your mistress in command?'

'Overall command rests in the hands of the Mordian general,
Luthor Dvorgin. He is a good man, a faithful man. It was truly
a blessing of the Emperor that you appeared when and where
you did, my lord,' said the palatine, her eyes shining with wonder. 'I see you have rescued one of the Emperor's martyrs. She
is blessed. I will present her to the canoness, for such grace
cannot be ignored.'

'Martyr?' asked Achallor. 'She lives.'

'My lord, since the Archenemy invaded, they have preyed
upon soldiers and civilians without distinction,' Emmanuelle
said. 'Whenever they turn their attention to the latter we honour the sacrifice of these Imperial servants by making martyrs
of them.'

'You allow them to draw the foe's attention so that you may
strike and eliminate them?' said Vychellan, apprehending the
implication immediately.

'Could you not instead intercede to save these Imperial servants from the Traitor Astartes?' asked Achallor.

'The Emperor saves those who save themselves, my lord,' she
replied with a zealot's certainty. 'It is His will.'

'Bones of Old Earth,' Vychellan said privately. 'Five hundred
years experience of their cold fanaticism and I will never get
used to it.'

Achallor muted his suit voxmitter so he could speak with
Vychellan. 'If these warriors' faith helps them fight, I see the
value in it. How they choose to express that faith is no business
of ours unless it hampers our mission.'

'To serve is all,' countered Vychellan, 'but service is best done willingly.'

'Enough. Any moment could bring the outcry of detection, and with it the risk of failure. The seconds race. Hold your silence for the moment,' said Achallor, reopening his vox to the Sister. 'Lead us to your canoness,' he said to the palatine. 'But make no mistake, we are taking the woman with us. She will not be left here to die.'

Emmanuelle looked confused. 'But of course, why would I leave her here to die?' Then she did something that surprised Achallor greatly. Slinging her boltgun on its shoulder strap, she went to Varsillian and held out her arms.

'Give her to me, so that I might ease your way and bear my sister in the faith.'

Varsillian looked to Achallor.

'Do as she says. We're wasting time.'

Gently, Varsillian lowered the injured female. Emmanuelle easily took her and cradled her.

'You would martyr her one moment and rescue her the next?' Achallor asked.

'This one will be honoured above all others,' said Emmanuelle, her tone communicating that she felt this self-evident. 'She witnessed the arrival of the Emperor's Custodians. You, my holy lords, have blessed her. She may yet be declared a saint.'

'Just what this world needs, another saint,' Vychellan muttered.

Chapter Nineteen

THE BALANCE SHIFTS

GOLDEN GIANTS

MIRACLE

The balance was shifting. Fort Bastabus had fallen.

Luthor Dvorgin looked over the casualty figures again. The Lodovians had nearly been wiped out. He put the missive paper down on the desk with the rest. None of them bore good news. He resisted rubbing the tiredness out of his eyes.

Never show weakness in front of your soldiers, he thought. Exhaustion, hunger, frustration, despair; these things stayed between you and the Emperor.

Dvorgin took up a stylus from the map table to update one of the orbital picts. It was getting difficult to read them for all the overlapping annotations. Canoness Imelda Veritas had several of her Sisters making updated copies, but the work was constantly outpaced by the changing face of the theatre.

Stylus... map table... jests as grim as this campaign. The stylus was a sliver of bone. The map table was a tomb. Even the chart desk was little more than a joke, its neat holos suggesting a level of knowledge they simply did not have.

The attack was coming soon. Dvorgin suppressed a sigh and tried to formulate a plan to reinforce the perimeter. However, he could not shut out the chatter passing between the command staff as they tried to make something meaningful of this slow defeat.

'...third supply party to make it through to the Clarion Spires. The cell there is well enough armed now, but the enemy and the blood-flux have...'

'No, we've not heard from Thirty-Five Platoon in six days now. I think it's time to...'

'...rebuffed from Cache Delphi-Kato with heavy casualties. Last contact the Sister Superior advised that she was going to try to lose their pursuers in the catacombs before...'

'...line of the Faithful Grace canal. If we can...'

'Anyone have any news on Sister Clarita's Seraphim? They were pushing north of the Processional Worthy Suffering and...'

'...more damned heretics! We'll need to...'

'...confirmed lost.'

Dvorgin swayed. He took a deep breath. The air reeked of incense, sweat and dried blood. The Sisters Hospitaller had set up a triage station high up in the sanctum the day before as casualties flooded in from a counter-offensive at Choral Cross. They had succeeded in holding the aqua-exchanger shrines, but the butcher's bill had been high.

His eyes strayed to the casualty lists again. *If we keep this up, there'll be more than enough food and water to go around,* he thought. Conscious he was staring blankly, Dvorgin stirred himself. He made his annotations, cross-checking with his flickering data-slate to make sure he had it right. Matters were bad enough without mistakes. Every pen stroke condemned men to death.

Lieutenant Stehner was suddenly at his elbow. The younger man proffered a flask.

'Spoils of war, sir,' he said, his tone dry as always.

Dvorgin took the canteen. The water inside was tepid and tasted of chemicals, but he was desperately grateful for it. He made himself drink only a modest amount before passing the canteen back.

'Anything to report, Stehner?'

'Successful reconnaissance of Saint Claytor's Span. The report's all in here.'

Stehner produced another data-slate and neatly swapped it with the one Dvorgin held.

'Sir...' Stehner paused.

'Yes, Stehner?' Dvorgin said, as he read.

'On a personal note, sir, I request an operational update regarding when you last had rations or took a sleep shift.'

Dvorgin frowned at the lieutenant. Stehner met his gaze with his infuriatingly mild expression.

'Veritas put you up to that little comment?'

'Why do you say so, sir?'

'I should write you up to the Commissariat for impertinence, lieutenant.'

'Very good, sir. Shall I locate Commissar Shaliim for you, sir? Last report has him overseeing the platoons within the Basilica of Grace two days ago.'

'Don't be an arse, Stehner, that's half the district away,' said Dvorgin with a scowl.

'Very good, sir,' said the lieutenant.

'The Emperor rewards the forthright with honest toil, lieutenant. I shall take your observation under advisement. *You*, meanwhile, will analyse the recon intelligence, cross-reference it with all other reports to date, and compile a concise and comprehensive strategic report to be delivered to myself and the canoness upon my waking. The enemy are probing our defences on all sides, but when they come, they'll come over that bloody bridge, I'm sure of it.'

'As the Emperor wills, general,' Stehner replied, taking the data-slate back from Dvorgin.

'Concise and comprehensive,' repeated Dvorgin, then turned away.

The lad will do well, he thought. *Provided any of us makes it off Gathalamor alive.*

With rationing becoming stricter, enemy forces pressuring their last strongpoints, and no word whatsoever from the wider Imperium, the chances of that seemed fainter by the day. The enemy were tightening their grip, and with Bastabus eliminated, they would have more of their strength free to squeeze the last of them harder.

Even if we manage to hold the damned void port, what then? he thought. *How long can we hold? It would take a damned miracle for...*

He stopped. There was a commotion coming from outside. Dvorgin sought out Canoness Veritas amongst the crowd of personnel. Their eyes met.

'What in the Emperor's name is that?' he shouted over to Veritas. 'Are we under attack?' He strained his ears. 'Is that... singing?' He pushed his way through the command centre to her.

'It is not the sound of battle,' said Veritas. 'Come.'

They went into the corridor. The sanctum had become increasingly crammed, with troops billeted as high as the peak after the collapse of various redoubts. Tired soldiers stood from their resting places in statue niches and from atop sarcophagi, suddenly alert.

'Those are your warriors singing,' said Dvorgin. 'Why?'

The canoness frowned, put her face deeper into her gorget and exchanged hurried words via vox that Dvorgin couldn't hear, but the look on her face told him something amazing had occurred. It lit up, physically so, he could have sworn it, radiating light that made her lined face appear young again.

She reached out for his hand, taking it in warm metal.

'Come with me, general, for I have glad tidings.'

She drew him to a door that opened onto the outside. The balcony was deep, the balustrade some yards from the door, and she took him to the edge so they could look down into Ascension Stair's broken streets.

He squinted. He could see movement on the road, more people than he'd seen out in the open since the invasion began. There was a line of black among the crowds, and golden light from the middle, but his old eyes saw it all as a blur.

'Glory, glory!' Veritas was saying. 'Glory, glory, praise be to Him on Terra that He sends His servants to us now!' Tears ran down her face.

'What is it? Imelda, what can you see?'

'Glory, glory!' she kept saying. 'Oh, glory, glory, glory!'

He extricated his hand from the canoness, pulled his magnoculars out of the case at his belt and brought them to his face. The crowd below leapt towards him, and he saw the rapt expressions on individual faces. They were passing lanterns and candles out, so that in the shadow of the deep street, a river of flame was spreading. All the people were singing now, taking up the hymn of the returning Sisters, so that music filled the city, and Imprezentia remembered what life had been like, not so long ago.

He pointed the magnoculars towards the middle of the road. He caught the Sisters first, their armour reflecting the dawn and the flames. Palatine Emmanuelle was at their head, a dazed-looking woman held up by her and another Battle Sister.

He moved his view back along the small procession. A dazzling luminance flared, hiding what was there, and he winced. When his eyes adjusted and he saw the source, he almost dropped the magnoculars.

'The Emperor's holy shit,' he said, quite forgetting himself.

Veritas didn't notice his blasphemy; she was on her knees now, sobbing, hands clasped in prayer.

'Praise be!' she was saying, over and over again. 'We are blessed, we are blessed, praise be!'

Dvorgin and Veritas met their guests at the east gate. Sandbagged positions manned by Mordians flanked the way in, but they stood in front of their heavy weapons, duty forgotten, mouths agape. There were civilians everywhere, singing, crying. Many had thrown themselves prostrate upon the ground and were wailing incoherently.

Dvorgin tugged at his uniform, suddenly, ridiculously mindful of how shabby he had become. *How does one greet a demigod?* he thought. The men he'd gathered as an honour guard were similarly scruffy. They were Mordians, and that meant they had a certain image to preserve, and he panicked that they were not doing so. Veritas was flanked by Seraphim, who sang hosannas in beautiful harmony.

Palatine Gracia Emmanuelle reached the bottom of the hundred steps leading up from the street. The injured woman was taken away by Hospitallers, and the party mounted the stairs, the giants towering over the Sisters of Battle.

Throne... Adeptus Custodes, Dvorgin thought. *The Emperor's saints, His boon companions, who guard Him as He suffers on the Throne of Terra for the betterment of mankind.* Dimly recalled myths. The rational side of him tried to reject the notion that they were actually there, to insist that his eyes must be mistaken. But they were there, His own angels, larger than life and as golden as the sun. Dvorgin blinked in bewilderment, unable to accept what he saw.

There was something else growing in him: the slow rising of hope.

Emmanuelle reached the top of the stairs and flung out her

arm behind her. She wore her helmet at her belt, and her face was full of rapture. 'Canoness,' she said excitedly. 'The Emperor has answered our prayers!'

The figures behind her were huge, taller than Emmanuelle and they had not yet reached the top of the flight. Their leader grew bigger and bigger as he ascended the last few steps. He was massively armoured in powered plate of red and gold, his conical helm capped with a crest as bright as blood. He stopped, surveying the group as his men joined him, flanking him two to each side. They were armed with shields as big as doors, and wore swords nearly as long as Dvorgin was tall. One carried a banner pole instead of a shield, bearing a hundred pounds of golden metal as if it were no inconvenience to him at all.

The leader passed his sword and shield to two of his companions, reached up with both hands, unsealed his great helm, and lifted it. Dvorgin had a sudden terror that he would go blind at the sight of the Custodian's face, so beautiful it would be, and he flinched, but the warrior was human-looking enough, though perfect. He showed a face like something carved from stone: a square jaw and a firm slash of a mouth; a flat, broad nose between cheekbones that looked as though they could shrug off a bolt-shell. Narrow, brown eyes hard as gems, their irises shot through with fine gold streaks. Cables ran into interface ports in his left temple across the side of his head. His skin was golden in the reflected morning light coming off his armour.

He was of middling age it seemed, but his eyes said he was far, far older than he looked. He moved with a grace that Dvorgin had never seen in a human being, even encased in that walking tank of an armoured suit, and though he had a warrior's presence, there was no mark or scar on his face, as if he were so skilled no enemy could touch him.

Dvorgin dropped to one knee without meaning to. There

was a divinity to this towering warrior. It took the general a moment to realise that every Mordian and Battle Sister had knelt too.

Am I doing this right? thought Dvorgin, semi-coherently.

'My lord, we are blessed indeed,' said Veritas, finding her voice. 'To think that the Emperor has sent us His own Custodian Guard to lead us to victory! We are blessed, blessed!'

Custodian Guard. An impossibility, surely, that this being had stood in the presence of the Emperor. The Emperor. The Master of Mankind Himself. Dvorgin couldn't stop thinking it.

The giant inclined his head in recognition of Veritas' words.

'We come not to perform that task, though we will help you if we can. The Emperor sends us to see that the gate of Gathalamor stands open, that Roboute Guilliman's avenging hosts might pass freely through it upon their road to war.'

'My lord,' Dvorgin managed to croak. 'The primarch is coming *here*?'

The giant looked down at him; it was an appraising look, the look a man gave a useful object.

'The Indomitus Crusade has begun,' said the giant, as though that explained everything.

'My lord? A crusade has been called?' asked Veritas. Dvorgin was glad she had; he wasn't sure he could have mustered the courage.

The Custodian – Dvorgin forced himself to think the word – smiled. Just a brief turning up of the corners of his mouth, but the effect was electrifying. 'The greatest crusade in mankind's history.'

A murmur of holy joy went through the crowd.

'You have been cut off here, have you not, fighting without sign of the Emperor's favour yet enduring nonetheless?' asked the Custodian.

'Our faith has never wavered,' the canoness answered fiercely.

'It is to all your credit,' said the Custodian, addressing everyone on the steps. Only the servitors standing sentry at the doors were excluded from the ripple of hope these words brought, but now Dvorgin realised even the mindless sentinels had not challenged this newcomer.

'I am Shield-Captain Achallor,' he said to them all, 'and I bring you word that you do not fight alone.' He looked about the rapturous crowd, before turning to Veritas and lowering his voice. 'We must take counsel. Privately. We have much to discuss, and time is growing short.'

Chapter Twenty

STRATEGIES DISCUSSED

AN EXCHANGE OF FAVOURS

THE MIST

'The Indomitus Crusade is the greatest military undertaking of our age, the counter-offensive that will see the enemy driven back into the raging storms whence they came,' said Achallor. 'Gathalamor is of utmost strategic importance.'

The command centre had been cleared of all personnel but the highest officers of the theatre. Dvorgin, Veritas, Princess Jessivayne, Colonel-Chieftain Jurgen and their immediate subordinates made a colourful display.

'The blows you have already struck will be immortalised,' Achallor continued, 'for they will be the first of countless more.'

Dvorgin heard prayers of thanks; the audience were too awed for anything more effusive.

'Your Emperor asks more of you yet, however,' said Achallor. 'We are but the heralds of this invasion. Barring the caprice of the warp, our comrades are but days behind us. There is scant time to act against the threat to the fleet.'

'A threat?' said Veritas. 'Of what kind?'

'That we do not know,' said another of the Custodians, the big one who had named himself Vychellan. He had removed his helm to show a stern face framed by white hair. 'Sorcery. Ambush. Who can say? We know only that it exists. We must know every strategic detail of your operation, and everything you can tell us of the enemy.'

Dvorgin moved forward to the chart desk. He willed his knees not to betray him.

'My lord, at once,' he said, gesturing at the cartolith. 'After the initial attack, we managed to hold Ascension Stair space port and other locales, but I am ashamed to say we have been losing territory steadily for the last few weeks. Today, we received notice that Fort Bastabus had fallen. This was one of the last major strongpoints we had in this part of the continent.'

'Where is it?' Achallor asked.

'Fifty miles up the coast. It was being held by a demi-regiment of Lodovians. They are all now dead. The enemy has been preparing to launch a major offensive from the direction of Saint Claytor's Span. I think now that Bastabus is gone, that attack is imminent.'

'I have faith that we have the strength to endure until the crusade arrives,' said Veritas.

'We are perhaps not lost,' agreed Dvorgin, pointing at the jagged slash in the landscape. 'If you were to lend us your support, we could pre-empt this attack, and push them back, and destroy the artillery threatening our void shielding.'

'What are your plans thereafter?' asked Achallor.

'They were to hold a line on the far side of the bridge, to give ourselves a little breathing room, but now you're here, we could retake the Blessed Bastion.'

Dvorgin refocused the map on a tall tower partway between Ascension Stair and the macro-cathedrum.

'The Blessed Bastion was Imprezentia's primary command-and-control centre. It should have been impregnable, but it was taken from us by treachery from within on the first day of the invasion. They have a vox-blunt in operation there, crippling our communications. With the bastion back in our hands, we would be able to better coordinate what assets remain on this world.'

'What are their numbers?' asked Vychellan.

'Many cultists, some Heretic Astartes,' said Dvorgin. 'We do not have exact figures.'

Jessivayne spoke up. 'House Kamidar sallies out daily to press the foe back from the canyon, but our wargrounds are increasingly limited,' she said. 'They overran the outer defences a month ago, and now we cannot dare Claytor's Span, but must pass south under fire, so we do not know their strength on the far side of the canyon any more.'

'It is deep and provides a formidable ditch,' said Achallor, looking at the map. 'The bridge is the only way across. It is a difficult assault for them.'

'Nevertheless I judge it their best chance for a quick victory,' said Dvorgin. 'You can see how the ground around the port limits their movements to the south, east and north. The western districts are most vulnerable. The equal elevation either side of the canyon gives them a marginal advantage, as they have more guns, and the bridge leads right into the heart of the void port. They have moved up their bigger artillery. The Princess Jessivayne attempted to destroy the guns several times, but was driven back, and our void shields are now sorely tested by them. Our power supply is on a knife edge. We possess barely enough capacity to power both defence lasers and shields simultaneously, and I am sure that as soon as the enemy become aware of that, the fleet will attack. Then we are finished.'

'So if you can push them back from the District of Heavens at the other end of Saint Claytor's Span, then you can remove the artillery that threatens your voids,' said Vychellan. 'Thus negating the threat of ground assault. That is your plan?'

'Yes,' said Dvorgin.

'My main concern is the orbital laser batteries,' said Jessivayne. 'If we lose those, Kamidar will be open to direct attack from orbit. My Knights would not be able to leave our drop keep, and we would lose one of the most potent forces still in play on this world.'

'They could have destroyed you already,' said Achallor.

'The enemy wish to capture this port intact,' said Vychellan. 'It is why they have not moved on you yet.'

'What is your void strength, if I may ask, my lords?' asked Dvorgin.

'You think to use our void assets to harry them in space, perhaps drive the fleet into range of your ground lasers? Discount the thought,' said Achallor.

'You would lose this port,' said Vychellan, 'your lives and the planet. You have made them cautious. Your strength is almost spent. If they knew how precarious your situation is, they would attack now. Fortune favours you, for the moment.'

'The Emperor favours us,' said Jessivayne.

'Do not think to test either fortune or the Emperor,' said Vychellan.

'Yet help is coming,' said Achallor.

'Most pressing is the threat to the crusade,' said Vychellan. 'The enemy's commanders have established themselves in the Emperor Exultant, the macro-cathedrum of Asclomaedas the Builder, yes?'

Dvorgin nodded, and shifted the focus of the cartolith again.

'That structure looks near impossible to defend effectively against concerted assault,' said Achallor.

'My lord, it is true my Sisters and I were unable to hold it,' said Veritas. 'However, we were outnumbered, facing betrayal, and burdened by the duty of salvaging the most holy relics. Our enemies possess far greater strength, Heretic Astartes and

Throne-alone-knows what numbers of faithless. They have had weeks to fortify the structure.'

'The macro-cathedrum is almost two days' march from our current location, my lord,' said Dvorgin. 'It would cost us dearly in lives to attack, and if we fail, we will lose everything.'

'Serving the Emperor is a costly business, general,' said Vychellan.

'If the cathedral were not a fortress before,' said Achallor. 'It will make a poor fortress still, no matter how well Perturabo's sons reinforce it.'

'You mean to attack?'

'We do,' said Vychellan.

'But you are only five,' said Dvorgin.

Princess Jessivayne laughed. 'They are the Emperor's own archangels, general.'

But only five, he thought again, nervous they might catch his thoughts and hold him to account for his lack of faith.

No divine judgement came. Achallor and his lieutenant were instead examining the macro-cathedrum closely.

'Wide open to attack,' said Vychellan.

'If that is so, why are they there? We need clarity before action. Vychellan, contact Mistress Sangar. Have her prepare Brother-Sergeant Lucerne's warriors for deployment. Can your void and aerial defences provide a covered approach vector?' he asked Dvorgin.

'Of course, my lord,' said Dvorgin. He hesitated. 'There are more of you?'

'Not us, Adeptus Astartes,' said Vychellan. 'Thirty of them.'

Murmurs went around the room.

Achallor ignored their excitement. 'Their numbers will not matter if they are blown from the sky. Hastius, what is the probability of safe landing, given the capabilities of the vertical defence grid?'

Vychellan looked over the representation of the port. 'Fifty-four per cent. There are enough ground-to-orbit batteries to establish a safe approach corridor in the void – the risk is in-atmosphere. Slim odds.'

'But good enough,' said Achallor. 'Tell Sangar to send down Master of Astropaths Ashmeiln with Sergeant Lucerne. She is to come, I will not accept any denial.'

Dvorgin couldn't imagine anyone refusing an order from the Custodians.

Achallor addressed the assembled officers. 'We will aid you in securing the bastion. But we must deal with this threat. Once the bastion is in your hands, we will require you to make an assault upon the cathedrum to mask our own attack upon it. You will provide us with all information you have regarding the macro-cathedrum and the catacombs. You have a prisoner, yes?'

'We do,' said Dvorgin. 'Though she knows very little.'

'Take me to her,' said Achallor. 'I will be the judge of that myself.'

Time ran dry for Ismadela. They had hurt her, and now she floated upon a mist of pain between the realms of life and death. Not long now for heart to beat and blood to flow.

'Great ones,' she said, though whether they were words or only thoughts she could no longer tell. A fleeting echo responded, making her own words mocking.

Great ones, it said, and she had a vision of the cold stone niche she had snatched a few moments of rest in, and knew the echo disapproved.

'Aid me!' she cried. There had been faith in her before, once for the Emperor, and then for the Great Powers. Now she was alone.

Aid me. Laughter bubbled under the echo. She could feel things moving in the mist. They were coming for her. She had failed in her service to the pantheon, and she would pay.

She was dimly aware of the room where her body sat, leaking out its life onto the floor, the place where the brides of the Emperor had spoken kind words even as they cut her and burned her. One watched over her now, her face hidden behind a mask of ceramite. The rest had gone.

'Please,' she mumbled through broken teeth, and she did not know whether she spoke to the Sister or to the echoes in the mist.

Please, the voices in the mist mocked. The glowing substance of it stirred. A scaled fin rose and plunged back within the vapours. Terrified now, she tried to push her way back into her body, but it was shutting down, part by part, and rejected her spirit. The mist waited, and drawing her into it with slow purpose, threatened worse beyond.

In the room of her death the door opened, and a blazing light shone through. Where it touched her failing form, the cult tattoos burned, spreading blisters across ragged flesh, but where it lit upon the brands the brides of the Emperor had given her, a coolness grew.

'Look at me,' a voice said. It used the high speech of the Emperor. For the first time she understood it completely.

Her head hung loose on dying muscles.

'Look at me!' the voice commanded, and it was louder than the peals of Asclomaedas' cathedrum before the holy ones had come and thrown down all the bells.

Against her will she raised up her face.

A golden giant stood before her, ablaze with salving light. She wept when she saw it, for she knew in an instant that she had taken the wrong path, and that here true judgement was.

A metal hand cupped her chin. Bloody tears ran down her ruined face.

'What were you digging for?' the voice said. She could not see its features. Light shone too brightly from its eyes. She felt the Emperor look upon her through him, and though she had turned her back upon Him, she knew that she was seen.

'Forgive me!' she thought to shriek, but her words were a painful mumble. The voices in the mist laughed.

The golden hand was cool and gentle.

'It is not in my power to forgive you anything, but I can take away your pain. Tell me, what were you digging for?'

Don't tell, the voices in the mist said. *Don't tell!*

Ismadela wavered between speech and silence, as she wavered between life and death, but in the golden light around this true angel of the Emperor, she could not stay silent.

'Bucharis,' she gasped. 'We were looking for something called Bucharis.'

Traitor! hissed the voices. *Traitor!*

'For what end?' asked the golden giant, who seemed to understand her language, as different as it was.

'Judgement...' she murmured. The mist was calling to her. She could not tarry. 'Judgement... on the faithless.'

'A weapon?' the giant demanded.

'I don't know.' Her muscles felt they would fail, but she managed to shake her head within the giant's hand.

'Do you know more than this? Answer truthfully. I shall know.'

'No, no, nothing,' she said.

The giant held her a moment longer, weighing the truth of her words, and Ismadela felt her soul measured along with them.

'Then be at peace,' he said.

The hand tightened, and twisted, snapping her neck.

No blessing was hers, nor salvation. The mist enveloped her, and the echoes laughed. She screamed as Chaos gave its reward, and the creatures of the warp began to feed.

Achallor answered the Battle Sister's unspoken challenge.

'She had suffered enough,' he said to her. 'She knew no more.'

He paused, then continued, burying his rage under a calm, commanding voice. The injuries inflicted on the woman in the chair were obscene. 'Think not of her as a heretic, Sister, and consider instead how you would have fared, were you in her place. There are many paths to unrighteousness, and they are far easier to find than those that lead to the Emperor's light.'

The Sister bowed her head, and called for one of her fellows to remove the body.

Achallor left the stink of bowels and blood behind, fury stoked, for though he had little pity for those who worked against the Imperium, he dearly wished humans would acknowledge their own weaknesses, and behave accordingly.

Chapter Twenty-One

A MOMENT'S REFLECTION

HOMUNCULUS

RECORD AND ARCHIVE

Shipmistress Ebele Sangar worried and paced the interior of her cabin.

It was well appointed, though not opulently, her furnishings being of quality without unnecessary adornment. All were bolted down against violent manoeuvring. She paced past the torsewood desk with its high-backed chair, its inbuilt cogitator unit, piles of books, papers, her dormant cyber-slave and ancient astrosextant.

She passed her bunk, her private head, three ornate firearms of Martian manufacture mounted on the wall, shelves housing her library and logbooks. Sangar had discovered long ago that if one wished to converse with the Adeptus Custodes, one required a solid grounding in a wide variety of lore.

She passed a beautiful painting by Asposean of Admiral Ravensberg's victory at Gethsemane. Then she was back around to her desk again.

She stopped, sighed, and ground the heels of her hands into

her eyes. The magi-omnissor who monitored the Custodians' life runes assured her not one had gone dark. She had never known one do so, in fact, for the Custodians did not die easily. Still, these were unusual times.

'That's enough of that,' she muttered. The emissaries were a subtle weapon. As such, Sangar was used to being a ghost until her masters called her. But although Ebele Sangar gloried in her duties, she was also acutely aware of their gravity, and she hated waiting. It was insane that she feel maternal towards the shield-captain, but sometimes she did. The Custodians were beings beyond compare but they could sometimes seem so... naive.

Clicking her tongue at herself, Ebele Sangar sat down at her desk. If sleep wouldn't come, she might as well work.

'Nobody ever talks about how much damned scroll-work there is in captaining a voidship,' she muttered, activating the cogitator's holo-reader.

There was a movement on her desk atop a stack of books. Small eyes lit up blue.

'Record and archive?' queried her cyber-slave.

She glared at it. It was a horrible thing, a small homunculus of hideous aspect, so old it looked like it was falling apart. It was little more than a brass skeleton and powercell wrapped about with leather. Maybe once the skin had given it the seeming of a living creature, but it was now so dry and cracked its metal innards poked through the stitching. She wondered what it was supposed to represent. It could have been a preserved animal or dwarfish xenos species, she thought, but it didn't match anything in any file or book she'd ever seen. It wore a little plaque on a chain about its neck, like the cuirassier's plate favoured by certain military orders. Upon this was a legend whose engraving was almost worn away: *Lest we forget what waits beyond the veil.*

'No,' she said.

The thing cringed at her tone. It had belonged to the last captain, and he'd said he had also inherited it. It was feasibly as old as the *Radiance* itself, and so she hadn't mustered the heart to dispose of it. Sailor's superstition, she chided herself, but she still heeded it.

The *Radiance* was currently in high geostationary anchor over the Ascension Stair space port, shrouded by the obfuscation field from the enemy, who were in turn hiding from the port guns.

She pulled in fresh datafeeds and consigned stale information to the archives. Then she consulted the repair reports from Magos Kzarch. All damage suffered by the *Radiance* during their translation into realspace had been made as good as it could, barring a few tertiary power couplings in sector quartus. Kzarch assured her these would be resanctified within the hour.

Officers Osmor and VenShellen had managed to contact three surviving Imperial warships. One, an Armageddon-class cruiser called the *Resolute*, was concealed in Gathalamor's lesser asteroid belt. The other two, a system monitor called the *Nil Desperandor* and the sorely wounded grand cruiser *Paladin*, were lurking at the system's edge.

Sangar had spoken with their captains at length. The picture she assembled of the enemy's void strength was daunting but not, she thought, wholly disastrous. She ran her finger down an annotated list floating before her.

'Record and archive,' she said clearly.

The small construct straightened. Mechanisms exposed by the drying of its skin ran swiftly, like it was eager to be useful. She sometimes felt a little sorry for it.

'Notation, enemy numbers beyond planetary orbit something between five and ten heretic escorts,' she said, 'scattered on out-system patrols and hunting sweeps. Consider possibility of catching them in ambush. Annotation, in a one-on-one fight *Radiance* would make short work of any frigate. Tactical posit, perhaps one or more of them could be wounded and left to bleat their distress calls into the void, to pull heretic warships out of position. Caution, danger of miscalculation. Caution, other Imperial vessels present heavily damaged. Caution, major enemy fleet presence around Gathalamor. Response times unknown.'

She paused. 'I wonder if the other ships are up to such subtle and precise manoeuvres,' she told herself.

A longer pause followed as she read on.

'Recorded and archived,' said the homunculus, prompted by her silence.

'What?' she said distractedly. 'Play back last twenty seconds.'

The thing gaped. Whoever had made it had thought it amusing to set vermin's teeth in its plaster gums. Her voice came out of its mouth, always higher than she thought it was.

'Delete last line,' she said.

'Deleting,' it said.

She took a sip of tepid water. She wanted something stronger, but needed her head clear. If she regretted one thing about serving the Emperor's guardians, it was that they made the smallest bad habit feel like the worst sin.

'Record and archive to shipmistress' log,' she said. 'Further appendage to enemy strength estimate. Main enemy fleet strength – five void craft of cruiser void displacement class, three originally of Adeptus Astartes design, the remainder Legion vintage.' Truly ancient, she thought. 'Appendage, further strength at anchor, non-Gathalamor orbit. Total four frigates, one over Rhanda and Chyrosius' Rest apiece, two over the oceanic agri world of Jhorr.' She leaned back. 'Pause recording,' she said.

'Compliance,' squeaked the hideous thing. It shifted, waiting tensely to be useful again.

'There's one more.' She paged through a number of other

documents floating before her. 'Aha! And then there is you, you filthy abomination,' she said, peering at a grainy spectral data-rubbing.

'Mistress?' said the thing. She could have sworn it sounded hurt.

'Hush, not you. This.' She put her finger through the holopage, and found herself explaining it to the homunculus. 'Something in its build suggests an Adeptus Mechanicus Explorator ship.' The thing crept forward. 'Do you see, these lines? Looks like a Ryza pattern, M38, doesn't it? But Kzarch says no. I think he's wrong. Whatever that thing hanging over Gathalamor is, it is no longer clean. These extrusions here.' She pointed them out. 'They're biomechanical in nature. Psy-auguries suggest empyric activity throughout the ship's structure. It's riddled with corruption. Now, if you forced me at gunpoint, I might say that the ship doesn't *appear* to be much of a combat craft, though I'd qualify that assessment was based upon gut instinct. What the vessel *is*, however, is an effective informational warfare weapon. We've detected augur energy signatures and empyric sweeps stretching out from it like solar flares. Terrific range. Mister Osmor describes the craft appearing on his instruments as a darkly burning star. Mistress of Astropaths Ashmeiln mutters about the ship's "foul animus" and how it churns the warp. Interesting, no? But it hasn't seen us, not yet.'

'Record and archive last?' asked the homunculus.

'Record and archive last,' Sangar said. 'So, we have to consider. What if that thing somehow picked up on Achallor's teleport signature? What if the heretics know where he made planetfall? What if they're even now besieged or, Throne forgive me, captured?'

She paused.

'I could contact him to find out. What would that help? It would give away our position, that's what. Stupid idea.'

She clicked her tongue again, shook her head and opened a fresh report from the ship's Navigator. She frowned, seeing that he, like Ashmeiln, spoke of strange whispers in the warp originating from Gathalamor.

'That can't be good,' she said.

'Record and archive?' rasped the cyber-slave.

'Record memorandum to self, interrogate both witches about the whisperings.'

She felt all the more urgency after reading the rest of the Navigator's report. *Substantial bow waves upon the warp tides, accelerated empyric currents, omens of substantial fleet presences approaching.*

'The battle groups are coming.' She looked the data over again. 'They're going to be here too soon.'

'Record and archive?'

'Throne blast it,' she said, reaching for the bottle in her desk drawer. 'I'm going to have a drink. I need a drink.'

'Record and archive?'

'Could you maybe learn how to say something else?' she said, uncorking the bottle and pouring herself a stiff measure.

'Record and archive,' it said decisively.

'Good health,' she said.

She took a swallow and sighed, letting her eyes close as the fiery liquid warmed her belly.

Her vox trilled. She reached up for her torc and pressed the receive jewel.

'Yes?'

'Forgive the intrusion, my lady,' said the voice at the other end, one of Osmor's men. *'But I have a coded message from Lord Achallor.'*

She felt a dizzying wave of relief.

'I'm on my way,' she said, and downed the last of her drink, and hurried out.

The homunculus shuffled about on its book, peered around,
then hunched low.

'Session ended,' it said, and the light in its eyes went out.

Chapter Twenty-Two

THE DARK CARDINAL

KAR-GATHARR EMPOWERED

GLORY OF THE GODS

Kar-Gatharr knew the place of mists that Ismadela saw, as he knew a million others. None of them were real; they were landscapes of thought and emotion, and nothing was less permanent than they, so apt to dissolution in the warp as soon as they manifested.

And yet, they had truth. Truth as much as any stone or breath or star. Reality was subjective, and so experience was all, Kar-Gatharr had learned long ago. Around the self could be found the true essence of reality.

His soul wandered close to the veil. Days or ages he had been gone, it did not matter, time was an illusion. Being was all. Being transcended time. He saw himself within his chamber and he saw himself in myriad landscapes. They were all the same, all false, all true.

The Hallowed Sacristy had been amongst the most holy places in the macro-cathedrum, for Cardinal Asclomaedas had offered prayers there before leading his first sermon in the great nave. Lies, like all else about the cathedrum, but lies had power, tainting the place from the start. Kar-Gatharr had erected altars in the four corners of the sacristy, one sanctified to each of the gods. There was an altar of brass, surrounded by skulls; an altar of gold, wreathed in incense; an altar of rusted iron, garlanded with diseased entrails; an altar of crystal in whose depths formless shapes danced.

All four had been slicked with blood during the days of his meditation. Sacrifice after sacrifice met their end beneath the daggers of Yheng and her coven. After each death, the still-bloodied knife was used to cut another holy rune into the Dark Apostle's flesh. His skin sang with hot, tight pain. His flesh was crimson, his blood mingling with that of the hundreds who had perished around him.

'In pain is power,' he whispered, as another victim gurgled his last, and the wet knife was pushed into Kar-Gatharr's skin again.

Elsewhere, he wandered awhile on plains of shimmering silk, where dancers leapt for tortured eternities, crossing rivers of boiling dreams that melted with soft weeping into nothing.

'My lord,' he called. 'Are you there? I come to you with news.'

Something moaned in ecstasy, something else in pain. His environs shifted to a pleasant forest, where trees with mossy faces slept.

'My lord, my cardinal. I have come.'

In the greater falsehood of reality, the knife pricked him again. There was a rushing sensation, and a touch of a soul upon his.

Kar-Gatharr, Dark Apostle, come to me.

'I hear you, Dark Cardinal, lord of mine.'

Space and time fell to nothing, and from their wreck stepped a figure both proud and terrible. Armoured in black Terminator plate, his ancient, withered face surrounded by sculptures of leering daemons, Kor Phaeron was the essence of majesty, the Master of the Faith, swollen by the power of the pantheon.

Kar-Gatharr knelt before him, his head bowed, blood falling

from his ritual wounds into the hungry void. From their drops, a dark fane built itself around the two priests, glossy black masonry and iron arching up to meet, with tall windows framing stars of some other realm. Soft hymns soothed the air.

Kor Phaeron placed his hand upon Kar-Gatharr's head, and it felt as real as anything could.

'Dark Apostle Kar-Gatharr, in the name of the Great Four, I bless thee, faithful servant of Legion, primarch and gods. Rise. Rise, my son, and be welcome.' Kor Phaeron's armour growled with animal voices as he lifted his hand.

'Thank you, my lord,' Kar-Gatharr said. He got to his feet.

'The ring is found,' Phaeron said. 'Lord Tenebrus' weapon is almost ready. You have done well.'

'Thank you, my lord.'

'My praise is genuine, my son, but be wary. Tenebrus is cunning and treacherous. The corpse-god's false son runs to spread his rage across the stars. This I have seen. Many ships come to Gathalamor. More than anticipated. Abaddon has stirred the hornet's nest. In the Hydraphur Sector the sons of blood suffered a great defeat. The final war has come.'

'The primarch attacks as two spears so distantly spaced?' asked Kar-Gatharr. He had expected a large assault, but not this. 'I have seen nothing to warn me of this.'

Kor Phaeron laughed. 'The Anathema shrouds the warp. Guilliman attacks on many fronts, not two, and each spear shall be further divided. His armies are beyond compare. Not since we went to war for the corpse-god ourselves have so many warriors travelled the stars. Guilliman seeks to pin every serpent head at once. He will fail, for Lord Abaddon's armies are as prepared as his. I have met him in battle. He is wanting. He is nothing compared to the Warmaster's power.'

'What of our goals?' asked Kar-Gatharr. 'What of our war of faith?'

'The Legion stands ready to move on Talledus. We shall answer the calls of the faithful there, and take it. When the false primarch moves through Gathalamor, we shall strike, and drive for Terra. They think themselves on the brink of victory, halting the Slaughter Crusade, but many blades are aimed at Terra's heart. We shall cut them and bleed mankind of souls, until only the faithful remain.'

'If you say you await Guilliman's further advance, you do not think we shall be successful here,' said Kar-Gatharr. 'We will not hold this nexus.'

'Fate is in flux. You may yet. The gods will decide, but know that the weapon must survive, beyond all other consideration.' Kor Phaeron looked down on Kar-Gatharr, his lined face glowing with power. 'There is something you would ask.'

'Yes,' Kar-Gatharr said. 'I feel something. There is a disturbance here. I sense the hand of our enemy. The Adeptus Custodes.'

'A flash of gold. The death of one of the faithful, yes, yes. I sense it too,' said Kor Phaeron. He closed his eyes. 'The corpse-lord's guardians have set foot upon Gathalamor. This I did not see before.' Kor Phaeron frowned. 'Unfortunate. This will make your task all the more difficult. If they are there, the Adeptus Custodes must have warning of our intentions.'

'How?'

'We are not yet the sole masters of the warp,' said Kor Phaeron. 'Guilliman has his own seers. Stop the Custodians. The weapon must survive.'

'My lord,' Kar-Gatharr said, and bowed. 'I pray to the Dark Gods to make me strong. If I must face the guardians of the corpse-lord, I must be blessed.'

'You would know how your prayers will be answered?' Kor Phaeron smiled. 'You sacrificed well. The souls you offer are well received, and the gods have judged you worthy.'

Kar-Gatharr let out a grateful sigh. 'At last.'

'Their boons may kill you.'

'If that is my fate, so be it. For the glory of the gods.'

'As the faithful must accept all burdens placed upon them, for pursuance of the one truth,' said Kor Phaeron.

'When shall I receive their blessing?'

'Their power is already in you. You are favoured. When the time comes for you to use it, you will know.'

The building collapsed into a howling spiral of shadow, with the two Word Bearers at its centre. Dark faces were dragged out into streamers of teeth and fear, the souls of Yheng's victims.

'The enemy comes. The warp is in turmoil. The process of meeting like this becomes more arduous,' said Kor Phaeron. 'You and I shall not speak again, Kar-Gatharr.'

He faded from sight.

His master gone, Kar-Gatharr felt the tug of the materium work upon his soul. Cold stone rose around him. Spirit nestled into flesh, and Kar-Gatharr took a breath. After days in trance, his eyes slid open and he looked upon mundane surroundings again.

He smiled through bleeding lips. The promise of power burned through his body. He felt invincible, poised to work a great destruction.

'The gods have their due,' Kar-Gatharr murmured, 'and so I have mine.' He unfolded his limbs and rose to his full height. He clenched his fist. Blood squeezed from it, and dark flame flickered at the edge of his sight.

'My lord, you wake,' said Tharador Yheng, starting up from her seat near the sacristy's door. She watched him nervously, fearful that what dwelled in his flesh was not he, but some other soul of more diabolical intent.

'It is I, Yheng! Cease cowering,' he said, and his voice now was a layered growl.

He stepped over the ritual circles carved into the floor. His feet adhered to sticky blood. Flies buzzed up from the ground. He spread his arms, and dark light glowed from his palms.

'I return to you blessed, Yheng, show your respect.'

She dropped immediately to her knees and bowed her head. Her silver chains jangled.

'Is it time?' asked Yheng.

'It is,' rumbled Kar-Gatharr. He could hear Yheng's heartbeat, hear the rush of blood in her veins, smell her fear, and he smiled. 'I heard it in the warp from my tutelary's own mouth. The enemy is coming.'

'We have had no word,' said Yheng.

'The powers and I play a game you do not comprehend.'

'Yes, my lord. I apologise for my ignorance.'

'The gods care not for apologies or for regrets. They favour only will and action. Have my slaves attend me. I require my armour, my relics, my weapons and my mantle.'

'At once,' said Yheng, bowing again before hastening from the chamber.

Slaves crept in bearing Kar-Gatharr's armour plates. His weapons arrived, guarded by his chosen warriors. It was an hour before the arming and prayers were complete, and Kar-Gatharr stepped from the sacristy fully clad for war. Over his armour was draped the cloak of nightmares, on whose chain baleful runes glowed.

'Come, Yheng,' he said. 'We go to see Lord Tenebrus.'

Chapter Twenty-Three

THE WEAPON

A GATHERING OF DARKNESS

ALL THAT POWER

The cannon was made all of bone, and the ivory glory of it was very fine to behold. As Yheng paced behind Kar-Gatharr, she breathed, 'Beautiful!' and again, 'Beautiful, master!'

It was beautiful, even though it was not quite finished, and scaffolding encased the device halfway up its three-hundred-foot length. The Iron Warriors were there in numbers, and the adepts of the True Mechanicum worked busily around the gun, molecular torches fizzing green sparks as they welded bone to bone.

Tenebrus' weapon was mounted on a turntable of dark steel that filled the chapel. Toothed edges allowed the cannon to be rotated, and long equilibrators gave it a range of traverse so it covered the sky almost down to the horizon.

Kar-Gatharr went to a set of fresh, semicircular steps hewn from granite tombstones that gave access to the platform. The top step was perfectly level with the steel, and when he stepped from the stone to the metal the turntable was solid as rock. The base seemed to have been cast in one piece, though it was over four hundred feet across, and Kar-Gatharr could not see how it had been brought under the dome. The base was decorated with images of leering daemons, the horns, tongues and sharp cheekbones of which tessellated perfectly.

'See, Tharador Yheng, the art of the sons of Perturabo. They have more talents than only fighting.'

But Yheng did not look; she had eyes only for the great cannon. Interlinked ribcages made up the breech, then a barrel first of long bones, then of stacked pelvises, and the last fifty feet of it made only of skulls, their eyes all pointed forward, and their jaws opened up in screams. Each component was part melted into the next to make one osseous whole.

'Beautiful,' she said again.

'You should be entranced,' said Kar-Gatharr. He rested a hand on her shoulder. 'You lived all your life among these worthless relics. While the worms of the Corpse-Emperor lived in the light, you suffered in poverty. You know these bones of old. They were family to you more than the dogs of Terra ever were. Now see them elevated to a just purpose. You found the key, Tharador Yheng, you helped choose the bones. You are blessed.'

To see someone give themselves so totally to the gods gladdened Kar-Gatharr's black hearts, so he did not kill Yheng when she had the temerity to reach up and clasp one of his armoured fingers.

'Thank you, my master, for the chance you have given me to prove my faith.'

They walked around the weapon. The breech was solid, with no shell assembly, and the end of the barrel had no aperture but the howling mouths of a thousand stolen saints. At the base of the gun were assemblies of delicate glass, and stacked tubes full of focusing crystals, while at the very rear was a cascabel carved of blue-veined rock, through which moved skeins of light.

In place of a firing station was an obelisk of dark stone, machinery and flesh. Eight thick pipes erupted from the obelisk's flanks and plunged down through a hole at the centre of the turntable, thence into a shaft bored through the chamber's floor. Those pipes ran down and down, and spread away in a great ring that ran beneath the planet's surface. The Ring of Bucharis, Tenebrus had named it. Dark pacts had been made to ensure its completion.

They went to the control station. The Mechanicum adepts bowed to Kar-Gatharr, and gave due respect to Yheng as the finder of the ring. Prevalent on the controls were rods of noctilith. In the centre of the obelisk, girt by weeping sores, was a cavity no bigger than a coin.

The Dark Apostle pointed to it. 'See here the place for the key, that will unleash all hell upon the Corpse-Emperor's dogs,' said Kar-Gatharr. 'The key you found.'

Yheng moaned in holy ecstasy. She was shaking again, sending her chains dancing, but not this time from fear.

'An impressive sight, yes?' said a voice at Kar-Gatharr's side. He heard a wet sniffing. 'You have grown mightier, Dark Apostle. Very impressive. I wondered what you were doing with yourself these last days, while I laboured here.'

Kar-Gatharr swung about, and he had the urge to snatch out his crozius and strike Tenebrus down there and then. But he refrained.

'Magus,' he said.

Tenebrus had his hood down, showing a smooth scalp the colour of a shark's belly, and a nose receding to nothing. Needle teeth glinted in his infuriating smile.

'You wished to see, yes? I know. Did not want to come a-creeping to me, but show your pride instead and come unbidden. Fairly done, Apostle. I acknowledge the favour you are held in.' He crooked his neck in a mocking bow. 'Now, we have business to be about, a communion with our war leaders.' He looked up at the cannon. 'The time approaches for us to show our power.' He leered at Tharador Yheng. 'Your acolyte is proving herself most useful. By our command, she will attend also.' He turned his back and walked away from the gun. 'Come now. Great things are afoot.'

'Stay behind me,' Kar-Gatharr said to Yheng. 'You must court great people to become great, but do not allow yourself to be drawn into his net. There is peril here for you.'

Once they were in the sorcerer's lair, Tenebrus went to his font.

'Will you join me, Apostle?'

The invitation was lightly given, yet it did not bear refusing. Kar-Gatharr stepped up beside the robed figure and directed his gaze down into the oily liquid.

'And what about your charming disciple?'

'She is not ready to partake of the warp conclave,' said Kar-Gatharr. 'She will remain here and watch only.' The oil moved sluggishly in the font. Lights stirred in the depths.

'I insist–' Tenebrus began.

'You asked her attendance, not her participation,' Kar-Gatharr interrupted. He lifted his gaze from the liquid and stared at Tenebrus. Black light flared around his eye-lenses.

The sorcerer chuckled. 'My, my, such new spleen you have, Apostle. Very well. You will observe, Tharador Yheng.' He winked at the acolyte.

Kar-Gatharr returned his attention to the font. The darkness called to him, rising up, forcing his vision into a tunnel.

'The rest of them await our pleasure,' came Tenebrus' velvety voice. 'Let us commune with them, yes?'

Suddenly Kar-Gatharr felt as though he were lurching forward. Instinct moved him to grip the rim of the font. Yet his body was gone, an absence left behind as his consciousness plunged downwards. This was not the smooth journeying of his own sorcery, but something harder, more unforgiving. There was a sense of acceleration, of falling, the building need to breathe, to move, to blink, to do anything at all except fall, but fall was all he could do.

Then all around Kar-Gatharr was calm. He hung in a void, a bodiless spirit unable to see or to move.

Then Tenebrus spoke.

'Here we meet in the bosom of darkness. Here we gather to snuff out the false light of Terra. Friends, do you hear my voice?'

'I do,' replied Kar-Gatharr.

'Aye, I hear you,' came the rasp of Torvann Lokk's response, and Kar-Gatharr was glad to hear his war-brother.

'Confirmatory,' came the many-layered whine of High Magos Vech Xyrax, a voice of scrapcode whispers and snarls.

Others spoke – Warpsmith Yutil; Warpsmith Casipiniax; commander of the fleet, Voidmaster Jhorgg Klordren; Grand Battery Master Fodov – until the darkness was thick with distant presences.

'A fine gathering,' said Tenebrus, in the tone of a man reunited with beloved friends. 'I come with grave news and good news. First, the good. The weapon is almost finished. The grave is that the enemy is coming. You have limited time to achieve your objectives. Warpsmith Lokk, how fares your hunt?'

'It continues,' replied Lokk with a poor grace that made Kar-Gatharr wish he could take his friend aside. Lokk and Tenebrus had no love lost between them, and Lokk was too blunt a man to hide it. 'We flushed out another pocket of corpse-worshippers before dawn. They were better provisioned and supplied than I might have expected.'

'Warpsmiths, did you not tell me days ago that you were on the verge of breaking them?' Tenebrus' voice was indulgent yet Kar-Gatharr heard the threat there all the same.

Yutil spoke up. 'It is a big city, with a continent's worth of surface structures and catacombs. The cultists Kar-Gatharr delivered to us are not worth a damn in a war like this. The best indication they give us of the foe's presence is when they show up dead. You said, Tenebrus, that you would deliver this world to us. Where are Kar-Gatharr's warriors? Where are the daemons we were promised? Without aid from the–'

'I have better than daemons to give you, if you would but wait,' Tenebrus interrupted. He didn't raise his voice but his intervention cut the veteran Iron Warrior dead.

'This cannot continue. The Imperials are heavily dug in to the space port,' said Kar-Gatharr. 'You warriors of iron take down their remaining strongholds slowly. You do not live up to your reputation. The Warmaster told us to take this world, and what do we have? Dead warriors and ruins.'

'The port of Ascension Stair is the key, yet it is well shielded,' said Casipiniax uneasily. 'They resist on the ground. The Emperor's dogs are persistent. We must take them from above.'

'While the defence laser batteries remain operational, you shall have no orbital support,' said Klordren. 'I am tempted to bomb this place to ruin and depart. We shall not take it now. The enemy will move on us. Best we leave them nothing but ash.'

'You shall do no such thing,' said Tenebrus. 'There are plans in play that must conclude. Bucharis' Gift will provide.'

'You put too much faith in the mystical and none in the physical. All the favour of the gods will do nothing if we are outplayed in war,' said Yutil.

'Give us more Possessed at least,' said Casipiniax. 'They have proven most useful in scouring the catacombs. I have volunteers who wish to host the Neverborn.'

'The Possessed are the most blessed of all our brethren. It is not an easy thing to fashion more of them,' said Kar-Gatharr.

'That is another thing,' said Lokk, sounding wary. 'War-brother, a pack of your gods-touched vanished from our vox-net yesterday. I sent a force to look for them, and they had been slain. They were dealt with quickly, and I found none of the foes dead.'

'It would have been the Sisters,' said Yutil.

'They were slain using a bolt calibre the same as our own,' said Lokk.

'Imperial Space Marines?' Fodov exclaimed.

'How?' said Klordren. 'I have had no notice of enemy ships entering the system. The remnants of their fleets are gone. We are in control. Nothing has emerged from the Mandeville points. They could not break in-system without my knowing.'

'Yet they did,' mused Tenebrus. 'Without my detection or Lord Xyrax's either. Curious.'

Kar-Gatharr knew, but kept his silence, for the moment.

'Additional advisory,' said Xyrax. 'No ships detected, affirmative. Nothing detected, negative.'

'No warp signatures?' asked Casipiniax.

'Negative.'

'It means nothing, the interference from Tenebrus' sorcery and the number of ships coming and going earlier in this war could mask their arrival,' said Klordren. 'Even were the warp here placid, it would be easy to miss the arrival of a small task force.'

'Is that what we are dealing with?' said Fodov.

'Possibility,' said Xyrax. 'No ship arrival detected, but possible warp disturbance logged here, on Gathalamor.'

'Speak,' said Yutil.

'At a time approximately eighteen hours and twelve minutes prior to present, *Paracyte* primary empyric augurs detected four nanosecond energy spikes from deep void, followed by resonance return located within Imprezentia.'

There was a pause as the others digested this information.

'What, in your estimation, would you say these anomalous pulses warned of?' asked Tenebrus, his voice a chill zephyr.

'Hypothetical – possible teleportation signatures, or empyric excitation from daemonic manifestation.'

'Teleport signatures? There's not an Imperial warship within a million miles of Gathalamor, or your damned daemon-ship would have detected it, correct?' said Klordren.

'Confirmatory. *Paracyte* is infallible. I would stake my life upon it.'

'No need for such dramatic declarations, I am sure,' said Tenebrus equably. 'Magos, is it possible that what your ship detected was just some unusual anomaly, perhaps an omen or fore-echo of our work?'

'Assessment – unlikely. Further evidence of slain daemon-hosts suggests possibility of hostile unknown entrants into theatre highly probable. Resonant pulse detection was close by last known location of missing Word Bearers Possessed hunting pack.'

'What? Why in the name of the Dark Gods did you not tell us this straight away?' barked Yutil.

'The information had to be fully analysed to ensure there were no errors, and then distributed via the optimal channel. Causal – my request to Lord Tenebrus for this communion.'

'Send me the coordinates and I will move on them at once!' said Yutil. 'Our forces are weakened after these months of fighting. A demi-company of loyalist scum could tip the balance in their favour. What if there are more?'

'Agreed, we need to discover the nature of this threat,' said Casipiniax.

'Calm yourselves,' said Tenebrus, and now there was none of the good humour in his tone. He sounded stern, a scholar rebuking lazy students. 'Warpsmith Yutil, you may send a force

to investigate but you will not allow this effort to delay your
assault on the void port, is that understood?'

'If the magus suggests,' said Yutil sourly.

'High Magos Xyrax, you will transmit all relevant data to the warpsmiths, but once that is done you will turn all your efforts to accelerating the completion of the cannon.'

'Confirmatory with expression of reiterated fealty.'

'The corpse-worshippers grow bold indeed to strike at us so,' said Fodov. 'Leave them to my guns. Keep those Knights off my batteries, Lokk, and those shields will come down, then the defence lasers, and Klordren will be free to act.'

'The Space Marines must be dealt with,' said Yutil.

Kar-Gatharr deemed now the time to speak up, and as he did he gloated a little that he knew something that Tenebrus did not.

'They were not Space Marines,' said Kar-Gatharr. 'The Adeptus Custodes have arrived here, in what number I know not.'

'Adeptus Custodes? Here? Why?' said Casipiniax.

'I can only infer they have learned something of what we intend to do,' said Kar-Gatharr. 'It is the only explanation.'

There was uproar in the dark as the assembled leaders all began talking at once. Their minds buffeted at Kar-Gatharr's own, and beyond them he felt malignant beings turn their attention upon the group.

'Their efforts will ultimately come to naught,' said Tenebrus lightly. 'Better to see this as a sign of what is to come, for if the Adeptus Custodes are here, their faithless master is not far behind. Guilliman is coming, and he will be here soon. That is our focus, not the thin-blooded mortals grubbing about in the ruins, or the so-called guardians of the Throne. Lokk, please, continue to harry the foe, yes? Keep them away from the macro-cathedrum.'

'If you were to allow me to move on the Knights–' Lokk began.

'Yutil and Casipiniax are tasked with taking the port,' said Tenebrus. 'It is the Warmaster's will. Matters move swiftly now, the stream gathers pace and becomes a raging river. I dislike that the enemy lingers here. Weak they are, yet they pose a risk even so. I know that the Warmaster would feel as I do that the planet is not yet ours. He would be...'

Kar-Gatharr heard the menacing smile in the pause.

'Disappointed,' Tenebrus finished. 'Do not make me apportion blame.' He loaded his word with threat.

'We will continue to make every effort,' said Yutil, and now he did sound rattled.

'Weak,' said Lokk. 'We are iron, we do not fail, and we do not fear disappointment.' Kar-Gatharr knew his war-brother well. Angering the Despoiler was not a notion Torvann Lokk would care about. He was too far along his own path now.

'Perhaps if my fleet could have the direct support of the *Paracyte*?' said Klordren. 'If we were to make a concerted attack together, we could overwhelm the port void shields. *Paracyte* is armoured enough to take the brunt of their defence fire for the few minutes it would require.'

'Dismissal!' blurted High Magos Xyrax in alarm. '*Paracyte* will maintain current position and operational parameters. Imperial force arrival imminent.'

'You will not help us, and yet we are considered to be failing and you are not?' asked Yutil angrily.

'*Paracyte*'s vox and augury monitoring is enhancing ground-force efficacy by projected factor of three,' retorted the high magos. 'Concurrent decrease in coordination of enemy forces due to risk of detection through vox or energistic signature at projected factor of three also. Detection of incoming assets at one hundred per cent probability while *Paracyte* remains in mid-lunar orbit.'

'Apart from those you have already failed to detect,' said Fodov acidly.

'My lords, my lords,' said Tenebrus with a laugh in his voice.

'You must rely on your own talents. Both the Word Bearers and the magi of the Mechanicum have their own duties to attend to. Those are progressing according to schedule, are they not?'

'They are. The macro-cathedrum is reconsecrated, and our labours in the catacombs are all but done,' said Kar-Gatharr. 'We have the favour of the Four.'

'Confirmatory – psychoreactive cabling and datashrine installation currently at seventy-two per cent completion,' blared Xyrax. 'Five of eight noctilith focusing arrays are online. Consecrated servitor maniples continue the work. Advisory – current labour pace will eliminate eighty-one per cent of available unaugmented labour force by completion.'

'Perhaps you could accelerate matters, high magos?' said Tenebrus. It didn't sound like a command, but neither was it a suggestion.

'Facilitating,' replied Xyrax, his mechanical voice emotionless. 'Completion projected in fifteen hours' time.'

'Very good then,' said Tenebrus, and Kar-Gatharr could imagine him clapping his worm-fingered hands together. 'If there is nothing else?'

No voice spoke in reply.

'Excellent,' said Tenebrus. 'Let us be about our divine work, the better to ensure the Warmaster's pleasure, yes?' Tenebrus' voice was light and friendly again.

The darkness whirled around Kar-Gatharr before anyone else had a chance to speak. He found himself on his hands and knees beside the font, retching sulphurous black ooze that drooled straight through his helm's vox-grille as if it were something not wholly material.

He looked up to see Tenebrus standing, untroubled.

'Yheng,' Tenebrus said condescendingly, 'see to your master. I believe something ails him.' Tenebrus tutted at Kar-Gatharr. 'All that power, too.'

The sorcerer departed the chamber in a whisper of robes, leaving Kar-Gatharr seething.

Chapter Twenty-Four

ARRIVAL

WAR-BROTHER

CORAX

The Thunderhawks coasted without power towards Gathalamor for a day, their systems at minimal output and flight shielded by the debris of the campaign's opening void battles. Only when they needed to make the rapid dash down through the atmosphere did their engines ignite. As soon as news was given of the final approach, Achallor and Vychellan hastened to the landing pads assigned to the Adeptus Astartes.

They crossed raised causeways over the fields that filled much of the space between the landing mounds. The larger facilities had been the arrival points for Gathalamor's legions of pilgrims. The galleons had fled when the invasion began, but some of the hangars still held their abandoned landing vessels, covered now in blankets of dust.

Seeing these prompted Vychellan to speak. 'I must say something, shield-captain.'

'Then speak, my brother. I listen attentively to all words said in good faith.'

'It is faith I speak of, Marcus,' he said.

'How so, Hastius?'

'I will say bluntly,' said Vychellan. 'I do not like it when you feed the superstition of our people.'

'I see,' said Achallor. 'You disagree with the use of religious language when dealing with our allies here.'

'Heretics, faith, the Emperor is watching – it's nonsense,' Vychellan said. 'You know it's nonsense. You have seen the Emperor. You know He is a man. Why do you insist on using their false terms?'

'Because they understand the world that way,' said Achallor. 'The Adeptus Ministorum is the second most powerful organisation in the Imperium. The faith of the people is our most potent weapon in this war.'

'Yet it is false,' said Vychellan.

'Is it false, Hastius?' said Achallor. 'Is it false when the Sisters pray and their belief in our master protects them? Is it false that the soldiers here draw on wells of courage that would run dry without belief in the Emperor's protection? Is it false when the cards of the tarot deliver the Emperor's will to His servants?'

Vychellan stopped, and put a hand on Achallor's arm. 'The Emperor is powerful. I have no doubt that He reaches out and touches those who will further His goals, just as He guides us. By the Throne, Marcus, there are whispers that He stirs and more hear His words. That is a wondrous thing, if true. But He is not a god, and when you use these words that impute divinity to Him so easily, it troubles me.'

Achallor stared at his friend a long time. The sound of distant battle rolled across the blasted city.

'I sometimes wonder if you are truly fitted for the Emissaries Imperatus, Hastius.'

Vychellan held his position, then laughed in rue, and turned aside. 'Someone has to break heads, when diplomacy fails.'

'You are an impatient man,' said Achallor.

'And you love me for it, my brother.'

'It is not for your impatience that I value you,' said Achallor. 'Do not be concerned. I judge the moral weight of my words as much as I do their effect. They are chosen carefully.'

'Do others see it that way?' said Vychellan. They recommenced walking.

'Hastius, for thousands of years the entente between the church and the state has held. It is useful. Nay, it is necessary. We should not burn the Imperium upon the bonfire of our principles. Take heart from this, that the primarch also finds worship distasteful. He is a son of the old truths, perhaps he can make sense prevail again.'

They were approaching the landing pads prepared for the arrival of Brother Lucerne and his men. Teams of human ground crew with servitor support stood ready, in case the ships should land aflame or with injured aboard.

'They are coming,' said Achallor. 'Hurry now.' They quickened their stride.

As they reached the pads, there was movement to the north, where the hills rose highest. The first defence laser ground slowly into action, followed by several others, the great orbs of their ball turrets, huge as basilica domes, aligning. Once in position, they began to fire in sequence, the flash-heating of the atmosphere by their beams sending whipcrack thunders across the city. The ground rumbled with the activity of reactors far beneath their feet.

'They are there!' a human port officer shouted, looking up from a pad-side cogitator and pointing skywards.

Three brilliant dots appeared above.

Achallor and Vychellan watched the ruby strobing of defence lasers as the Thunderhawks came in.

The enemy were quick to respond. Alarms wailed from every

quarter of the void port as enemy aircraft raced to intercept the gunships. The net of defence lasers was ill-suited to bringing down such small vessels, but Icarus lascannons joined their bigger brethren, and their delicate fire grid kept out the daemon engines and pursuit craft that would dare the skies over Ascension Stair. With a crackling ripple, a ceiling of flak bursts filled the middle airs with shrapnel. Higher up was where the danger lay. Lascannon beams were made ineffective by atmospheric diffraction, and the solid munitions did not have the energy to soar so high. For crucial minutes after they first hit the atmosphere, the Thunderhawks were vulnerable.

Achallor's helm displays gave him a real-time graphical view of the ships' progress, and he saw their ident runes dart and spin around interceptors rendered as fanged skulls. The Space Marine pilots fired on their pursuers and several of the ships disintegrated, for though the pursuers were faster than the gunships, the Thunderhawks were heavily armed.

Vychellan gave a sharp intake of breath as one Thunderhawk was set upon by half a dozen fighters, slowly divided from the flight, and forced into a corkscrewing dive. Though it made good account of itself, it was riddled by shells, and came apart in an explosion visible as a yellow blotch in the sky.

The other two Thunderhawks came into the safety of the anti-aircraft net, whereupon their attackers were driven off, and they hurtled down towards the landing pads with their bright yellow hulls scorched and steaming from the rigours of re-entry. They fired their thrusters at the last possible moment, coming to a hover when it seemed certain they would crash. Heat buffeted the welcoming party. Landing struts extending, they drifted a little with minor course correction, until steel touched steel and they settled into their hydraulics. Engines spooled down from an excited scream, leaving the sky to the shrieks of the departing enemy and the last few explosions of flak.

Hulls pinked as they cooled. Then all the hatches and ramps opened onto an interior soaked in ruddy lumen glow.

Lucerne emerged first, daylight changing his armour from sanguine red to the rich yellow of Rogal Dorn's livery. Mistress Astropath Ashmeiln followed, flanked by two more of the Unnumbered Sons; then the rest debarked in ranks of two, split as they came out, and filed out to ring the main landing pad. The mortals gaped to see the Angels of Death come among them, more even than they had at the Adeptus Custodes, for there were twenty of the Space Marines, and their legends were better known.

'Sergeant Lucerne,' Achallor greeted the Space Marine.

'Ten lost on the way down, along with one Thunderhawk,' Lucerne said. He looked over the city. 'Acceptable fatalities for insertion into a warzone like this. The Emperor is with us.'

'Come,' Achallor said.

'That's it? You drop me into this nightmare with a one-in-three chance of death and I get no greeting?' said Ashmeiln. She was pale-faced and trembling.

'Apologies, mistress astropath,' said Achallor, 'the hour is late and politesse eludes me, for we must soon go to war.'

'Yes, you don't have much time,' said Ashmeiln. She pulled a scroll case from her robes and held it out to Achallor. 'Message from the shipmistress. I'll give you the short version – the fleet's coming early, you'd better move faster.'

'Now?' said Vychellan. 'That's days ahead of schedule.'

'They will be here in two days, at the outside.' She pointed over the horizon, in the direction of Asclomaedas' macro-cathedrum. 'You should be heading there, Custodian,' she said.

'We shall,' said Achallor. 'But why do you say that?'

'Because the empyric interference that's giving me the worst headache I've ever had and stopping every teleprayer from leaving this system emanates from there, my lord, and if you had the Emperor's sight as I do, you would see upon the horizon a tower of unnatural colour, and the faces that scream within it. If there is any threat to the primarch and the crusade, I'd wager my second sight it is to be found there. That's why.'

'Aye, well,' said Vychellan. 'We've other business to be attending to first.'

'You are being serious, I take it, Lord Vychellan?' said Ashmeiln. 'The danger is in the cathedrum!'

'As serious as the Emperor Himself,' said Achallor. 'To win a war, one must fight more than one battle.'

Lokk drowsed in his tank. Night was heavy over him, full of smoke and bursts of light. The sound of Fodov's guns rocked the city, and the flash of the void shields resisting the shelling sent nightmares crawling across the sky.

Cradled in *Dracokravgi*'s warm embrace, Lokk's present receded, and he remembered another day, and another world. A war of a different age.

Isstvan V.

Boltguns flashed over black sand. Lokk's company roared after the fleeing Raven Guard. Corax's sons rode swift combat bikes, but for all their skill at evasion, they could not resist the guns of the Iron Warriors tanks. Las-fire lit up the night. Heavy bolter rounds cut fiery tracks over the black.

He remembered with a Space Marine's perfect clarity every kill, the bikes hit and flipped into the air, the bodies blasted to pieces. They fled, the sons of Corax, but they were doomed.

'Finish them!' Captain Kayth commanded. His voice came to Lokk as if he heard it again, right then, nine thousand years later. He had a singer's voice, Kayth. He and Lokk had been friends once. 'Finish them!'

Lokk, a driver then, accelerated.

The sons of Corax split and split again, weaving complex

too many, their bloodlust too great. The end was in sight.

And then it was not.

One of the Predator tanks lifted up to Lokk's front as something large hit it. Lokk had the impression of sparks and claws, and blue-hot jets, spread wings and a vengeful white face, and then his own vehicle stopped, rammed hard into the back of the stricken tank.

'*Corax! Corax is here!*' one of the others voxed.

He could see him. Corax was not two yards away, feet planted on either track guard of the stricken Predator. Its tracks churned up black sand, and it shifted, but Lokk's tank was tangled with it, and the two were locked in place. Lokk's commander shouted from the turret, urging him to pull back. The tanks slewed about, threatening to toss the primarch from the roof, but he stood firm, face straining as he heaved at the Predator's domed turret, power claws carving through plasteel. He stood up suddenly with a roar Lokk felt in his bones, and flipped the turret clean off. Lightning burst from ruptured power lines. Corax thrust his arm into the exposed cupola and tore out the tank commander there, skewering him on his claws and hurling him away into the dark.

Some of the tanks in Lokk's group had roared on after the fleeing Raven Guard. Others fled before the anger of the XIX primarch, yet some could not resist the prize of this most mighty of kills, and they circled the stricken tanks, firing at the giant atop them. Autocannon shells ricocheted from his armour. Lascannon beams scorched the air around him, but Corax stood indestructible in their fury.

Then he turned his attention to Lokk.

'Move!' Lokk's commander said. Long dead now, his name was Asorios of the Pentatuach. 'Move!'

Rarely had Lokk heard an Iron Warrior panic.

He rammed the drive sticks back. The tank fishtailed, its ram stuck firm in the dead Predator's rear door. Corax jumped onto the glacis, driving the machine down with his weight. Lokk thought that had saved them, because the ram point dislodged, though it did not seem so when a sable fist punched forward, claws alive with disruption lightning, and burst through the tank's front.

Lokk barely stopped the engine from stalling as the tank suddenly lurched backwards. Corax clung to the front one-handed, the claws inches from the mask of Lokk's helm, and with the other he swept back and forth, ripping at the glacis, carving up furrows in the ceramite. Cables sputtered. Smoke filled the cabin. Lokk swung the tank from side to side, but Corax would not be moved, his enraged god's face becoming more visible with each swipe of his claw.

Asorios spun the turret round. Powercells hummed as the twin-las powered to fire, but Corax swung his fist, and cleaved the barrels. A flash of power burst behind Lokk, and Asorios shouted. Fires caught in the cabling. Alarms trilled all around him. The Predator accelerated to full reverse speed, Lokk driving blind, but still Corax would not let go.

He drew back his fist again. Black eyes flashed in a corpse-pale face.

The fist flew forward, obliterating the rags of metal left between the primarch and the future warpsmith. It continued on, severing controls, and into Lokk's armour, whereafter the tip of one claw found and blew his primary heart.

The tank rolled to a halt. Fire was blazing all through the rear compartment. Hatches slammed as Asorios and the secondary gunner tried to escape. Lokk tried to breathe, his secondary heart still not yet fully engaged, his lungs filling with blood, his body close to failure from the shock.

Corax could have finished him then. Every night, for thousands of years, Lokk had wondered why he had not.

Lokk gaped. Blood flowed from his mouth and pooled in his helm. He was closer to death then than he had ever been, and he remembered well the look on the primarch's face. The look of horror, and of betrayal.

Then Corax was gone, a flash of armour and wings, and night took Lokk.

A soft rap on the side of the tank brought Lokk back to himself.

'War-brother? War-brother, it is I.'

'Kar-Gatharr?' Lokk said. He shifted himself. His bones hurt with a fever's cold.

'Come out, my brother. Let us speak.'

Lokk was in no mood for conversation, yet something made him get up. 'A moment,' he grunted. He yanked at his interface cables. A machine bleeped, as if in pain. He pulled again, and felt the spikes break in the sockets in his armour, obliging him to fish out the spines. What he cast out onto the deck was made of gristle.

He made his way out of *Dracokravgi*, and found Kar-Gatharr waiting, helmless and solemn, a few yards behind the tank. Lokk stopped when he saw his friend.

'You are changed,' he said.

'You will be too, soon, my war-brother,' said Kar-Gatharr.

Lokk limped towards the Dark Apostle. He had not changed physically, yet seemed larger somehow. Once, this would have alarmed Lokk, but he had seen far stranger things in the Long War.

'Then,' Lokk said, 'you have your wish.'

'My wish has only ever been to serve the gods,' said Kar-Gatharr.

'You have done that well,' said Lokk. He limped past his friend, and went to a stowage bin on the back of *Dracokravgi*. It was a simple metal box, surprising by its quotidian nature, when one considered what lived within the tank. From inside, Lokk took out a glass bottle protected in a net of twisted cord.

'Drink?' he said. Speaking was becoming more difficult for him.

Kar-Gatharr nodded. Lokk thrust the bottle at him, and took off his own helm. It was so hard to remove now. The joins kept sealing over, like fresh skin, and the shape of his face made disentangling himself from it awkward. He took the top off, then removed the distorted mask, tossing both onto the top of his tank.

Kar-Gatharr had not seen his war-brother's true visage in some years, and now he looked in wonder upon the blessings the Dark Gods had bestowed. Lokk stood in discomfort as he looked him over, the bestial lines, his jaw heavy and distorted by the suggestion of tusks, the vestigial horns which jutted from his temples. Below them, Lokk's eyes were amber, his pupils black slits.

There was murder in those eyes.

'Such fine acolytes we are. Both blessed,' said Kar-Gatharr.

Lokk's twisted mouth smiled. 'You perhaps. I bear their blessings with discomfort.'

'It is a test, brother,' said Kar-Gatharr. 'Pass it and know real reward.'

'Like you?'

'Not like me,' said Kar-Gatharr. 'Better.'

Lokk retrieved the bottle and uncorked it. He handed it back to his friend.

Kar-Gatharr drank, pulling a face. 'What is this?'

'No weakling's wine,' said Lokk, with a real smile now. 'Olympian slozo, or at least an approximation of it.' He took back the bottle and drank long, finishing with a gasp. 'Burns like I remember.'

'It tastes like engine lubricant.'

'That may be one ingredient,' Lokk admitted. 'It is good to see you. To what do I owe this visit?'

'Comradeship,' said Kar-Gatharr softly.

Lokk looked again at his friend, knowing immediately why Kar-Gatharr had come. 'You have come to say farewell. You think you are going to die.'

'We all die, war-brother.'

'Don't give me your priest's riddles!' Lokk said angrily. The rush of emotion surprised him. 'When? When did you know?'

'The power I hold within me will consume me.'

'Then why take it?' said Lokk. 'Why now?'

'The weapon. Tenebrus. The war. The Adeptus Custodes are here. They will not be bested by mortal means.'

'So? There's nothing but war,' said Lokk. 'What makes this one so special you must surrender your life to it?'

'Faith,' said Kar-Gatharr without hesitation. 'Matters here must go according to the will of the gods. The Warmaster. Abaddon...'

'Ach, Abaddon, another vainglorious fool,' said Lokk. 'He's the same as Horus, a liar who has deceived himself.'

'Maybe,' said Kar-Gatharr. 'But he will triumph. Victory must be won correctly. It must be done with faith. Abaddon does not honour the gods, not as he should, not yet.'

'Nor does my primarch,' said Lokk.

'Would you have an eternity of rule by the Lord of Iron?'

'I would have no eternity under anyone,' said Lokk.

'Then why do you go on?' said Kar-Gatharr.

'I don't know,' said Lokk. He stoppered the bottle and put it away, his thirst forgotten.

'Mankind was made to worship, that is Lorgar's creed. If Abaddon takes the Throne of Terra, insisting on his own supremacy, the gods will destroy him, and mankind will endure a living hell.'

'Mankind already endures a living hell, Kar-Gatharr,' said

Lokk. 'Do not pretend any of us are in this for anything but ourselves. If you taught me one thing, it is that Chaos has no mercy. We have been lied to by everyone. All we can do is fight. That is all there is.'

'It is not true. Lorgar had a vision,' said Kar-Gatharr. 'Mankind living in harmony with the gods, as supplicants, and willing vessels for their power. All the potential the Emperor sought to deny us, and keep for Himself. When you speak as you do, Torvann, you outline the Emperor's path, not mine. You have known their gifts. You have lived nine millennia, you have seen things of such sublime glory. Could the boy you were have imagined such a thing? We all have that potential. If the strong are allowed to prosper, humanity will rise to glory, but the gods are fickle, and they must be propitiated. It is the duty of my Legion to make Abaddon see this. It is our duty to make the victory the right one.'

Lokk laughed. 'You're all deluded. There is nothing but death and suffering, so it has ever been, so it will ever be. You can't control Abaddon. You can't control what manner of victory he will have. You can't reason with the gods. What is this that we fight for? We were dupes under the Emperor's banner, under Horus', and still under Abaddon's, while the gods laugh all the while.'

'Yet the gods honour you,' Kar-Gatharr said stepping forward. 'And yet you still dedicate your kills to them. Why, if you are so full of doubt?'

'Because there is nothing else,' said Lokk quietly. He looked around his camp. His men sat by fires, their machines silent, hidden by the walls of a roofless building. It could have been any night in his miserably long life.

Kar-Gatharr broke the silence. 'I have new gifts. New insights. I can help you, one last time, war-brother, to find the glory I know you still seek.'

Lokk glanced back at him. 'Truly?'

'You know it.'

Lokk paused a moment, staring out into the night, then turned to his friend. 'We know the enemy will move against us. We are prepared. They will not wait for their relief force. It is in the nature of them, to push forward when inspired. The Emperor's own mewling chaperones are here. Their arrival will have lit a fire of righteousness under the weaklings. They will be eager to die on our swords to show their faith.'

'They will,' agreed Kar-Gatharr.

'They will move over the bridge, seeking to strike at us before we do the same. I have tried to tell Tenebrus this, but he will not listen.'

'He is concerned with higher matters. But I will always heed you,' said Kar-Gatharr.

Lokk nodded. 'I have examined the ground. I expect several attacks. They may make an advance towards the cathedrum, but I expect they will try to retake the Blessed Bastion first. I have sent warriors to reinforce it, but I personally plan to ambush them. If you are willing to help, I want you to draw on your favour and shroud me. I will set my trap in the commercia nearby. If they go for either target, some of them will go that way. I wish to conceal myself so completely they will not notice I am there until it is too late. A shroud, a shadow. You know these things. Hide me.'

Lokk expected to make his case, to argue even, and he dearly wished not to, for he'd had his fill of conflict, but Kar-Gatharr surprised him.

'I shall lend your cabal the necessary art. I shall contact Osmoch, if you haven't had him killed yet.'

'The worm still leads my sorcerers.'

'Then consider it done, war-brother.'

Lokk smiled sadly. 'I remember when you first called me that.

Before you came, I was thinking of the night you saved me, do you remember it?'

'I do,' said Kar-Gatharr.

'That night you pulled my body from that wrecked tank, my brothers slaughtered all around me. I thought I was going to die.'

'I knew you were not, though it took me hours to find you.'

'Yes,' said Lokk. 'You have told me a thousand times you went there because the gods sent you.'

Lokk looked up into his friend's eyes. They were a solid black now, like those of the Lord of Ravens. There was no escaping what they were – the Space Marines, the primarchs, the powers of the warp – he thought. They were all parts of the same cosmic jest.

'Is that really true?'

'The evidence speaks for itself,' said Kar-Gatharr. 'You live.'

'No, brother, I mean it, did the gods really send you?'

Kar-Gatharr paused, then he said softly, 'They aided me, but only because I asked them to.'

They held each other's eyes a long time, until Lokk broke the silence with a small laugh. 'There is a primarch coming here. Can you imagine it, after so long?'

'It has been ordained. This is the last war.'

The smile faded from Lokk's deformed lips. 'You can never understand how much I pray that is true, brother,' Lokk said. He looked away again. 'This power you have taken. I know you, Kar-Gatharr. You seek to face things you should not. You will fight the corpse-lord's lackeys. You should leave. Let us fight again, on other worlds.'

'It is my fate,' said Kar-Gatharr. 'My story ends here, but do not mourn me, for I go on to greater glory. Hold true to the faith I have given you, Torvann Lokk, and you will know power untold of.'

'Another possibility?'

'A certainty.'

Kar-Gatharr embraced his friend.

'Fight well, Torvann. This shall be our last meeting. In honour of our friendship, you shall have your shroud of shadow.'

Chapter Twenty-Five

A MIRACULOUS FISHER

SAINT CLAYTOR'S SPAN

A NEED TO BE SEEN

Achallor and his Custodians waited in a cloister overlooking the Canyon of Countless Blessings. The early evening light slanted between the ragged spiretops, painting the ruins of the other side of the bridge with shifting patches of black and red.

The canyon was deep, formed in ages past by a river encountering the barrier of the Ascension Stair hills and forced to burrow its way through to the sea, though most aspects of this creation were obscured. The cliffs were carved into a fantastic confection of tombs, domes and statues, and the giant buildings built either side raised the lips thousands of feet over the natural ground level. But for the first time in millennia, the river ran in the open again, for the grand culvert constraining the river had been broken, and the flow dammed by fallen masonry into a filthy lake. The escape of the river reverberated around the canyon in a rising mist and a voice that drowned the rumble of artillery.

Saint Claytor's Span crossed this chasm, a tall suspension

bridge a mile long. The main cables ran through the hands of paired statues atop two piers which plunged like swords into the canyon depths. Claytor had been some kind of miraculous fisherman, Achallor gathered, and the hangers that held up the bridge deck were crossed over so they made nets of plasteel. Most were still in place and the bridge deck was stable, though the statues were pockmarked, and bodies littered the road.

The far end of the bridge was formed by the slopes of a macro-ossuary. At the Imperial side was a hab-block. Both were craggy with abutments and promontories of stone. The Processional Hope Abundant cut through both mountainous buildings by way of sizeable tunnels, joining the District Immaculate and the District of Heavens over the bridge. The cloister was next to the processional, giving the Custodians good sight lines while concealing them. The void shield limit went right up to the edge of the canyon, and the building was only just on the inside. Achallor's group were relying on the shields to hide the power signatures of their armour from enemy auspex.

Vychellan sheltered behind a pillar and peered into the canyon, making noises of distaste at the profusion of skulls, reapers of souls and similar grim monuments laid out before him. 'This is a place of blood and bones,' he said. 'Death venerated at every turn.'

'Mortal lives are short,' said Varsillian. 'Long have they made monuments to that which they fear most.'

'They placate things that should not be paid attention to, Pontus,' said Vychellan. 'Fear only feeds the things we fight. Take these poor fools who oppose us. Somewhere down there in that chasm, under that lake, was a pilgrim shanty. Many of its inhabitants are among the traitors holding the District of Heavens. What good did appeasing death in this way do them, or us?' He looked at Varsillian. 'The Imperium failed these people.'

'What is your point, Hastius?'

Vychellan looked back down into the depths. 'When we must abandon our duties and become involved in these wars, have things not gone too far? That is my point. Perhaps we should have left Terra millennia ago. We have been blind to what has been happening.'

Achallor let them talk and looked over the gap to their targets. Their primary was a squat blockhouse built out of the bridge. It was little more than a sentry post for enforcers to watch over pilgrims from, not a true military fortification, and even had a large window fronting its command deck. Little threat to the guardians of the Emperor, it nevertheless presented an obstacle to the mortals, for it housed a generatorum powering what was left of the local defence grid, and was a command centre for the traitor forces.

The secondary target was the barricade stretching across the centre of the bridge deck. Old prayer flags still hung from the cables around it, but they were tattered and burned, and the foul brass icons jutting above the barricades declared the changed faith of those who guarded the bridge. Achallor could see the mortals manning the defences there, but they did not see him.

'I see no Traitor Astartes,' said Amalth-Amat. 'This does not look overly troublesome for us,' he said. He leaned on the pole of his vexillum, gripping it with both hands as he watched the far side. 'Yet that which motionless and meek doth repose, may yet a predator be,' he quoted.

'We shall make an impact here. We will spread fear, and force them into action, but even once we have the far end of the bridge, crossing is going to be bloody for the mortals,' said Vychellan. He looked upwards, to where traitor positions nestled on balconies and walkways. 'Many loyal subjects of the Emperor will die today.'

'We cannot help the losses,' said Aswadi. 'We must set up this situation so that when our allies move on the cathedrum, it occupies our enemy's attention. What better end could any mortal servant of the Emperor hope for than to die in His name, and truly, what other purpose do their lives have?'

'Try telling them that, Menticulous,' said Vychellan.

'This is no time for ethics. Our concerns are of a larger scale than individual lives,' said Achallor.

'A little caution never hurts our cause, shield-captain,' said Amalth-Amat.

'Truer words rarely said,' said Achallor. The guns cut out, leaving the waterfall to roar unaccompanied. Achallor had an eye on a countdown on his helm display. 'Thirty seconds, then we go,' he said. 'Are there any thoughts, challenges or suggestions arising from observations here?'

'I see nothing that merits changing our original plan,' said Amalth-Amat. 'Of course, once we're through the void shield and my auspex might see, it may be different.'

'It's always different,' said Vychellan with a sudden burst of mirth.

'Your mood improves,' said Aswadi.

'Whatever our reasons for being here, I look forward to the fight.'

The counter hit zero. Time seemed to hang, then the bombardment recommenced. This time, the guns aimed not for the Iron Warriors' batteries deeper in the District of Heavens, but at the macro-ossuary on the other side of the canyon. Shells screamed down, and chained explosions erupted across the uppermost levels, sending masonry thundering down in avalanche. Heavy weapons fire from the Imperial side joined the shelling, autocannons, heavy bolters, missiles and lascannons hitting the blockhouse and sending the enemy racing for cover.

'To battle, then,' said Achallor, taking up his sword. 'Terra's fortune go with you all.'

* * *

Only one sentry watching the maintenance walks beneath the bridge's deck kept his post while the others ran for cover. A single bolt-round felled him, his death drowned out by the pounding of the guns hitting the ossuary, and he fell unremarked into the canyon. Achallor and his Custodians then set out under the bridge. Above, the mass of Saint Claytor's Span swayed as rubble bounced from the western end. Shells rained down. Crude alarms sounded, bent metal hung from wire beaten with rebar. Shouts reached the Custodians' ears, but they were not seen.

Under the cover of the bombardment, they reached a ladder leading up to the midway point of the main deck.

'Undeyr Amalth-Amat, Menticulous Aswadi, to your task,' Achallor ordered. 'Slay any you come across.'

The vexillor nodded. The pole on his standard collapsed into itself, and he slung the icon across his shoulders. Aswadi maglocked his shield to the back of his armour, and the pair of them hurried upwards, climbing with one hand, swords ready in the other.

Out from the canyon sides it was gusty with ocean winds. Air sang around the hawsers and snatched at the Custodians' cloaks. Achallor's group passed the second pier. The base of the blockhouse was near, where an armoured door gave onto a ledge that provided access to the maintenance walks.

Taking the blockhouse was not the sole reason they were there. They had to be seen. The enemy had to think the Custodians intended to attack the cathedrum above ground. Their actions there would seed that thought, and take the enemy's attention away from the catacombs.

'Hastius, lead us in,' Achallor ordered. Vychellan nodded and moved ahead. Achallor followed. Behind him came Pontus Varsillian. All had their shields up, though there was no firing slit in the bunker's base, and no enemy visible.

Vychellan reached the door. He paused while his battleplate's auto-senses swept for life signs on the other side, then cleaved the door down with a blow of his sword. He crouched behind his shield and vanished into the bunker.

'Fields,' ordered Achallor. He and Varsillian activated their power shields and followed Vychellan into the generatorum, which was long enough that it must have gone far under the ossuary, and was dominated by three large promethium generatoria in a line down its centre. Fuel pipes fed in through one ferrocrete wall, while bundles of cabling led away through several ducts around the edges. The air was hot, heavy with electrical charge and fumes. Several spidery-looking maintenance servitors scuttled around the machines, clucking to themselves in binharic like concerned parents.

They took no notice of the Custodians.

A metal stairway was bolted to the far wall, leading up to a heavy door set twenty feet above the deck. Vychellan climbed the stairway with his blade forward. Achallor adopted a covering position. Varsillian went between two of the generatoria and unclamped a haywire bomb from his leg. The canister-shaped device looked small in Varsillian's hand, though it was the size of a Guardsman's ration tin.

Varsillian activated the release sequences. As soon as he did, one of the room's cyborgs detected the threat, turned its head towards the device and moved in Varsillian's direction, mechanical arms flexing, servo-tools whirring. Achallor paid it only cursory attention. It was no threat to them.

'Awakening,' said Varsillian. The haywire device emitted a piercing whine. Skeins of energy erupted in a sudden storm, lancing out to claw at Varsillian's armour, at the generatoria to either side and the approaching servitor. The cyborg shrilled and reeled back, emitting showers of sparks and a waft of roasted flesh, before clanging against the machine and sliding dead to the ground.

White light drew in towards the device in a sudden pulse, then raced back outwards. The Custodians' armour and weapons were hardened against such disharmony. Nothing else was.

The generatoria shuddered like wounded bull-groxes, belched black smoke and cut out. The other two servitors collapsed in tangles of metal limbs. The strip-lumens along the ceiling died, as did every light on every control panel in the chamber. The only remaining illumination was the spill of daylight coming through the ingress.

'The enemy have lost their lights, power, and all vox capabilities,' said Achallor. 'They are blind and unable to call for help. Hunt well, my friends.'

Vychellan swung his sentinel blade in an arc that severed the door's hinges in a burst of sparks, then raised one foot and gave the slab of metal a kick. It fell with a dull clang.

Achallor was already following Vychellan up the steps as he vanished through the doorway, Varsillian at his heels. They emerged into a dark corridor defaced with cult graffiti. Vychellan turned left. Achallor went right. Each of them would now disperse as he saw fit, individual warriors fighting their own battles. It had always been thus.

Achallor activated the blood tally of his armour's sensorium. He had taken three steps when a doorway opened with a groan of metal. Several cultists spilled through, clad in grey, rubberised boiler suits reinforced with scraps of stolen flak armour. They clutched autoguns and wore crude iron masks. Achallor saw their eyes widen within the viewslits as they saw him bearing down upon them.

'By the great gods!' cried one. The other two had more presence of mind, but they got their guns less than halfway up before they were dead. The first, Achallor lunged at one-handed, and drove his blade though the skull, obliterating the man's head in an explosion of greasy smoke. Simultaneously, a blow from his shield caved in the other's chest, driving him into the wall hard enough to burst his body, leaving a splatter of blood. The third heretic stared up at Achallor in wordless terror. Achallor disdainfully drove Prosektis' point into the coward's sternum. The width of the blade alone was enough to split him in two. The power field annihilated his flesh and bone noisily, throwing his steaming remains all over the corridor and Achallor's golden plate. The shield-captain walked through the mess.

<Three kills, two point zero five seconds,> the blood tally informed him.

Achallor pressed on down the corridor, ignoring the doorway the cultists had emerged from, and broke into a servo-assisted run, gathering speed as he clanged towards another heavy portal. He dropped his shoulder, hitting the door hard enough to rip it from its hinges and send it cannoning into the chamber beyond. Screams tore the air as the hurtling slab of metal crashed into living bodies.

Daylight fell through the small, grubby windows of a machine-shrine. Achallor saw work-altars stained with oil, several of them with pieces of machinery held in clamps. Tools hung from hooks along the walls, a wide array of devices all festooned with Omnissian seals. Incense braziers sat in the room's corners. A chain-rig dangled from the ceiling, empty. There was no sign of machine-priests here now, only a mass of shocked-looking traitors.

All this, Achallor absorbed in an instant. His foot slammed down on the broken-in door, squashing the bodies beneath. Prosektis sang through the air, trailing a crackling after-image in the gloom, cleaving into the shoulder of one cultist, obliterating the top of his torso, and carrying into the head of another. A flash of light, and the man fell, his head reduced to blood mist that fizzled in the field corona of the blade. Achallor ran forward then, shield first, crashing through the cultists with the impetus of a freight hauler. The power shield made no distinction between incoming munitions and the human body, reacting as violently to both. Cultists were flayed down to the bone by the field, before being smashed to pieces by Achallor's weight. They offered no resistance. He was a tank charging through grass. Bodies exploded before him, and the room was full of the stink of blood. A cultist screamed as she crumpled, and Achallor stamped her skull flat as he passed. The blood tally's number grew quickly.

Several of the enemy managed to raise their weapons and the sudden roar of gunfire filled the machine-shrine. Muzzle flare strobe-lit the gloom. Achallor favoured his shield only as a weapon here. He had little need of its protection from simple autoguns. Their bullets rang harmlessly from his auramite.

Achallor flicked out with his blade, wielding a weapon the weight of a grown man as easily as a mortal might a switch of wood. Another cultist died in a flash of atomic dissolution. Achallor ducked slightly, putting his weight behind his shield, catching the nearest work-altar, and with a quick heave, sent half a ton of metal spinning into the air. It hit a knot of heretics, killing them instantly.

A bullet grazed the cheek-guard of his helm. In return the shield-captain sliced one of his attackers in two at chest level then spun amidst the resultant welter of blood and impaled another. The cultists looked on the bloodied giant, and his sentinel blade cooking gore to steam. They broke and ran.

The shield-captain followed, running them down. One leapt and scrambled frantically up a ladder going up a shaft. He didn't even dirty his blade with her blood. Ramming Prosektis into the floor, Achallor grabbed her foot and pulled her from the ladder. He swung her down into the decking with such force that she was killed by the impact. Her remains lay amidst those of her luckless fellows.

<Seventeen kills, seven point six-four seconds. Total dead, twenty. Total combat time, forty-eight seconds.>

He let the others flee. Let them take news of the Custodians' coming. He could hear them shouting deeper in the bunker.

'It is the Emperor! He has come! The Emperor is here to offer His judgement!'

Vychellan emerged from another door, his blade steaming and golden armour stained red. 'I've swept the outer corridors. They're all dead. Varsillian is working his way towards the rear.'

'We go up,' said Achallor.

'It's a tight fit,' said Vychellan, looking up the shaft and the hatch at the top.

'I'll make room,' said Achallor.

'Then the shield-captain has the honour,' said Vychellan.

'Generous,' said Achallor, tone dry. He left his shield at the base and climbed the ladder one-handed, keeping his blade ready as he pushed himself up and grabbed each rung. The ladder bent beneath his armoured weight. He braced himself and shoved at the hatch. It resisted, barred from above.

Achallor lowered himself a little, then drove Prosektis into the hatch. The blade sliced through the metal with ease. Achallor dragged it in a smooth curve, sending fountains of sparks everywhere. He cut through the hatch, and into the plascrete, opening up a hole big enough for the Custodians to negotiate. The noise was tremendous, a raucous rat-a-tat-tat banging of breaking atomic bonds.

He reached the end of his cut, and pulled Prosektis back.

'Ware below,' he called, and swung aside as the neatly sheared and still-glowing hatch fell past him.

An autogun barrel thrust down. Achallor squeezed his trigger and sent a round from his blade's boltcasters up through the hole. There came a wet explosion, a slapping fall of gore, and the autogun bounced from his armour, the severed hand of its wielder still gripping the stock.

Achallor got one hand over the rim of the hole he had cut.

With a servo-assisted heave he pulled himself up and out. His reactions were fast enough that he saw the metal table swinging towards his head and moved to take the blow on his shoulder guard. It hit with a resounding clang that staggered the shield-captain sideways.

'Ogryn,' he voxed, when he caught sight of his assailant.

'That's a surprise,' Vychellan replied. *'Need some help?'*

'No,' said Achallor.

The abhuman made another swing. It was huge, taller than Achallor, and more heavily muscled. Perhaps it had been a pilgrim, he thought, or a bodyguard for a high-ranking priest, for its skin was covered all over in devotional tattoos and lines from Imperial scripture that it had not bothered to deface. Against a mere standard human, the ogryn would have proved a terrifying opponent, but Marcus Achallor was a different order of being. Prosektis scythed the table in half straight down its middle. As the abhuman struggled to form an expression of surprise, Achallor punched it in the face hard enough to stave its nose backwards into its brain. It fell loudly.

<Kill twenty-one, one point three-seven seconds,> the blood tally reported.

Bullets began ricocheting off his armour from every direction. He was in the blockhouse refectory. The tables had been tipped over to serve as barricades, behind which figures crouched.

'You can come up now,' he voxed.

Turning from the hatchway, Achallor strode into the chamber with his sentinel blade up. More autogun fire rang from his armour, but it was as stones flung at a wall by impudent children. He sliced and stabbed, kicked and punched, every blow smashing cultists into bloody pieces and hurling them hard into the refectory walls. The carnage intensified as Vychellan joined the fight. Achallor's keen hearing picked out the din of battle raging through other chambers of the blockhouse.

A door in one wall clanged open and the long barrel of an auto-cannon was thrust through. The crew let fly in panic, blasting apart several of their own warriors. They managed to score two hits on Achallor, one rebounding from his chest with enough force to drive the breath from his lungs, the other hitting the elbow joint on his right arm. He felt a sharp pain shoot up to his shoulder. The shock almost shook Prosektis from his grip.

Achallor snarled and levelled Prosektis before squeezing both triggers. Its boltcasters roared and the autocannon crewmen detonated in bloody sprays.

Beyond the autocannon was a makeshift armoury. Standing amidst the racks of guns and blades was a figure in gunmetal power armour decorated with black and yellow chevrons. Curling brass horns rose from his daemon-faced helm, and a heavy chainsword hung at his hip.

'Traitor Astartes,' said Achallor.

The Custodian felt the hatred burning in the Iron Warrior's gaze. He felt nothing but contempt. Space Marines were flawed creations, each and every one.

Achallor surged forward. The traitor drew his own blade and came to meet him, but his movements were painfully heavy and slow in comparison to Achallor's.

The haywire has killed his power pack, Achallor thought. The notion disappointed him; he would have preferred to humble this traitor properly, not while he was weighed down by crippled armour.

To his credit, the Iron Warrior managed to parry Achallor's first blow as he came out of the armoury and bulled his way past to get more space. He even managed to turn aside a second swing, though this time Prosektis drew a line of fire down the Iron Warrior's flank.

'The Dark Gods will devour you, Throneslave,' spat the Iron Warrior.

'I need no deities to slay my enemies for me, traitor,' replied Achallor. He lunged and drove his blade right through the Iron Warrior's throat. Blood boiled from the wound and the traitor tried to gurgle some last word of hate, but Achallor twisted Prosektis and his enemy fell dead to the floor.

<Kill twenty-seven, four point five seconds.>

Vychellan finished the last of the cultists. 'Next time, let me have a big one,' he said.

'There will be plenty more,' said Achallor. There were klaxons sounding now. 'They know we are here. Come, the command centre is this way.'

They went down a short corridor, the roof low enough that they had to crouch a little. A set of double doors opened without trouble, and they emerged into the blockhouse's empty command centre. Achallor strode to the long armaglass windows that made up one wall and looked out, back along Saint Claytor's Span. The blockhouse shook to the pounding of Phyroxian guns. The bridge was empty. Amalth-Amat and Aswadi had done their work. Only bloodstains remained of the small squad that had guarded the deck.

'The battle begins,' said Achallor. He snapped off the power field on his sword and rotated his shoulder. There was a little stiffness in his arm from the autocannon hit. 'The Imperial assault force will fall upon the Blessed Bastion in a few hours, assuming the plan proceeds as intended.' He opened his vox-channels. 'Custodians, regroup,' he said. 'We push on to the bastion. General Dvorgin, you may give the order for general advance when you wish.'

Dvorgin was quick, for not moments later the mournful blare of war-horns sounded across the canyon deeps. Moments after that, the bridge decking shook to the thunder of Questoris feet as House Kamidar made their advance, but by then Achallor and his warriors were already gone, heading deeper into the city, and their next objective.

Chapter Twenty-Six

LYING IN WAIT

DVORGIN WATCHES

KNIGHTS OF THE IRONHOLD

'Squads in position, eighth level, hab three,' crackled Casipiniax's voice over the vox. Lokk sent a vox-pip of acknowledgement and felt anticipation stir within him. He allowed himself a moment to gloat. His ambush was placed to perfection.

'They are coming straight to us, as I predicted,' he said.

'What of the fighting around the canyon, lord?' asked Harvoch.

'Leave that brawl to the cultists and the traitor militia,' replied Lokk dismissively. 'The Emperor's bitches have left their fortress and gone over the bridge. They will come this way and attempt the bastion from the south. We will finish them at our leisure.'

'My lord's plans are without peer,' said Lorgus obsequiously.

'You are a tedious sycophant,' growled Harvoch. *'I remember the assault on the Cult of the Raw. So do you. Lord Lokk failed that day. No one is infallible.'*

Lokk should have enjoyed Lorgus' devotion, and punished

Harvoch, but he found himself agreeing. He had failed. Harvoch's honesty was welcome. Lorgus he would have happily disembowelled.

'*Their numbers are great, lord, many times our own,*' said Harvoch. '*Surely they represent the lion's share of the Imperial forces remaining on Gathalamor.*' There was no hint of concern in the champion's voice at this, but it was a challenge to the plan.

'We will take them unawares, and we shall smash them, and with them what remains of the corpse-worshippers' defiance,' said Lokk. 'Then let Tenebrus prate when he witnesses the true might of the Lord of Iron's sons.'

'*I take back my comment, my lord,*' said Harvoch, laughing. '*And instead advance my agreement with Lorgus. This is a good plan.*'

General Dvorgin stood in a hab-block, staring through his magnoculars at the dark mass of the Blessed Bastion. He stood firm as stone as a stray missile whipped down and exploded against the roof above him. The structure, already damaged by long weeks of conflict, shuddered violently. Dead lumen globes swung and clinked together. Dust spilled down upon the command staff.

Some of the local adepts flinched, but if any of his men did, Dvorgin did not see it. *Not my Mordians*, he thought proudly. *That famous iron resolve.*

The night was advancing into morning. The flash of gunfire leapt in the dark. Phyroxian tanks fought their way through the streets, while from the rubble heaps and ruins the Mordians kept up a disciplined, punishing hail of fire as they pushed further on towards their objective.

The Blessed Bastion rose above the skyline atop a ridge of high ground busy with bombed-out hab-blocks and minor shrines. It had clear sight lines for miles, huge guns set in outsized casemates facing in the four cardinal directions, all now spitting fire.

The void port, the sea and the macro-cathedrum could be seen clearly from its battlements. It was perfectly sited, and should have been an invincible lynchpin in the Imperial defences.

It should never have fallen.

Time to rectify that, thought Dvorgin.

Not quite trusting their limited augury capabilities, Dvorgin glanced to the sky. If the enemy fleet was going to dare the defence lasers, he wouldn't be able to tell until they were on top of them. There was not a star alight up there. The fog of war was too thick.

That was all right with Dvorgin. He didn't much like looking at the sky since the Great Rift had poisoned the night.

He returned his attention to the streets around the bastion's southern arc. The enemy were in disarray. Their artillery was silent, position unknown, their traitor cultists were no match for properly drilled troops, and their Heretic Astartes were largely absent. *Those in the area must be trapped within the bastion*, he thought, though he had scout units scouring the ruins for signs of a counter-attack, just in case one came before the fortress was theirs again.

'Otherwise, it's all going swimmingly,' he said to himself. The enemy had not expected this breakout, and they had taken them unawares. He smiled.

Give us some luck, he thought, *and Princess Jessivayne will be able to begin her run in a few minutes.*

The room he watched from had been a dining hall, with a single large table and a scattering of wooden chairs. Most of the furniture had gone for firewood, burned by desperate civilians, and the remains of their campfires could be seen as scorch marks on the stone floor. But though the table bore the marks of blades, it had proven too tough to break, and the command staff had their charts spread over it. Large gallery windows looked down from some height over the surrounding urban sprawl, giving Dvorgin a good view over the southern approach to the bastion. Vox-operators kept up a constant buzz of reports and relayed orders, though they struggled so close to the vox-blunt's source. Heavy weapons teams occupied a few of the bays in the long window, the intermittent barking of their guns disrupting conversation. The power was out in the whole district and portable lumen poles in the corners of the room gave just enough light for them to see by.

Running footsteps rang against stone flags. Dvorgin lowered his magnoculars and turned from the window as a Mordian skidded to a halt in the broken doors. There was so much counter-electronic warfare going on they could not trust their vox-net, so runners were a useful supplement. As the saying went, the older the way, the better the way, and you didn't get older than human feet.

'Sir, report from Captain Dvasky, sir,' said the Guardsman, offering the sign of the aquila. His left arm was troubling him and the salute shook. Dvorgin squinted at him, his ageing eyes struggling in the half-light, then he saw the blood soaking the Mordian blue around a tear in the runner's sleeve.

'A flesh wound, sir,' said the runner, following the line of Dvorgin's gaze. 'Nothing to worry about, sir, a graze.'

'Very well. Proceed,' said Dvorgin.

'Nineteen Platoon has advanced to mark four-seven and is dug in around the western plaza edge as ordered,' said the Guardsman, standing ramrod- straight even though he was breathing heavily from his run. Blood trickled down his hand, and fell in a fat drop from his little finger. 'A small band of traitors attempted to intercept, but we put them down with minimal casualties. The captain has diverted Eighteen Platoon and established a secondary position overlooking the Processional Virtuous Silence. They are watching for any attempt to relieve the Blessed Bastion from the sea, as ordered. Other enemy forces encountered broke and ran.' The man allowed himself a small smile. 'They're panicking, sir.'

'Thank you, trooper,' said Dvorgin with a tight nod. 'Get yourself some water and a ration block and have Medicae Hesp check that arm, then you can return to your platoon with somewhat less haste. There you will tell Captain Dvasky to hold.'

'Very good, sir. Thank you, sir.' The veteran offered his clumsy aquila again.

Dvorgin frowned. 'Have you seen any sign of the Heretic Astartes?'

'None, sir. Is that all, sir?'

Dvorgin nodded. The man moved off. Dvorgin beckoned Stehner to him.

'Sir?' the lieutenant said.

'Send a runner to Seven Platoon. Have Lieutenant Frans move up to mark one-nine to reinforce Eighteen Platoon. If the enemy are going to try any last-ditch breakouts, it will be to seaward. They may try to escape once Achallor moves in. And make sure they set up proper weapons nests. I'm concerned these armoured companies of the Iron Warriors might show. Make sure that is well known by all, but don't put that out by vox. If they are going to come at us, I want them to think us unprepared. The gap in the west must look like a deliberate error. They'll come that way from the cathedrum, where Veritas will catch them.'

'Very good, sir,' said Lieutenant Stehner, swiftly scribing the orders with an auto-stylus then handing them to another messenger who waited nearby. The trooper set off at a run. The general returned to studying the fight through his magnoculars.

'I'd dearly like to get in at them,' said Chedesh. His standard stood in a holder, the flag limp. 'It doesn't seem right, us waiting here, circling the bastion like this.'

'Little enough for us to do,' said Dvorgin. 'I'm not sorry. If the Custodians and the Battle Sisters wish to storm ahead like something from a preacher's sermon and vent their fury on the heretics, then it's best not to get in their way.'

'We're missing out on the honour, sir,' said Chedesh.

'Preferring front-line operations is one thing, colour-sergeant, but one has to know when to step back. If the very attendants of the Emperor ask me to provide a ring of iron about something while they win all the honour, then a ring of iron they shall have.'

Stehner returned and handed Dvorgin a data-slate. The general lowered his magnoculars, and tried not to squint at the writing swimming before him.

'Very good,' he said, and handed the slate back. 'That's the last. All platoons are now in position. Vox Princess Jessivayne. Tell her that the approach is secure, the perimeter is established to the south, east and north, and that she may begin her attack run on the bastion turret ring. Tell her to prioritise the south gate, as Achallor is moving up, but that she is not to neglect the turrets to the west for Veritas will come that way soon. If she can breach the west gate, then tell her to do that also, but prioritise the south, it's key. We have to get the Custodians in there.'

Stehner clicked his heels and turned to go.

'Actually, wait,' said Dvorgin. 'Contact Jurgen's artillery first and have them throw a few more salvoes at the bastion to encourage the enemy to keep their heads down, then signal the princess.'

Stehner went to Yenko and had him disseminate the commands via vox. A couple of minutes later, shells fell from the night, lighting up the side of the bastion in fiery golds and reds.

'Don't fret, Chedesh, we'll have the bastion soon enough,' Dvorgin said. 'There'll be bloody work to come for us after that.'

As he spoke, a shell launched from within Ascension Stair hit the bastion top. Several merlons broke free from the crenellations, and bodies tumbled to the kill-plaza around it a hundred yards below.

'Not long at all.'

Princess Jessivayne thundered around the giant colonnade that fringed the edge of the Blessed Bastion's kill-plaza. Everything about the precinct was hugely scaled, so much that her Knight felt shrunk to human size, and the traitor foe were as mice as they fled before her.

The fortification towered to her right, a mile away over the open ground, the blaze of guns lighting up the night in all directions. Its perimeter turrets, her primary target, tracked her. She kept *Incendor*'s ion shield angled to the side, intercepting a turret shell and causing it to detonate in mid-air. Smoke and flame from the blast wreathed her as she ran. A cable whipped up from a covering of dust in front of her, catching *Incendor*'s ankle. It strained, and she stumbled, but it broke, the ambush failed, and she regained her balance as a rabble of enemy infantry surged from a monastic house to her right. They screamed terrified oaths and sprayed small-arms fire at her Knight. Jessivayne brought her conflagration cannon to bear, intoned a prayer of immolation, and fired. Three columns of flame leapt forth, transforming living beings into charcoal scarecrows. The few survivors fled, and she swung the torso back round to face front, her ion shield still taking a pounding from the right.

Alarms squealed. She found herself staring down the barrel of a Vindicator siege tank, hull down between a transmitter tower and the long, low bulk of an auto-benefice. She dodged aside as it fired. The shell glanced from her pauldron without detonating, and caromed off into a windowless tower. The explosion brought it down, a thousand tons of stone heeling over and toppling in seeming slowness to the ground, where it broke into pieces.

The hit staggered her into the colonnade, her left arm drawing sparks from the stone before she bounced free, and half stumbled back to the right. The tank had a clear shot at her, less than two hundred yards down a straight line. She'd been lucky the first time. It was no doubt even now cycling its autoloaders to chamber another shell.

She couldn't switch her shield facing. The ground turrets of the Blessed Bastion continued to track her, their fire causing her ion shield to flare and spit, half blinding her.

'Go around!' Sheane voxed her. *'It's about to take another shot. Get into the ruins, out of the fire line!'*

'Negative,' she said. Jessivayne fed more power to *Incendor*'s actuators and pushed the Knight into a run. Ferrocrete shattered and the ground shook as she closed the gap between her and the heretic siege-tank. 'I risk those that come behind me, and too many have fallen already.' Her anger was echoed by her ancestors within the Throne Mechanicum. 'The turrets must be neutralised before Canoness Veritas approaches. We've lost two engines already. I will not allow this fight to slip any further from my grip. We will not fail our queen, nor our God-Emperor. The tank dies now.'

She could imagine its crew racing to arm their weapon, to resolve a firing solution and–

Jessivayne tilted her shield to the front, pouring power into it, half a second before the tank fired. Autocannon shells hammered her unprotected right side, but greater danger was presented by the Demolisher, and her shield sent the massive projectile skidding away across its ethereal surface and twenty yards to the rear, where it hit the ground and detonated, leaving a large crater in the ground.

Alarms peeped at her as the weight of fire from the bastion chewed into *Incendor*'s exposed piping and cables. She felt shadow pain from the hits, but pressed on, closing the gap between her and the tank in a dozen pounding strides.

At the last moment the tank tried to reverse, rubble spraying from beneath its tracks. Too late.

'Kamidar!' she roared, raising *Incendor*'s gauntlet high then bringing it down like a comet into the Vindicator's top. The tank's sides buckled outwards. Its ammunition stores exploded with furious force.

Jessivayne ripped her Knight's fist backwards. Shrapnel pinged off her armour, fire engulfed her torso and she reeled under the force of the explosion, yet she kept her feet, and she swung her shield back to cover her right, and the needling bites of the turrets subsided. Jessivayne took a moment to flex the digits of the gauntlet and mutter a benediction to the weapon's machine-spirit, ensuring it was still operational. Then she strode *Incendor* deliberately past the tank wreck in the direction of the fortification. The killing ground around the Blessed Bastion opened up before her. Fire poured down from its emplacements onto her ion shields. The bastion wasn't having it all its own way, as artillery shells were tracking in from the space port, aimed for the bastion's larger guns.

'Lady Nimue, what says *Battlehound*?' she voxed her herald.

'*Enemy armour nullified. Emplaced turrets twenty per cent destroyed,*' replied Nimue, her voice tight with concentration. Jessivayne pulled herself back a little from union with *Incendor*, allowing her eyes to flick over strategic maps, data-screeds and auspex imaging. A glance at her auspex told her that the herald was working with Sir Laughlain Y'Kamidar to hunt out an enemy missile nest.

'Any sign of the alpha target?' she asked.

Fifteen Knights were still fully operational. More than enough. She sent messages to the worst damaged to fall back to the rear.

'*No, princess,*' Nimue replied. '*Token Heretic Astartes presence here. Imperial infantry support is moving up and securing the southern assault corridor. Western approach is free of foes and ready for the canoness' assault. We are guarded. You have a clear run at the turret ring. Once the south arc is taken care of, the south gate will be at your mercy.'*

'Then we go forward and accomplish our mission. Knights of the Ironhold!' she ordered. 'Form up!'

She pushed on into the teeth of the enemy weapons. Weapons that had, until only a few months ago, been in Imperial hands. It pained her to destroy them.

More Knights emerged onto the plaza, shouldering their way through the colonnade and the ruins behind. The blaze of solid shot and energy beams coming at her reduced as the bastion divided its attention between the new targets. Sheane led one lance, her uncle Gerent the other, coming towards the bastion in a broad arc that encompassed nearly half the plaza.

'Armigers, cover our rear and flanks. All other Knights, concentrate fire upon the turret weapons. Banish their machine-spirits and shatter their corpus metallicus before they can speak again.'

'Risk and more risk, dear cousin,' said Sheane. His own ion shield was a white blaze of deflective energies.

'You know this is the righteous course, cousin,' she replied.

'Oh, that I do,' he replied, and she heard the familiar, wolfish smile in his voice.

She raised the gauntlet and pointed. 'Ironhold! For Kamidar! For the Emperor! For the primarch!'

'Kamidar!' they replied, and broke into a lumbering run. Sir Tolven Y'Kamidar's Knight Gallant was hit full on by a macro-cannon, its ion shield failed, and the shell exploded on his chest, sending the Gallant's reactor critical. A boiling hemisphere of plasma swelled into being, whiting out displays and making the Knights nearest to it stumble. When it vanished, a perfect circle of molten ferrocrete marked the place of Sir Tolven's death.

By then, the Knights were at full charge, their blood singing with the thrill, the Blessed Bastion rearing over them as they closed like a snake poised to strike.

The next instant, the air filled with a blistering storm of rockets, las-beams and high-explosive shells as the Knights of Ironhold unleashed their fury. Turrets exploded under the barrage, their ornate plasteel spires collapsing under the weight of fire.

'Swing left, ion shields right, circle and destroy!' Jessivayne ordered.

Perfectly coordinated, the Knights pivoted, their legs carrying them forward, while their torsos remained facing the bastion. They ran at full gallop around the base. Where they destroyed the lower turret ring, they tilted backwards, aiming their guns higher up, raking the emplacements and casemates there. Fire and fury pounded the sides of the bastion, pulling the fortress' teeth. Most deadly were the great Castellans, their plasma decimators and volcano lances gouging molten furrows across the surface of the bastion, bringing plumes of fire from secondary explosions.

'Steady, uncle,' she voxed Baron Gerent. 'We are to take this bastion back for our own use. Try not to reduce it to rubble.' She received a laugh in return, and she laughed with him.

Message chimes alerted her to power armour signatures moving in from the south-west. She swung about a little to see, and caught sight of golden figures carving their way through a horde of cultists seeking to trap them at the plaza's edge. Though surrounded, their height and the splendour of their panoply made them easy to see. The Emperor's light shone from His Custodians, and she felt her heart soar at the sight. Their battle spilled further onto the plaza, drawing away from the ruins, and gunfire from the bastion immediately began to track them, slaying the ragged hordes besetting them, but leaving no mark upon the golden giants. They moved through plasma blast and las-storm unmarked, their weapons rising and falling in sprays of blood and searing displays of weapon lightning.

'The Adeptus Custodes are here,' she said, her voice full of triumph. 'Cover their approach. Baron Gerent, Castellan Folgil, the turrets are clear, the south gate awaits you. Sheane, take your lance, continue the circuit. Clear the western side of weapons to enable the Holy Sisters' advance.'

Jessivayne's lance slowed while Sheane's accelerated off around the side of the bastion. One of his squires took a hit that blew out the ion shield, and the Armiger was hammered into scrap a moment later. Sheane's warriors ran on, still firing.

Gerent's Castellan, *Lance of God*, aligned itself with the south gate, his attendants at his side. Castellan Folgil followed him. The gate was a massively reinforced piece of adamantium. It would have kept the Heretic Astartes at bay, if it had not been opened from the inside. Another asset they must destroy to retake what was theirs.

Folgil and Gerent set their stance, and lowered their weapons. The ground around them vibrated as their reactors drew on their full power.

Firing together, the volcano lances struck the adamantium gates. Heat bloomed across the metal, and molten rivulets began to pour from the surface.

By then the cultist horde had had enough of sentinel blades and their comrades' fire, and scattered. Shield-Captain Achallor's warriors passed by the great war machines without slowing, heading directly for the entrance. Jessivayne turned her attention back to the gate. It was glowing white-hot, and the centre sagged. Her uncle and his castellan ceased firing with their volcano lances. Again their machines shook as their reactors crept up to dangerous draw levels.

Then they unleashed the power of their plasma decimators. White-blue lances of energised gas streaked at the gate, hitting the glowing metal with the force of an exploding star. Gobbets of adamantium were flung outwards. The beams snapped off. Hot metal smoked, the gates fused into semi-molten slag, yet they still held.

Lance of God sagged as a heavy shell got through its ion shield and tore off its left shoulder turret. *'Terra's ancient dust damn it all, again!'* Gerent voxed. Once more the volcano lances fired.

The exterior of the bastion was ablaze by now, scored by melta-tracks, and the upper storeys cratered by the Militarum's big guns. Jessivayne judged the fire coming down from the top to be negligible.

'Lance, lend your fire to the baron,' she said. Her Knights switched targets, those with thermal cannons moving up until they were in optimal range. The air shimmered with heat haze around the gate, obscuring it completely.

Jessivayne swung her ion shield to cover her rear arc, and moved into the plaza. The Mordians were moving up through the ruins, flushing out the cultists. Those that didn't throw down their arms and plead for mercy were far gone enough to come running at her, screaming praise to their gods, and her conflagration cannon belched fire again and again.

There was an immense explosion from behind.

'Gate breached,' Gerent voxed.

A chorus of triumph went up from the Knights' war-horns. Before the smoke had cleared, ruby beams of las-light were stabbing out from the dark of the breach.

'We are commencing our assault,' Shield-Captain Achallor voxed. He said no more than that.

Yet Jessivayne felt uneasy. She was awed to fight alongside the Emperor's own guardians, and she would not dare gainsay them, but something was not right. The main strength of the foe on Gathalamor were the Heretic Astartes, and she had seen little sign of them.

She voxed her herald, the Lady Nimue. 'Any sign of the alpha target?'

'Still none, your highness.'

Foreboding sank cold tendrils further into her. Where were the Iron Warriors' main forces?

'Any notice of Canoness Veritas' approach?'

'Central command reports she is making the turn onto Processional Abandoned Doubt, and will be making her attack on the west gate soon.'

Jessivayne immolated a mob of screaming cultists. She saw horrible mortifications of the flesh and the wildness in their eyes before they were blown to ash on the wind.

'Send her a message from me, highest encryption level.'

'Ready,' said Nimue.

'Tell her minimal Heretic Astartes presence detected. Tell her to be careful. Tell her...'

She stopped. Alarms sang throughout her cockpit, drawing her attention to the southern sky. Long lines of bright yellow fire were climbing upwards, mellow in the smoky air.

'They've repositioned their artillery. Incoming bombardment. All Knights turn ion shields to face, and brace!'

'Princess, any further content for your message?'

'Tell her it's a Throne-cursed trap,' Jessivayne hissed.

Then the first shells were falling among her warriors, and the plaza filled with fire. *Terra's Bargain* took a trio of hits that beat it down to the ground. An Armiger disappeared in a geyser of broken metal and stone.

'Retreat into the lee of the bastion. Head for the northward side! My regrets, Shield-Captain Achallor, but you are on your own.'

No reply came.

Through the fire and fury of exploding ordnance, *Incendor* ran.

Chapter Twenty-Seven

SONS OF DORN

A TRAP SPRUNG

OLD ENEMIES

Racej Lucerne and his Primaris Marines rode in transports loaned to them by the Sisters of Battle. They were cramped spaces for warriors of their stature, forcing him and his brothers to eschew the tiny, mortal-sized benches and crouch on the floor; even so there was only space for four of them in each.

Lucerne allowed himself to think the situation amusing. For thousands of years, exactly how long he did not know, he had been prepared for war. His mind had been emptied and refilled with the practice of violence, a lot of it hopeless in nature, for Cawl's hypno-training had inculcated in all of them the need for self-sacrifice. But not this.

He laughed.

'Sergeant?' Ghorias Kesvus Bheld was a man alive to problems. He did not like Lucerne's sudden mirth.

'It is nothing, brother,' said Lucerne.

'Share with us,' said Khastus Omecro. 'I could do with a little amusement,' he added, and did not mean it. This one was phlegmatic to the point of misery. It was funny, Lucerne thought, that though Cawl had changed them all, he could not erase their fundamental characters.

'It is this, then,' said Lucerne. 'Of all the last stands, beggar's choices, hopeless rearguard actions and doom-filled scenarios Belisarius Cawl put us through in our millennia in stasis, not one of them involved riding to battle bent double in the back of an inadequately sized vehicle.'

Omecro snorted. The fourth, Sulin, laughed out loud.

'I fail to see what is amusing,' Bheld said.

Thus far the advance had gone well, the Battle Sisters voxing in as they found each new coordinate empty of foes. The Knights had advanced on the bastion, the Mordians rolling up behind them. Through the armour of the transport, Lucerne could hear the thunder of artillery.

'Any return on auspex?' Bheld asked. 'Anything untoward?'

'Nothing,' replied Sulin.

'You are concerned, Brother Bheld?' asked Omecro. 'Why? It matters not if we are doomed to die.' He paused. 'Unless it is a pointless death.'

'My instincts,' replied Bheld. 'And common sense.'

'Explain,' said Lucerne.

'Our enemies have void craft, aircraft, some manner of diabolical spy ship, not to mention numerical superiority. And what do they do with all these advantages? Nothing! It rings false, does it not?'

'Their void craft are wary of the port lasers,' said Sulin. 'And their eyes are, perhaps, elsewhere?' he suggested. 'The shield-captain spoke of a concentration of assets at the macrocathedrum. If Dvorgin's intelligence is accurate then the enemy have committed substantial ground forces and armour to retaining its outer defences. Last we heard, several other conflicts still rage elsewhere on this continent.'

'Nowhere today do we see the hand of the Heretic Astartes,' exclaimed Bheld. 'These Iron Warriors are the foes of our gene-line. We should seek them out.'

'It is theoretically possible that their numbers were miscalculated by the planet's defenders,' said Sulin. 'Space Marines have ever struck awe into the hearts and minds of mortals.'

'Speak for yourself,' said Omecro. 'I feel no awe in your presence.'

'Or perhaps they have left this world to fight elsewhere,' added Sulin. 'We may be waging a war for a world they are already done with, even as they menace another. They might have gained warning of the approaching battle groups. If that is the case, might they not recognise the superiority of the Imperial forces coming against them and turn tail like the cowards they are?'

'Their ships are still in orbit,' said Bheld. 'They are here, somewhere. I fear there are pieces to this puzzle we do not yet see.'

'And if it is so, what then? He that cannot see peril has but two choices,' said Sulin.

'To cower or to strike forth,' said Lucerne. 'We know this, brothers, as I know Shield-Captain Achallor follows the only course open to us. This is our first war. We have much to learn. We must trust the decisions of the shield-captain and the general.'

'Yet I misgive,' said Bheld. 'We could have taken the bastion alone.'

'Like the sergeant says,' said Omecro mockingly. 'It is our first war.'

'What if the Mordians fail to take the bastion?' said Bheld. 'If we are held back from the attack only to find that the enemy has struck at and annihilated much of our strength?'

'Is this a game of consequences, brother, or were you misbuilt, and show us fear?' said Omecro.

'I am not afraid!' snarled Bheld.

'Stay your insults, lest they move your hand to violence,' said

Lucerne warningly. 'I say Bheld evinces the great characteristic of Rogal Dorn and thus of our gene-line – the ability to
assimilate large amounts of detail and simulate every outcome.'

'Would that Achallor allow his shipmistress into the fray,'
Bheld muttered. 'If we were assured of orbital–'

Whatever Bheld had been about to add, it was cut off by sudden thunder from ahead. Lucerne heard the distinctive thump
of bolters firing, the whoosh of rockets and the hollow crack
of lascannon beams.

'That was close,' he said. He moved until he could look
through the transit compartment's periscopes, and he saw the
flash of muzzle flare from the buildings either side of the road.
Dirty smoke sprouted above the ruined cityscape then blew
away upon brisk winds.

'Those were armour kills,' said Omecro, shifting his bolt rifle.

'But we registered no enemy,' said Sulin in disbelief.

An explosion sounded close behind them.

'Head and tail attacked. Principal armoured column ambush
tactic. They aim to trap us,' said Sulin.

'Throne of Terra,' cursed Lucerne. The transport lurched to
a halt. 'All Sons of Dorn, out!' he voxed. He banged on the wall
dividing the transport bay from the driver's compartment. The
ramp at the rear clanged down onto a dusty night strobed by
gunfire. More explosions sounded. 'This could still be a chance
encounter.'

Yet even as he said it, Lucerne knew that it was not so.

'You are wrong, brother-sergeant, my instincts don't lie. This
is an ambush,' said Bheld, and they ran out into the battle.

Torvann Lokk clenched his fists with satisfaction as his helmplate display filled with fire. His warriors exhibited all the
discipline he demanded of them, waiting silent beneath their
sorcerous shroud. With the main strength of the Imperial forces

strung out along the processional, the Iron Warriors struck with merciless precision.

Beams of laser energy and armour-piercing warheads impaled Imperial tanks. Several exploded into flaming wreckage. Others slewed wildly as their tracks were mangled and their engines slain, ploughing into the ruins. The armoured figures of Battle Sisters spilled out, some aflame, and did what they could to take cover and return fire.

As Lokk watched, salvoes of bolts and tongues of flame reached up towards Casipiniax's position. Missiles leapt from the war organs of Exorcist artillery tanks. Astra Militarum Leman Russes inclined their turret guns and let fly.

'*Some of them are breaking into the arcade on the far side of the processional,*' observed Lorgus. Lokk saw Seraphim using their jump packs to smash through the windows of upper storeys. Meanwhile, squads of determined warriors exited their burning transports and plunged into the commercia arcade's ground floor.

'Expected,' replied Lokk dismissively, his attention dancing from one image to the next, his ancient mind assembling a picture of the engagement. 'Casipiniax will intercept.'

'*They are on their knees, we should attack now,*' said Harvoch.

'We will only reveal ourselves when the enemy's second wave enters the engagement area,' Lokk said.

Even now, appointed squads of Iron Warriors would be relocating from their original ambush positions, rappelling down elevator shafts then moving to earthworks that flanked the Imperial line of advance. Others would be leading their squads higher up the buildings, making every effort to draw their enemy's attention after them. Imperial zeal could be relied upon to doom them, leading them into traps. The next step of the ambush would come when the rest of the foe's column moved up, and the Obliterator Cults engaged. Only then would Lokk land the final blow in person, leading his armour in a strike that would tear the heart from the corpse-worshippers' forces.

'*My lord, the veil is fading,*' voxed Osmoch, Lokk's most exalted sorcerer. He sounded hoarse with exhaustion, his words quavering. '*We can no longer maintain the shroud.*'

Lokk suppressed a surge of irritation. 'Do what you can to veil us until the appointed time,' he replied.

'*As you will it, my lord. It may necessitate... a sacrifice...*'

'Do what must be done, Osmoch,' he commanded, knowing that he had just condemned the least accomplished of his sorcerers to the gods' knife.

'*Of course, my lord,*' Osmoch replied, then cut the link.

When the veil failed, the Iron Warriors' position would be revealed. His enemies would be able to see the extent of the battle taking place here. That was of no consequence, as the Imperials would be fully invested around the bastion by then, and this column trapped. Thanks to the *Paracyte*, Tenebrus would know too. That mattered much more.

Let him see, thought Lokk defiantly. *Let him bear witness to our victory.* Lord Fodov had repositioned unnoticed and begun bombarding the forces around the bastion. The Knights were caught in the open there. The Sisters of Battle would perish here. Then they would move on the Mordians and this pitiful war would be over. Not even the Custodians would be able to stop them.

'*My lord, look!*'

Lokk turned his attention to the holofeed Harvoch sent him. His annoyance drained away at what he saw there, replaced first by surprise and then, amazingly, by a feeling he hadn't known in long years.

Excitement.

He watched as tall warriors in golden yellow stepped around a burning Rhino, their bolters thundering. More of them came.

Bolt-rounds flashed from their power armour as the other Iron Warriors marked their hated foe.

'Now there is prey worthy of the hunting,' he breathed.

'*The Imperial Fists,*' said Harvoch, sounding almost reverent.

'Perhaps,' Lokk said, squinting at the feed. 'They appear different somehow...' His words trailed off as he watched them closely. The armour was a new mark, the guns were different. They appeared too uniform to be his enemies of old. Their armour was lacking the personalised ornamentation common to the Adeptus Astartes, and the few markings they did bear were strange. He would investigate why later, after they were dead.

'Ready the armour strike,' ordered Lokk, feeding power through his armour to rouse the machine-spirit of *Dracokravgi*. 'The plan has altered. The sons of Dorn belong to us. Beasts of Steel, break cover now.'

Lucerne advanced up the rubble-strewn processional, firing his bolt rifle sparingly to conserve his ammunition. At his side, fourteen Primaris Marines of the line of Dorn marched. Their guns outranged the ancient patterns wielded by the Iron Warriors. Furthermore, although the processional offered a fine ambush site due to its narrowness, that very quality put the ambushers at risk from Lucerne's brothers. Two of them were armed with Stalker-pattern rifles, and held back, sniping ruthlessly every time a heavy weapon opened fire.

The Space Marines reached a group of Rhinos bunched up into a loose corral, bolt-fire spanking off their roofs. A shoulder-mounted lascannon put a hole through the top hatch of one, but the traitor bearing it paid with his life, Brother Task Ulandin blowing out his chest at two hundred yards. The dead Iron Warrior toppled from his perch and hit the rubble with a dull clang.

'Canoness!' shouted Lucerne. He scanned the buildings either side, taking shots only when his kill-marker gave him good hit percentiles. 'Canoness!'

He found Imelda Veritas supporting a wounded Sister with one arm, pouring bolter fire into the foe with the other hand. Around them her warriors were falling back in good order. Their surviving tanks served as mobile bulwarks as one squad after another pulled back and provided covering fire for the next. Several were retreating to the shelter of the commercia's mercantile centre, a grand arcade now mostly in ruins. Fierce fighting was already breaking out there.

Punishing fire still rained down upon the Imperial forces from the higher windows of the hab-blocks, and from well-sited stone banks that hemmed them in on both flanks. Perturabo's sons had lived up to their reputation with those, for they had seemed but features of the ruins until the trap was sprung. The processional was thick with the bodies of the slain, and with blazing hulks that had once been proud Imperial tanks.

'This will become a defeat if we do not act soon,' said Lucerne.

'There shall be no defeat while the Emperor watches,' replied the canoness. Bolt-shells cratered the roadway near her feet. She fired back in the direction from which they had come.

'Indeed, Sister,' said Lucerne.

'You are a believer?' she asked in surprise.

'I was to be a priest until the agents of Belisarius Cawl found me. I never lost my faith. Though I wear Dorn's yellow for the moment, one day I hope to change it for Sigismund's sable, and find my place among the Black Templars.'

Lucerne paused to reload his gun. A flight of jets streaked overhead, unleashing a salvo of rockets that exploded a street or two distant.

'Help me,' she said, and together they pulled the groaning Battle Sister back into better cover. Blood leaked down the warrior's ruptured armour, leaving streaks along the processional.

'The Archenemy employed sorcery of remarkable power to veil their presence,' said Veritas. 'The worshippers of Chaos employ lies and deceit as easily as the servants of the Emperor draw breath. We should have predicted some trickery on their part, and sent scouts ahead.'

Jump jets screamed as a squad of Seraphim took to the air. They were aiming for the roof of a shrine, from where Iron Warriors played their heavy bolters upon the trapped Imperial force. Evidently, the Iron Warriors had anticipated this, for no sooner were the Seraphim airborne than twisted Raptors leapt from the building, and they clashed like wheeling birds in the air. Aircraft roared past in the sky, strafing the centre of the road.

'And if the enemy had not been in position here? We would have wasted precious time while Fleet Primus drew ever nearer. I doubt neither your faith nor the divinity of your provenance, my lady, but even the holy Sisters of Battle are not omniscient.'

'We still have one road to victory,' she said.

Lucerne checked his auspex and gauged the distance between his retreating forces and the towering hab-blocks where the enemy hid.

'And what is that, Holy Sister?' He spied an enemy raising his gun, put stock to shoulder, and took his head with a single shot.

'The ship you came on. Call it in. Flatten the hab-blocks. We will shelter in the mercantile arcade.'

Four autocannon shells hit the roof of the nearest Rhino. One of his Space Marines let out a gurgling cry and fell.

'Achallor will never agree,' said Lucerne.

'You have influence with him. Call the fires, my lord,' said Imelda Veritas.

'We are barely at a safe distance, and if the *Radiance* does this then it exposes itself to the enemy fleet,' said Lucerne. 'It would be lost.'

'The Emperor protects,' replied the canoness, rising from her bloodstained knees to stand at his side.

A mechanical roar sounded, as though some monstrous beast had been sorely wounded.

'Tanks,' said Lucerne. 'So this is where the enemy armour has been hiding. It is strange. They attack too soon. They will find themselves fighting our rearguard on open ground.'

'That does not matter to us,' said Veritas.

'I concur,' he said. 'We cannot stay here.' He looked to the buildings around them. 'We must fall back into cover. The arcade is a good suggestion. We should get your wounded Sister up again.'

She looked at him sternly. 'If you do not call in orbital support, we will die in there.'

'We will not,' said Lucerne, picking up the wounded woman with one arm. 'I will attempt to contact Achallor, and if I can get through the enemy's vox-blunt, I will do what I can to sway him, I swear, but if we do not move now, then it does not matter one way or the other.'

Lokk's tank crested the ramp that led up out of the hangar. Its tracks bit into broken ferrocrete and accelerated. The enemy rearguard of tanks was rapidly approaching, but he dismissed almost all his strategic feeds, focusing upon the strange Imperial Fists. *Dracokravgi*'s eyes showed his prey dead ahead down the road. The rest of his armour roared up the ramp behind him, breaking left and right as they dispersed.

The Imperial Fists had linked up and were serving as a rallying point for the enemy's forces. They stood in a ring within a cluster of Rhinos, their guns aimed upwards, hammering volley after volley into hollow windows. Lokk saw several Iron Warriors hit as they leaned out to blaze away at the loyalists. They fired on the atmospheric attack craft, bringing one down into a tower that shook with the impact. Taking advantage of this punishing covering fire, Battle Sisters were falling back towards the arcade, or else working themselves into position to add their guns to the fusillade.

'Formidable,' said Harvoch.

'Still just prey,' said Lokk, then switched channels to address his lieutenant. 'Soften them up, K'gharl.'

He received a binharic-laced snarl in response. The lascannons of the Predator trailing *Dracokravgi* fired. Ruby beams of energy leapt across the diminishing gap between Lokk and his prey. One took the head from an Imperial Fist. The warrior's corpse toppled over backwards, trailing smoke. A second Space Marine fell, a hole burned through his armour. Lokk chuckled, then stared in surprise as the warrior staggered back up to his feet and recommenced firing.

What are these warriors? he wondered, for as he drew closer to them, he saw more novelty in their appearance.

His thoughts were interrupted as an Immolator support tank swerved into his path and sent a wall of flame against him. Lokk sneered as the fire washed harmlessly over *Dracokravgi's* hull. He accelerated, and fired at point-blank range, the laser destroyer burning clean through the side of his attacker. He slammed into the Immolator, half crushing it as *Dracokravgi* rode up over the wreck. Lokk had a fleeting glimpse of the pulpit-gunner spitting defiance before her armaglass screen shattered and her body was pulped by the Vindicator's churning tracks.

When his view cleared again, he saw the foe retreating. He snarled in frustration as the last of the bright yellow warriors disappeared from view inside. The rearguard tanks were approaching, opening fire. The fight would be harder now he had broken cover early.

'Obliterators, prepare to engage,' he ordered. His hearts were thudding as they hadn't in decades. Lokk was going to enjoy this fight.

Chapter Twenty-Eight

THE ARCADE OF NOBLE COIN

OBLITERATOR

ORBITAL STRIKE

Bolter fire roared from every quarter. Lucerne led his surviving men into the commercia arcade. The building had been an open space, full of balconies draped with greenery. A pleasant environment to strike deals and perform the duties of commerce, a terrible place for a gunfight. Bolt-fire whipped down at him, and he shot up at a bridge over the atrium, aiming for the walkway, not the Iron Warrior sheltered behind its parapet. His bolts thumped into the plascrete, blasting chunks out, and the bridge gave way, taking the traitor down with it.

Lucerne checked his retinal displays. They were fuzzy with static as the enemy vox-blunt hampered the data-sharing systems within his squads. The Imperial column was spread across the processional and the commercia, and scattered into the streets beyond. Imelda Veritas' warriors took up position, dug in as best they could. Sisters Hospitaller were hastening from one wounded soldier to the next, doing all they could to staunch wounds even as enemy fire still fell amongst them. On the street, enemy tanks duelled with the advancing Phyroxian rearguard. Ordnance rained periodically upon the Imperial positions around and about, sending plumes of rubble skywards.

'Shield-Captain Achallor, do you hear me?' voxed Lucerne.

He received no response but the crackle of the vox-blunt. A glance up towards the Blessed Bastion showed him fire and the flash of heavy weapons.

'General Dvorgin, do you hear me?' he tried on another channel.

Again, Lucerne received nothing but the rasp of aggressive jamming.

'Insupportable,' he muttered to himself. Imelda Veritas looked up from where she knelt by the side of her wounded Sister. A Hospitaller was leaning forward to close the fallen warrior's eyes and speak the prayers that would send her soul to the Emperor's side.

'They are still blocking us,' the canoness said.

'They are,' said Lucerne.

There came a sudden thundering of guns from the open floor of the atrium, and shouting of female and transhuman voices.

'*Sergeant,*' Khastus Omecro voxed him. '*We have a problem.*'

Lucerne brought up Omecro's helm feed onto his retinal display.

'Dorn's bones,' he said. He got up, taking a burst of fire on his pauldron the moment he showed himself. 'Stay here, canoness, hold position. Cover my men from the fire coming from the upper galleries.'

'We should not hang back, but fight together.'

'This foe I think is beyond you.'

'What do you mean?'

'Obliterators have entered the building,' he said, and ran for the stairs.

* * *

Achallor slammed his storm shield forward, flinging back the
Iron Warrior coming at him. The traitor's chainsword flew from
his hand, carving white lines in the soot-blacked tunnel. The
entryway was a mess of melted adamantium and plascrete.
Water was pouring from a broken pipe. The lights were dead,
cables fizzed with earthing power, and his enemy was a crowd
of horned monsters lit by bolter flash. An artificial wind blew,
generated by the fierce heat of the Knights' weapons. It was hot
as a furnace in the gate tunnel and choked with swirling ash,
yet still the Iron Warriors stood.

They would not stand before him.

Achallor rammed the edge of his shield down on the warrior's throat, mashing the soft seal and his neck both. He left
him writhing, the blade of Aswadi finishing him as he stepped
over. Relocking shields with Vychellan and Varsillian the Many-
Gloried, they pushed forward. Bolt-shells by the score exploded
upon their power fields, as the Iron Warriors retreated a step for
every one the Adeptus Custodes took forward, firing relentlessly.

'Ready?' he asked his fellows.

Varsillian gave a nod.

'Always,' said Vychellan.

'Break shield lock,' said Achallor.

The three of them charged forward, taking the Iron Warriors
off guard. Close assault with shields by the Adeptus Astartes
in either voidship or fortress would have been conducted step
by step with return of fire, as dictated by Roboute Guilliman's
great codex, only followed by a charge when the enemy line
was disrupted.

They were not Space Marines.

The Custodians hit the Iron Warriors with the Emperor's
own wrath, swords wielded with practised economy. Despite
the close confines of the tunnel, not once did the three Custodians collide with each other. Not once did their blades nick

the tunnel wall. They fought around each other, their individual styles making a complex dance. Their armour flashed gold, their plumes streamed behind them, and the Iron Warriors died.

Genetically altered to be physically superior to all men, with thousands of years of experience and granted strength by the Ruinous Powers, the Traitor Space Marines were among the most fearsome warriors ever known.

The Adeptus Custodes were better.

Faces flashed before Achallor. Horned helms, fanged maws, angled faceplates. All fell. Armour dating from the dawn of the Imperium split at last, cleaved by Prosektis. They fired at him from point-blank range, filling the combat space with blizzards of micro shrapnel. Few bolts got past his shield. Those that did detonated on his superior armour.

They pushed through the traitors, knocking them down. Varsillian took the only serious hit, his shield pincered in half by a champion wielding a power claw. Neither Achallor nor Vychellan took a scratch. Amalth-Amat and Aswadi fired between the comrades, each shot timed perfectly to pass between their bodies and strike down their foes. Achallor brought Prosektis around to finish one of the last, but the Iron Warrior's chestplate erupted in white sparks and fire before the blade could bite, blood spraying after as he fell down into the deepening flood on the floor.

'That was my kill, Amalth-Amat,' Achallor said.

'Apologies, shield-captain,' said Amalth-Amat. 'The shot was too challenging to resist taking.'

The blood tally chimed.

<Engagement concluded. Six kills, twelve point four seconds. Battle total, one hundred and thirty-six.>

Drenched in filthy water and blood, cloak tattered, Marcus Achallor allowed himself two deep breaths.

'South entrance clear,' he voxed. He received no reply. In the

quiet, he could hear the bombardment falling on the square
outside.

'Those are not our guns,' said Varsillian.

'And they are still jamming our communications,' said Vychellan.

'The main uplink-shrine is two floors up,' said Aswadi. 'They'll be blunting us from there, that's what Dvorgin suggested. I believe he is correct.'

'Victory is close. We advance,' said Achallor.

Not one ache or pain did he feel as his superhuman body powered into a sprint.

They were coming towards the open front of the building: three twisted monsters, once Space Marines, whose form now only mocked the sacred pattern of humanity.

They were immense, hulking things. Their faces hinted most at their lost mortality, for in their eyes was the gleam of a hateful intelligence all too human, but they were nearly lost in the mass of machinery and flesh that had grown up around them. Armour plates blended with warty skin. Power cables transitioned to throbbing, veinous tubes halfway along their length. Their arms were held out before them, their fingers a profusion of barrels from which issued bolts on strangely coloured plumes of fire.

Lucerne's Space Marines occupied a barricade of broken statues filling the open front of the building. The glass that had glazed the front was a slippery mess of shards on the ground.

Four of his Space Marines knelt by the barricade, led by Omecro. A fifth was dead on the floor. The Obliterators advanced into the full fire of their bolt rifles slowly but relentlessly, miniature warheads exploding within the masses of flesh-metal leaving craters that healed with supernatural speed. The Obliterators played their guns over the whole building, expending ammunition at a rate that would have left Lucerne and his men relying on their combat knives in a minute, and yet the Obliterators did not reload, and their guns seemed to have no magazines. When their bolts exploded they did so with violent blue flashes.

'Go for the head!' shouted Lucerne, sliding into position by Omecro. 'Concentrate fire. Bring them down one at a time!'

His men switched targets to the leftmost foe, the nearest, filling him with so many bolts that he was pushed back, and his chest and head were reduced to an oozing red ruin. The Obliterator swayed on his feet, then pushed on, his raw, eyeless face sweeping about as he fired blindly.

The rightmost Obliterator stopped. His body shuddered, like a canid before it retches; the shaking spread down his arms, and they spasmed, and flowed, and the boltgun fingers melted and ran like quicksilver, re-forming into a missile launcher on the left, a meltagun on the right. The melta fired with a sound like screaming, turning the head of a saint on the barricade into red-hot slurry. The missile launcher barked, and a krak round hit the stone near the top, the force of the blast throwing back Bheld, who fought by Omecro. Bheld hit the ground, and skidded over the shards of glass into a support pillar, where he lay still. Lucerne glanced quickly at his vitum monitor. Bheld was alive, but unconscious.

Omecro flicked his bolt rifle into single-shot mode, drew a bead on the blinded Obliterator, and put a round into its right eye socket. The missile passed into the head. Impossibly, still it lived, until the bolt blew, putting out a little column of crimson. The Obliterator stopped, face smoking, then fell forward to the ground with a loud clang.

'One down,' said Omecro. He fired three more rounds and then ejected the empty magazine.

The central Obliterator was still advancing; the third hung back, face gurning with pain and arm shivering, before its missile launcher sent another rocket at them.

'I'm out,' said Omecro. He took the ammunition from the dead brother. 'We can't keep this up long.'

'Keep firing!' Lucerne said, hammering the lead Obliterator on full-auto.

The battle in the street had become more clear-cut. With the Imperial infantry now embroiled in close-range firefights in the commercia, the lines on the street had solidified. Sisters of Battle and Phyroxian tanks exchanged fire with the advancing Iron Warriors, but they were being pushed back, leaving the infantry in the commercia exposed to both the tank fire and the warriors still attacking from the hab-blocks on the other side of the street.

Lucerne noticed a Phyroxian tank firing down the processional a mile away and opened up a vox-link. 'Brother-Sergeant Lucerne, requesting fire support. Target heavy assault troops. My mark.'

A squall of static greeted him, full of active jamming patterns, yet a faint, accented reply came back to him.

'Target marked. Prepare.'

The Leman Russ brought its turret to bear. An eructation of smoke, followed a fraction of a second later by the noise, then the impact. The shell hit a few feet away from the Obliterator pinning the Space Marines down with its missile launcher, lifted its enormous weight from the ground and tossed it through the air. The Obliterator slammed down hard, and did not rise. The tank drew the attention of a Rhino-variant tank hunter; crimson light flashed, missed, and the Leman Russ retreated. Lucerne could count on it no more.

The last Obliterator registered the death of its kin, and snarled. Then it began to jog, slowly at first, building into an unstoppable charge, guns blazing as it came at them.

They emptied their weapons into it. As it approached, its fists morphed again, becoming lethal power claws that sparked with arcane energies. The Greyshields split and ran before it hit the barricade, kicking aside heavy lumps of masonry as if they were sticks. Omecro was not fast enough, and the Obliterator slew him with a backhanded slap, pitched from the waist, which slammed the Space Marine's broken corpse clean through a support pillar.

Lucerne stopped, drew his pistol and shot the thing in the face until its head sagged in. But the Obliterator would not die. It staggered, the raw mess of its face pulsing. From its broken jaw a gun's muzzle pushed out, slick with blood.

'For the Emperor!' Lucerne cried, dropping his spent pistol and flinging himself at the corrupted Space Marine, his combat knife gleaming in his hand. He dug his fingers into its broken skull and hung on, driving his knife repeatedly into the join between the back of its neck and its armour. There was no differentiation between flesh and battleplate. The knife jabbed almost uselessly into the strange meld of materials, scratching across it as if it were ceramite, but drawing blood all the same.

Lucerne stabbed repeatedly. The muzzle in the thing's mouth finished growing, becoming a plasma gun. It burned hot, and Lucerne moved his head aside as it discharged, vomiting a stream of superheated gas that burned the yellow from his helm. Lucerne's skin scorched through his armour. Desperate, he jabbed into the flowing mess of flesh re-forming over the Obliterator's eyes. It made a noise of pain deep in its chest, plucked at him, and flung him aside.

Lucerne rolled violently over the ground, arms flung out. His remaining warrior threw grenades at the Obliterator, but it walked through their explosions as if they were gentle rains, the plasma gun in its mouth charging to fire again.

Lucerne offered his prayers, and prepared to die, sorry more than anything that his life as a Space Marine had proven so short and so useless.

A fusillade of boltgun fire came from the right, hammering away the Obliterator's pauldron and making it grunt. Canoness Veritas was coming towards him, firing all the while, her Sisters behind her, and they were singing.

Lifting his groggy head, Lucerne beheld a nimbus of soft light surround them as they chanted their praise to the God-Emperor. It grew in brilliance, and he thought that he could see a tall warrior behind them, almost indistinct in the glare, his eyes brighter than suns.

He threw up an arm to protect his eyes. There was a scream halfway between a human shout and the grinding of gears. Then the Sisters were helping him up, and the Obliterator was a twisted hunk of smoking metal.

'The Emperor hears us,' said Veritas.

'Praise be,' mumbled Lucerne though a mouth full of blood. 'Have you reached Achallor?'

By way of answer she voxed, 'This is Canoness Imelda Veritas. Shield-Captain Achallor, do you hear me? West Gate task force under heavy armour and infantry attack. We have been driven into the Arcade of Noble Coin. Enemy target concentration in hab-blocks facing the arcade. Requesting immediate support.'

They waited.

'Nothing,' she said.

'Try again,' he said, then he looked out of the building front where enemy tanks were approaching. He stood up, his body and armour working in unison to drive the pain from him, and switched his own vox-channels to widecast. 'All Imperial units, fall back!'

The melta bomb roared. Achallor was through the slagged door before it had a chance to cool, kicking droplets of molten plasteel free as he ran into ruddy firelight. The comms hub occupied a tall chamber with a mezzanine running around it. Fourteen men and women manned the stations, all Traitor Guard. A solitary Word Bearer watched over them. Achallor supposed the turncoats' new faith was shakily held, and needed to be guarded, but it would not save them.

One mortal went for his pistol.

Achallor's boltcasters roared, splashing the remains of the man against the room's enormous oculus, which showed the battle raging outside. This was a false window made up of vid-screens, and they hissed under the gore.

The Word Bearer was shooting by then. Vychellan made a great roar, and charged headlong into the barrage of bolts, his shield catching most. He slammed out with the edge, the power field ripping free the warrior's mask. Vychellan spun around, his sentinel blade out at full stretch, the impact of it cutting the warrior nearly in two. The Word Bearer fell, and Vychellan yanked the weapon free.

The remaining adepts in the room remained in shocked silence. Those standing held out their hands before them, as if they were attempting to placate some wild creature. Those sitting were twisted halfway around in their seats, unsure what to do.

Vox signals burbled from a dozen emitters, all traitor. The bastion shook with artillery hits. The false oculus showed a landscape full of flashing lights as weapons of all kinds discharged in every quarter. Achallor saw fires raging unchecked, the descent trails of enemy rockets, explosions, laser tracks vaporising particulates in the air.

He took off his helmet.

'Listen to me. I am Shield-Captain Marcus Achallor of the Emissaries Imperatus Shield Host of the Adeptus Custodes. I come with the Emperor's judgement and the Emperor's word. You have all turned your backs upon the rule of Terra. In doing so, you have embraced a darkness beyond your understanding.

That is your error. Heed me now, and your deaths might yet be clean.'

He strode forward. Aswadi and Varsillian covered the door. Amalth-Amat hauled himself up the creaking ladder to the mezzanine. Vychellan went to stand by the main control board, where embedded servitor torsos twitched to the click of a giant runeboard. One woman glanced sideways at the glowing buttons.

'Do not move,' said Vychellan, holding the edge of his sword near her cheek.

'You will close down the vox-blunt,' said Achallor. 'You will shut down all relay systems carrying traitor vox traffic.'

The traitors stared back, none of them daring to move. The woman Vychellan menaced sobbed.

'Now,' said Achallor.

They went into sudden action, calling orders and check signs to one another. Machines were consulted, power rerouted. Vychellan let the woman up to work her part of the station, but as she and her terrified fellows depressed the buttons, the servitor choir began chattering and snarling, and balefires shone in their eyes.

'It won't work, it won't work,' she said, gibbering in fear, 'they're stopping us.'

'Get back,' growled Vychellan. He surveyed the cyborgs thrashing about in their input niches. He swept his sword through the lower row of servitors, then rested the blade on the edge of his shield, and slew the upper tier with bolts.

Power lines spat. The servitors' pulped remains shuddered, pumping blood, oil and preservative fluids onto the floor.

Softly at first, one Imperial vox-channel after another became audible, and Achallor attempted to piece together a strategic picture.

'...ntral command, this is Lieutenant Frans, Fifteen Platoon.

I repeat, a group of Heretic Astartes is pushing up Processional Glorious Repentance. I repeat, Fifteen Platoon is under attack, do you...'

'Heretic Astartes armour has surrounded the orbital laser silo on the north-western edge of the void port...'

'...orbital vox-uplink is secure and operational. Phyrox Fortieth, Ninth Squadron and Mordian Twenty-One Platoon holding but we require immediate reinforcement. Do...'

'...they're coming over the...'

'Listen to this. They meant to trap us,' said Vychellan.

'They will fail,' said Achallor. 'These messages come from all over the continent, not just this vicinity. The enemy's failure here will ensure our victory.'

'The Emperor protects, the Emperor protects...'

'Sisters, drive them from their position. Let holy flame cleanse...'

One vox-stream caught his attention.

'...anyone? This is Canoness Imelda Veritas. Shield-Captain Achallor, do you hear me? West Gate task force under heavy armour and infantry attack. We have been driven back into the Arcade of Noble Coin. Requesting immediate support!'

'That one,' said Achallor, and crooked his finger at one of the adepts. 'Bring it to the fore.'

The man isolated Veritas' communication.

'Open a channel.'

With shaking hands, the adept complied.

'Canoness, this is Shield-Captain Achallor.'

'Captain! Praise the Emperor. We are in dire need of support. A large portion of the Iron Warriors force here has us trapped. Please, order an orbital strike.'

'Options?' he asked Vychellan.

'Bring it up,' said Vychellan, nudging the woman. She moved to a different console. 'All of it. The whole district. Show me the battle.'

capture of the battleground. Runic designators flashed up, showing the warring sides. They were thoroughly intermixed, with
the task force meant to advance on the west gate embroiled a
few miles short of its objective.

'We stand on the precipice,' said Vychellan. 'If we do not get
them out, we are going to lose half the remaining forces in this
sector. They will not hold the space port.' He looked directly
at Achallor. 'And we will get bogged down.' He turned back to
the cartograph. 'Artillery is too imprecise. The Mordians are
too strung out, we are too far away, and the Knights are occupied here. We are going to have to call Sangar in.'

'She will be exposed.'

'I know you do not want to do it, Marcus, but it is only for
the time it takes to fire one round of lance strikes.' Vychellan
pointed to the display. 'The Iron Warriors are concentrated
on the western side of the processional. We could knock out
twenty to thirty per cent of their fighting strength in one blow.
They will not expect it. Sangar is canny enough to get herself
out of this. If she shrouds fast enough, which she will.'

'Where is Brother Lucerne?' Achallor asked the canoness.

'*I am here, my lord,*' he said. Achallor could hear the furious
sounds of battle loud behind his voice.

'Stand by,' said Achallor. 'You. Give me a line to orbit, maximum gain.'

The adept obeyed, and a vox-feed interrupted by the whoop
of energetic weapons discharge came online.

'Mistress Sangar, respond,' said Achallor.

She must have been waiting for his signal, for she answered
immediately. '*Shield-captain.*'

'Prepare to drop the shroud. Immediate orbital support
required at these coordinates.' He datapulsed the location to her.
'Be advised, the Traitor Astartes employed sorcery to ambush

our advance short of Ascension Stair. Canoness Imelda Veritas is making every effort to break through the Iron Warriors' lines. It pains me to say it, but the renegades prepared their positions with skill. Casualties are mounting. Bombard the enemy-occupied hab-blocks to clear her advance.'

'*As you command,*' she said.

'Canoness, mark the target,' Achallor said, speaking to both Sangar and Veritas briefly. 'Mistress Sangar, I give you permission to fire upon the surface at your discretion thereafter, provided you are able to withdraw safely.' Then to the operatives he said, 'Step away from your stations. Gather upon the lower floor.'

The traitors lined up before Achallor. He surveyed them all coldly.

'You were taught that the Emperor was your god. He protected you, and you turned against Him. I would have you wait here to receive the proper judgement, and to have you assessed to see if any of you might be saved by repentance. But thanks in part to your efforts, this world is in the grip of war, and I cannot afford the luxury of mercy.'

The Custodians raised their weapons, blades rested upon shields, boltcasters forward.

'Know this last truth. The Emperor is not a god. He is a man, but He is not a forgiving man. Nor am I.'

Their guns blared, three rapid rounds apiece. Fyceline drifted through blood vapour.

'Amalth-Amat,' he said. 'Bring out your standard. It is time the aquila spread its wings over this bastion again.'

Alarm tolls rolled through the bridge of the *Radiance*. Emergency lumens strobed.

'We have been noticed, my lady!' called Osmor. 'Mass torpedo launch from the far side of Gathalamor. Estimated time to impact ten minutes.'

'Scutum control, shields up,' barked Shipmistress Sangar from her throne. 'Mister Osmor, cogitate enemy targets. Helm, positional manoeuvres.' Her officers responded smoothly, rolling the *Radiance* so that her spinal weaponry and the port broadside were facing down to the planet.

'Another torpedo wave is away, my lady. The enemy are attempting to interdict with fighter craft also, wide spread.'

Sangar sucked air through her teeth, already plotting a way out of the racing missiles and ships coming at her.

'Miss VenShellen, do we have analysis of interdiction patterns?'

'Yes, my lady.'

'Transmit to helm. Formulate safest path out. Magos Kzarch, prepare to re-engage obfuscation engines on my mark. Miss VenShellen, let us offer all the fire support that we can while we are in the open. Have the targeting cogitators ready for ground fire against the targets as Lord Achallor commanded, select others at will. We fire the moment Veritas' force gives coordinates, understood?'

'Of course, my lady,' replied VenShellen, her fingers dancing over her runeboard.

'First wave of fighter craft expected in six minutes, my lady,' Osmor said. 'They're outpacing the torpedoes.'

'They're using the munitions to box us in, in case we vanish again. Clever,' said Sangar. She clicked her tongue and sat forward a little further in her throne.

'Weapons ready, my lady.'

'Prepare to fire, Miss VenShellen,' Sangar said. 'Get me a channel to Sergeant Lucerne.'

Communications were opened, and a nod was given.

'Brother-Sergeant Lucerne, this is Shipmistress Ebele Sangar. Preparing to deliver orbital support. Please give precise coordinates.'

A squealing of troubled vox made her wince, then Lucerne's bass, transhuman voice was ringing out loud and clear.

'Direct a full bombardment against the hab-block at these coordinates,' he said. A data packet followed. *'Be advised we are at absolute minimum safe distance, shipmistress.*

'Then you might want to duck,' came her response. 'Miss Ven-Shellen, open fire, spinal lances and port batteries, immediately.'

The *Radiance* shook. Beneath the ship, the clouds burned away like morning mist as the fires of the God-Emperor fell upon the Iron Warriors' positions.

Torvann Lokk raged as crimson beams of light speared down from the heavens. The first lance struck the rightmost hab directly and drove down through it; fire erupted through the building's windows and it detonated from the top down as it was blown apart from within. The blast wave rolled outwards in a hot and howling gale. Chunks of rubble the size of battle tanks tumbled through the air and smashed down upon the ruined cityscape. One such block hit the ground mere feet from *Dracokravgi*, crushing three Iron Warriors into the ground in a spray of gore.

The second and third blasts stabbed down to cut another hab-block apart, one shearing away its pinnacle before the next struck at a slight angle and caused it to fold at its midpoint. Thousands of tons of ferrocrete and plasteel toppled into the ruins of the commercia, taking Iron Warriors with them, burying them alive.

Yet even as he endured his brothers' demise, Lokk was fighting for his own life. A withering storm of ordnance rained around him and raked the collapsing flanks of the hab-blocks.

'Casipiniax?' he barked, sending his tank into swift reverse. The Leman Russ he was hunting vanished behind a billow of dust. Bright tracks of vaporised rockcrete followed him out as his foe fired its hull lascannon blind.

'I live,' came the other warpsmith's voice, underlaid by the roaring of explosions. *'Where did that come from? There were*

supposed to be no Imperial ships in orbit! Curse Xyrax and his viper's tongue. Where by the primarch are Klordren's shi–'

A rain of barrage bombs followed, slamming into the cityscape and sending black clouds of smoke billowing hundreds of feet into the air. Shockwaves battered *Dracokravgi*. Lokk watched as life-runes winked out on his strategic overlay by the handful. Pict-feeds vanished in flares of light. Vox-channels gasped and died.

Casipiniax's voice disappeared in a wash of static.

Lokk's hearts pounded. His mouth was filled with bile. He felt hatred as only an Iron Warrior could: hatred for whatever Imperial ship's captain had bombed his warriors out of existence; hatred for Tenebrus for having them linger on this miserable world; hatred for Klordren's timidity in withholding the support of his warships and hatred for himself, for overreaching in his need to hunt, and kill, and win.

Snarling, he slammed the drive levers opposite to each other, turning *Dracokravgi* on the spot. It exposed the tank's weaker rear armour to their enemy, but he was past caring.

'Let them have this victory, for what good it will do them,' he spat over the vox. 'All who remain, we retreat, rally-point Asmor.'

Retreat would involve running back to Tenebrus with his tail between his legs, but better that than lead the last of his legionaries to their destruction for the sake of his pride.

'Besides, there is yet Tenebrus' way to victory,' he told himself as *Dracokravgi* rumbled up over the shifting spreads of rubble, explosions still blowing all around him.

Torvann Lokk retreated, leaving the Emperor's dogs mauled but very much alive.

'Are they dead?' Stehner asked nervously.

'They are the personal guard of the Holy God-Emperor of

Mankind, lieutenant,' replied Dvorgin. 'We should have more faith in them, don't you think?'

'Of course, sir. My apologies,' said Stehner. 'I worry that they will be unable to succeed with the Sisters of Battle pinned down.'

So did Dvorgin, but he was not about to let on to that.

He scanned the firefight ongoing by the bastion's feet. A Knight lay broken and ablaze. Two more stalked past, rotary cannons peppering the walls with bullets. The enemy were still fighting, but the battle was moving off, back in the direction of the macro-cathedrum and the main nest of heretics. That could, he supposed, mean the enemy were retreating.

At that moment several lance strikes stabbed down from the sky and hit the city in the area where Veritas was embroiled. A moment passed, and a second rippling series of explosions lifted away an entire section of the bastion's upper north battlements. Blazing figures spilled from the parapet and plunged to their deaths.

There was nothing but smoke for a moment. Then, as Dvorgin watched, a golden standard rose from the fire.

The aquila atop it gleamed.

'And there you have it,' said the general. 'Men and women of Mordian, make ready to relocate field command to the Blessed Bastion.'

'Throne alive, they did that alone?'

Dvorgin shot a sidelong glance at Lieutenant Stehner, whose mask of composure had cracked for a moment. He forgot sometimes how young this lad was, how few wars he'd seen in the Emperor's service. That dry demeanour he had was a mask.

'Stehner, respect.'

'Yes, sir. Very good, sir,' said the lieutenant, hastening to be about his duties. Around Dvorgin his command staff hurried to pack up portable auspex consoles, strategic cartographs and heavy weaponry.

'That's it,' said Dvorgin as he folded down his magnoculars and stowed them in the pouch on his belt. He would feel far better once his soldiers were inside a good, defensible structure. Surely it couldn't be long before the heretics moved to counter their offensive, and he didn't want his platoons exposed when they did. 'The day is done.'

Chapter Twenty-Nine

RADIANCE RETREATS

NEW COMMAND

A GENERAL'S DEFIANCE

Ebele Sangar watched intently as the *Radiance* extracted itself from the pursuit over Gathalamor. The ship ran on minimal systems. The inverted void shields operated on far lower sensitivity settings than when turned outwards to deflect attacks. It was a finely tuned system, devilishly hard to manage, and no wonder to her that it had never been used more widely by the Imperium. It could absorb only so much energy before detectable leakage occurred, and at that moment all allowable power was being funnelled to the realspace drive.

To save energy, the command deck was soaked in the disorienting red of emergency lumens. The air was cold, the gravity weaker. She always felt much closer to the void when they ran silent like that, and also to the warp. She tried not to think of the echoes of her life shunted silently by the voids into the empyrean, where who knew what might observe them.

The crew operated in a hush. It wasn't necessary, but the sense of oppression the obfuscation field brought made them all behave that way. Their actions were matched by those of the ship. Every movement was slight. The enemy knew they were there. Dropping a payload of macro shells and lancing the surface with high-energy weapons tended to do that, she thought. But they did not know where the *Radiance* had gone. The enemy craft patrolled the high void, sweeping the planet's orbit.

Ebele Sangar was not happy. This was nothing unusual for the shipmistress, who privately felt that if one was not worrying then one had probably missed something important. This day, though, she felt a deep-rooted conviction that something dreadful was approaching. The worst part was that they still did not know exactly what their enemies were planning. Sangar swore to herself and to her Emperor that she would be ready for it, whatever it was.

Even now, Sangar was half tempted to abandon caution and make a run on the macro-cathedrum. She might be able to cause enough damage to that mountain of a building to foil the enemy's plans.

Impatient foolishness, she thought. *It'd take days of bombardment to crack it, the enemy have five cruisers in the black, plus whatever that spy ship can do. So instead we creep away and wait for Fleet Primus to translate from the warp, and hope that they get here before... Before what?*

Her eyes flicked back to a screen displaying the last orbital pict they'd snatched of the cathedrum. It was immense, two miles high and several across. It was one of the great wonders of the segmentum, for although there were larger constructions in the Imperium, and many larger churches, there were few that could boast its bewildering number of statues. It was said, and she took this to mean the information was entirely apocryphal, that every saint that had ever lived was represented on that building. It was so big that if she did opt to assault it, from the outside.

Her throne rotated and she swept her gaze around the bridge of the *Radiance*. Osmor and VenShellen were monitoring their stations with hawkish focus, faces underlit by flickering vid-feeds and auspex screens as the ship inched its way up into the inter-lunar void. There was little else they could do for now, and though she maintained an outward veneer of composure, inaction was wearing on Sangar's nerves.

'My lady, movement from the enemy void craft,' called Osmor.

'Details,' she said, spinning her throne to face him.

'They're forming into a close pack, my lady, and...' He frowned. 'Confirm, they're pulling away from high void anchor. Mechanicum ship also is moving off.'

'Their heading?' asked Sangar. 'Are they following us?'

'Cogitating, my lady,' said VenShellen, clipped and urgent.

A minute crawled past, then two, then three, filled with the click of fingers across rune-keys and the rumble of the *Radiance*'s systems. On her vid-screens, Sangar watched the enemy ships light their engines, pull up from orbit and haul their unclean bulks away from Gathalamor.

'What are they doing?' she said. 'Do you have a destination yet, Miss VenShellen?'

'Still cogitating.'

A soft amber light began pulsing over the empyric monitoring desk.

'My lady,' said one of the operators, a woman named Choorvi. 'I must inform you we've detected multiple incoming warp translation signatures at the trans-Gathalamorian-Rhandan gravipause.'

Adrenaline surged through Sangar. One of her hands reflexively tightened on her throne.

'That's far in-system,' said Sangar. The further in one risked translating, the greater the danger of mishap due to the gravitic fields exerted by planetary bodies. To break warp so far from the safety of the Mandeville points suggested either daring or some convulsion of the empyrean.

'A gravipause jump, with that mass of ships? Easy enough to overshoot I suppose, but...' said Osmor.

'No speculation please, Mister Osmor. Details, Miss Choorvi.'

'Empyric translation signatures are multiple, my lady, and still incoming.'

'Confirm origin,' ordered Sangar. 'Is it our fleet or more foes?'

'At this distance, we will not hear the choral beacons for another five minutes, twenty-six seconds, my lady,' said Vox-man Phryke. 'Monitoring'.

'Inform me the moment you have identity,' said Sangar.

'Confirmed,' said Phryke.

'It's a clean jump. Minimal warp tearing. I suggest Imperial ships.'

'Very good, Miss Choorvi,' Sangar said. 'Miss VenShellen, where are those heretic craft headed?'

'Six-six-nine, upper elliptical-three, counter-rotational sling-shot past Gathalamor and making for open void.'

'They're putting the planet between them and us, moving directly away from our incoming reinforcements,' said Sangar, frowning. 'They knew they were coming.'

'They're cutting and running, leaving their ground forces to our mercy like the cowardly heretics they are!' cried Helms-man O'Casver from helm throne two. His words brought several 'Hurrahs!' from other crew members, but Sangar held up a hand to stop them. The sense of wrongness was only increasing, her premonition of doom now a band constricting her chest.

'They began their manoeuvre *before* the translation signa-tures of our craft registered,' she said, her stern voice cutting through the cheers of her crew. 'How would they know to do that unless...?'

'Unless they somehow knew when and where the battle groups would exit the warp,' VenShellen finished the thought for her, looking up from her station.

'Disputational – the difficulties of precisely monitoring void craft transit while those craft lie beyond the empyric veil are proven,' droned Magos Kzarch.

'And yet,' replied VenShellen, her tone sharp.

'There's that unholy Dark Mechanicum ship,' suggested Osmor. 'Throne alone knows what capabilities it has.'

'They have more warships in orbit over the other worlds,' said Sangar. 'If they had that sort of forewarning, why not engage us here to keep us pinned while they moved those assets into position to ambush our ships as they translated? They could have wreaked havoc before the ships had awakened their shields, weapons and auspex, then withdrawn.'

'Maybe these newcomers are the enemy, my lady,' said Osmor.

'The Iron Warriors fleet has recalled its strike craft,' Ven-Shellen said. The level of activity on the command deck was increasing. Voices were getting louder.

'Then why aren't they linking up?' said Sangar. 'They'll be able to read the incoming empyric track of Fleet Primus as well as us. Scattering themselves like that is the best way to die, and quickly. They're not running. We're missing something,' she said, half to herself. 'What are we missing?'

She watched the enemy ships departing, then looked back at Gathalamor. The last of the torpedo fans were spreading off into the void. The flights of fighters and bombers were looping back and speeding after their carrier craft. Sangar clicked her tongue, and drummed her fingers on the arm of her throne.

'Magos Kzarch, prepare to drop obfuscation field and revert to voids. Enginarium, begin cycling of plasma to full reactor capacity. I'm tired of sneaking about. The *Radiance* will out-run any of those lumbering behemoths.'

The deck's activity increased again.

'Obfuscation field ready to drop,' said Kzarch.

'Stand by,' said Sangar. 'I'll have confirmation of who these ships belong to before we move.'

A few more minutes passed. The Iron Warriors craft were accelerating. They were so big and space so vast that they didn't seem to be moving at all to begin with, but they were moving fast.

There was a chime of bells from the vox-station. Phryke's frown of concentration transformed into an excited smile. 'Confirm Fleet Primus signifiers, translated within a day's full burn of Gathalamor orbital space. Battle Group Orphaeus, strike groups alpha, beta and gamma.'

'Is the groupmaster with them?'

'Lord Kseyvorn's signum is being broadcast. Vox-channels open and encrypted. Standing by to return message.'

'What's their heading?' Even as she asked this question Sangar had a sinking sensation in her chest. Kseyvorn was a hothead.

'They're making all speed for Gathalamor.'

'Of course he is,' she sighed. 'How many ships?'

'I'll have an asset list for you within a minute.'

'Very good,' said Sangar. 'Come to new heading, rendezvous intermediate of Gathalamor and gravipause ingress. Get me within stable hololithic communication range.'

The ship rumbled. Agonisingly slowly its prow lifted away from Gathalamor's ecliptic plane.

'New course set,' the helm reported.

'Drop obfuscation shields. Realspace drive to full,' ordered Sangar. 'Break vox silence. Contact Lord Achallor. Tell him the fleets are beginning to arrive. Send it on an open channel. Let's put the fear of the Emperor into the enemy. Then get me point advertising where we are. I will compose a missive in my cabin, then take rest. Notify me of any changes. If not, summon me at watch change. Lieutenant Osmor, you have command.'

Her throne lowered itself to the floor. As she rose from it and strode for the door, Ebele Sangar could not help but think, *Emperor, if this is the aid I prayed for, you've a wicked sense of humour.*

A new day was coming.

Dvorgin sat behind a heavy brass desk in what was once the office of a high official. Located near the heart of the Blessed Bastion, the chamber boasted solid furniture, several working holoscreens and a minimum of heretical graffiti, and had therefore swiftly recommended itself as his new field headquarters.

Though the office was spacious, his command staff filled it. Officers brought a constant stream of data-slates to him: casualty lists and current operational strengths of his forces within the bastion; reports from the officers whose platoons had dug in to defensible positions outside, and who had been charged with watching for what Dvorgin was now thinking of as 'the inevitable enemy counter-attack'; Munitorum tallies of armaments, ammunition, medical supplies and the like; and, most pleasingly now the vox-blunt was gone, reports from other officers' commands spread across the continent.

Dvorgin stifled a yawn as he worked through the contents of another data-slate. Once more he found himself deprived of sleep, settling for a carefully administered dose of stimms from Medicae Hesp. He still felt exhausted but full of jittery energy. The office's cot bed called to him constantly.

'Vox-officer,' called Dvorgin as he finished the slate and set it atop a teetering stack of its fellows. A Mordian appeared at his side.

'Sir.'

'Take this down,' ordered Dvorgin, and waited while the man readied an auto-stylus and slate. 'Chieftain Secondary Jasmal of the Phyrox Fortieth reports that he has three units of armour moving up to reinforce this position. Commissar Shaliim is also en route with what remains of our own Sixteen, Twenty-Two and Twenty-Four platoons. Further, take note that Chieftain Quintary Yespar, Lieutenant Orms and Celestian Gervaine all report that they have engaged enemy around the periphery of Mozver City. Advise caution to all officers. A counter-attack is coming – it won't necessarily fall here.'

'To whom should I bear this missive, sir?' asked the officer after a long pause. Dvorgin blinked and realised that he had neglected to say.

Tired, dangerously so, he scolded himself. *As soon as the stimms wear off you're taking a few hours' rest time no matter what's going on. You're no use to your officers without your edge.*

'It's for Canoness Imelda Veritas,' he said. 'You should find her in the bastion's fane-primus.'

'No need, you will find me right here.' Imelda Veritas' voice cut across the noise of Dvorgin's command staff. Heads snapped around. A Mordian trooper hovered behind the canoness in the doorway, looking apologetic.

'Canoness Imelda Veritas of the Order of the Argent Shroud, sir,' he announced belatedly.

'Thank you, Rhepser, virtually prescient,' said Dvorgin with a scowl. 'Canoness, I have an operational update for you here, accrued from external reports.'

'As the Emperor wills,' she said, taking the data-slate from the officer and casting her eyes over its contents. The canoness' armour bore fresh scorch marks and bloodstains from the fighting. A new, angry-looking scar ran across her right cheekbone.

An inch higher, and whatever did that would have taken her eye, he thought. If the wound bothered Imelda Veritas she showed no sign of it.

'This is good,' said Imelda Veritas, handing the data-slate back to the officer. 'My Sisters are in readiness, general. By the Emperor's will we were able to replenish our ammunition supplies from this bastion's stockpile. We have performed the appropriate devotions and intoned our thanks to the Emperor for our victory to come. What of your own warriors?'

'We shall be marshalled,' he said. 'Give us the room,' said Dvorgin to his men. At once, his assembled aides filed out. Trooper Rhepser closed the door behind them.

Dvorgin rose from behind his desk and moved to a cabinet. Opening it he took down a half-full bottle of amasec and a pair of crystal glasses.

'A gift from whatever luckless adept called this chamber their own,' he said, inclining the bottle towards her in question. Imelda Veritas nodded.

'I prefer dhar,' she said, accepting the glass in her armoured gauntlet. 'It has a certain bite that I relish. But I thank you for this.'

'Have you seen the shield-captain at all since we occupied this place?' asked Dvorgin, sipping from his glass and pacing a little. Thanks to the stimms he found staying still difficult.

'I have, albeit briefly,' Imelda Veritas replied, raising an eyebrow. She sipped then spoke again. 'I believe he was gathering his men to discuss the next stage of the campaign. He informed me that, by his estimation, the battle groups of Fleet Primus should now be no more than two days from making translation. Emperor willing, we shall have to keep the foe busy no longer than that.'

'Let us hope that is the case,' said Dvorgin. 'We've had fortune thus far.'

'We have the Emperor's own guardians at our side,' the canoness replied. 'Fortune has nothing to do with it.'

'We still lost a lot of good people,' said Dvorgin.

'Their martyrdom will be honoured,' said Veritas. 'But I concur, this is not a war that we can sustain. Now we have this bastion, I have faith that we will hold Ascension Stair until the crusade forces arrive.'

'And yet the enemy still do not show their full strength,' said Dvorgin.

Veritas sipped again. 'That there has been little sign of the Heretic Astartes concerns me,' she agreed. 'I wonder,' she said. 'What if they are massing, observing our efforts, planning where to undo us at a stroke? We should push on immediately to retake the macro-cathedrum.'

'Should we?' he snapped, setting his glass down hard on the corner of the desk. The stimms had made his movements jerky and the glass spilled off, hitting the rug with a soft thump. 'So says Achallor, but what should we do to decide? Pray for guidance? Throne knows we're fighting blind. Or should we throw ourselves at the enemy? I seem to be the only officer with any interest in keeping our soldiers alive to see their victory!'

Realising that his voice had risen, Dvorgin took a slow breath and composed himself. Veritas' expression hadn't changed.

'Do not make the mistake of thinking that I and my Battle Sisters are mindless zealots, general,' she said, her voice quiet. 'We do not fear a martyr's death, but nor would I see these women throw away their lives. I know every face, every name. There is not one amongst them whose loss would not wound me.'

Dvorgin gave in at last and rubbed at his eyes.

'Of course, of course,' he said. 'I apologise, canoness. I feel as though I am fighting in the dark, and to be frank Shield-Captain Achallor does not appear inclined to provide any light. We have won a victory here, but at great cost, and I fear it may be in vain if we push on immediately, as he desires.'

'As I thought,' said Imelda Veritas, setting her own glass down unfinished. 'You are tired. Do you not think I am tired, Luthor?'

'Yes, yes I do,' he said.

'But I do not feel it, not because I have strength, but because I have *faith*. I lean upon the Emperor. The Argent Shroud prizes deeds above words, as does He.'

'I know,' said Dvorgin. 'Forgive me,' he said. 'I mourn my men. I mourn that it has come to this. My faith is weak.'

'Your faith is strong, and I cast no aspersions upon it!' she said passionately. She leaned across to him, gripping his wrist tightly, and he felt a modicum of her strength flow into him. 'I know it. I feel it. So does He. We are all moved by the spirit of the Emperor. It is not for either of us to deny His will. Though it may lead to death and suffering, we do holy work. This is an eternal struggle, Luthor. How we feel about it is irrelevant. All that matters is that we serve Him. He is our salvation, and the light in the darkness. I will not tell you to have faith in Him, because you have it in abundance, but I will tell you that you must also have faith in yourself. Only in that way shall you prevail.'

Dvorgin nodded.

'Better?' she asked.

He nodded again. 'Better than my regimental priest was. Much better.'

She smiled. 'Do not be too hard on him, general, he was only a man.'

Dvorgin snorted in amusement. 'Quite.'

Veritas' smile deepened.

'Besides, can you honestly tell me that stiff-necked Mordian pride of yours doesn't have something to do with it? I've come to know you well, Luthor. Do not think I haven't noticed, you strongly dislike any suggestion that others might be capable of feats that your own soldiers are not. I mean no offence,' she said, in answer to his frown. 'Only that neither you nor I should compare our deeds to those of demigods. The Custodians are far more than we are or will ever be. You must be more open to the spiritual guidance of those who are closer to the Emperor than you. The Emperor's own blood runs in their veins, and the light of His life shines in their souls.'

'Praise be,' said Dvorgin.

'Praise be indeed. More sacrifice is to come before this over,' she said. 'The Custodians will leave us soon, to complete their own mission. We must be ready to give them the diversion they need, and attack the cathedrum, no matter the cost.'

'We shall fight together then, one last time.'

'Alas no, Luthor.'

'No?'

'I have appointed Palatine Gracia Emmanuelle to lead the Argent Shroud in my stead,' she said.

'Your stead?' said Dvorgin.

'I was, naturally, the first to volunteer to support the Custodians,' she replied, speaking quickly before Dvorgin could interrupt. 'I must go with them into the catacombs. It is what the Emperor wishes of me. He needs you to be strong. *I* need you to be strong.'

He nodded. 'Another drink?'

'I have dallied here too long,' she said.

'I make you neglect your duties.'

'Spreading the faith is my duty,' she said. 'But you are right that I have others. I will see you soon.'

'Would you be so good as to send my command staff back in upon your departure, canoness?'

'Of course,' Imelda Veritas said. 'Thank you for the victory libation. See you upon the battlefield, General Dvorgin.'

With that she was gone. Dvorgin's command staff filed back in. Dvorgin stooped and picked up his glass, looking at the spilt liquor with a sigh. He reached over and finished the canoness' drink for her.

thought. *I want to know what the enemy were up to in the damned
catacombs. But I fear that, even if we have the answers to those
questions, we will have little enough strength to act upon them.
Either the Custodians will deal with these matters, or we will all
suffer the consequences.*

Achallor beheld devastation. Ash blew thick on hot winds, coat-
ing the living and the dead alike. The bastion roof was a mess
of blast-cratering, yet it was as nothing to the broken carcasses
of the buildings around the kill-plaza, and the firestorms still
raging in them. Pre-dawn skies hung leadenly overhead.

'You would think there would be nothing left to burn, after
all this,' said Vychellan.

'The whole galaxy is afire,' said Achallor. 'The void itself will
ignite should the primarch fail.'

'I hear the tribune thinks otherwise,' said Vychellan.

Achallor turned to look at him. 'It is our division as a species
that dooms us, not the returning Thirteenth,' he said. 'Roboute
Guilliman offers a figurehead that we may rally around. That is
why we do what we must.'

He took one last look over the city. The macro-cathedrum's
spires could be seen jutting over the horizon, and for a moment
Achallor imagined the column of psychic energy Ashmeiln had
described.

'Come, the hours grow short. Battle Group Orphaeus is here,
and Ashmeiln says the bow wave of Fleet Primus' approach
waxes near. The enemy will be recovering as we speak. All
things move in conjunction. The confrontation approaches.
We must leave soon.'

They approached the door leading into the bastion via a small
ornamental spire. Hollow-eyed Mordian sentries stood to attention and offered tired salutes, though a few just stared, frozen by

awe. Achallor passed them and made his way into the building. Here he found many more Mordians, some preparing the bastion defences, others engaged in bringing shrouded corpses out on stretchers. They went into a large hall being used as a makeshift morgue. Traitors were piled by one detail to be carried out by another. Mordians lay in neat lines, each bagged in a royal-blue body shroud. He spotted General Dvorgin standing amongst them.

Achallor had seen countless mortals endure the horrors of war. He could read every nuance of unaugmented human emotions like an open tome. In Luthor Dvorgin he saw weariness beyond measure.

'General,' said Achallor. Dvorgin did not respond at once, but seemed fixed on the rows of bodies on the floor. Achallor frowned. He understood loss, sympathised even, but now was not the moment for the commander of the Astra Militarum forces on Gathalamor to waver.

'General Dvorgin,' repeated Achallor, and this time he hardened his tone.

It was enough. Dvorgin looked at him and offered a salute.

'It is time for us to go,' said Achallor. 'We have contacted the other elements of Imperial resistance on this world and given them their orders. You must liaise with Princess Jessivayne and Colonel-Chieftain Jurgen and begin preparations for your advance immediately. The crusade is arriving. Already a battle group approaches through the void. There will be more coming soon. Whatever the enemy have in that cathedrum must be destroyed. Amalth-Amat and Pontus Varsillian the Many Gloried will fight with you, so that the enemy believe us to be leading the advance, while I, Vychellan and Aswadi take the attack to them through the catacombs.'

'Yes, my lord,' said Dvorgin. 'I will ensure all intelligence that we have on the catacombs is given to you immediately.'

'With your permission, we would also take a guide.'

'A guide?' Dvorgin said. He became a little paler.

'Pathfinder Sergeant Kesh,' said Achallor. 'Canoness Veritas recommended her, she says that Kesh has the most experience under the ground here among your soldiers. I am afraid I took the liberty of approaching her myself, and she has agreed to accompany us. I trust that is acceptable?'

Achallor said these words as a formality, but they were well meant. He understood respect must be given to the existing power structure. There was no reason to offend people if there was no need to, though not all Custodians were so considerate, not even among his own shield host.

He did not expect the general's reaction. Dvorgin stared at him in horror.

Achallor paused. 'General?'

Dvorgin blinked, seeming to come back into himself. The mask of Mordian discipline slipped easily back over his face, but his eyes exhibited such pain.

'I am sorry, my lord. I would say it is simply tiredness, but...' Dvorgin tailed off. He took a sharp breath, and forced himself to look into Achallor's eyes. 'With the greatest respect, Lord Achallor, you ask the impossible.'

Achallor looked down at the man in growing surprise. The general stared back, his eyes dark-rimmed with exhaustion. Achallor could see it had cost him a lot to speak up, but now that he had forced the words out, he would say his piece.

'Your warriors may be suited to such unrelenting operations, my lord, but mine are not. Nor are the Phyroxians. Nor, I suspect, are the Battle Sisters. Mordian discipline is a wonderful resource but we are not indefatigable. My soldiers have seen weeks of constant battle. We have lost more in the few days since your arrival than in the month before. You spend our lives as though they have no other meaning and Throne knows that is your right, but what do we have to show for it? Stretched supply lines, exhausted reserves, and a half-ruined bastion. Now you ask us to march at once upon the enemy's greatest stronghold without food, or rest, or a chance to mourn our fallen, and to send others into certain death below the ground. I condemn my soldiers to a pointless end. To do so would be an inexcusable waste in the sight of the Emperor. Strike me down for my insubordination if you must, my lord, but I speak only the truth as I see it.'

Dvorgin delivered his speech with quiet dignity and, when he had finished, he removed his cap and set it under one arm, revealing the thinning hair of his scalp. Somehow that made him look a decade older, and immeasurably more vulnerable. The silence that settled around the hall was thick and heavy as the prelude to a thunderstorm. All eyes turned to Achallor.

'Are you telling me you will not do it? Do you know who you are speaking to? Do you not think we risk our own lives as well?' Vychellan hissed, taking a step forward. Achallor put out his arm, stopping his comrade. Dvorgin shrank a little, yet stood firm.

'I am not saying that, my lord,' said Dvorgin defiantly. 'You ask the impossible, but I tell you that we will do it. We are Mordians, loyal soldiers of the Emperor, each and every one. We will march while our throats are parched, our bellies empty and limbs are bleeding. We will fight until we die, and we will do it because the Emperor demands it. You command, and I shall obey.'

'Then what is your objection?' asked Achallor.

'There is no objection. I state these facts because I would use them to strengthen my request for a favour, from you who ask so many brave men and women to go to their deaths so your mission might be achieved.'

'And what is that, General Luthor Dvorgin?' Achallor asked.

'Do not fail,' Dvorgin said. Some of the stiffness went from him. 'Some would call it blasphemy to even think you could, but you are flesh and blood, though mighty, so I ask that you do not allow yourselves to be killed, and that you do my warriors the honour of winning quickly. Please. I would dearly like as many of my men as possible to live to see the arrival of Roboute Guilliman.'

Achallor stared down at him. Dvorgin stood his ground, sweat springing from his brow. His eyes twitched when Achallor's gold-clad hands swung in front of him and made the sign of the aquila. He bowed to this brave, tired little man.

'As you command, general,' said Achallor. 'If the Emperor had but a few more men as bold as you, we would not need to be here at all.'

'We leave in two hours,' said Vychellan, rather more frostily. 'You will begin your assault an hour after that.'

'Yes, my lords,' said Dvorgin, and his salute was as crisp as it had ever been.

Chapter Thirty

AN ARMADA APPROACHES

THE WEAPON UNLEASHED

THE TOWER OF PROCLAMATION

There were Imperial ships coming to Gathalamor, the first in an armada to conquer the galaxy.

Songs rose up around the osseous barrel of the weapon, the screams of sacrificial victims shrieking through the deep plainsong of eighty-eight Word Bearers. A choir of mortals accompanied them, making the air shake with their devotions. Vitae flowed down the weapon's barrel from the corpses held in frames above it, soaking into ancient bone. Tenebrus looked on approvingly. The air was charged with baleful power. Behind the skin of reality, a presence writhed in torment. The cardinal of yore, summoned again, the spiritual resonance of his apostasy put to proper use. Roboute Guilliman was on his way, and the fate of humanity hung in the balance.

The moment to give Bucharis' Gift had come.

The last captive's screams finished abruptly. Kar-Gatharr stepped back from the mutilated body, and handed his knife to Tharador Yheng. He took the cloth she offered, and wiped his hands.

'It is done,' he said. 'Bucharis' Gift is consecrated to the pantheon. It awaits your command, Lord Tenebrus.'

He said the words in time to the music filling the cathedral dome.

'Prepare to bestow the cardinal's beneficence,' Tenebrus said. He stood near the obelisk. His eyes glinted beneath his cowl. His voice was soft as the flesh of a drowned corpse, yet it carried to every corner of the vast space.

High Magos Vech Xyrax stood at the obelisk's other side, his compound eyes regarding Kar-Gatharr from the stitched nightmare of dead flesh, leather and pipes he called a face. The high magos' augmetic limbs twitched beneath the robe that covered his bulk. His eagerness to see his machines unleashed was clear.

The great bell in the dome tolled. It was a signal, long awaited, and as its echoes rolled away a sharp expectancy fell across the chamber. Xyrax's emaciated acolytes scurried into action, spinning valve wheels and flicking banks of switches fashioned from finger bones.

'Target selection required,' Xyrax said.

Kar-Gatharr intoned simple spatial coordinates that, when sung thusly, carried the power of the warp. These were input into instruments where ectoplasmic faces writhed behind the glass. Motors engaged, elevating the barrel. The turntable rotated the weapon a quarter-turn, and with a loud clank the weapon came to its bearing.

'Prime soul siphons. Begin excitation of corposant storage,' Xyrax said. These last operations were carried out by barechested men in black hoods.

A rasping noise rose from the base of the gun. The bone began to radiate an unclean heat that made Kar-Gatharr sweat under his armour.

'Weapon ready,' said Xyrax.

His smile widening, Tenebrus twisted the ring around his finger and then turned to the obelisk.

'This world was a locus of faith for the False Emperor. Billions upon billions have let out their tears upon its barren ground. Their unrewarded faith is gathered in the warp. Now is the time to excise this burden of lies, to cut out the black cancer of false belief. Let us release those condemned by the Emperor. I say to you all, you suffering masses, you lied-to, you dead, let your madness and hate serve the true gods now.'

Xyrax ground forward on his armoured tracks. Swaying mecha-dendrites and flesh-tentacles slithered from beneath his robes. They mated with sockets across the obelisk. A high whine emanated from the machine. Silver-green light pulsed faster and faster through the mechanisms.

'Fire,' Xyrax said.

With a flourish, Tenebrus raised the ring, displaying it to his gods, then brought his hand down and slid it into the dripping cavity set into the obelisk.

A moment of sublime Chaos followed, where all thought was extinguished, and Kar-Gatharr was at one with the primordial energies of the immaterium.

Then the world split, and pain flew out, true and deadly as a spear.

Dawn's light crept over the Thunderhawk flying low through the ruins of Imprezentia. Broken spires clawed the sky on every side.

Achallor, Vychellan and Aswadi stood within the Thunderhawk's troop bay, riding out the turbulence of the craft's passage with subtle shifts of their weight. Imelda Veritas and the remainder of their strike team – some twenty Battle Sisters, Sergeant Kesh and two other mortal troopers – occupied folding seats.

Jinking around the remains of a pillar, the ship dropped into a trench almost the rival of the Canyon of Countless Blessings. It had perhaps been a sub-street cloister opened by bombardment.

It was a dangerous road and a mortal pilot would have dashed themselves on the sides, but Space Marines were above such failings, and it offered a route below the level of enemy scans.

Achallor watched his helmplate readings intently. Should he catch the slightest sign of enemy movements he would order them to break off at once. They were too close now to risk detection. If spotted, they would find their target flooded with traitors.

He had thought that he and his comrades should land and make the final approach on foot. Yet Ashmeiln had told him that time was of the essence. Every minute wasted would carry a prohibitive cost in Imperial lives.

Their destination was a once mighty edifice. Orbital fire had toppled the Tower of Proclamation at the start of the invasion, but enough of it remained for it to be impressive, and its broken base still jutted over the ruined skyline. The tower was perhaps six miles from the macro-cathedrum, whose mountainous shoulders hunched upon the horizon.

The trench sides smoothed off to an area that was supposed to be open to the air, and a wide canal appeared. For the first time on the world Achallor saw a significant amount of greenery. The Thunderhawk dropped low, jets sending up a glittering spray and buffeting the trees lining the water.

Across Gathalamor, Imperial forces rose up, guided by Achallor and Vychellan's plans. The more distant conflicts would be in full flow by now, for Achallor had ordered the other enclaves to attack before Dvorgin's advance on the cathedrum began; a diversion from the diversion. Not for the first time, Achallor wished for an orbital relay to show him the strategic picture. But they could risk no communications. Instead he scanned the horizon with his own keen senses. Smoke rose off Imperial positions to the south, and the sound of pounding artillery echoed from some distant place. To the far north-east, up towards

Gathalamor Exegis, where the enemy fleet were safe from the void-port guns, the clouds were churned by titanic ruby beams stabbing down like the sword of some wrathful god.

As the shadow of the tower fell over them the Thunderhawk slowed suddenly, jets blasting on reverse, and the landing cycle began.

'Destination in two minutes,' the pilot informed him.

Achallor turned on close-vox with a thought.

'Groupmaster Kseyvorn is impetuous. He will attack at once. We have only a few hours before he is here,' said Achallor. 'Perhaps less.'

Vychellan grunted. 'I was wondering how much longer our luck could hold. As it is, I expected this craft to be shot down within minutes of taking to the air. It is hardly our most subtle infiltration.'

'Speed is of more import than secrecy,' replied Achallor.

'The Emperor offers us His divine protection in this moment of need,' said Imelda Veritas. 'I and my Sisters pray for His beneficence to continue.'

'May it extend to us all,' said Achallor softly.

Vychellan's helm tilted towards him in disapproval at his words.

'Expediency is the sharpest blade,' said Achallor in response. 'In action there is hope.'

He brought up a map based on ancient charts, annotated by Kesh. An aqua-tunnel led most of the way to their target. It was this they would take. He sent the schema to the party, highlighting the route.

Vychellan surveyed Achallor's runemarks as they flashed on his strategic cartograph.

'Daring, decisive and glorious,' he said, and Achallor was glad to hear his old friend's smile resurface.

The pilot's voice issued from the voxmitter set into the troop bay's wall.

'Canoness, lord Custodians, we are reading power spikes ahead.'

'Where?' asked Achallor.

'Emanating from the macro-cathedrum, my lord. There's a...
Throne!'

The Thunderhawk gave a tremendous lurch as though it had
been kicked, the engines coughed, then it dropped like a stone.
Sparks erupted from overloaded power junctions. Everything
shook and Achallor heard a rustling hiss like waves rolling up
a shingle shore. A pale, poisonous light flooded the troop bay
as the sound rose to a roar.

'Brace yourselves!' shouted Aswadi.

Then the ship crashed with tremendous force.

Chapter Thirty-One

A DELAY

GHEISTS

FAITH'S SWORD

Princess Jessivayne was in the vox-uplink shrine with Sheane and Lady Nimue when the sky turned to white fire. A gaggle of adepts were busy in the room, readying the attack on the cathedrum. Though she had wished to leave an hour earlier, Dvorgin had his way and they delayed to wait for more men to join them. All turned to look as a sickly silver-green glow filled the room.

'What in the Emperor's name is that?' asked Sheane as they hastened to the false-oculus. Bodies shifted aside for Jessivayne as she strode her servo-frame to the screens and pressed one hand to the plex-glass.

'You know what it is, cousin, what it must be,' she said with dawning horror. 'The shield-captain was right. This is the weapon of the enemy.'

From the cathedrum across the city glowed a pillar of unnatural light. Its glare silhouetted the teetering shrine-spires and hollow-eyed hab-stacks, the tattered strings of prayer banners, creaking ossuaries and shattered domes.

'Unclean,' hissed one of the Battle Sisters, making the sign of the aquila.

As they watched, the column swelled larger, wider, higher.

'It is an unholy star born before us,' said Jessivayne. 'What have the traitors unleashed? Oh Emperor, let us not be proven weak!'

The column of witch-light pulsed and a shockwave rolled out from it, racing across the cityscape to topple weakened towers.

'Get back from the screens!' yelled Sheane, spinning himself in front of Jessivayne to shield her body with his. The shockwave rushed towards the Blessed Bastion, raising a wave of cinders. It slammed into the bastion with punishing force. The walls shook. The panels making up the false-oculus spider-webbed with cracks but for a miracle they did not shatter, and nor did their images fail.

'We are safe here, cousin,' said Jessivayne as she shook off Sheane. 'You are no more use to the lance riddled with shards than am I.' She was grateful, nonetheless, and his quick smile told her he knew as much.

'Warning – vox disruption,' blared one of the vox-servitors from its station. 'Severe atmospheric interference. Contact lost with the *Radiance*.'

'Warning – vox disruption,' chorused two more servitors, and then all of them were blaring their alarm calls.

'Warning – vox disruption.'

'Warning... warn.... warrrrrraaaagghhhhh!' the servitors' announcements distorted, their voices warping and transforming into wails and shrieks. Many of the adepts and sacristans cowered. The Battle Sisters raised their weapons, muttering prayers. Jessivayne glanced up as the lumens flickered, several bulbs whining bright then bursting with dull pops. She felt the hairs rising on the back of her neck and knew in that instant that they were in mortal peril.

'Nobles, draw your oighen!' she commanded, reaching back and fetching out her longsword from its scabbard. She thumbed the activation rune in the weapon's hilt, causing blue light to shimmer along its blade. Shadows crawled about the chamber's edge. Another shockwave rattled the screens and caused the servitors to wail all the louder. Smoke was issuing from their eyes.

A piercing scream cut through the gibbering of the servitors. Jessivayne spun to see a young adept wrestling with a being that defied comprehension. She had an impression of clawed hands that squirmed up out of the floor, grabbing handfuls of the adept's robe to haul itself higher. Flames danced about the thing, flaring silver, red and black. An indistinct head emerged, its face a skull. Then Lady Nimue was lunging, bringing her oighen down. The blade wailed, the microchannels etched into the shaft making it sing the war dirge of Kamidar.

To Jessivayne's shock, the weapon passed straight through the glowing thing and bit into the decking. The adept screamed. Nimue cursed, pulled back her blade and stabbed. This time the oighen bit home, piercing the apparition through its skull. As it fell the gheist disintegrated, leaving smears of reeking slime.

'Emperor preserve us,' said one of the priests. As though his words had been a signal, a mass of the spectres erupted from the floor and walls.

Pandemonium reigned.

Gibbering servitors rose from their stations, eyes glowing silver, joints leaking slime. Adepts panicked as spectral figures grasped at them with talons or sunk phantom teeth into their flesh. Gunshots rang out as Battle Sisters and Mordians discharged their weapons. Some shots struck the apparitions, but others passed through them. A priest was blown backwards, disembowelled by a bolt-shell. A Mordian fell to another's las-fire.

'No guns!' roared Jessivayne.

It was a nightmarish fight, the lumens flickering, writhing

bodies all about her. Her longsword was far from the ideal weapon for such a press. With every blow there was the danger that the blade would pass straight through its intended target and strike an ally by mistake.

'Foul spawn of damnation!' bellowed a Battle Sister to Jessivayne's right. 'Benighted and unholy spirits, may you be purged in the holy light of the God-Emperor!' The warrior fought her way into a knot of writhing gheists with nothing more than her armoured gauntlets, yet Jessivayne watched with amazement as the Battle Sister's every blow struck, and scattered the stuff of the ghosts.

'Pray,' Jessivayne yelled, staggering as a body slammed into her from behind. Only her servo-frame spared her from being spilled onto her face. 'Pray as you strike them! Make faith your weapon!

'I call to He who watches over me!' Jessivayne said, spinning her oighen over her head into a gheist clad in the vestments of a priest. 'Oh, holy Emperor, see now the travails of your faithful!' she bellowed. 'Let your light be upon them, and within them, and let it shine forth that their enemies might be blinded by its righteousness!'

Hate twisted the face of the phantom as it writhed on her sword point, but as she shouted out her devotions, it changed; the light flickered, the expression became more human, one of horror and confusion. She dragged her oighen down, feeling resistance as if it were embedded in flesh, cutting deep into its torso, and the ghost shredded with a despairing wail. A surge of the things came at her, their expressions tormented, their bodies burning in spectral fires. She met them with her blade, and found a Sister of the Argent Shroud fighting to her left and Lady Nimue to her right.

Prayer echoed through the shrine as the Imperial commanders took up the words of the faith. Children's catechisms, warriors' hymns, whatever they could call to mind. Immediately, there was an effect, and gradually, bloodily, they banished the tide of spectres, until a moment came that Jessivayne looked about and saw only the living within the shrine. Many dead were sprawled upon the floor. She herself felt the fiery pain of talon-slashes down her right cheek, though she couldn't remember receiving them, and her left arm ached where it had been pummelled in the crush.

When the shrine's doors banged open, every warrior present turned and raised guns and blades. But no more foes were there, for it was General Luthor Dvorgin who came through them, a harrowed band of Mordians at his back.

'What by the Throne was that?' he said.

'The weapon of the enemy,' said Jessivayne. 'The thing Lord Achallor warned us of.'

He and Jessivayne shared a look of mutual understanding.

'Can we raise the shield-captain?' Dvorgin asked. Jessivayne gestured to the servitors and their burnt-out consoles.

'Not from here, not for a while. What of your own vox-sets?'

Master Voxman Yenko was amongst Dvorgin's group. He set down his master vox and spun the dials, one hand clamped to his earpiece, and shook his head.

'Whatever the enemy have done, it has thoroughly disrupted the vox-waves,' he said. 'There's nothing but gibbering and moaning. It's fading though. I'll make contact with him as soon as I can.'

'Keep trying, but be cautious,' ordered Dvorgin. 'We don't know what that was. It may manifest again.'

Yenko saluted and bent to his task.

'We were too damned slow to stop it. Too cautious,' said Jessivayne. 'We should be in the field.'

Her statement irritated Dvorgin. 'With respect, princess, if we had left an hour ago as you wished, we would have been barely halfway to the macro-cathedrum by now,' he said, straightening his cap. 'We would only have been closer to the epicentre of whatever power the Archenemy unleashed. For all we know, our choice to organise first was moved by the hand of the Emperor Himself that we might live to fight on.'

'Perhaps you are right,' said Jessivayne, but she couldn't believe it. She pictured her mother's proud expression on the day she had set off. Her queen had placed her trust in her. Jessivayne felt as though she had betrayed that trust with overly cautious actions.

She walked to the cracked screens and stared out over Gathalamor Imprezentia towards the cathedrum. The evil light was fading from the skies.

'They will unleash that power again,' she said.

They looked to the heavens. 'What about the crusade?' said Dvorgin. 'What if we were never the intended target? Did you see the energy beam? Most of it went skywards. What hit us was backwash. Yenko, try to get confirmation. Order the platoons to wait for orders to advance, I want some certainty before we–'

'No!' shouted Jessivayne. 'No more delays!'

Silence fell. Dvorgin looked shocked.

'I am sorry?' he said warningly.

'If they have hit the fleet, what then? If we cannot raise Shield-Captain Achallor, what then? Do we hold back from our attack for fear no help will come? Do we cower? We are the righteous servants of the God-Emperor! His Custodians themselves have given us their command. We came to this blessed world to purge the taint of Chaos and by the light of the Golden Throne we shall do just that!'

Murmurs rolled through the group. Faces shadowed by the grey light spilling from the screens stared at her, wanting, *needing* to act.

'We must attack as planned!' cried Jessivayne, and murmurs turned to shouts of agreement. 'We will take this fight to the foe. We shall smash down their doors, drag them out into the cold bastards to the sword!'

More shouts of agreement. A scattered handful of cheers.

'We are ready to depart,' said Dvorgin. She could see the cautious side of him warring with the officer who relished front-line battle. 'But this weapon changes everything.'

'It changes nothing,' Jessivayne said. 'We weather the storm as best we can, and all those who fall do so with faith in their hearts and the Emperor's name on their lips. We must show faith, Dvorgin. That is what will defeat these tortured ghosts. Faith will bring us victory.'

Dvorgin considered for a moment longer, and then offered her a salute.

'As you suggest, princess. You are correct. We have our orders. We have our faith. We shall advance on the macro-cathedrum at once. No more delays.'

'My lady,' Voxman Phryke informed Sangar. 'We are in good range to attempt a secure hololithic communication.'

'About time,' Sangar said. 'Send the hail. Prepare the device.'

Her throne dipped low to the ground and Sangar got out. A pair of cherubim, tall and armour-clad, floated down from their roosts in the ceiling. They looked upon her with white, pupilless eyes set in wooden faces. Their jaws unhinged, and from them protruded lithic band scanners that played light upon her body. A third and a fourth angel came down from on high, their sword arms mechanically cranking back, revealing projection lenses in the pommels.

'I have confirmation from Lord Kseyvorn's command that he is ready.'

Sangar straightened her uniform. She'd taken extra care over her appearance for the conference, and had her hair wound about her head in a tight braid. She cleared her throat.

'Engage lithocast.'

The angels scanning her parted, allowing her to see in front. The second pair hummed, and the figure of the seated Lord Kseyvorn was painted onto the air, line by line, until he was a seemingly solid being with a faint luminescence about him. He was a tall man, with a long nose, and strong jaw. His skin was almost as dark as the wood of the angels, and gleamed as if polished. He wore his hair in long ringlets, freshly oiled, and his beard was turned into one long curl. His uniform had the sober look that everything stemming from the primarch's will seemed to have, but he wore over it a broad sash of cloth of silver, with his many battle honours there displayed.

As soon as his image was complete, the groupmaster began to speak.

'*Lady Sangar,*' he said. The gentle buzz under his voice took a little from the projection's verisimilitude, but to all purposes it was as if he was actually there. '*Would not vox have sufficed?*'

'I can't stand the lag,' she said. 'And it's too dangerous. The enemy have been playing hell with communications in this system since we arrived. They would have intercepted and heard whatever we exchanged.'

Kseyvorn smiled. '*Let them listen. I see precious few enemy assets in this system. We've all been apprehensive about what we might find here, now I arrive to discover a fragment of a broken Legion. We shall crush them in a matter of hours, before the primarch comes.*'

Sangar's misgivings grew. She could see the glory hunger in Kseyvorn's eyes. He wanted to be the man to liberate the warp nexus.

'There is a threat as the xenos suggested,' she said. 'Lord Achallor is dealing with it as we speak. It would be best to retreat to the system's edge to wait out the result. As I understand the situation, the arrival of the Custodians has stabilised may be so bold.'

'*Bold to ask after stating,*' he said. '*I'll give you that. My strategos give another opinion, that if we hold back we risk allowing the Iron Warriors and their allies an escape, such as they are. If we move now, we shall remove their stain from the galaxy forever.*'

'My lord, please, if you attack into the face of this threat, you could be in grave peril.'

'*And what is this threat?*'

'Unknown, a weapon of some kind,' she said. 'But Lord Achallor is highly concerned. Our empyric readings are well into the highest threat ratings across the board. My psykers give me nothing but evil news. Whatever they have, it is a weapon of the warp, and therefore unpredictable. It may be nothing, but if the attack on Terra and the opening of the Rift have taught us anything, it is that we must be prepared for the worst.'

Kseyvorn's elegant nostrils arched. '*If it is as powerful as you fear, then we are in peril anyway. We have come early. I take this as a sign of the Emperor's will. He moves us as pieces are moved upon the regicide board. We are meant to be here. I will not have you, though honoured and highly placed as you are among His servants, to gainsay the will of the Master of Mankind. We advance. Follow or do not, as your own conscience dictates. It is time the enemy relearned the power of the Imperium. This conference is–*'

He was interrupted by an urgent ringing from the *Radiance*.

'What is that?' Sangar asked.

'The astropathicum, my lady,' one of Phryke's underlings reported.

'Answer them,' she said.

The woman hit the receive button and they were met by a barrage of screams. Over them came a voice, urgent and alarmed. Sangar recognised it as belonging to Adept Osori, one of Ashmeiln's attendants.

'My lady, our astropaths are in seizure. Two have manifested psychic phenomena and the psy-baffles won't hold long under this pressure. My lady, what are your orders? I fear they have become unstable and present a clear danger to the ship. Do we have permission to euthanise?'

'Shipmistress, hails from the battle group,' called Phryke, his tone alarmed. 'They report sudden seizures amongst their astropaths and Navigators. They are requesting immediate intelligence on the phenomenon.'

'Lord Kseyvorn?'

The groupmaster looked off to the side, conferring with a man only part of whose face Sangar could see.

'The same here. A psychic attack? Is this the weapon they have developed? Raise all voids,' Kseyvorn said.

'I don't think this is it,' said Sangar, her misgivings growing.

'Void shields up,' her Master Scutum reported.

'Shipmistress, I'm reading immense energy spikes coming from Gathalamor,' reported VenShellen.

'Empyric readings are high,' said Choorvi. 'Psy-auguries show multispectral emissions, crossing physical and psychical energy ranges.'

'Get the voids up!' Kseyvorn was shouting. His hololith buzzed and broke into a jagged pattern, before snapping back.

'Specifics, Miss VenShellen. What in the Emperor's name are we dealing with here?' asked Sangar.

'It's... it's like nothing I've ever seen,' VenShellen gasped.

'Oculus!' croaked Osmor, pointing at the ship's viewport. 'What *is* that?'

Sangar looked. The point of Gathalamor flashed brightly. As she watched a sickening glow laid itself across space, a broad stripe which reminded her strangely of a road. Lines of white fire raced around it. Madly churning energies filled the black, and alarms shrilled through the bridge.

'*Group, break formation, break formation!*' Kseyvorn commanded, before his hololithic presence was disrupted and the angels projecting it fell down sparking to the floor.

The glow on Sangar's oculus grew so bright that she could barely look.

The energy flare hit the lead elements of Battle Group Orphaeus, first striking the *Lord Sewar*, dispelling the grand cruiser's shields with insulting ease and breaking the craft's spine. The *Lord Sewar* arched its back like an angry felid, lazy plumes of fire billowing from within. Moments later, saviour pods and drifting wreckage fell away from the dying ship into the void, but they were swallowed by the beam. It spread and took the prow of an escort craft. The smaller ship shuddered as ferocious explosions rippled along its length then blew out its engines. Another in the same squadron heeled violently to starboard, thrusters burning so hard it threatened to break its own back, before its engine stack went out, and it drifted, lights flickering.

The *Radiance* was at the edge of the wash of light. Sangar didn't think that would matter.

'Close the oculus, get us clear of the fleet!' she shouted. 'Voxman Phryke, priority alpha warning to all Imperial void elements. Tell them to break formation! In the Emperor's name, tell them to get clear!'

The shutters squealed towards closure. The armaglass suddenly cracked with a sound like a gunshot. Sangar threw up her hand as breaking screens showered her with stinging fragments.

'Oculus holding. Shutters closing in three, two, one,' said Osmor. The shutters boomed closed over the fractured glass. 'Closed. Bridge secure. Atmospheric pressure maintained.'

'Miss VenShellen, analysis,' Sangar barked. But when she turned to see, VenShellen had fallen back from her station, her face a mask of blood. Across the bridge, Voxman Phryke gave a piercing scream and wrenched his headset off with shaking hands. Sangar heard the dreadful cacophony of voices spilling from the device. Phryke staggered up from his station, data-tethers snapping from socket-ports and blood drizzling from his ears. His eyes rolled up and he collapsed with a groan.

'Get a medicae on the command deck!' shouted Sangar.

A din of gibbering voices issued from voxmitters all over the bridge. It sounded like damnation might, like all those who had sinned against the Emperor crying out in pain.

'Helm, why are we not under way?' she yelled over the rising cacophony of voices. The armsmen were tearing off their helms and hurling them aside, raising their shotguns but unsure where to target them.

'Enginarium report massive power fluctuations in the real-space engines!' Helm Adept Pheng shouted back.

'Cautionary – Helm Adept Pheng is correct,' blared Kzarch, vox-amplifying his voice to be heard over the screams. 'The machine-spirits are in torment. Shipmistress, I do not believe that we can achieve sufficient motive power to escape the beam effect.'

'Someone, anyone with eyes on a working auspex, tell me that the battle group is holding!' ordered Sangar. The lumens failed, blinking out to leave only the light spilling from cracked, static-furred vid-screens. The wailing grew deafening. Sangar went back to her throne and sought the saviour chest beneath it. There were chem-lights in it, and she felt the instinctive need for light. It was getting colder. Her breath billowed before her in a cloud and her skin goose-pimpled.

And then there was light – not the clean, mechanical light of the bridge lumens, but a leprous glow that spilled from everywhere. Sangar got a hand to the saviour chest as the first shotgun blast sounded, cutting through the wall of wailing like a thunderclap. She got a chem-light out, its feeble blue glow doing nothing to dispel the horror she witnessed.

There were figures dragging themselves through the hull into the ship. They were human in shape, but exaggerated in form, as if all the hateful aspects of humanity were accentuated, and the gentler elements dissolved. Their eyes were blank white orbs in skeletal faces. Their malformed teeth gnashed around black tongues. As Sangar stared she took in the vestments of Imperial preachers, the rust-rotted armour of Battle Sisters, the plain garb of pilgrims. Most horrifying of all, she saw that every last spectral figure was wreathed in cold flames that ate away at their flesh and, she was sure, goaded them with their agonies. These were the faithful, yet they were not at peace, they were not bathed in the light of the Emperor. Far from it.

Hundreds of them flooded aboard, tangled together into compound horrors. The crew were firing. Some shots tore at the ectoplasmic stuff of the gheists. Many more simply passed straight through as though they weren't there. These wrought havoc on the bridge. Sangar saw Osmor plucked from his feet by one such wild shot, his chest torn to bloody rags. The gheists writhed over one another in a gnashing, clawing tide, and though Sangar's crew struggled to harm them, the maddened spectres suffered no such disadvantage. The damned of Gathalamor crashed down upon her devoted crew. Talons tore through robes and flesh; rotted teeth sunk into the unprotected skin; clawing hands wrapped around throats, blistering and burning with unnatural fire even as they strangled.

Somewhere deeper into the ship something exploded with a muffled roar. The artificial gravity of her beloved *Radiance* faltered.

'Emperor, protect your faithful servants!' cried Sangar as she brandished the silver aquila she wore about her neck. It did nothing to ward off the wave of gheists cresting over her, and she saw that many of them wore aquilas of their own.

She closed her eyes and waited for the end.

Abruptly it was over. The gheists faded to nothing. The wailing stopped.

'Emperor save us,' said Ebele Sangar. She looked about her, hardly able to believe she was alive, but the ghosts were gone.

Of her three dozen command crew, more than half were dead. Others stared in shock. Hardened veterans were rendered mute. It wasn't just the apparitions or the violence. Sangar felt as if her soul itself were poisoned.

She went to the controls of her throne, and opened ship-wide vox.

'All off-watch bridge crew attend immediately. Section commanders give me casualty reports,' she said. 'Kzarch!' she shouted. 'Tech-adepts to provide an immediate estimation of damage. Do you hear me?'

'Affirmative, my lady,' said the magos. He had come through relatively unscathed, but for the first time, Sangar heard doubt in his voice. She opened hails to the rest of the fleet.

'Battle Group Orphaeus, please respond. Lord Kseyvorn, do you live?'

Her surviving crew were getting up, attending to the wounded.

'Lord Kseyvorn?'

She waited the few seconds a reply would take to cross the void by vox, but only the cosmic sleet of particles hissed back.

'Lord Kseyvorn?

Some semblance of order was being restored. Someone opened a near-scan holo of their surroundings.

'Lord Kse–'

She stopped halfway through his name. She could not believe what she was seeing.

Battle Group Orphaeus, a force grand enough to conquer a subsector, was all but destroyed. Ships floated, reactors out, their formations scattered. Energy markers blandly indicated where reactors had blown, leaving nothing but radioactive dust.

Damage indicators tagged every ship within a band a thousand miles across. Only those at the edges had escaped damage. They were precious few.

She pressed her vox button again. 'Lord Kseyvorn, do you hear me?'

Finally, the vox buzzed, and a different voice answered her.

'Lady Sangar, it is good to see the Radiance *lives.'*

She knew that voice. It filled her with dread as much as hope.

'You will fall in with the remnants of the battle group. The weapon is everything Lord Guilliman feared. There is nothing to be gained by hiding. We must attack immediately.'

'Yes, my lord,' she said. 'I trust Shield-Captain Achallor will perform his duty.'

'As much faith as I have in Achallor, I prefer not to leave our fates to his actions alone. I, Tribune Colquan, have spoken, Lady Sangar. Fall into formation.'

Sergeant Kesh blinked blood from her eyes and found herself dazzled by a pale silver light. She recognised sorcery when she saw it, and it sent a shock of adrenaline through her body. She tried to rise but she was pinned. A plasteel panel had folded itself around her restraint cradle, trapping her near the floor. The glow of flames and emergency lumens reached her, yet still the silver light, though feeble, was somehow brighter. She slapped at the cradle release, but the mechanism was broken, and she was left hanging there.

'Help!' she called weakly, coughing on rising smoke. 'Help me!'

A glowing form rose up through the buckled deck, a phantom, she could only think, its cadaverous face contorted with secret agonies and flesh burning in fire that gave no heat, but which gave out a light the same silvery green as that from outside. Hands on bone-thin arms reached out, locked about her neck, and squeezed.

Kesh instinctively swiped her hands at the thing, trying to grab it. Her alarm increased as her hands passed straight through it. Brutal cold seeped into her flesh. Her vision greyed at the edges, the centre filled with the phantom's bulging white eyes.

There came a roar of chainsword teeth alarmingly close to Kesh's face, and the phantom disintegrated with a silent shriek. An armoured hand reached around and mashed at the buckle on Kesh's restraint harness until it gave, and she fell to the floor, where she gasped for breath and wiped stinking slime from her face.

Canoness Imelda Veritas stood over her, her chainsword chugging in one fist. She held the other hand out to Kesh.

'Sergeant Kesh,' she said. Kesh grasped her wrist gratefully and allowed the canoness to haul her to her feet. 'You yet live. This is good news.'

'What happened?' she croaked.

'Outside,' said Imelda Veritas, already turning away. 'See for yourself.'

Kesh heard the thump of bolter fire beyond the flames, accompanied by a cacophony of wailing. She had lost her fusil but she had her pistol still at her hip, and she drew it, taking comfort from its familiar weight.

Not all her companions had been so lucky in the crash. Several armoured forms in the silver of the Argent Shroud lay pinned amongst the wreckage. Of the two troopers she had brought with her, she saw only blood and a single hand poking from mangled metal. She looked away, following Veritas through the wreck, and exited through a side hatch blown off by its emergency bolts, emerging onto a slope of rubble. The Space Marines flying the transport had managed to guide the craft down more or less in one piece, but a glance at the crushed front section told her she would never get the chance to thank them.

A little way down the rubble slope, a mass of spectral figures pushed up towards the crash site. Holding them back was a thin half-circle of Battle Sisters and Custodians. Bolt-shells hammered down into the spectres. Blades sliced into those that got too close. They were already fading, their advance petering out, until the blades and bolts had nothing to fell.

'Why couldn't I hurt them?' Kesh asked.

'Faith, sergeant. His full miraculous might is manifest within we, His brides and His guardians. Next time, pray harder.'

'What are they?' she asked.

'Tell me what you saw, my child, and answer your own questions.'

Veritas and Kesh scrambled down the last few yards of scree and joined the others, now warily scanning the empty landscape.

'They were... ghosts,' she swallowed. 'They looked like us. They were preachers, pilgrims...' breathed Kesh.

'There you have it. These tormented souls are the dead of Gathalamor.'

Kesh felt a chill run though her. She thought of the thousands of miles of catacombs, the endless myriad shrines and fanes, ossuaries and burial sites that formed the planet's geological strata. She pictured again the empty niches and broken tombs she had seen down there in the dark. She thought of the promise of the Emperor's light. Wasn't it true, what happened to them after they died?

'I fear, my lords, that we understand better now what the weapon might be,' said Veritas, addressing the group. 'Madness, torment, and unwilling servitude for every pious soul Gathalamor has ever known. Bucharis' revenge upon the world that spurned him, and our enemy's weapon – denying the dead the rest they deserve.'

'They must be targeting the fleet,' said Achallor.

'Could they hit it, with that?' Kesh asked.

'There was a beam with the likeness of an anti-orbital weapon, though wholly profane in sort,' said the other Custodian, Menticulous Aswadi. 'I saw it strike for the sky. We must assume the fleet is their target.'

'They live or they do not by the strength of their faith,' said Imelda Veritas. 'There is nothing that we can achieve for our God-Emperor by languishing here waiting for the tormented dead to come for us again. We have our duty still, and we are but miles from the objective.'

The macro-cathedrum was close enough that they could see the streamers of supernatural energies trailing from its statues and the flickers of corposant dancing about its spires.

'We have a little luck left,' said Vychellan. 'Sergeant Kesh lives, and she knows the way.' He pressed a button on his gauntlet, bringing up a small cartolith. Kesh saw a rune marking their position, winking steadily only a small distance from one of the ingress points she had chosen for them.

'What about those we left behind us?' she asked, her voice so small and impure surrounded by these paragons. 'Do you think they live?'

'We can but pray for their safety. Many of my Sisters remained with them, and the faith of the Knights of Ironhold is strong,' said Imelda Veritas, and Kesh took comfort from her words. 'If any could endure this disaster and strike back against the heretic foe, it is they.'

'As Harostese puts it, let us not wait until the grass grows green beneath our heels,' said Vychellan. 'Let us venture down into the catacombs where the massed dead of millennia lie in wait, now unquiet and baying for our blood. Really, Marcus, this can only end well.'

No one else shared his humour.

'The Emperor protects, Lord Vychellan,' said Veritas serenely.

'He will need to,' said Achallor. 'Sergeant Kesh, lead the way.'

Kesh nodded. The sky was black and it had become cold, and she was glad she'd kept her coat and hat when they crashed. She patted at her equipment belt as she had done a score of times before venturing down below: canteen, ration blocks, holster, knife, rope, rebreather and stablight. All was in place.

'Please, my lords, this way. I do not think we have much time left.'

'We are in agreement there,' said Aswadi.

As ash fell like snow from the skies and vivid aurorae streaked the troposphere, Kesh led the way, three golden heroes and a handful of Sisters following her steps. All hint of the coming day was smothered. *The last hour has come,* the general often said the day before a battle. Victory had always followed. She thought it might not this time.

She tried to be brave for these gods among men, and the Sisters who honoured their father. She thought of Dvorgin, of how he'd always been kind to her, though it led to unpleasant jests from her comrades. Darker thoughts surfaced, of failure, leading the Custodians awry, and perishing under the ground, where her bones would rot with a trillion others and her ghost would be hurled screaming at the sky, but she crushed them. Kesh would not lose herself to despair. She would fight, and push forward, lead these holy beings to the place they must go, and punish the heretics who had despoiled this world, for that was the Mordian way.

Whatever came after, if anything, well, she would face that in due course.

'One impossible thing at a time,' she said under her breath.

Chapter Thirty-Two

THE TRUTH OF THE NOW

FIRES OF VICTORY

A NEED FOR LIFE

Spectral energies roared about the macro-cathedrum. Poison-ous aurorae streaked the skies. Yet within Tenebrus' sanctum it was still, the fury of the weapon unable to penetrate its cold gloom. Kar-Gatharr stood a pace away from the font, Yheng as ever by his side. Tenebrus stood to his left, Magos Xyrax directly across from him. About the chamber's edge, the shades shifted restively.

Tenebrus dabbled his deformed fingers in the pool, calling forth an image of Gathalamor as it would appear if one could see its soul, as a green-tinged orb of bone. Silver-green striated the planet's skies, shifting like the ocean tides. Those same energies stretched up from the planet in a fading column that had to be thousands of miles across and that reached forever into space.

The font's view shifted, showing Imperial warships floating broken in the void. Further out drifted yet more hulks. Kar-Gatharr counted a dozen bright gleams of light where ships still lived with some number of smaller, dimmer motes drifting aimlessly about and away from them. The wrecked vessels far outnumbered the whole.

'Is this a scrying, or do we see the truth of the now?' Kar-Gatharr asked.

'We see through the eyes of the *Paracyte*,' answered the high magos, his blare jarringly loud in the sanctum. 'A fusion of Tenebrus' gifts and the Omnissiah's knowledge. You see the Imperial fleet as it is. They are dead.' The words echoed flatly.

'Bucharis' Gift is terrible indeed,' said Kar-Gatharr.

'Analysis supports this conclusion,' replied the high magos.

'What was the effect here, on Gathalamor? How it did touch our forces?' Kar-Gatharr asked.

'I am notified of sixteen separate spectral breaches throughout the macro-cathedrum,' said Xyrax. 'Casualty reports amongst our non-legionary forces are pending, but projections are acceptable. The light cruiser *Talons of Archuthis* did not leave the zone of effect before the weapon's activation and was subsequently depopulated. This weapon is tremendously powerful, but it is indiscriminate and therefore hazardous.'

Kar-Gatharr frowned at Tenebrus, attempting to pin the sorcerer's dark eyes with his own. Then slowly, grudgingly, he smiled. Despite his distaste for both company and surroundings, Kar-Gatharr felt triumphant.

'You are pleased, yes?' said Tenebrus.

'I am. Your weapon worked,' he said. 'How sweet is the corpse-lackeys' suffering.'

'Then perhaps we can let our enmity burn lower, while the fires of victory burn high?'

'We have not yet won,' said Kar-Gatharr brusquely. 'There are more ships on the way.'

'Many more ships,' said Xyrax.

'If this is but the vanguard of Guilliman's fleet, then...'

'Disaster.' Tenebrus' ghoulish face was unreadable, half lost in the shadow of his hood. 'But the weapon works. We have our chance at Guilliman. What of the enemy's ground forces, those fools we've been fighting down here?' he asked Xyrax. 'Magos, did any survive the Gift?'

'Insufficient data,' responded Xyrax. '*Paracyte* was forced to retreat to extreme sensor range in order to avoid destruction. However, long-range augury suggests enemy troop movements across the planet. I predict a high probability of assault against this location before the arrival of incoming Imperial warships.'

'How long until Bucharis is ready to offer his beneficence again?'

'There was damage – noctilith sinks fractured, empyric capacitors burned out, phantasmic interference to soul siphons necessitating further cross-dimensional patching,' Xyrax said. 'My magi are at work. Estimated time until proper function – hours, rather than days.'

'We cannot stand against an attack of this magnitude,' said Kar-Gatharr. 'If we wipe out every one of the Emperor's lackeys currently here and in the void, we will still be overwhelmed when the main body arrives.'

'We must only hold until the primarch may be targeted. Lokk's warpsmiths have seen to the macro-cathedrum's fortification. Your warriors are all but untouched by battle. We will hold until Bucharis' Gift be given to the corpse-god's get,' said Tenebrus.

'There is the current advance from Ascension Stair to deal with.'

'These are your concerns, my lord,' said Tenebrus. 'You were created for war. I leave the defence to you.'

Tenebrus dipped a finger into his pool, stirring for so long that Kar-Gatharr felt moved to speak. Before he could, Tenebrus withdrew the digit and sucked the filth from it.

'Kar-Gatharr, do you understand that this moment is crucial?

We stand at a tipping point in the Long War. To one side waits annihilation, to the other, final victory. Will you serve your Warmaster at this fated hour?'

Kar-Gatharr narrowed his eyes. 'I serve him always.'

'Well then,' said Tenebrus, suddenly brisk. 'The Custodians will come for us by other ways, and my shades must be prepared to greet them. You are dismissed. Do not stray too far, Kar-Gatharr, you will have a role to play when the appointed time draws nigh.'

'Yes, my lord,' he said, and his tone was contemplative.

Kar-Gatharr and Yheng departed. As he strode the corridors of the cathedrum, the Dark Apostle thought. He faced a destiny centuries in the making. He stood at the crossroads from which would spring the last, bloody road to Terra.

It would be his last act in this life. He would not have it spoiled.

'Yheng,' he said.

'My lord?' asked Tharador Yheng.

'We come to the end. My time is almost done. I must rely on you one last time. So listen to me. Firstly, I do not believe Tenebrus will be successful in slaying the primarch.'

'My lord, but...'

'He is no fool. If it appears that he will be captured or slain, he will depart, and he will take the Gift with him. Whatever happens, the Gift must survive what is to come. He can see this as well as I,' said Kar-Gatharr. 'But there is more at stake here than Bucharis.' He paused, and glanced down at Yheng's rapt face. 'The Long War is almost done. You heard him say that, and he is right. Everything we have worked towards for ten millennia comes to fruition. I must tell you now that what kind of victory Abaddon wins is more important than the victory itself, do you understand?'

'I think so, my lord.'

'Lorgar dreamed of a universe where mankind served the

gods, not one where they consume us. The gods' victory is inevitable. What happens after that is dependent on the actions of the faithful. To achieve the best possible outcome, that is our goal. We would give mankind the power the Emperor denies. Power you have taken yourself. Do you see?'

'Yes.'

'Those are my orders from my lord, the master of the faith himself. We are but part of a larger scheme, a scheme you have earned a place in. I pass these orders to you.'

'But, my lord, how can I possibly–'

'Silence,' he said. 'I understand now that fate has chosen you. You must stay with Tenebrus. His weapon is more than something to kill a primarch. Do you understand? If he is successful in his ultimate goal, he will become exceedingly powerful. You must be there to influence him, and through him, maybe the Warmaster himself.'

Yheng's eyes widened in alarm. 'How can I do this thing?' she said. 'You are immortal. You are powerful. I am not.'

By way of reply, he offered her a wintry smile.

'I am not immortal, and your power grows, Yheng. I see greatness in your future. Already you attract Tenebrus' favour. Nurture it. Become his confidante. Let him feed your growing might. There is nothing certain in what I say, but I sense a certain destiny about you...' His words died. He began again. 'For the time being, I need only one thing from you.'

'Anything, lord! Name it, and it is yours.'

'I need you to live,' he said.

Chapter Thirty-Three

CATACOMBS

THE GREATER RING

SHADES

There were signs of skirmishes in the ruins, though the evidence of large-scale ground warfare was scant, and when Achallor's party came across a score of blackened tanks, it was evident that they had been broken months before. Their armour was rusty, and in the turret of one, half sunk in the canal, wild-flowers bloomed in corpse soil.

'This way,' said Kesh, leading them on. 'There was an entrance open to the tower here. We went in in the spring, before we were driven back, when I was looking for a way to get back into the cathedrum.'

It had been a massacre, and afterwards the sectors fell, and every patrol that had gone underground was lost, but Achallor knew that anyway.

The upper part of the Tower of Proclamation was draped across the landscape, the brittleness of man's designs revealed, smashed like a broken column in some temple on Old Earth. Kesh gave an audible sigh of relief when she saw the entrance to the tower stump.

'It's still open,' she said.

'Wait,' said Aswadi. He pointed to the side of the building. 'See the wreckage where it rises?' he murmured. 'There is a ship there, under the rubble. I would wager that was a pilgrim hauler. It looks as though it collided with the tower and they both fell together.'

'An impact like that will likely have destabilised the entire structure,' said Vychellan. 'The building might come down upon our heads.'

'Sergeant Kesh?' asked Veritas.

'My lord is correct. The ground is dangerous, and things hunt down there, but there is no other way.'

'These things... the constructs you told us of?' Vychellan said.

'Yes,' said Kesh.

'Servitors designed to evade auspex. Some sort of cyber-construct melded with unclean sorcery,' said Veritas. 'One was sufficient to kill Sergeant Kesh's patrol when she took the prisoner. Only Palatine Emmanuelle's intervention saved her.'

'Daemon machines,' said Vychellan.

'That is what the palatine said,' said Kesh. She blanched at the memory. The thought of facing those things made her want to run and hide. If it weren't for the Custodians' presence, she feared she might have.

'Neverborn or not, we go on,' said Achallor.

Kesh nodded, and led them to a point where the canal side had caved in, leaving a steep slope of rubble, metal and bone. They climbed into the shadow of the tower, and checked their auspexes again.

'Two traitor patrol groups,' said Aswadi.

'Neither of them looks to be moving this way, and if the enemy has eyes higher up the tower, we can assume they have not yet spotted us,' replied Achallor. 'We will slip in on the ground floor and strike downwards at the first opportunity.' He looked to Kesh. 'You have guided us well.'

Artillery boomed to the north-west, where the macro-cathedrum dominated the land.

'Let us be about it then,' said Vychellan. 'Battle is joined. Dvorgin makes his move.' With that he strode up the rubble and into the debris field around the shattered tower.

They passed from one rubble pile to the next, staying in shadow out of the groping fingers of the morning. Achallor kept one eye on his auspex, yet it seemed luck was with them. They reached the tower's entrance without detection, and passed beneath a skull-studded lintel into deeper darkness beyond.

'No wonder the enemy have no spotters up there,' muttered Aswadi as he looked up.

The upper floors had collapsed into the lower, hollowing out the entire structure except for the bottom, where compacted debris blocked the passageway a dozen paces inside. Water was running from somewhere, sluicing down one wall and vanishing into the yawning cracks in the corridor's floor.

'Blocked?' asked Vychellan.

'It was not the last time I was here,' said Kesh. 'But there is more rubble than there was.' She was alert now, listening for the sounds of the thing that had killed her squad mates. 'We must go through the fissures.' She looked at them. 'I am sorry, my lords, I did not take your size into account, and the path was wider than this before.'

Achallor crouched by the widest fissure, tracing its line to the rubble fall where there was an opening. He consulted the subterranean returns from his auspex.

'Canoness, your armour is somewhat lighter than ours. Could you and the Sisters descend through that gap?'

'We can try,' replied the canoness. 'If there is a way beyond, I will widen the gap enough that you can follow.'

A Sister moved forward, but the canoness stopped her, and went herself, handing her chainsword and bolter to another.

'It is fortunate that we do not suffer such frailties as claustro-phobia, no?' she observed. 'Though I have no desire to end my days trapped beneath this tower's carcass. If this goes wrong...'

'We shall not abandon you here,' said Achallor.

Veritas stepped forward and crawled into the crack. Achallor watched her feet vanish into the darkness, find purchase and push deeper. Her armour scraped against stone, then nothing. They waited, listening to water trickle and the distant gunfire.

'Is there another way?' Aswadi asked Kesh when some minutes had passed.

'No, my lord,' she said.

Achallor had started to fear that the canoness was lost, when he felt a shudder run through the ground. The stone dropped several inches. Vychellan shot a look at the shield-captain.

'Cave-in!' he hissed.

Achallor dropped to one knee next to the hole and gripped the rock. He would tear a path down to the canoness if he had to, never mind the noise it made.

There was another lurch, and the fissure crumbled inwards. A silver gauntlet reached up through the gap.

'There is a passageway down here,' came Veritas' voice. 'Help me to widen the gap and I shall set each chunk of rubble down so that it does not fall.'

Soon the gap was wide enough that the rest of the party could drop down to join her. They were in a minor access passage-way, ankle-deep in the water flowing down the building. It was low enough that the Custodians had to bend to avoid banging their heads on the ceiling.

Reclaiming her weapons, Veritas nodded.

'Delightful is it not? The passage is blocked not far in that direction, but it seems to go this way without serious obstruc-tion. Shall we attempt it?'

'Kesh?' Achallor asked.

'I will go first,' Achallor said.

As they progressed, the Custodians were forced to crawl through half-collapsed sections of passageway. The darkness was such that even the Custodians' augmented vision struggled to make out detail, yet they eschewed light for fear of revealing their presence. Skulls leered up at them from beneath the water. At one point they were forced to pause again and clear away debris before they could proceed. Twice, the tunnel shuddered and dust fell before the tremors settled.

'One more like that and we turn about and seek another route,' Achallor decreed, mindful of the thousands of tons of rubble pressing down above.

Not long afterwards they heard the gurgle of falling water ahead. The tunnel evened out, and ended in a spiral stairway which the water raced down. Achallor led the climb down, water foaming over his boots, past slimed murals, and emerged in a bigger tunnel at the bottom. Pathways ran down each side of a square channel eight feet deep. It was empty, but for the shallow stream coming in from the staircase.

'This is the aqua-tunnel. Now we are getting somewhere,' commented Vychellan.

'Which way?' asked Aswadi. 'It is so damned dark I can only see a handful of paces in either direction.'

'The cathedrum is this way,' said Kesh, pointing. 'This route was considered for a counter-attack before things got too bad.'

'A poor fortress indeed if there are tunnels like this into it,' said Vychellan.

Achallor switched out his helmplate display for his auspex. There was no sign of the enemy. 'Let the Emperor guide us.' He lowered himself into the empty channel where he might go more easily, Vychellan and Aswadi following. Kesh, Veritas and the remaining six Sisters stayed on the walkways.

So it went on, the group pressing ahead into Stygian depths. The tunnel was blocked off by a rockfall a mile short of the cathedrum. The canal opened into the catacombs below, where all its water had flowed, and they were forced to submerge to pass through a flooded crypt. Power armour kept the Custodians and the Sisters safe, but Achallor noted with concern how badly the water chilled Kesh. Once they were out he allowed her a moment to wring out her uniform, before insisting they push on.

They had delved three hundred feet beneath the city streets by Achallor's estimation. Amidst a warren of diverging passageways, they encountered first one dead end and then another, and Achallor's concern deepened. In his mind's eye the sands of time trickled away.

His relief was great when Aswadi spoke.

'Readings on auspex, energy signatures below us. Here,' Aswadi said from within a faintly lit side-chamber. A hole had been made in the stone floor, and a reinforced iron ladder rose up through it.

'This has been las-cut recently,' noted Vychellan.

'Hints of artificial light from somewhere down there,' said Aswadi.

'No movement on the auspex, only energy readings,' said Achallor. 'I will lead. Gunfire as a last resort only.'

Holding Prosektis loosely, Achallor climbed down the ladder. He found himself in another space defaced with heretical sigils. Lumen light filtered through an archway in one wall and he crept up to it, watching his auspex all the while. The passage beyond was twilit and, continuing to follow the source of the light, Achallor found himself at the junction of another catacomb tunnel. This one had been used recently. The dust on the stone flags was disturbed. Cabling ran along the floor, powering widely spaced lumen poles. Somewhere up ahead Achallor could hear the chug of a mobile generatorum.

He felt a hand on his shoulder and turned to meet Vychellan's stare. He gestured at the walls, and Achallor realised that he had been so intent on seeking the foe that he had overlooked an act of vandalism.

Here the walls were lined with inscribed slabs covering niches and upright sarcophagi. All had been broken open, and the bones removed.

'What do the heretics want with centuries-old dust and bone?' asked Aswadi.

'Nothing good,' Achallor replied.

'It is their nature to profane the holy,' said Veritas.

'Movement, next corridor, hundred yards and closing,' said Vychellan. 'Two contacts, reading power armour signatures, moving at walking pace.'

'Traitor Astartes,' said Achallor.

He led his comrades in a swift advance. The Custodians could rely on their superior armour to conceal them from their enemies' auto-senses, but the others trusted to luck. The sound of heavy footfalls upon stone came to them, along with the thrum of compact reactor packs and the whine of servos.

There were two of them, clad in the dried-blood crimson and silver of the Word Bearers. Achallor rested Prosektis and his shield noiselessly against the wall, and drew his misericordia, the sacred power knife all the Emperor's guardians carried.

Achallor stepped out into the corridor directly behind the enemy, grabbed his victim's helm and drove his misericordia into the vulnerable joint between respirator and gorget. The powered blade went deep. Blood spurted over Achallor's fist. He caught his victim as the second tried to bring his bolter up, but before he could open fire, the shield-captain stabbed the point of the misericordia through his left eye-lens.

Achallor caught the second Word Bearer in his other arm and laid the two dead warriors down with difficulty – even for him, the weight of two fully armoured Space Marines was considerable.

'Finely done,' said Veritas, her voice little more than a murmur.

'If there is one thing that the Adeptus Custodes do better than anything else, it is slay Space Marines,' said Vychellan.

'We need to move swiftly now,' said Achallor. 'Leave the bodies. If the alarm is raised, it cannot be helped.'

'Shield-captain, there are odd energy signatures from ahead,' said Aswadi. 'I do not know what to make of it.'

Achallor consulted his own sensorium.

'Perhaps something empyric in nature? Sorcery?' Vychellan suggested.

'The enemy have been doing a lot of digging down here,' Kesh said. She was shivering, her lips were pale. 'A lot of searching too. A few weeks ago they changed their operations. We saw them collecting bones last time we were out.'

'Let us look upon their source, and then we shall know,' said Achallor. 'You are cold,' he added.

Kesh hesitated. 'No, my lord.'

'Your body temperature is dropping. My eyes and my instruments show me this.'

Abashed, Kesh nodded. 'I am cold, my lord.'

Achallor reached behind himself and wrenched his cloak free.

'Wrap yourself in this,' he said.

Kesh stared at it, her expression alarmed. 'I cannot sully the cloak of a Custodian as if it were a camp blanket. No!'

Achallor threw up the cloak, grabbed it, and cut a neat hole in the middle, making the cloak a poncho. He placed it over Sergeant Kesh's head.

'Lo, and His servants shall show their mercy, and from their hands largesse come, and all shall be rich and provided for, by the light of the Lord of Man,' said Veritas worshipfully.

They went on, blades ready, moving swiftly and as close to silently as they could, keeping wary eyes on their auspexes.

They ascended a flight of crumbled ferrocrete steps. Kesh slew a cultist who stood sentry at the summit of the stairs, then hid the corpse in an alcove to one side. She beckoned the others, and led the way for a time, through a great hall where empty stone coffins marched off into the black.

'I still do not understand these readings, but they are intensifying,' said Aswadi. 'Is that movement amongst them, or is the source itself in motion?'

'Perhaps something is disrupting the machine-spirits of our equipment,' suggested Vychellan.

They rounded another corner, alive for sudden enemy contact, and Achallor found himself staring into a spill of faint, silvery illumination. Starlight, he thought. But it could not be.

The light was shining up from an access shaft in the middle of the coffin hall, and as he peered into it, he realised that the ladder was sheared off halfway down. The entire shaft ended abruptly over a wider space that was lit by the silver luminescence.

A much larger, sloping tunnel had been bored through the honeycomb of the undercity. Dark apertures showed where smaller passages had been cut neatly through. Running along the centre of the tunnel was a mass of cables and tubes, their combined diameter perhaps fifteen feet across, held aloft at intervals by tall obelisks of rune-etched gold. Liquid flowed through the tubes; some carried blood, while others were filled with a substance that gave the unnatural glow. That light was wrong, the shadows it threw too jagged and vigorous, and the liquid churned with sinister motion.

'This must be part of the weapon,' said Vychellan.

'We could destroy it here,' said Aswadi.

'What if that only alerts them to our presence?' said Veritas. 'Evil must be struck through the heart or the head. If we attack only the limbs, all is lost.'

'These readings...' said Aswadi. 'There are clear empyric spikes.'

'We are close,' said Achallor. 'Be on your guard now.'

They dropped down to the tunnel. For the Custodians it was a short distance; the Sisters had to jump. Vychellan caught Kesh, then they took the route upwards towards the Macro-cathedrum. The tunnel went in a spiral, Achallor judged, with each turn becoming tighter. They had not progressed far when he spotted a machine ahead through which the pipeline plunged.

'Contacts... some sort of movement from the tunnels around us,' reported Aswadi, frustrated at his inability to get clear readings, and after Amalth-Amat, there were none as good with the auspex as Aswadi. Achallor glanced swiftly about and led his warriors into the concealment of a shrine cut clean in half. He strained his senses but he could neither see nor hear anything.

'That is noctilith, I have no doubt at all,' said Aswadi, staring in revulsion at the machinery.

'What?' said Kesh.

'It is a stone, a xenos thing,' said Vychellan. 'From what the Martian magi have so far discerned, it has a psychoreactive quality that can be polarised either to repel the energies of the empyrean, or to arouse them.'

'What if they intend to open a warp rift?' asked Achallor. 'If they know of our approaching battle groups, might they intend to tear reality asunder in response? They have done it elsewhere.'

'I do not think so,' said Veritas. 'This is something worse. The deliberate vandalism of a shrine world, and the enslavement of the souls of the honoured dead. It is no warp rift.'

'Shield-captain, I have contacts approaching!' hissed Aswadi.

They came in supernaturally fast from behind, Aswadi barely

avoiding the downswipe of a trio of long, wickedly sharp blades. A gruesome, hunched thing of pallid servitor flesh and dark metal limbs came screaming past, a field of energy dancing around. Achallor's sword was already swinging up. Prosektis sliced and sent the head tumbling. Sparks and ichor flew. It crashed to the ground, where it spasmed wildly.

'More of them, closing fast,' said Aswadi, recovering his feet and raising his own blade and shield.

'We cannot be trapped here,' said Achallor. 'Follow me. We make for the cathedrum with all speed.'

They pushed their way around the machine. Passages opened up off the smooth tunnel in every direction. Kesh skidded to a halt, and whistled for Achallor's attention.

'Shield-captain,' she said, pointing out a dripping culvert. 'That way.'

The Sisters of Battle started firing behind them. Bolt-flashes lit up the tunnel, and otherworldly shrieks echoed. Kesh went up first, then the three Custodians. Veritas and her Sisters followed, firing all the while. They ran, and in their wake came hunting cries and the skitter of bladed limbs.

Achallor loped ahead. Aswadi was two paces behind. The Sisters just managed to keep pace, but Kesh was struggling. Vychellan grabbed her around the waist and hauled her off the floor.

'They come again,' said Aswadi. Achallor gritted his teeth. They halted, turned, stood side by side in the darkness with their shoulder guards scraping the walls. They raised their bolt-casters over the heads of the Sisters. Vychellan let Kesh down and she took aim with her pistol.

They waited until they could hear the servitors close before they opened fire. Muzzle flare lit the passage, illuminating the monsters surging at them. Bolts hit the close press and detonated with devastating force. Blood and entrails painted the walls as the shades were blown messily apart.

'More coming!' said Aswadi.

'Curse it all,' said Achallor matter-of-factly. 'My boltcasters are almost dry.'

'Bladework then,' grunted Vychellan.

'No space here,' replied Achallor.

'How about this?' said Kesh, pulling a grenade from her belt and tossing it at the ceiling, where it adhered. A single lumen upon it blinked faster and faster. 'Get back!' she shouted.

They ran, and the device blew behind them, bringing down the ceiling in a rush of black dust and stone.

The fall ceased. The last rocks bounced down the heap. The corridor was blocked. Kesh leant with her hands on her knees and coughed.

'For the Emperor,' she said.

Behind the rockfall they heard the shrieks of the hunter-servitors rise again, then fall away.

'They will find another route,' said Achallor.

'We should lose them for a while,' said Kesh. 'It's not far now.'

Chapter Thirty-Four

NIGHTFIGHT

CATHEDRUM

YHENG'S COURSE

Night had fallen over Gathalamor. To Jessivayne Y'Kamidar it felt as though it would last forever. Ash fell across the ruins. It settled thick on the Processional Hope Enduring, only for *Incendor*'s footfalls to send it whirling into the air again. High above, the sky was streaked by silver-green luminescence.

'*A fine night,*' voxed First Blade Sheane.

'Full of all the horrors one would expect from a world meeting its end,' she said in return. 'Let us not stint in our efforts. We have oaths to fulfil here. No true child of the Ironhold would shirk this duty.'

'*Well said, niece,*' said her uncle. She could almost feel his warm presence behind her. From her earliest days he had been there for her, and she felt reassured by him, even now she was grown.

Within the mind interface of the Throne Mechanicum, Jessivayne's ancestors clustered close. Surrounded by her family, her cockpit swaying her with *Incendor*'s long strides, she felt invincible.

'Courage, honour, fealty,' she said as she urged *Incendor* on to a swifter stride.

'You are nearing the cathedrum, princess.' General Dvorgin's voice was scratchy over the vox.

'One could hardly miss it,' she replied, though without rancour. The macro-cathedrum of Cardinal Asclomaedas was truly vast. It loomed out of the night afire with the light of countless lumens, still glorious.

Jessivayne glanced over her read-outs, muttering a prayer to the God-Emperor as she did so.

'Once again, oh Emperor, we stride out to battle the enemies of humanity in thy name.'

Her surviving Knights were split into two lances, hers advancing down Processional Hope Enduring and Gerent's down Processional Splendour of the Throne.

'We beseech thee, in this hour of trial, lend us thy strength and thy glory, thy heart and thy fury,'

Two columns of armoured fighting vehicles followed behind the lances, Adepta Sororitas armour transports, the last of the Mordian Chimeras and the dregs of the 40th Phyroxian Tankers.

'Let us spread the light of thy cleansing fires to every shadow so that the heretic, the mutant, the alien and the witch might have no place to cower.'

Behind them went companies of infantry, force-marched through the day, already weary from yesterday's battle when they set out, now wearier still.

'Aid us, oh Emperor, for we are but thy humble servants and only in the light of thy regard do our deeds gain worth.'

That was it. That was everyone that remained from Ascension Stair who could be spared.

'There are a lot of energy signatures ahead, your highness,' Lady Nimue voxed. *'The enemy have not been idle.'*

Jessivayne flicked through Nimue's sensorium feeds. The foe had raised a maze of defences about the feet of the macro-cathedrum. They had built walls, turrets and bunkers, laid minefields, and blasted trench lines out of the ferrocrete. She considered how many guns might nestle in the cathedrum's towers and domes. She refused to be intimidated.

'Their weakness is the sheer size of the fortress,' voxed Jessivayne, 'Their forces will be strung out around it. We are not the only Imperial forces on this world, and soon there will be many more. They cannot defend all of it.'

'They can't have missed our advance, princess,' cautioned Dvorgin. *'Were I them, I would be stripping defenders from every unthreatened wall and moving them to meet our attack.'*

'That will take time,' said Jessivayne, hands flickering over controls that roused *Incendor*'s weapon-spirits. Ahead, a towering arch of gold and marble was resolving itself, a portal in the cathedrum's flank through which a Warlord Titan could have stridden. It was heavily defended. Among the hordes of cultists, Jessivayne saw the war engines of the Heretic Astartes.

'General Dvorgin, are you receiving our datafeeds?'

'Clearly,' responded Dvorgin.

'I recommend you fan out and deploy infantry forces into the ruins on either side of both processionals,' said Jessivayne. 'Palatine Emmanuelle's troops would best sweep the ruins to safeguard our left flank then move up. They'll stand up better to the Heretic Astartes than Militarum troops. There's the possibility they could outflank my Knights with their tanks. I would prefer if that were not allowed to happen.'

'I shall see it done,' replied Dvorgin.

'By the Emperor's will,' said Emmanuelle.

Jessivayne keyed off her close-in views, and the cathedrum dropped back. Although it was still several miles away, it dominated the horizon.

She opened a household-wide hail.

'Knights of the Ironhold Protectorate, champions of House Kamidar, by the light of the Golden Throne we charge!' cried Jessivayne, feeding more power to her steed's motive actuators. *Incendor* accelerated. Around her, close behind her, her comrades followed. Two mighty spears of adamantium bore down upon the enemy's defences. The first shots whipped out to meet them. Rockets and las-blasts flickered against ion shields.

'Return fire!' she commanded.

The Knights' weapons roared, causing ferrocrete bunkers to erupt in flame and gun towers to topple.

This was the moment she had been born for. This was her appointed task.

The Knights were running now, approaching maximum speed.

'Courage, honour, fealty!' roared Jessivayne Y'Kamidar through her Knight's vox-amplifier. 'In the Emperor's name! Glory or death!'

War-horns bellowed, and the attack began.

Tharador Yheng's powers shrouded her presence from human sight as she followed Tenebrus. The hood of her robe stilled the jingle of her braids. Her heartbeat was steady. Somewhere in the distance the sounds of battle rumbled, but in the dusty ways of the macro-cathedrum, Tharador felt as though she were back in the catacombs again, stalking her next meal.

She maintained a cautious pace, not drawing too close to the grotesque figures ahead, unworried by her footsteps. High Magos Xyrax made as much noise as a light tank, and the gaggle of servitors that accompanied him were scarcely quieter: two enormous, grumbling hulks of armoured vat-flesh carrying heavy cannons; a trio of scuttling, spider-like creatures that bore the black casket containing the ring; and a hovering flock of skulls from which blurted a babble of vox-intercepts and binharic signals.

The only one she was truly nervous about was Tenebrus. The sorcerer glided along at Xyrax's side, mutant hands clasped behind his back, head inclined towards the high magos in conversation. As he neared each electro-sconce it dimmed and flickered back to life only once he had passed.

He is powerful, thought Yheng. She didn't believe for a moment that Tenebrus was a mere mortal. What she did believe was that Tenebrus had power, more power than the master; the sort of power in whose presence opportunity flourished.

They went into the chamber of the Gift. Yheng followed and secreted herself in the shadows. Kar-Gatharr had given her a vox handset. He would be at the gates, commanding the defence against the corpse-worshippers. She could hear the battle outside the cathedrum growing in ferocity.

'The weapon must not be lost, whatever happens,' he had said. 'If its survival is in doubt, summon me.'

As Tenebrus and Xyrax roused their servants, Tharador Yheng watched, ambition boiling through her veins.

Chapter Thirty-Five

STENCH

BONE HEAP

THE PEOPLE OF GATHALAMOR

Shield-Captain Achallor swayed aside as the hunter-servitor leapt at him. He swung Prosektis up, impaling the construct and running it through with the force of its own momentum.

Achallor kicked the body free in time to bring the weapon about to deflect a set of talons aimed at his head. The shade screeched, slashing with incredible speed, forcing the captain to retreat, until Hastius Vychellan appeared at Achallor's side and smashed the servitor's skull with his blade. Achallor nodded in thanks.

They had returned to the main tunnel, where the journey had become a running fight. Boltguns boomed, the sound mingling with the whoosh of a flamer and the chanted prayers of the Battle Sisters. Pale nimbuses of psychic power outlined the Sisters of the Argent Shroud, manifestations of their faith. It seemed to Achallor that was all that was keeping the daemon-machines from rushing them en masse. The Custodians used this to their advantage, cutting down the servitors that braved the aegis of faith, while Kesh fought in the shadow of Aswadi, snapping off shots with her laspistol.

The weight of fire proved too much for the cyborgs.

'They are retreating!' Achallor shouted. 'Cease fire!'

Immediately, the racket of boltguns stopped. The servitors fled into the dark on whirring contra-grav. The shrieking receded.

The party wasted no time. Prayers were said for the fallen. Empty magazines exchanged for full. Achallor counted his surviving warriors: Kesh, the Custodians, Veritas and five Sisters remained.

'Again and again we drive them off,' said Vychellan. 'Again and again they come at us. If their aim was to slow our progress, then they are most assuredly succeeding.'

'Their aim is to slaughter us, and in that they continue to fail,' replied Achallor, wiping gore from his blade.

'They shall not prevent us, for we do the Emperor's work,' said Canoness Veritas. Her voice was steady despite the casualties her Sisters had suffered.

'How long have we been about this?' asked Vychellan. They set off again, following the incline of the tunnel up to the macrocathedrum.

'A count of hours,' replied Achallor. 'How do your warriors fare, canoness?'

'Where the body fails, the spirit takes the burden, shield-captain,' Veritas said.

'It must be dead of night by now,' Vychellan said. 'We must make haste. As Pollandrius puts it, "no corpse ever thanked the cautious rescuer".'

'There is nothing of caution about this advance, only necessity,' said Achallor. 'We cannot control the arrival of Fleet Primus.'

'My lord, if I may, we're nearly there,' said Kesh. 'We never came this way, but there was an access shaft beneath the a gasp, covered her mouth, and shied back.

'The stench of death is strong here,' said Achallor.

'Wait,' said Kesh. She lifted up her jacket, and not wishing to further damage Achallor's cloak, tore a strip from her shirt instead. It had dried to a warm dampness, so she soaked it anew in water from her canteen, and wrapped it about her face. Then she took her rebreather from her belt, and fastened it as tightly as she could over the top. Thus protected, she took them on another quarter of a mile. The stench grew worse, the thick, sweet smell that told of life's end.

The tunnel ended suddenly, and the piping and cables took an abrupt turn to the left, through a breach cut into the bone-rock. The wan light of the machine was stronger there, spilling in a ghastly square. In this light, Kesh paused a moment, steeling herself, before passing through into the chamber beyond.

When he followed her, Achallor understood well enough why she had hesitated.

Before them was the domain of the dead.

The shaft marked on the maps had gone, and an enormous cavern gaped in its stead, gouged out by industrial equipment from the catacombs. Skulls lay about on ledges of smashed mosaic. Sarcophagi teetered on the brink of falling. So many tunnels had been laid open by the works, it looked like someone had scooped huge handfuls from the heart of an insect hive. Scattered around the chamber's edge were piles of hand tools, rock drills, mounds of spoil and bone, portable generatoria still linked to lightless lumen stands.

All this desecration faded into inconsequentiality when set against the mound dominating the cavern.

At the centre of the chamber's ceiling there was a freshly cut hole, down through which went the great braid of cables and tubes that wound through the spiral beneath the cathedrum.

Between the entrance and the hole, these cables passed through the most titanic mountain of human remains Marcus Achallor had ever laid eyes on.

'The people of Gathalamor,' said Vychellan simply.

The remains were skeletal, but raw, their flensed bodies clung about with enough gobbets of flesh to putrefy. The bones were still connected by sinew, and heaped without form or order into a pyramid three hundred yards each side. Thousands upon thousands, if not millions, had been slaughtered to make this vile charnel heap. Black fluids from their deliquescence gathered in a stinking lake around the base. At the pinnacle, directly below where the tubes let into the cavern ceiling, were twenty complete skeletons, grey and green with slimed decay, each dressed in high-priestly robes bound together with steel wires. From this vantage, eyeless sockets stared out over the wreck of humanity, white teeth horribly prominent in peeled faces.

The canoness took off her helm and let it dangle in her hand.

'Emperor grant peace to these numberless souls,' said Imelda Veritas. Her seamed face had set into a stony mask. Her eyes burned with fury. 'To be so slain by heretics you once named friend and neighbour. To have your mortal remains despoiled even as your soul is ripped from the bosom of the Emperor. I have seen many terrible things in my life, but this is the most unforgivable.'

There was a soft sound coming from Kesh. It took Achallor a moment to realise she was weeping.

'You know we must climb that mountain,' said Vychellan.

The canoness nodded. She was pale from grief. She put her helmet back on.

'There must be countless routes up through the strata of catacombs to either side,' said Achallor. 'This might not take our weight.'

'Time-consuming routes,' replied Vychellan. 'This is the fastest way. If we cannot prevent the enemy from unleashing their weapon when the main body of Fleet Primus arrives...' He left the rest unsaid.

'Canoness, auspex reads more servitors closing upon our position,' said one of the Battle Sisters.

'We must make haste,' said the canoness. 'I wish that it were not so, but the Emperor asks for our service.'

'Once we get to the top, we can scale the pipes and cables easily enough,' said Achallor, looking up. 'If this must be our course then let us be about it.'

Achallor locked his blade and his shield to his back and advanced upon the gruesome mountain. He did not imagine the silver-green flickers dancing in eye sockets, or the subtle shifts of bones moving of their own accord. They were real. His mind was not made to allow flights of fancy.

'We shall do this because we must,' he said.

With that, Marcus Achallor started to climb. It was as torturous as he had expected. The remains were tangled solid, until a loose section was reached, where they would slide free, sometimes causing an armoured warrior to fall down twenty or thirty feet, and throughout the remains were slick with disintegrating meat.

Kesh clung uncomfortably to the storm shield mag-locked to Aswadi's back, unable to climb herself, for her unarmoured body was at risk from the edges of broken bones. The Sisters prayed as they ascended.

Stubbornly, Achallor climbed. The hole in the cavern's ceiling grew closer. Then came skittering from below, and the keening shrieks of hunter-servitors.

'They are here!' he called. A dozen of the servitors entered the cavern and made straight for the bone mountain.

Bracing themselves as best they could, Battle Sisters and

Custodians turned about and fired their bolters. A few servitors were blown apart. The others weaved around the corpses of their fellows and charged onward, their flickering stealth fields making them hard to hit, and clawed their way madly upwards through fountains of exploding bone, and yet more were arriving.

A servitor reached one of the Argent Shroud and pounced, its talons flashing. The Battle Sister managed to ram her bolter's muzzle between the creature's jaws and blow out the back of its head, but not before its power talons had burned through her armour at the thigh and gut. Blood sprayed from severed arteries as the servitor fell away, only to be replaced by another. The Battle Sister and her attacker fell away in a tumble of bones and flailing limbs, and were lost in the pile. Kesh half turned on Aswadi's back, laspistol cracking as it flicked beams of focused light at the enemy.

'Keep climbing!' Achallor bellowed over the gunfire and screams. 'Do not let them slow you! If we make the peak, we can fight as one and drive them off!'

He turned and clambered higher, hand over hand, jaw clenched. Behind him he heard more reports of gunfire, more scrambling and clattering.

'Keep climbing,' he shouted again. He was only a hundred feet from the crest, then ninety, then eighty.

The tubes ahead pulsed with light and the shield-captain recognised the poisonous silver-green tinge that presaged the weapon's discharge. From all around came a whine of machinery, turning by degree to the hissing of a million voices. The pyramid of bone shook. The air vibrated. He turned around as best he could, one foot braced in a mesh of cracked ribcages, one hand gripping a spine buried in the heap, hoping it would hold. His warriors were still climbing and, for a mercy, none had fallen.

Yet now the gheist-light was flowing in ribbons from the cave mouths all around, forming ghostly shapes, which in turn gathered together into multi-limbed horrors. One of these agglomerations lashed down like a club, swatting a Sister into the air along with the two servitors that had been trying to drag her down. All three were caught up in the squirming grasp of a thousand hands, and rent apart by ghostly claws. As they vanished into the morass of spectral energy it spasmed inwards. There was a metallic bang of armour caving in, and blood drizzled upon the bones like rain.

Another tendril speared downwards into the bone mountain, flowing into the mass as if through water. A third tendril followed it, then a fourth, and Achallor saw witch-light shining in the eye sockets of countless skulls. The spine he gripped flexed. Achallor crushed it. The energy was pouring into the mound, animating the remains, and an awful screaming rose from empty jaws.

'In the name of the Golden Throne, climb!' he roared. 'Fighting will not avail us! We must get clear!'

Above him a glowing limb of spirits exploded outwards from the bone. He unclamped Prosektis and sliced through a hundred wailing phantoms, and the limb fell away into shreds of vapour.

The mountain shifted underfoot, trying to drag them down into a maw forming out of stabbing bones.

'Unclean things, I abjure thee!' cried Veritas. 'Enslaved souls, I shall save thee!'

Achallor climbed hard, snarling at each fresh convulsion of the bones beneath him. At last he got a hand to the cables and hauled himself clear. Strands of gheist-light came with him, wound about his ankles, thick with rasping bone-scraps. He kicked them away and looked to his comrades.

Achallor watched powerless as another Battle Sister was launched away from the slopes by an eruption of ghosts. Aswadi was impaled through one eye by a needle of bone that punched through his helm lens. Without breaking his beat, he smashed the spar and kept climbing, blood sheeting from his face, only for a hunter-servitor to latch onto his legs and drag him back down. He kicked it free into a heaving wash of spectres, where it was torn apart.

Imelda Veritas reached Achallor first, her prayers driving back the unholy energies seeking to kill. She was gasping for breath, her armour covered in scratches and filth. Yet as soon as she had pulled herself up onto the mass of cables she swung around. She leaned out and carefully aimed her bolt pistol then started snapping off shots to support her still-climbing Sisters.

Achallor was out of ammunition. Unable to provide covering fire he leaned down, perilously close to the threshing mountain, grabbed Vychellan and hauled him up onto the cable-mass.

'Climb, make room,' Achallor ordered and Vychellan headed upwards, finding footholds on brass binding hoops. Veritas was next, then the first of the Battle Sisters reached them. The shield-captain and the canoness sent them all clambering upwards.

Last was Aswadi, twenty feet down and struggling furiously with Kesh clinging to his shield. Aswadi punched and snarled, smashed with his fists as best he could. Phantasmal energy snaked about him, squeezing close, spectral teeth biting at Kesh's unprotected head.

'Aswadi!' shouted Achallor, making to drop back onto the bone mountain. Imelda Veritas grabbed his arm.

'You cannot, my lord,' she said. 'The heap is collapsing.'

Aswadi struggled onwards. The bones were tumbling away in wet falls. But he made the pinnacle just as it started to slip. Leaping high, he locked hands with Achallor.

Grunting with the effort, Achallor heaved, but their gauntlets were slick with corpse matter, and their fingers slipped.

The whirling storm of ghosts fastened onto Aswadi's legs, and dragged hard at him.

'Let me go,' he grunted. 'Take Kesh.'

Achallor's muscles burned with the effort of holding up his comrade. The enraged dead of an entire world pulled at him.

'Kesh,' he said. 'Now!'

Kesh scrambled up Aswadi's back, but the weight proved too much. As she reached, Aswadi let out a frustrated snarl, and with a squeal of auramite, his hand slipped from Achallor's.

'My lord!' Kesh yelled. Achallor swiped for her. He only just missed, snagging her folded cap from her shoulder as she was ripped away from him, and nearly fell himself. He saw her plummet, a look of perfect terror in her eyes. Aswadi fell beside her, already turning to fight.

They hit the stinking bones, and the mountain collapsed upon itself, tides of bone splintering across the chamber floor far below. Kesh and Aswadi were dragged down and swallowed.

The pulsing light in the tubes diminished. The screaming subsided to hissing, then died as the spectres faded from view.

Achallor stared for several heartbeats at the wreck. He did not think he would ever forget the look in Kesh's eyes.

'I am sorry,' he breathed.

'The Emperor mourns their loss, as He mourns all those who fall in His name,' said Veritas. 'Now we must climb, before the servitors that took our friends think to pursue us up this shaft. We must make our enemies pay for every life they have cost us.'

For the next twenty minutes they climbed. The strata of the catacombs crawled past. The lip of the shaft was at last in view, some thirty feet above and limned by sconce-light, when Veritas shouted.

'Shield-captain, above!'

Marcus Achallor looked up in time to see a pair of heavy servitors appear over the rim of the pit. They pointed their shoulder-mounted autocannons down. Their augmetic eyes projected targeting beams that flickered active target locks across his armour.

With a chugging roar, the servitors opened fire.

Chapter Thirty-Six

Kar-Gatharr directed the defence from a contemplation chamber over the cathedrum's east gate. Ash blew through the night air, flashing in the flare of weapons that, along with the smoke and flame, obscured the field. He flicked through the filters of his auto-senses to better see.

The Imperial Knights drove hard up the processionals leading to Saint Pyrophus' Arch, breaking open the outer defences, the heavier walkers directing artillery fire in support of their lighter brethren. Now inside the defences, the Knights moved in tight formation, wreaking devastation. Back along the line of their attack lay those war engines that had not endured. Kar-Gatharr counted three fallen Knights, ash already settling over them like shrouds.

Elsewhere the fight was harder to decipher, a confusion of close-quarters gun battles flickering through the ruins, while on the broad roads Imperial armour elements pushed on through punishing fire. Vox-communication chattered through his systems. He selected one strand or another, especially careful to chart the progress of the Adeptus Custodes. They had been seen, accompanied by weakling mortals. Where they went came death, and then silence.

None of it mattered. He let his sight rise heavenwards, to the flame-licked clouds. Somewhere, up there, the ships of the Imperium drew nearer. He could feel the tensing of the world as Tenebrus' machinery sucked at its soul, the gun ready to spit hollow faith back into the Emperor's face.

'Bucharis' Gift offers itself again,' he said, unhooking his crozius from his belt.

The cathedrum shook. He tasted bone dust, though his armour was sealed, and heard a great lament rising from a million damned throats. The great soul spear roared up, seeking out the carrion-god's servants in the void.

An expanding dome of ghoulish light swept out.

Kar-Gatharr uttered words of power, and spread his arms, black fires burning around the head of his sacred mace. A crowd of shadows embraced his men the moment before the spectral horde struck. The shadows made figures of their own which held the silver-green at bay, and the tormented dead swept on, out into the battle, where more of them erupted from the ground, until the district about the cathedrum was alive with spirits, and corpse-light supplanted that of fires.

Coiling tendrils writhed through the battle. They plunged through tanks and left the vehicles dark and dead. They rose up and crashed down in gruesome waves upon opposing groups of infantry. One wrapped around the legs of an Imperial Knight, flowing into its body and causing it to stiffen. Kar-Gatharr knew a moment of satisfaction as the enormous machine toppled backwards, the pain of the pilot rendered as a mournful blast of its war-horn, though his pleasure was tempered when another spectral tendril plunged into a bastion held by his own warriors, and their weapons fell silent.

The shockwave passed on, leaving phantasmal eddies behind, like the pools of a receding tide, then these sank away, or were blown apart on the winds, and only mortal conflict remained.

Kar-Gatharr dropped his arms, banishing his protectors.

'Tenebrus' weapon harms us as much as them,' complained Vorr-Dashk, one of Kar-Gatharr's warriors.

'They suffer more,' replied the Dark Apostle. Burning wrecks of tanks made islands of fire in the night.

'The corpse-worshippers press hard. They may break our lines,' said Vorr-Dashk. He leaned out of the window to discharge his plasma gun at the lead Imperial Knight. The shot flashed against its ion shield.

A volley of rockets hammered the cathedrum gates some two hundred feet beneath their chamber. Fire boiled up about the windows. With a crash, a section of the ceiling fell in. Two of the Chosen Sons were pinned under the rubble.

'Get them out of there,' Kar-Gatharr ordered. His brothers were already hefting chunks of ferrocrete and rebar aside, dragging their wounded fellows from under the fallen stone.

'Tenebrus' sorcery has opened the way for the carrion lovers. Look,' said Vorr-Dashk.

He pointed up the road. Two squat towers that had been pouring fire up the processional were silent. The foe were not slow in seeing the opening: Knights and tanks surged forward.

'This world is lost,' said Vorr-Dashk.

'The war is not,' said Kar-Gatharr. And yet he felt his faith waver. He could feel the promise of a bloody road to Terra waning in his hearts. They had nearly subjugated this planet. A handful of Custodians had come, and that had all changed. Kar-Gatharr knew their power was not in their weapons, but in their worth as symbols, but he had been taken aback by their effect nonetheless. The Imperium's faith in its false god was powerful.

He thrust these unworthy thoughts aside. His destiny awaited.

Signals announced Lokk's counter-attack. No words, but a coded cant, short and harsh.

'Glory to the Four, War-Brother Lokk,' said Kar-Gatharr. Below, in the plaza, tank engines roared. Smoke snorted from exhausts. Stab-lumens cut the darkness as Lokk's iron-hued tanks rumbled out from their positions to meet the Knights. Squads of Iron Warriors advanced around them. A cheer went up from the cultists packing the trenches, redoubling in volume as a hail of Iron Warriors fire brought another Knight crashing down.

'Misguided, short-lived, and ultimately doomed,' said Vorr-Dashk of the cultists.

'Despise the fools below for their hope if you must, but remember it is our duty to be strong for them, and all of men,' said Kar-Gatharr. 'For we are the Bearers of the Word.

'All squads, provide what cover you can to the Iron Warriors but do not risk yourselves,' he said to his warriors over the vox. He had a mere handful on the world – a couple of hundred, no more – but his might was not measured by men or guns. 'The Dark Gods reward the living, not the wasteful dead.'

He watched Lokk's tanks, but he could not pick out *Draco-kravgi* amid the confusion.

A vox-chime sounded loud in his ear.

'Yheng,' he said.

'Master,' she said. *'The device is under attack. The Adeptus Custodes are in the building.'*

Kar-Gatharr sucked in air through his teeth. Not unexpected. He must face them. This was the moment Kor Phaeron had spoken of. The power in him shifted, readying itself for the confrontation.

'The battle without is a deception,' he said. 'The true battle is here, in the cathedrum. Chosen Sons, with me. We go to do battle with the carrion lord's greatest lackeys.'

He was going to die, he knew it. It was strange how ambivalent he felt. After all the millennia, the end came, but he didn't care. As he marched for the weapon dome, he thought he understood Torvann Lokk a little better.

Torvann Lokk hunched in the crimson gloom of his cockpit. *Dracokravgi* was shouldering its way through ruins around Processional Unquestioning Servitude, followed by the Beasts of Steel.

Excitement and bitter anger churned within Lokk.

'The Knight witch is ahead,' Harvoch voxed him.

'I have already sighted her,' snarled Lokk.

'Our lord's tracking skills are superior to ours, brother,' gurgled Lorgus.

'Silence,' said Lokk. 'About your task,' he said, turning off the feed. His fingers flipped toggle switches greasy with fluids weeping from the instrument. 'Lord Klordren, respond.'

'Warpsmith Lokk, to what do I owe this pleasure?'

'This war of Tenebrus' is almost done.'

'He will prevail.'

'No. He will not. What does that black-eyed little worm know of a hunter's instincts? He's no warrior. He has failed.'

'He is the emissary and the Hand of the Despoiler.'

'He may be, but he does not give the Iron Warriors orders,' said Lokk. 'If you are so certain of victory, tell me, what is the status of the Imperial fleet?'

Klordren paused. *'More of them are destroyed by the Gift,'* he said. *'Yet many remain. A battleship, most of the attendant support, with a host of warriors coming behind.'*

'The world is lost.'

'The world is lost.'

Reaching up for another panel, Lokk compelled the tank's infernal spirit to holoproject a map of the district. Yellow runes marked the location of the attacking Imperial force. Pulsing silver skulls indicated Lokk's own force and those of his lieutenants ploughing through the cityscape, converging on the sign designating the Imperial princess.

Dracokravgi rumbled on through the streets, rolling over corpses and shoving aside the wrecks of loyalist battle tanks.

'Prepare to evacuate us,' he said to Klordren. 'All of us. Send withdrawal signals to all Iron Warriors elements. Return to close orbit and prepare your landers.'

'*What of the weapon? It is as big a risk to our ships as it is to the Imperials.*'

'It's an extraction. I am not asking that you linger.'

'*We will be open to fire from the void port.*'

'Don't tell me you are afraid, Klordren?'

'*Never.*'

'Do not be concerned. I do not think Tenebrus will give the Gift again. It is done. Be ready to move over the horizon and offer orbital support to cover our retreat, then reprieve us.'

'*Yes, warpsmith,*' said Klordren. '*I shall follow your recommendations.*'

Recommendations. He can never bring himself to call them orders, thought Lokk, *though he never refuses me.*

'*What about you, do you fight on? Lokk? What shall–*'

Lokk turned off his vox, and brought his attention back to the battle. Upon his feeds he saw her, nearer now, the last sacrifice he would dedicate to the gods upon this blighted world.

He murmured to himself. 'We have one more prey to hunt.'

Shells whined from Marcus Achallor's armour. He and Vychellan went up the cables first, shielding the others with their storm shields.

Foot by foot they ascended, the three Custodians and the last of the Battle Sisters. They neared the iron collar of the shaft opening under fire. The servitors backed away, shooting relent-lessly. As their drum magazines ran dry, and the whine of empty barrels spinning took the place of gunfire, Achallor uttered a wordless war cry and heaved himself up the last few feet. He snatched Prosektis from his back, and thrust upwards, taking one of the heavy servitors through the chest. A blue-white thun-derbolt of destruction met meat and armour and sliced them apart like parchment. The servitor fell apart, bifurcated by the blow, blood and oil fountaining. Bolt-shells ripped up from the shaft and perforated the other servitor as it tried to retrain its guns upon him, disembowelling it. Its hyper-muscled legs fal-tered, and it slumped into the steaming coils of its own viscera.

Achallor emerged into a despoiled prayer chamber, now occupied by a gargantuan weapon fashioned of welded bone, its snout nuzzling at the chamber dome. Close at hand was a biomechanical obelisk – the control mechanism, he thought – but it was inactive, and the tubes that led from below had lost their silver light.

Beyond, even now vanishing through a high arch set with a huge bell, he saw a knot of figures: three spider-like servitors bearing an ominous black casket, a bloated tech-priest borne on rumbling tracks, and a slender mutant in dark robes.

This last turned slowly towards Achallor and surveyed him with eyes like beetles dug into fleshy white pits. Achallor saw the malice in the mutant's stretched grin. He knew instinctively that this thing, this sorcerer, was behind the weapon, and felt the press of evil radiating from the casket.

'In the name of the Master of Mankind, this ends now!' roared Marcus Achallor.

'This is but the prologue, shield-captain,' hissed the sorcerer. A rush of ragged black figures poured through the archway, obscuring him, racing into the chamber with such force that they tolled the bell with their passing.

Whatever was in that box was the key to the destruction wrought on Gathalamor. Achallor ran forward, but was engulfed in a storm of shades. Crimson eye-lenses stared at him from all sides. Malevolent cold washed over him.

Achallor brought Prosektis around in a crackling arc. Black cloth parted. Leprous flesh split. Worms of coiling metal fell away and lenses shattered beneath his blade. The bolters of the last few Sisters smashed holes in the fluttering mass.

'The Emperor protects!' he heard Canoness Imelda Veritas bellowing. 'The Emperor protects!'

A tendril whipped across his helm, knocking his head to the side. Another coiled about his sword arm, forcing him to drop his shield and draw his misericordia. He slashed with the short, powered blade until his limb was freed, then pushed forward, only to snarl in frustration as he saw his quarry had made their escape. More servitors fell on him, and he killed and killed until they were all broken on the ground, and the way was clear.

He ran through the arch.

The sorcerer and the magos were already leaving the next chamber, a high, octagonal space with a dozen exits.

'We must reach the casket!' he shouted, sprinting after them, flinging open the door, only to be met with a tremendous blow of psychic force that lifted him up and sent him skidding back into the room on a trail of sparks. He struggled up onto his elbows, his chestplate half caved in and the auramite split.

What came through the door had been a Traitor Astartes. His armour was that of a Dark Apostle of the Word Bearers. But now he was something else. He was huge, swollen with the warp. Black smoke trailed from his outstretched limbs, and when he spoke it was layered with another voice.

'Custodian,' he said. *'You are too late. The weapon is beyond your reach.'*

The creature drew himself up, sighing with pleasure as his

armour split and ran, re-forming itself over freshly bulging muscle. The cracks in the plates glowed with fell light, and droplets of flame fell from them. His helm burst and fell to the ground, and horns sprouted from the temples of his exposed face. His respirator mask re-formed into a long, metal-fanged snout. The stabilisers on his back flexed and grew, stretching out, forming knuckles and long fingers, between which membranes of night flexed into being, giving him dark wings. His feet arched with the cracking of bone, metatarsals stretching; toes became hooves, while about his growing mace a wicked fire ignited.

'*My name is Kar-Gatharr,*' he growled, his warp-laced voice painful to hear, '*and I am your end.*'

The doors opened around the room, and Word Bearers appeared in each one, bolters ready. Achallor got to his feet, Prosektis at guard.

'*Kill them all,*' said Kar-Gatharr.

Chapter Thirty-Seven

ALPHA TARGET

DARK APOSTLE

TRIBUNE

Torvann Lokk snarled as autocannon shells tore up the ferro-crete then hammered against *Dracokravgi*'s frontal armour. The Knight Armiger ran insolently past Lokk's tank, swinging about to hammer at *Dracokravgi*'s weaker rear. The tank's daemon-spirit coursed furiously around the subsystems at this outrage, causing them to spit.

Lokk sneered. 'Caution, Throne-cur. You may be faster than I, but you are a far less perilous foe.'

Lokk turned his tank around. He couldn't bring his laser destroyer to bear, but he made a show of trying while Harvoch's Predator lined up a killing shot. The Armiger took the bait, running in an arc to come about for another pass. Expecting Lokk to fire, it rotated its ion shield to face *Dracokravgi*, leaving its vulnerable reactor exposed.

'Harvoch, punish this presumption,' Lokk ordered.

Harvoch let fly from all four lascannons at once, striking the Knight in the back. The reactor housing went from gleaming white to scorched black then bubbling, molten orange. Leaking plasma screamed from the wounded engine. It staggered about to face Harvoch, autocannons firing wide in panic, swinging its ion shield to the fore and showing its left side to Lokk.

Lokk took his chance. The laser destroyer was already primed, and with a howl of triumph he discharged it. The blast cut off the Knight's left arm, hit the left facing, cut through the ancient machinery into the pilot's cockpit and directly into his oh-so-fragile flesh. An explosion inside jolted the Armiger, and it fell to lie burning on the ground. Lokk shivered with the rush of the kill.

Then he saw her through the smoke and fury, and his pleasure grew. The princess. He gunned his engines.

'In formation,' he commanded the Beasts of Steel. 'She is ours.'

Jessivayne Y'Kamidar swung her Knight's gauntlet, punching through the bunker. Ferrocrete and reinforced plasteel exploded out from the blow, the mangled forms of armoured traitors mingled with it. The avalanche crashed down upon a knot of cultists cowering below. Jessivayne was already wheeling *Incendor* away. She levelled her conflagration cannon at a trench full of cultists firing on advancing squads of Battle Sisters. Flame erupted from the cannon and boiled along the earthwork. The enemy were blasted to ash before they could even scream.

A salvo of rockets slammed into *Incendor*. The Knight rocked on its gyros and alarm hymns rang through the cockpit. Jessivayne spotted her attackers, a band of Iron Warriors who had taken cover in the rubble of a bunker. Another fusillade of rockets exploded on her ion shield.

'Cousin, if you would,' she voxed, shunting targeting data to Sheane Y'Kamidar.

'*My pleasure, princess,*' came the reply.

The Iron Warriors' position disappeared in a cloud of evaporating matter.

'My thanks, First Blade,' said Jessivayne.

'*I live to serve, princess,*' replied Sheane.

Jessivayne tilted her shield towards the cathedrum and ran into the cover of a burning shrine. Threat runes winked all around her. Her vid-displays were crowded with crimson wire-frames of gun turrets and enemy warriors. Green frames showed her Knights cutting their way deeper into enemy lines. The enemy were launching a counter-attack. A formation of battle tanks was surging towards her like a mailed gauntlet up the processional. She saw one of her Armiger Helverins overwhelmed, and with a thrill of excitement recognised its destroyer.

'Alpha target sighted,' she voxed. 'Knights of Ironhold, re-form, prepare to receive enemy armour charge.' Her shield deflected a blistering storm of lascannon fire. One of the beams punched through and put a hole in *Incendor*'s hide, causing Jessivayne to hiss in shared pain. 'Form on me and meet them head-on. Lady Bronaech, Sir Cohaiegn, covering fire on these coordinates.'

Assent runes and cries of fealty flashed back to her. The blood thundered in Jessivayne's temples as her warriors massed to meet the enemy. She felt the weight of the circlet of iron upon her brow and swore a silent oath to her queen.

'*Princess Jessivayne, you have substantial enemy armour inbound,*' voxed General Dvorgin, his words urgent. She heard the crack-thump of his bolt pistol over the vox.

'I see them, general. We shall meet their blow and shatter them,' she replied.

'*Princess, I wouldn't advise it,*' replied Dvorgin. '*Pull back, draw them onto our guns and together we will advance and cut them apart. Without those tanks the enemy won't hold the gates forever.*'

'Shield-Captain Achallor and his warriors are inside the macro-cathedrum now,' she voxed. 'If we give the enemy room to breathe, they will turn their fury on our comrades within and overrun them.'

'The enemy's counter-attack is reckless. We shouldn't answer it in kind.'

'This is not recklessness. This is not valour for valour's sake. This is the righteous course of action. A Knight's duty is to be the shield of their people,' said Jessivayne, runes flashing in her peripheral vision as Knights fell into lance formation and confirmed readiness. 'A Knight's oath is to pledge their sword in defence of the weak. When asked to fight, a Knight must answer without hesitation. Now is the time to fight. My oath is to protect this world, as my ancestors did, and I shall not break it.'

'Princess, I am ordering you–'

'The primarch is coming, General Dvorgin. I will not fail the Emperor's last loyal son.'

With that she cut the vox-link and sent a single runic command to the nobles drawn up on her lancepoint.

Charge.

War-horns blared. The ground shook as they gathered speed. It took a certain calibre of warrior to stand their ground against the charge of Imperial Knights.

The Iron Warriors were of that calibre.

Boltguns roared from every door, cutting down one of the Sisters. Explosions blew all over Achallor's armour, driving him back.

'Shield-captain!' Vychellan called. 'We must move!'

The Adeptus Custodes went into action while the canoness was still reacting. They exploded outwards, each taking a different path. Vychellan hit first, his longer stride lending him a modicum of additional speed, slamming aside the boltgun of one of their assailants with his shield, and driving his power sword deep into the Space Marine's abdomen. He wrenched it free, bringing out a torrent of dark blood.

He was already moving on to the next foe before the first had hit the floor. He hurled his shield with such force that it stove in the faceplate of the next traitor, sending him stunned to his knees. Taking his sword in both hands, he lopped the bolt-gun of another Space Marine in half, causing the ammunition to explode and taking the legionary's hands, then he turned on his heel, his blade a blur in the air, and sliced the heavy sword through stone, door jamb, ceramite and flesh. By the time Vychellan was past, his enemy was dead, and the wood of the doorway was aflame.

Achallor went for the Dark Apostle. Screaming chimes warned of building psychic energy. He raised his sword, but his foe flung out his hand, and black wind blasted from his palm, slowing Achallor to a stop.

'You are a fool,' said Kar-Gatharr. *'Yet I pity you, for you were ever the least free of all of the Emperor's slaves.'*

The wind had Achallor, pushing through his body, his soul, ripping at the essence of who he was, what he was. He gritted his teeth, and put one foot in front of the other, nearing the warped Dark Apostle.

'Look at this galaxy the Emperor has bequeathed our species with open eyes, and tell me we were not all deceived.'

Achallor pushed on, another step, then another.

'As sorrowful as mankind's state is, it is as nothing to what your gods would inflict,' said Achallor. The wind was weakening, giving out before his indomitable advance. 'All our woes are by their design. We are playthings to them.'

Kar-Gatharr laughed. *'They are stern. They test us. They reward the strong. The weak are consumed, as has always been.'* He whirled his mace around and around, so that the unnatural fires roared in a circle. *'It is cruel, but it is right. Your Emperor does not even give you that.'*

'No,' said Achallor, as with a last step he broke the gale, and stepped forward with his sword raised. 'He wishes to end the cycle. He wants to set us free.'

Achallor was a golden blur. A smear of light. His blade cut towards Kar-Gatharr's shoulder. The Dark Apostle's crozius blocked the sentinel blade. Disruption fields and fell sorcery met with a force that ignited the air. A shockwave of power burst from the contact, blasting Word Bearers back, knocking Veritas and her last Sister down, and staggering Vychellan. Achallor was sent stumbling backwards, dangerously off balance. Kar-Gatharr slid back, leaning to touch the floor to keep balance, his hooves drawing lines of glowing slag from the stone.

Vychellan saw the opening, barged past a recovering Word Bearer and ran at the Dark Apostle, sword held two-handed like a spear. Kar-Gatharr swung out his hand the instant before he hit, and a wave of telekinetic force lifted the Custodian off the ground and slammed him into the wall. He fell hard, chunks of broken sculpture thumping off his auramite.

Veritas fired, raking the wall near Achallor, hitting a Word Bearer in the pauldron, knocking him aside as he ran to fall upon the downed Vychellan. The armour plate disintegrated under Veritas' fire, exposing his shoulder. More bolts thumped into the thinner armour beneath, finally penetrating, and with a trio of wet bangs, blew off the Word Bearer's arm.

Vychellan staggered up. Achallor regained his balance. The Custodians began their charge at the same instant. To their enhanced minds, time was a crawl, each speeding bolt a silver candle on a spike of flame, the movements of the Chaos Space Marines sluggish and easily countered. Achallor, moving to engage the Dark Apostle again, was more exposed, and the fire of three of the Word Bearers punished him. Decorations centuries old shattered under their attack, and Achallor felt a stab of pain as a bolt lodged under the cracked auramite of his chestplate and exploded, forcing slivers of metal into his body. Still he came on.

Vychellan went for the remaining Word Bearers, discharging the last of his own bolts as he ran, killing one then two of those shooting at Achallor. Their threat indicators winked out, leaving only three with Kar-Gatharr. Vychellan attacked the next hand to hand, trading blows with his foe and forcing him back as the others continued to fire.

Achallor only had eyes for the Dark Apostle. He came in shouting, his words a war cry ten millennia old: one once shared by his opponent.

'For the Emperor!'

Only Kar-Gatharr could counter the Emperor's guardians. His reactions speeded by the warp, he was ready and his crozius came down as Achallor closed. Achallor shifted his attack, switching from the high line to the low. His sentinel blade cut deep into the Dark Apostle's leg, bringing forth a rush of scalding smoke instead of blood.

The crozius followed Achallor's movement, and hit the shield-captain on the shoulder. The tremendous impact drove Achallor to his knees. The lion-headed pauldron was obliterated, snapping his head sideways, shrapnel punching through the side of his helm. His ear rang. Blood ran down his face. His arm went limp, the shoulder shattered.

'Marcus!' shouted Vychellan. He finished his opponent and ran to his stricken brother. The remaining two Word Bearers switched their fire to him so that he ran through a blizzard of metal fragments. He cut one down as he passed. Veritas and her sole surviving Sister accounted for the last.

Achallor drove upwards with his sword, his grip clumsy one-handed, yet true and sure.

Kar-Gatharr snarled, and twitched his finger.

Achallor's sword stopped, thrumming, an inch from Kar-Gatharr's chest. The Dark Apostle looked to Vychellan, his eyes flared, and the white-haired Custodian was lifted up from the ground, where he hung choking in the air.

'You are nothing, you corpse-guardians.' Kar-Gatharr lifted his hand, and squeezed. Vychellan kicked, clawing at his throat. *'Misguided servants of a lying god. I pity you.'*

'You will never prevail,' panted Achallor. His ribs were broken, and his breathing hard.

'Whether or not I do, you will not live to see it.'

With a thunderous blow, the Dark Apostle brought his crozius down on Achallor's head. The Custodian's proud golden helm was laid open, and his skull turned to mist.

Marcus Achallor's headless corpse toppled to the side.

Vychellan let out a strangled cry, helpless in the air, his eyes fixed on the ruin of his friend.

Kar-Gatharr turned to Veritas and the surviving Sister.

'If you would live, acknowledge the true gods. Kneel, and be spared.'

'Here is your answer,' said Veritas. Both Sisters levelled their bolters. 'There is only one god, and He resides on Terra.'

Kar-Gatharr laughed. *'Your Emperor is powerless,'* he said. *'You cannot harm me.'*

'I think not,' said Veritas.

They fired together, the last Sisters of the Argent Shroud. Their bolts streaked across the room. There was no fire or thunder, no great show of light. They flew as bullets do, struck flesh, and killed as bullets will.

Kar-Gatharr looked at the smoking ruin of his chest in amazement. His twin hearts, both black and exposed, shuddered their last. He looked at Veritas, his face a question, and fell down dead.

'The Emperor protects,' Veritas said.

Vychellan hit the ground. He took in a great shuddering breath.

'The weapon,' he gasped, and ran.

The Iron Warriors and the Knights of Kamidar closed on one another. Las-fire, plasma and solid rounds filled the space between the two forces. A heretic battle tank flipped onto its roof and exploded. *Incendor*'s sheeting flames leapt out, transforming a band of Iron Warriors into collapsing sculptures of molten metal.

Knights met heretic war engines with a titanic crash. Battle tanks were sawn open. Armour-killing weaponry fired point-blank, reducing proud Knights to flaming ruin. Ahead, Jessivayne saw the alpha target, the rare Rhino variant that had slain so many Imperial tanks, and had evaded her so many times.

'Finally,' she snarled. 'Face the Emperor's judgement, you heretic filth.'

She stomped forward, the cathedrum gates now just a few hundred yards away, and brought *Incendor*'s fist crashing down. The tank was nimble, and moved back. Her size worked against her, and she found herself overbalancing as she sought to hit it. Every time she leaned down to punch it, it slewed back. She was being drawn into a kill box of tracked heavy weapons stationed around the cathedrum entrance, but she was blind to it, her fury stoked.

Artillery fire screamed overhead, fired by her support Knights in the back lines at the macro-cathedrum gates. Missiles blasted gaping rents in stonework and melted metal supports to slag. The way was opening, and the enemy's armour charge was in ruins, though it had cost the Knights of Ironhold dear.

The laser destroyer fired, its triple beam cutting past her right leg and demolishing the portico of a lesser chapel. For although she could not hit it, neither could it bring its gun to bear, and they continued on their dance.

She hosed the Vindicator down with flames, thinking it a poor and feeble machine for a warlord to command, yet it evaded her again. Until, by chance, a rocket landed near, and with a great clap of earth and fire stopped the tank a moment.

She drove into it with her fist.

Track links sprayed through the air like broken teeth. Armour crumpled. Something exploded inside and flames ate their way across the tank's hull.

'Vengeance,' cried Jessivayne, stepping *Incendor* sideways. 'Vengeance!'

Jessivayne continued to pour fire onto the wrecked vehicle, watching with savage satisfaction as its ceramite plating glowed red, became friable and weak, and its cannon barrel became a searing white. She raised *Incendor*'s fist to bring it crashing down again, but at that moment a melta blast speared from the back of the tank, fired from within the guard of her ion shield, and into her Knight's right knee joint.

Alarm hymns sang. She cried out, sharing *Incendor*'s agony, as though someone had taken a blowtorch to her kneecap. Jessivayne fought the urge to step back away from the pain, knowing that the damage to *Incendor*'s limb was too great. Trying would likely shear the right leg off and see her topple.

Beware this foe, whispered her ancestors.

The alpha target came out of the flames, a hulking shape covered in blazing promethium and yet still somehow upright. She directed another blast of fire at her enemy, swinging her Knight's stubber to target him as well, unable to risk the gauntlet in case the force of the blow broke her Knight's leg. At any moment she expected another melta-blast to reach out and burn its way into her cockpit, yet Jessivayne knew no fear, only a righteous determination to scour the foe from this blessed world.

'In the Emperor's name, accept your fate and die!'

Still the figure stepped closer.

Tharador Yheng ran from the thunder of gunfire. She could not aid her master. To do so would be her death.

Live. Kar-Gatharr's last order to her. She felt him fall, when the gunfire stopped. She knew he had gone.

She found Tenebrus and Xyrax walking down a long, dusty corridor as if they were taking the air on a pleasant day.

'Lord Tenebrus!' she shouted, and surprised herself at the strength in her voice. 'He is dead! My master is dead!'

Tenebrus stopped, and ever so slowly, he turned to look at her.

'Kar-Gatharr has fallen?' he said, as if it were no surprise at all. 'That is a terrible shame.'

Xyrax laughed, a horrible, grating, mechanical noise. It enraged her.

'We have lost,' she said. 'They are coming.'

'They are coming,' agreed Tenebrus. 'But have we lost?' Although he was some way away, when Tenebrus took one step towards her, he appeared to jump across the intervening space, and he was suddenly right beside her, his pale face leering, his long fingers twitching. 'You are quite talented to survive this long. Good at hiding, too.' He came closer, and caressed her cheek. His touch revolted her.

'Where are you taking the weapon?' she said. 'We could kill the primarch. We could win. Now. But you've taken the ring. Bucharis' Gift cannot be given.'

Tenebrus laughed softly. The sound of it was sinister in the forgotten hall.

'Could we kill him? Bucharis is very generous with his boons, so it is possible, but I think we missed our chance, and that now we might die, and that is not a part of my plans.'

'You'll die anyway,' she said, and dared to look into his eyes.

What she saw swimming in the depths of those featureless black orbs repelled her, but she could not look away.

'I will not die!' he scoffed. 'I am the Hand of Abaddon. One does not kill me. No. I and the Magos Xyrax are leaving.' He walked away from her.

'Then what was all this for?' she called after him. 'Why fight for Gathalamor at all? Why not burn the world and take the ring from its ashes?' She was shouting now, her anger overcoming her fear.

Tenebrus stopped and tensed, and for a moment Yheng feared she might have gone too far, and that he might end her with a word, for it was surely within his power, but he turned, and he smiled again.

'Because it did not suit me to do so. My dear young lady, this was never about Gathalamor, or the primarch.' His grin grew wider. 'The weapon is what matters. Did your master not tell you so? My target is much greater than a mere primarch. I said I intended to slay a god, did I not?'

He walked away, humming to himself, and the corridor grew darker. Shadows were creeping up around the magos, growing thicker and thicker as Tenebrus receded. He went to the servitors, and took the casket holding Bucharis' ring.

'Guilliman will be here soon, you can stay and meet him if you like,' Tenebrus said. The shadows curled up around him. A strange thrumming filled the corridor. 'Or, my dear, you can come with me.' He held out his hand, and the hideous fingers uncurled, seeming to grow longer and more knotted in the wavering dark. 'You have potential. You have courage. I would not see either wasted.'

She heard the clang of armoured boots ringing through the cathedrum labyrinth behind her.

'Be quick, one of the corpse-guardians is coming, and he will not be merciful to you, I think,' said Tenebrus.

Xyrax was flickering out of being. Where the shadows passed

over him, it was as if they erased him from existence, slice by slice. At first the wiped-away portions of him returned, but then they did not, leaving him in strips on the air, while Tenebrus too was being consumed by the dark.

'I know what Kar-Gatharr told you to do,' Tenebrus said. 'I know he told you to live. I know everything. Come with me and do so, forget what he taught you. Forget what he said. All he offered was another form of slavery.' His smile grew broader and broader, until the width of the passage seemed lined by his teeth. 'Come see the true nature of the victory I shall make. Come find eternal power at my side.'

She hesitated but for a moment, as the clank of boots came nearer, then ran headlong for the dancing shadows.

Together, she, Tenebrus and Xyrax were borne away by shadows to the *Paracyte*.

Vychellan arrived to see the sorcerer blink out of existence.

Finding himself alone with Tenebrus' abandoned servitors, he roared, and cast down his sentinel blade in fury.

Torvann Lokk should have been dead. His body was ablaze, flesh running like wax, agony so great that it washed out his senses entirely in a white-noise scream.

But then, Lokk could no longer feel anything properly, not even his bitterness. It was all as if it happened to someone else.

I will not die, he thought simply, *not now, not like this.* Burned skin cracking, blackened tendons holding together only through the blessings of the Dark Gods, Torvann Lokk stepped forward. He grasped the shin plate of *Incendor*, hauled himself up from the ground, and swiped Cruelty through the damaged knee of the Knight.

The blades flashed through the metal. The knee blew out, the Knight's overburdened right leg folded underneath it, and it fell sprawling on top of *Dracokravgi*. Grunting now at the pain, Lokk climbed atop his tank, stamping flat the barrel of Jessivayne's heavy stubber. The Knight was trying to rise, pushing against the ground with its giant gauntlet. Lokk grabbed the Knight's head, and fired his meltagun point-blank into its sensor cluster, then wrenched at it until it was hanging uselessly from its mounting. Clambering onto the chassis, he came to the access hatch atop the carapace. He braced his feet against the handrail, drew back Cruelty, and slashed a great cut into the hatch, then another. The jerking of the Knight became more frantic as he sliced his way within, but he would not be dislodged, until, with a shower of sparks, he had enough of the door cut away that he could look inside.

Princess Jessivayne stared up at him, her face twisted in hatred.

'You may have bested me, but you shall never defeat the Imperium!' She reached for a curved blade strapped to the wall.

Lokk cast aside his meltagun, and clawed down at her with his empty hand, swiping for her head.

'To Khorne, to Slaanesh, to Nurgle and to Tzeentch,' he said, bashing his shoulder into the breach, denting armour, forcing metal aside with inhuman strength. 'I dedicate this kill.'

The hatch caved in, nearly pitching Lokk atop his prey. She cut at him, but he did not feel the blade's bite, and his armoured fingers closed around her face, the heated ceramite burning into her skin. She forgot resistance then, and thrashed about screaming, the Knight mimicking her movements, threatening to toss him from the carapace, but he held fast, and squeezed, until with a moist pop her skull broke.

Knight and princess went limp.

Strength fled Lokk. He had enough left to push himself free, but thereafter weakness took him, and he bounced down the dead Knight's armour, onto the wreck of *Dracokravgi*, and fell from there to the ground.

For long minutes he sprawled, and felt life ebb as battle raged around him.

'To Khorne, to Nurgle, to Tzeentch, to Slaanesh,' he slurred, 'I dedicate this kill.' His eyes were dimming, and he found that he did not wish the Long War to end after all.

'To Nurgle, to Tzeentch, to Slaanesh, to Khorne, I dedicate this kill,' he said. And his voice grew stronger.

A new pain took hold, but he did not stop his chant of the Great Powers' names. 'To Slaanesh, to Tzeentch, to Khorne, and to Nurgle,' he gasped, his voice rising, 'I dedicate this kill!'

The pain grew. A heat far beyond anything the Knight's cannon could induce started in his bones, and radiated out through his flesh, deep into his organs and beyond, into his mind, and into his soul.

'To Kho–' His litany became a roar. His spine arched fiercely, breaking bone and armour both, as his body flowed and re-formed, ceramite running into flesh and flesh into ceramite, until Torvann Lokk was remade.

He stood, bigger, stronger, with a skin of plasteel and a heart of iron.

Iron Within, Iron Without, a voice that was not his own echoed in his mind, and beyond, down the halls of eternity.

'*Captain Klordren,*' he said; his voice carried across the vox-waves by uncanny means, and now it was deep and wild. '*Begin the evacuation.*'

'*Lokk? Lokk, is that you?*' Klordren replied.

'*You heard me. Obey,*' said Lokk, and strode away towards the extraction point, already taking his next step upon the path to glory.

'Fall back to my position!' Dvorgin shouted into Yenko's vox-horn. 'Fall back!'

Confusion is the natural state of war, but rarely had General

Dvorgin felt more powerless. Shells rained on his men from the cathedrum. The Iron Warriors had melted away, but there remained thousands of cultists and Traitor Guard, driven to a frenzy of slaughter. He had a position on the ground floor of a blasted palace. On the far side of the processional was a grand garden, now a crater-pocked wasteland. It seemed as good a place as any to make a last stand.

Boltguns boomed near him as Sergeant Lucerne and his Unnumbered Sons of Dorn fired into the screaming masses of cultists. They had become more bestial in action as the campaign had progressed, until today, when the last vestiges of humanity slipped from them, leaving nothing but husks animated by hate.

'Yenko, see if you can reach House Kamidar. If they can re-form their engines and bring them back to this position, we might last a little longer.' He slapped the master voxman on the shoulder and went at a crouch past his men, coming alongside the giant form of Sergeant Lucerne.

'General,' Lucerne said, not taking his eyes off the enemy. He kept his shots single, tracking every target with rock-steady aim before loosing the bolt. Dvorgin saw a crazed man explode on the far side of the processional.

'Have you heard from Shield-Captain Achallor?' asked Dvorgin. The Space Marine's vox-systems were more reliable than his, but he knew his hope was forlorn before the words had left his mouth.

'I have not,' said Lucerne.

'It would be nice to be able to die knowing his mission was a success,' said Dvorgin. He looked out for something to shoot, but his own bolt pistol felt like a toy compared to the Space Marine's massive bolt rifle; it lacked the range and he lacked Lucerne's skill.

'Have faith,' said Lucerne, cracking off another shot. 'The Iron Warriors have withdrawn.'

'You are certain?'

'I am certain.'

Dvorgin did not think it would be enough. 'What about Amalth-Amat, and Varsillian?'

'They live. They hold the north wing of this building,' said Lucerne.

A shell hit the building facade, bringing down a rush of dust that choked them. Through it, all Dvorgin could see were the bright flashes of weapon shots sparkling all over the front of the cathedrum, and the front ranks of the ragged horde advancing upon them. His own command included a few hundred Mordians, a few dozen Sisters of Battle and Lucerne's surviving Space Marines.

It would not be enough. The traitors numbered in the thousands.

'This is it then,' said Dvorgin.

'It appears that way,' said Lucerne.

The firing slackened off from the cathedrum, allowing the horde to advance. They came slowly, deliberately, murder in their faces. At two hundred yards wide, the processional would take them no time to cross. Gunfire still crackled across the Imperial front, felling the enemy in swathes, but they came on, fanatics with broken minds.

But they were still men, still women. They could still fear.

'If we can break their morale...' Dvorgin said to himself. 'Cease firing!' he shouted.

The guns stopped, one by one.

'Present arms for mass volley!' Dvorgin shouted, his voice carrying in the sudden quiet. If they could drop enough of the enemy at once, they would run. They would flee. They were cowards. He must remember that.

Then why were they still advancing?

Boltguns and lasguns rattled on piled stone. Tired faces caked in dust looked out from behind shattered statues and pieces of broken furniture, and yet their grips were steady and their aim was true. On the other side were civilians clutching lengths of pipe and street signs, or clubs of stone and wood. Only a few had guns. There were catacomb dwellers and artisans, priests, adepts, menials and lordlings, men and women both. The traitor planetary regiments they had fought these last months had lost all discipline, and were freely intermingled with the whole.

We can break them, thought Dvorgin. *They have no order. They have no commanders. We can break them.*

'Make ready to give fire! Select targets! Give fire on my command!'

Down the line the orders were repeated by Mordian and Sororitas officers. Far off, he heard the clear voice of Amalth-Amat doing the same.

He waited. At one hundred and fifty yards, they would get three volleys, he thought, if the enemy charged. Better to fire all at once. Bigger psychological impact.

'Morale, morale, morale,' he whispered to himself. The first and last lesson of battle. 'Fire!' he shouted, and the order was repeated down the line, and the guns spoke.

Las-beams and bolts took down two hundred of the enemy at once. They fell like cut grass. Still they came on.

'Fire!' he shouted again. More of the enemy dropped, those hit by lasguns falling like children playing at battle, those hit by bolts annihilated. The enemy let out a moaning, wordless roar, utterly mindless, utterly hopeless. Dvorgin knew then that he would not break them.

They moved into a trot.

'Fire!' he shouted.

The cultists were running, screaming, mad with loss and pain and all the things the Emperor had failed to shield them from.

'Fire!' Dvorgin shouted. He drew his power sword.

They were close enough now for him to see the madness in

The enemy were on the Imperial line.

The world disintegrated into screams and blood, where each moment existed as a thing discrete, distinct from every other moment. Dvorgin saw the battle from outside himself. His blade rose and killed, his gun fired. People exploded, were eviscerated, were stabbed. They fell clutching holes in their guts. They lost their faces. They lost their limbs. They lost their humanity, becoming brief incidents of pain and hate that were wiped away by violence.

A bullet skimmed the meat of his thigh, and he staggered, clutching at the wound while fending off an attack with his sword.

As the last moments came, and the defenders were reduced to desperate knots of resistance, something changed. Lightning leapt over the heads of the horde, jumping from particulates suspended in the air, throwing them down in showers of orange sparks. Dvorgin's teeth ached. His eyes hurt.

The lightning gathered into bright clumps in a dozen places, two dozen, then three, growing into loose balls of light that coalesced into solid orbs, and from them stellar violence erupted, laying out the combatants in neat patterns upon the floor, and allowing Dvorgin to see the fifty golden giants who had appeared standing amid the crowds of the fallen.

One, more glorious and mighty than all the rest, raised up his halberd and proclaimed, 'Warriors of the Imperium, be of good heart! Your salvation is at hand! The Indomitus Crusade has come!'

So speaking, trailing streamers of icy vapour and corposant, Stratarchis Tribune Maldovar Colquan led the charge that saved Gathalamor.

Chapter Thirty-Eight

PERSON OF CONSEQUENCE

POLITICAL RESPECT

FUNERAL

'Historitor Guelphrain, it is a real pleasure to see you again.'

The voice was familiar, but the figure was not. The armour the Space Marine wore was blackened all over and covered in chips that exposed the dull, leaden grain of raw ceramite. Dust clung to every recess, and only in a few places could the rich yellow of his livery be seen. Thirty Space Marines had set out from Fleet Primus, nine remained. Their insignia and colours stripped away, they looked all the same.

'Brother-Sergeant Lucerne?' said Fabian unsurely. He came down the gangway stairs of the lander, stopping on the bottom step.

'The very same,' said Lucerne.

'Then you live,' Fabian said lamely, too overwhelmed to speak well.

'Apparently I do,' said Lucerne.

'I'm sorry,' Fabian said, gathering himself. 'I didn't recognise you.'

'War changes a man, and not only on the surface,' Lucerne said. 'We have come to escort you. The city of Imprezentia is mostly secure, but there are dangers here beyond those posed by the enemy, and a few of them also yet remain.'

Fabian looked past the giant figures. Lucerne was putting it mildly. All he saw were ruins, in every direction that he looked. He had been told Ascension Stair was in a fair state, the space port already receiving a steady stream of landing craft from the fleet, but few of its buildings were free of damage, and the reclamation crews working everywhere to bring its facilities back into use were faced with a hopeless task.

'What happened here?' he asked.

'Victory,' said Lucerne drily.

'Then I would not like to see defeat,' said Fabian.

'Come,' said Lucerne. 'I will show you about, and we can start planning your duties.'

'Do you not get to rest?' asked Fabian.

Lucerne laughed. 'Rest is not something we crave, historitor, not while duty calls.'

Fabian looked down past the lighter's last step. The landing pad was made of ferrocrete, but covered over with the fine grit of ash and debris.

'This is the first planet I have ever set foot on that is not Terra,' he said.

'Then I shall pray to the Emperor that it is but the first of many, and that all of them welcome you in triumph,' said Lucerne, and held out his hand.

Fabian stepped down. Beyond the Space Marines was a group of wan-looking adepts, skinny with famine under their official robes. All of them were exhausted. All of them were haunted. More than half of them had ash painted on their faces in signs of repentance, and had torn the decoration from their robes in shame. They looked like the dead.

This place is thick with ghosts, he thought, and suppressed a shudder.

'Welcome to Gathalamor, historitor,' their leader said, and knelt. His fellows followed his example. 'Forgive us,' another said.

Fabian looked to Lucerne in question.

'You come with the authority of the primarch,' said Lucerne. He came closer and bent down, his lowered voice growling softly from his voxmitter. 'Remember, Fabian, that you are a person of some import now, and that you must act accordingly.'

A spread of shells had got through the void shields towards the end of the fighting, bringing down a vast hangar into a field of rubble, and Fabian, Lucerne and his small honour guard were forced to detour south and then swing east to avoid it. Fires burned in many places, and though the sky was clearing now the battle was days done, smoke still billowed from pits where stone had yet to cool, forcing Fabian to use his respirator more than once.

As they made their way through the battle-damaged void port, the adepts gave Fabian a brief history of the world, though it differed significantly from the truth he knew, with no mention of Bucharis. There was a hint of pride in the leader's voice as he spoke of the world's importance, but it was tarnished much by shame, Fabian thought, and a little fear. Not for what had been, but for what would come. Someone would have to answer for the betrayal here.

Fabian's unease deepened. Wrecked vehicles, blasted rubble and heaps of corpses were everywhere. A huge, still-glowing crater was sunk into the edge of the primary landing field. Fire suppression servitors were at work spraying retardant from integrated tanks, to no discernible effect.

'Is this facility even viable?' asked Fabian, his voice already roughened by smoke.

'Eminently,' replied the adept. 'The Logisticarum and Munitorum are here, laying grand plans for the port's resuscitation. What you see there is a bone fire. The remains of ancients beneath the surface were ignited by energy weapons in the last stages of the battle. We have experience with such disasters and will bring it under control. Lord Vychellan has already assessed the damage and deemed the port workable. It is troublesome, but not enough to prevent the landing of troops and armour.'

'And supplies,' prompted Fabian. 'To feed your people.'

'If the primarch deems us worthy,' said the adept tightly.

Fabian didn't wish to damage the adept's morale further, and so said nothing more.

They passed Mordians sitting quietly around campfires and Phyroxians seated upon their tanks. Sisters went about, their guns set aside, bringing succour now to the small groups of civilians daring to venture above ground. The soldiers saluted Lucerne as they passed, and called out to him, as if Fabian and the adepts were not there, and he found himself glad of the lack of attention. Gaggles of support serfs and logistical adepts hurried to and fro across the cracked ferrocrete, and as the minutes passed more and more landers came down from the fleet hanging in the sky, and more ground haulers growled out from the cargo bays of ships.

They approached the western edge of the port, and the drop keep of House Kamidar came out of the smoke, its forest of antennae and vox-shrines reaching towards the turbulent heavens. Several white-and-gold Imperial Knights encircled it. More of the war engines were encased in plasteel gantries concertinaed out from the keep on heavy track units. Tech-priests in strange garb busied themselves about these Knights, their servants swarming over them with tools, paint-sprayers and sacred unguents, repairing battle damage and reapplying markings, all undertaken to the singing of machine-soothing hymns.

As Fabian and his small group neared the main ramp of the keep, one of the less-damaged Knights took a step forward. Its head angled down, and a voice boomed from its voxmitters, accented and lilting.

'Brother-Sergeant Lucerne and Historitor Guelphrain, I presume?'

'Correct,' said Fabian. 'Whom do we address?'

'I have the honour of being First Blade Sheane Y'Kamidar, of the House Kamidar,' replied the noble enthroned within. 'Princess Jessivayne of the Ironhold Protectorate bids you welcome. She awaits you within.'

The princess would forever wait, thought Fabian when he saw her. She sat upon the battered throne taken from her war machine, surrounded by candles, murmuring priests and, sourced from who-knew-where, thousands of flowers. The hall was a war-deck, a place where battles were begun and victories celebrated. Fabian saw the locking cradles for the Knights arrayed around the hall, seven rows in a circle, in three ranks. A few were occupied by war engines of various sizes. Most were empty. Fabian did a silent count, adding the total to those outside, and saw that most of the cradles would remain empty for the journey back to Kamidar.

For now, the hall was a mausoleum. Jessivayne Y'Kamidar's lifeless body stared out through the gate she would never ride through again, coins over her eyes. The mortuary skills of her people were considerable, and a veil had been laid over her face, but neither could hide all the damage, and even in the low light of the candles the wreck of her skull was readily apparent. Another noble of solemn countenance stood vigil at her side. Fabian nodded respectfully at him. He stared back, as if searching for an excuse to draw the blade upon his back and run the historitor through.

The First Blade's Knight stalked in, the thrum of its engines and hissing pistons loud in the confined space. Fabian had seen vids of Knights in combat; they were fast, and daunting to behold in their skill at arms, but here, now, after the war was done, the First Knight's mount seemed tired, nothing but a worn-out piece of machinery as it stalked back to its cradle, reversed awkwardly into position and let its flight clamps take it. A gantry with steps pushed against the carapace. The hatch atop the machine swung up, and Sheane Y'Kamidar clambered out to join them.

He looks haggard, thought Fabian. *He has a face that seems more used to joy, but all his joy has gone.*

'They tell me you are the primarch's lorekeeper,' said the First Blade.

'In a manner of speaking that is true,' said Fabian. 'I am one among many, and there are differing sorts. I am simply the one that has been sent here to record the story of this victory.'

'Then you have the primarch's ear?' said the First Blade.

'As much as any man has, yes,' said Fabian.

'Then I want you to tell him something for me.'

'I shall do my best, First Blade,' said Fabian.

Sheane stepped close to Fabian. Once he would have stepped back, or even cowered at such an aggressive move, but he had learned to stand his ground and did so as the First Blade spoke right into his face.

'I want you to tell him how my cousin died defending this world. I want you to tell him her oaths were upheld. I want you to tell him how she fought.' Sheane looked upon the corpse, and his eyes gleamed with more than tears. 'I want you to tell him...' His voice cracked, and some of the aggression left him. 'I want you to tell him how glorious she was in battle, and I want you to write it, so that it will be known for all time.'

Fabian looked at the princess' body and the grim noble at its side. He could tell the First Knight of the politics that had sent him here before other places. How the honour done House Kamidar was purely a strategic consideration. The Ironhold Protectorate had been identified as a good place to site a hub-fortress to supply the crusade. That was all.

He did not say those things. Instead, he said, 'Do not fear, First Blade. The primarch Roboute Guilliman has heard of her valour, and he mourns her loss. It is why I came here first.'

The citizens of Imprezentia emerged in small groups, and when they came out they gave their thanks to their saviours, and set themselves to work to show their repentance.

Within a few days they were done, clearing by hand the route from Saint Claytor's Span all the way to the macro-cathedrum some twenty miles away. The entire length of Processional Hope Enduring was made fit for passage. When they were finished, they sent envoys, dirty, emaciated and half-dead, to plead with Gathalamor's new authorities.

Their request, much to Vychellan's disgust, was granted.

Vychellan and Maldovar Colquan watched as the cortege was made ready. They were given the position of honour, as representatives of the God-Emperor Himself, viewing the proceedings from a bullet-riddled balcony high over the processional. A hundred more of the Custodians lined the road, five to a mile, golden winks of light in dark crowds.

'This is not right,' said Vychellan.

'No, but it is expedient,' said the tribune.

A thousand Gathalamorians in ashes and sackcloth pulled the sarcophagus on rollers made of broken columns. The coffin and its effigy had been carved within days, a testimony to the skill of the world's sculptors. Ten thousand more civilians marched either side and in front, whipping themselves, singing dolorous songs of penance. Behind the cortege was a river of light, thousands upon thousands more people coming behind bearing torches, and wailing loud enough to shake the ruins.

There were other civilians too, those who had cast their lots in with different gods, and there could be no forgiveness for them. They were shackled to iron posts either side of the processional. At the very head of the cortege went Canoness Imelda Veritas and her Sisters. They sang hymns of victory. Young girls, orphaned by the war and selected to be raised within the Sisterhood, ran ahead, soaking the traitors with promethium from decorated buckets. Ordained Sisters wielding flamers set each alight with a short burst of fire as they passed, so that the wailing of grief, the songs of repentance and triumph were accompanied by thin screams. Those waiting to burn were praying. Though their words were lost in the noise of the funeral, the combination of Vychellan's enhanced eyesight and his battleplate auto-senses allowed him to read the lips of some.

The word they said most often was 'Emperor'.

'Faith is a poison,' Vychellan said. 'The Emperor was right to suppress it. Faith empowers the enemy, and enchains mankind. It is blind. It reduces us to beasts.'

The crowd turned their faces up as they went past the tower where the Custodians watched. Their hands raised beseechingly to the tribune, who looked over their heads the whole time.

'They are praying to us. That is wrong. It will affect us, eventually,' said Vychellan. 'We have been isolated for a long time, and we are not perfect.'

'We shall not fall,' said Colquan.

'This charade makes it more likely. Allowing him to be buried like this, here, in a church, to all this worship. It's wrong.'

'It is wrong.' Colquan turned to look at Vychellan. 'But it is also necessary. Achallor died fighting to defend this world. The whole character of the place is bound up in faith. It has a power of its own. You have fought with the Sisters of Battle. You have seen how their belief protects and enhances them.'

'A psychic effect that they would, in any other, denounce as witchcraft,' said Vychellan.

'We are not here to judge the galaxy for its hypocrisy. We are here to save it. Faith may yet prove to be our greatest weapon,' said Colquan. 'Faith is a psychic effect, but it is one like no other, and whether we like it or not, it is connected intimately to our lord.

'You do not understand, Vychellan. All this, the saints, the visions, the tarot, they are tools – they are a means by which we may exert control. They are *useful*. We have shown any who might waver in their loyalty that the Emperor's forces are abroad. They know now that His servants will smite those who turn from Terra, and His servants will be saved. Achallor's interment here is a symbol of that. Let them venerate him as a saint for a while. They would anyway. Best we make use of it. This world is a lynchpin, not only for this segmentum, but also for the crusade.'

'It is still wrong,' said Vychellan.

Colquan nodded. 'It is, but it will not last. When all this is done, the church will fall, and this long era of idolatry will finally pass. For what is the one truth, Hastius Vychellan?'

'The Emperor's truth,' Vychellan breathed.

'A primarch walks among us,' said Colquan. 'Though I question the wisdom of following him blindly, it gives me hope, for if one such being may return from the ages of wonder, our master may follow. I have faith of my own, Hastius. Faith in the Emperor's plan. Look upon this and do not see it as the plan gone awry, but as our master at work.'

The sarcophagus ground slowly along the processional towards the cathedrum's mountainous towers, traitors igniting before it, light following it, human grief and pain bathing it.

So it was that Shield-Captain Marcus Achallor came to be laid to rest in the Temple of the Emperor Exultant, the macro-cathedrum of Asclomaedas the Builder, a deception to gild a brazen lie.

Chapter Thirty-Nine

DVORGIN'S FATE

ANOTHER DAUGHTER

START AT THE BEGINNING

General Dvorgin limped down a corridor in the macro-cathedrum. Its bare walls amplified his footfalls and the clunk of his crutch. Alcoves stood emptied of defiled statues. The air stank of burning. The walls were black where thrice-blessed flamers had scoured away blasphemous marks.

Three days and already the faith spreads its cleansing fires across Gathalamor, he thought. Dvorgin should have felt pride at his role in bringing those fires here, but then he glanced back at Lieutenant Stehner and Master Voxman Yenko, and their exhausted faces, and he thought, no, there was no pride. Instead he felt loss, bone-deep exhaustion and a smouldering anger. That last, at least, kept his feet moving and his spine straight. It would have to fill in for hope and faith until... if... they returned.

He checked his pocket chron, saw the inscription there again.

Luthor,
Make us always proud, my fierce protector,
Marie.

A stab of guilt there. Another dear face never to be seen again. If there was any comfort to be found, it was that he always felt this way, after the victory.

'The Ecclesiarchy have done remarkable work so swiftly,' said Stehner.

Throne, he's trying to offer me encouragement, Dvorgin thought. The idea that his Mordian stoicism could have slipped so much Stehner noticed was quietly horrifying. Dvorgin answered with a carefully neutral, 'Hmm.' Stehner took the hint.

They continued in silence. They passed groups of Battle Sisters and priests at work scouring away the filth of the heretics. Work maniples of servitors lumbered past, hauling carts piled with corpses.

As they moved deeper into the wing that had been designated Temporary Crusade Command: Gathalamor, they encountered Astra Militarum sentries in regimental uniforms Dvorgin didn't recognise. They saluted Dvorgin's small party as they passed, some with fierce pride, others with wide-eyed expressions bordering on veneration.

All Dvorgin could think was how young the soldiers all looked, how untried and untested.

Make us always proud.

They passed, too, the scented torches burning along the walls of those sections declared purged to the priests' satisfaction. Whatever was in the brands threw fierce light. They forced the shadows back to the furthest corners and made Dvorgin squint.

At last he stumped up a flight of marble steps to their destination. The chantry of Saint Cassimus boasted an ornate arch set with skulls.

'Look,' said Stehner. 'They left it alone.'

'It's a very big place,' said Dvorgin. 'Not even those lunatics could get round to every single carving.'

Standing solemnly before the arched door was one of the Custodian Guard. There were so many around the temple and the void port that their presence had gone from the unbelievable to the merely astounding, though they would never become mundane. The giant stepped wordlessly aside, admitting them to the chamber beyond, where various officers waited in various states of tiredness. Voices floated from the room past the vestibule.

'Wait here,' Dvorgin told Stehner and Yenko. 'This will not take long. I'll make sure of it. Then you'll have your turn, and we can go and rest.' *After,* he thought to himself, *I've drunk a bottle of whatever I can get my hands on.*

He hobbled into the chantry, sparing barely a glance for the representation of the Emperor enthroned staring down from the dome, though it too represented a minor miracle in its unsullied state. *This world has blinded me to the holy,* he thought dismally.

Within the chantry, Dvorgin found Canoness Veritas and Palatine Emmanuelle, Lady Nimue and Lord Sheane Y'Kamidar, and Custodian Hastius Vychellan.

'...will not be ready for at least two more days,' Imelda Veritas was saying, but she halted and turned as she noticed Dvorgin. They all looked around, and for an instant the general was gripped by an unexpected surge of jealousy, as though he had walked in upon a group of friends holding a gathering to which he had not been invited.

Ridiculous thought, he told himself, and offered them an aquila salute. Its dignity was lessened by the necessity of propping himself on his crutch as he made the gesture, but all present returned it with the respect it deserved.

'General,' said Vychellan. Within the frame of his beard, his mouth was set. His expression was unreadable; his eyes looked upon matters beyond mortal concerns. Dvorgin was a little surprised. He had expected to see more grief there. Sir Sheane was the exact opposite. Grief wept off him like rain. It seemed that the galaxy had at last dealt Sheane Y'Kamidar a blow he could not shrug off with a smirk.

My fiercer protector.

'Is it true, what I have heard?' asked Dvorgin. 'That House Kamidar is to depart tomorrow?'

'We are,' answered Sir Sheane. 'Jessivayne's...' He started again. 'The princess' body is to be returned to Ironhold in state. It is my duty as First Blade to see that she and her Throne Mechanicum find their proper place within the sanctum of House Kamidar. Queen Orlah would expect no less for her daughter.' His jaw clenched. 'The primarch himself gave me this honour.' Sheane was unable to say more, his scarred face twisting with sorrow.

'We have no ship to bear us and our fallen hence,' Lady Nimue said for him. 'Thus, Lord Vychellan suggested and sought permission for Battle Group Praxis to steer a course that will bring it to the Ironhold Protectorate.'

'A very grand gesture of thanks,' said Dvorgin, and it sounded petty when he didn't mean it to.

'A deed, not a gesture, and one of absolute pragmatism,' Vychellan replied. 'My counsel has been ratified by Stratarchis Tribune Colquan himself on behalf of Primarch Guilliman. I make no secret of my belief that the Ironhold Protectorate would make a worthy redoubt for the crusade.'

Dvorgin felt shame at his tone. Duty felt hollow now, after all that blood.

Make us always proud, my fierce protector.

'I have not had the opportunity to express to you my gladness that both our lord the primarch and your own tribune remain safe,' said Dvorgin, and managed to sound sincere this time.

'The entire Imperium would no doubt express its gladness, had they but the chance,' said Veritas.

'Nonetheless, if we had been defeated, and the weapon free to fire over and over again...' said Dvorgin, letting the sentence hang. 'I am glad the lives of my people did so much to safeguard the Lord Guilliman.'

'Do not regret either your caution or your pragmatism during this conflict, general,' said Vychellan, softening slightly. 'Those qualities won us victory. Throne knows this campaign was costly enough.'

Vychellan's words threatened to plunge Dvorgin back into that ash-choked, nightmarish battle again, to conjure up the gheist-haunted darkness, the roar of gunfire. And still it was not done. There remained an eternity of battles to fight.

Dvorgin managed a smile. 'And so, the rest of you? Are you to accompany Praxis also?'

'I shall,' replied Vychellan. 'As a mark of honour to the princess' sacrifice.'

More politics, thought Dvorgin. More sacrifice. More daughters and sons to feed into the bloody mills of war. He felt his face tighten, and forced himself to look to Veritas.

'And you, canoness?'

'The Sisters of the Argent Shroud will not be departing,' she said.

'I would have thought that you would be the first to join the crusade,' Dvorgin said.

'And we would, Luthor, if our work in this system was done,' she replied. 'It will be weeks yet before even this one structure can be purified. Months before Gathalamor can be declared free from the taint of the heretic. Fleet command has graciously provided us with the assistance of the Eighteenth Korlian Tunnelsnakes and several missions from the Order of the Ebon Chalice. There remains hard fighting ahead to root out the most deeply buried cults, here and elsewhere in the system, and Gathalamor is vital, as much to the faith as it is to the crusade. What about you?'

Make us always proud.

The question hung in the air like the echo of a bell. Dvorgin felt as if he had nothing left to give, but his duty remained, always hungry, always demanding more of him.

'In a galaxy this bloody, there's duty enough for a soldier upon every world. And maybe, if they're lucky, a death worth the dying. We'll be heading out with the crusade...' He paused.

My fierce protector.

'Lord Vychellan, perhaps I might make a request?' Dvorgin asked.

'If I can accommodate you, general.'

'I would like to petition that what remains of my regiment be allocated to join Battle Group Praxis,' he said. His thoughts flickered momentarily to the torches burning in their sconces beyond the chapel door. 'I have made good comrades here. Friends. I would see us carry the light of the Emperor out into this dark galaxy and drive back the shadows. Ironhold seems like a good place to begin.'

'It is not my place to make such decisions,' said Vychellan.

'I know, I know,' said Dvorgin. 'But with respect, my lord, I do not know Groupmaster Ardemus and he does not know me. Whereas you have seen the quality of my regiment first-hand. A word of recommendation from you would secure the groupmaster's agreement with a surety no amount of Departmento Munitorum paperwork could guarantee.'

Vychellan smiled a small, hard smile. 'A fair observation, general. You and your soldiers are a credit to the planet of Mordian.'

'May we find her hale and whole beyond the Rift,' said Dvorgin automatically.

Marie.

He shrugged that thought off quickly. He was carrying enough on his shoulders without his homeworld's possible demise to think on.

'I will make the recommendation,' said Vychellan.

Dvorgin lightened a little at the thought of getting his soldiers off Gathalamor. He could not wait to escape its ghosts. 'Thank you, my lord,' he said.

'If we are done here, we have arrangements to make with Magos Rho-Theta Fideles before he can begin the loading of our Knights,' said Sir Sheane.

'You have spoken to the historitor?'

'All of the senior officers have,' said Sheane. 'He was saving you until last. He's a pleasant enough man. Now, if you will excuse us – come, Lady Nimue.'

Lady Nimue clicked her heels and bowed. Vychellan looked from the canoness to the general and back, then said, 'I shall accompany you, if I may, First Blade. You must tell me of your home.'

'It would be an honour, my lord.'

They left Dvorgin and Veritas alone in the chancery. For the moment the door was open, and Dvorgin saw the lower ranks outside waiting to be interviewed, and heard the murmur of conversation, then the door closed after the Custodian and the nobles, and silence fell.

'Well then,' said Dvorgin eventually. 'I suppose this is farewell.' He turned to the canoness. 'I am glad to know that this world and its safety remain in your hands, Imelda Veritas.' Dvorgin surprised himself with the emotion in his words. 'Holding the Gate of Gathalamor took more faith, and more lives than I believed possible. It has been an honour to fight alongside you.'

The canoness offered him the sign of the aquila in recognition of his compliments, but her brow furrowed.

'You did the Emperor's work here, Luthor, just as much as

I. If we still had that bottle of amasec I would toast your victory without hesitation, and I would not be alone in offering thanks to you.'

'That victory took a terrible toll, canoness,' he sighed, feeling terribly weary. 'Throne knows I have watched soldiers younger than me, better than me, die in their thousands these past years and I have always known that they and I did our duty both. Yet this conflict... so many gone, and here I am, still continuing on, unworthy as I am.'

The confession shocked him. He was glad that he had spoken quietly, and that Stehner and Yenko remained out of earshot. Still he cringed inwardly at having cast aside his Mordian reserve, even for a moment, even to one of the Battle Sisters of the Emperor. He expected reproach from the canoness.

Instead, Imelda Veritas gave him a frank look and grasped his shoulder.

'You made the right choice today, Luthor,' she said. 'Your faith is a pure and brilliant diamond that no travail can erode. You strike out on crusade and carry the light of the Emperor with you. Those who bear His word into the darkness cannot help but be bathed in His light. I believe you will find more than duty beyond the stars, my friend.'

Friend. That word, coming from this woman, shook Dvorgin. He found to his surprise that he was smiling for the first time in days. He felt a surge of gratitude and, with distinctly un-Mordian emotion, he gripped the canoness' wrist.

'Thank you, Imelda Veritas. May the Emperor watch over you, now and always.'

'Remember, Luthor, do not pity the dead. Their labours are done. What you witnessed here was an aberration. The faithful rest eternal and honoured at the Emperor's side.' With that, Imelda Veritas departed. Dvorgin was left alone in the small chapel.

She hadn't meant to chill him with those words, but she had. He thought of the writhing spectres that had assailed his soldiers in the last, nightmarish hours of the war. He thought of his fallen suffering the same fate as those tortured ghosts, then looked up at the Emperor in the dome above.

'Take no more of mine, oh God-Emperor,' he said fervently. 'Please, no more of mine.'

The far door of the chantry opened, and a man in a uniform Dvorgin now knew to be that of the Logisticarum came out. He looked to be in his thirties, and as if he had recently returned to good health after a long illness.

'General Dvorgin?'

'Yes?'

'Sorry to keep you waiting,' he said. 'I am Historitor Fabian Guelphrain. I am here to record your testimony of the campaign,' he added, though Dvorgin knew that already.

Dvorgin hobbled away towards the door, unable to shake the conviction that, whatever had transpired upon Gathalamor, darker days lay ahead.

Nor could he quite dispel the sensation that the heavy gaze of the Emperor followed him from the small chapel, and in that gaze was judgement.

Fabian Guelphrain had established a small, temporary office in a deacon's room. It was totally undisturbed, and dusty vestments still hung from their hooks on a worm-eaten rood screen. There was a desk, and piles of papers, neatly arranged, and data-recording technologies of various sorts, some of which were familiar and some of which were not. Another man, older and scruffier than Fabian, sat at a folding desk at the back of the room, an autoquill at the ready. Despite his shabby air, he looked alert.

'Please,' said Fabian, gesturing to the chair in front of his desk.

Dvorgin sat down in it, his wounded leg stiff off to the side, while Fabian took the chair opposite. He gave a businesslike sigh and straightened the utensils of his trade.

'You know what we are about here?'

'You just said yourself that you are here to record an account of the campaign,' said Dvorgin a little sharply. He paused, breathed. 'I'm sorry. I am very tired. Look, my lord, I know a debriefing when I see one. May we proceed quickly?'

Fabian smiled and tilted his head to one side. 'Well, yes, we can – but also no, it's not a debriefing. That's not exactly what this is.'

He laced his fingers together and peered over them at Dvorgin.

'What would you say is the one commodity we lack in the Imperium?'

Dvorgin could name many: mercy, kindness, joy, just for a start. He didn't. 'Why don't you tell me, my lord?' asked Dvorgin.

Fabian frowned when he failed to engage the general, but spoke on. 'It's truth,' he said. 'We are mired in lies and super-stitions. The primarch is a stranger to our times. He wants to learn everything he can about us – history, how we think, what is valuable to us – and from that he will learn how we will act, and how we must be ruled.'

'You know him then?'

'I don't know if anyone can know him,' said Fabian.

'You've met him, though. What's he like?' asked Dvorgin.

'Alone,' said Fabian, an answer whose frankness took Dvorgin aback.

He sighed, and shifted his leg into a more comfortable posi-tion. 'I don't really know what I can add. You have my combat logs, and my colour-sergeant's records. We mustered here at the primarch's command a week before the enemy invaded. We had no time to prepare before the Iron Warriors translated in-system. We were surprised by the uprising among the civilian the port despite heavy casualties.'

He took his hat off and dropped it on the desk, and smoothed
over his thinning hair.

'I would like to say that we drove the enemy off, but really
they simply withdrew. They could surely have finished us. In
truth, their strategy baffles me. It hardly matters anyway. A lot
of my regiment were lost.'

'You know, or you ought to, that this was a victory against
the Heretic Astartes,' said Fabian. 'A death in the Emperor's
service is always a good one, but your foes here were particularly dangerous.'

'And what do you know about fighting?' said Dvorgin tersely.

'Nothing. That is why you are here with me now.'

'It's no good,' said Dvorgin. 'You won't understand. You won't
understand if you've never seen men and women you are responsible for blown apart in front of you. If you've never seen a world
burn. If you've never seen the sky turn black with the enemy's
malice – and I don't mean that as some kind of metaphor,' he
said, gesturing dismissively at the papers and books. 'I mean that
as an actual, literal truth. You don't know what it's like.'

'Ah,' said Fabian. 'Actually, I do. I witnessed...' He stopped himself. 'I saw things, on Terra. I saw the attack on the Lion's Gate.'

Dvorgin felt a bolt of shock. 'Terra was attacked?'

Fabian nodded. 'By xenos, at least, that's what they said they
were.' He gave a meaningful look. Dvorgin thought he knew to
what the historitor referred. It wasn't safe to say.

'Did you fight?'

Fabian shook his head. 'I only saw for a few moments, but
it was enough.'

'With all due respect, it is not enough. You have no idea.'

Fabian shuffled his papers and had the good grace to look
embarrassed. He sighed. 'Shall we begin again?' he said.

'Yes, my lord,' replied Dvorgin. He paused. 'I am sorry. I am sorry for my behaviour. It has been a long campaign. I lost many good men and women. I am sorry if my faith seems lacking.'

'I'm not a priest,' said Fabian.

'Then I'm sorry if my dedication is also lacking.'

'Nor am I here to judge you.'

Dvorgin let out a snort of laughter.

'No, really, I'm not,' said Fabian.

'I am sure you are sincere, my lord...'

'Please.' Fabian pulled a face. 'Please don't call me that. I'm no one's lord.'

Make us proud, my fierce protector.

Are you safe, Marie? he wondered. *Who protects you now?*

'What should I call you, sir? "Sir"?'

'Call me Fabian, that is my name.'

'Then I don't know where to start, Fabian.'

'I find the beginning is a good place.'

Dvorgin frowned. He reached into his uniform, hesitated, then pulled out the cap he kept by his heart.

'This cap,' he said. He tossed it onto the table. 'This cap belongs to my daughter.'

'You have a daughter?' said Fabian, beginning now to take notes.

'Figuratively speaking, and I don't mean in the way that a general is a father to all his soldiers. She is special, this one. She is a good marksman, the best I have. Brave too.'

'And she feels like a daughter to you because of this?'

'No, not really,' said Dvorgin. His eyes began to brim and he coughed to cover his emotions. 'It's... it's complicated. Before I left Mordian, my wife asked me to give her a child. I refused. Who would want to bring a child into this age?' he said. 'I take hold of my duty with both hands, but what right have I to insist another do so?'

He stared at Fabian defiantly. In certain quarters, dealing with a certain kind of person, this admission would be a death sentence.

'It is the one time I failed in my duty to the Emperor. The one time my faith wavered. It never had before, and never has since.'

'Not even now?'

'I am sad. I am tired. I will get over it, and I will fight again. So no, not even now.'

'And does this relate to this...?' Fabian let the question hang.

'Sergeant Kesh, Sergeant Magda Kesh. That is her name.'

Fabian noted the name down. His servant transcribed everything said.

Where will it end up? Dvorgin thought. *What stains am I blotting my record with?*

He found he didn't care.

'How does your supposed lack of faith relate to Sergeant Kesh, then?' said Fabian.

'She is the same age as my child would have been had I chosen to provide one to the Emperor. I'd been thinking about it for years. She is impressive. As she grew under my command, I found myself questioning my decision.' There was a loose splinter in the desk. Dvorgin picked at it. 'I suppose I show Kesh a little favouritism, and I know some of the men talk, but it isn't like that. And then she went on a mission with the Adeptus Custodes, and I was horrified. I should have been glad. Think of the honour! But all I could think of was losing her, and, well, that's that.'

'Is she dead?'

'I thought she was. We all thought she was.' He picked the splinter free, wiped it off on his trousers. 'She's in the infirmary, wounded, more in mind than in body. She was with Shield-Captain Achallor. Lord Vychellan saw her fall, but she limped back into camp with a one-eyed Custodian a few days after the last battle. They say she was buried in bones, that she fought daemons, and ghosts, but she lived. Some people are surprised. I'm not, because that's Kesh. I'm proud of her.'

He glanced up and smiled.

'And so, I find myself thinking, if she could do that, what right did I have to decide that my real child could not? I never gave them the chance, because I did not let them be born. And so I failed my Emperor. No faith, you see?'

'You should not judge yourself harshly.'

'You're not in a position to make that kind of statement, I think.'

Fabian put aside his pen, and laced his fingers together again. 'Kesh, eh? Sounds like a good story,' said Fabian. 'Why don't you tell me about her first?'

'Why would anyone be interested in that?'

'Because she is a person. Because you care. That's why.'

'Alright,' said Dvorgin with a shrug. By the Emperor, he was so tired.

'Tell me about her, then you can tell me about what happened here.'

'Which part?' said Dvorgin.

'Tell me all of it,' said Fabian.

So Dvorgin did.

Appendix: Notes on the Crusade

It is said by some adepts that when the Indomitus Crusade's assets are fully calculated, they will exceed those gathered by the Emperor for His Great Crusade of galactic reconquest at the dawn of the Imperium. Whether or not this is objectively true, and many have disputed the facts that form the basis of this opinion, the Indomitus Crusade was undeniably vast, involving billions of men and women from hundreds of thousands of worlds. Orchestrating such an ambitious venture, across an Imperium that was suffering from warp travel problems and temporal upheaval, was a challenge even for the strategic genius of the returned primarch, Roboute Guilliman. Nowhere is this clearer than at the very beginning of the endeavour.

THE OPENING MOVES

The first months of this unprecedented military effort were concentrated on capturing the so-called 'warp nexuses' proximate to Terra. There were eight of these in total, only one of which, Vorlese, was in the hands of the Imperium as the war began.

After the turmoil unleashed by the opening of the Cicatrix Maledictum, established warp routes were severely disrupted. A number of major nexuses vanished, isolating previously strategically vital worlds, while new ones formed under a number of other worlds. Some of these were already of importance, others backwaters. Using sorcerous divinations, Abaddon's forces struck at the eight systems having the largest confluence of swift warp currents – the reasoning being, later strategists surmised, to box in the fleets of the Imperium and force them to take slower, more dangerous routes through the immaterium.

Following the successful defence of Vorlese by the Talons of the Emperor, Roboute Guilliman determined to retake as many of these vital systems as possible. Fleet Quintus was due to depart first under Lord Fleet Commander Tronion Prasorius. His mission was to retake Lessira, deep in the south of the Segmentum Solar. Fleet Tertius was marked to leave soon after under Fleetmistress Lady Cassandra VanLeskus for Olmec, a world largely abandoned for millennia. They were to operate swiftly, while Abaddon the Despoiler's forces were distracted by Fleet Secundus' direct attack on the Eye of Terror. Only when these two worlds had been retaken was Lord Guilliman himself to set sail, leading Fleet Primus against Gathalamor, a crucial cardinal and shrine world to the galactic south-west. The strategy being that key nexuses in an arc from the galactic west to the galactic east would be in Imperial hands, allowing rapid deployment of battle groups to multiple sectors. These would have reinforced Imperial-held space while purging enemy presence from the quieter regions of the Imperium Sanctus, allowing humanity to recover from the terrible galaxy-wide attack.

Alas, plans do not survive long in the maelstrom of war.

STRATEGY REWRITTEN

The first signs of disruption came with numerous setbacks for Fleet Quintus, including plague, logistical missteps and outright sabotage. An assault from the Eye of Terror towards the strategic system of Hydraphur – the Navis Imperialis' key base in the galactic north-west – threatened to tear the Rift wider, opening a road of unstable space into the heart of the Segmentum Solar. With Quintus delayed, and the attack of Tertius upon Olmec postponed to allow VanLeskus' crusade fleet to tackle this new threat, Guilliman's strategy was hanging by a thread. As it was, Quintus' departure was put off. Tertius was rapidly despatched towards Hydraphur. Secundus' sailing followed, beginning its slow Road of Martyrs. Guilliman made himself ready to take Gathalamor, without which the entire crusade might come to a crashing halt.

Although heavy casualties were inflicted upon Fleet Primus, Gathalamor was retaken, and thereafter Fleet Primus split, rapidly deploying across the Segmentum Tempestus and Segmentum Pacificus, with Guilliman's own battle group swinging north to take advantage of recent news that Imperial holdings persisted on the far side of the Rift.

Meanwhile, Fleet Tertius drove south, stabilising systems as it went, and finally took Olmec. Fleet Quintus eventually departed, but was beaten to the prize of Lessira by lead elements of Fleet Tertius, whose rapid advance gave cheer to citizens of the Imperium everywhere. Guilliman's opening moves had been accomplished, so to history's eyes the first, successful stages of the crusade hid the disaster that almost befell it.

* * *

ANDY CLARK

Notable among the fleet's many armed forces was the presence of the Adeptus Custodes. Although members of the Emperor's Legion had been active away from Terra on numerous secret missions since the Emperor's incarceration, the Indomitus Crusade represents the first time they openly left the Imperial Palace, and they had certainly not departed in such numbers since the days of the Horus Heresy.

Following the actions of Shield-Captain Valerian and Sister of Silence Aleya in securing Vorlese before the crusade began, the Adeptus Custodes enacted the Vorlese Precedent, formally dissolving the Edict of Restraint that had bound them to Terra.

Though present across all fleets as emissaries, commanders and shock forces, the bulk of their number was to be found in Fleet Primus, at least for the first few years of the crusade. This great host was commanded by Stratarchis Tribune Maldovar Colquan. One of only two tribunes in the entire legion, the Stratarchis Tribune held responsibility for all off-Terra operations of the Custodian Guard. A vocal critic of the returned primarch, Colquan was nevertheless to prove instrumental to the war.

THE IMPERIAL FAITH

The Sisters of Battle were to emerge as one of the Imperium's key assets during the era Indomitus, their faith in the Emperor a potent weapon in the fight against Chaos.

Psychic effects of all kinds increased markedly across the Imperium after the opening of the Great Rift. This coincided with incidences of great feats of faith within the orders of the Sisters and the armies that fought alongside them. Despite talk of the Emperor working directly through the faithful being regarded as dangerous by the Custodians, and Roboute Guilliman finding the

Imperial Faith distasteful, he was too canny not to bow to some of the Adeptus Ministorum's demands regarding his own purported divinity. And as the war proceeded, the Adepta Sororitas' faith was only to become more important to humanity's survival.

ABOUT THE AUTHOR

Andy Clark has written the Warhammer 40,000 novels *Fist of the Imperium, Kingsblade, Knightsblade* and *Shroud of Night*, as well as the novella *Crusade* and the short story 'Whiteout'. He has also written the novels *Gloomspite* and *Blacktalon: First Mark* for Warhammer Age of Sigmar, and the Warhammer Quest Silver Tower novella *Labyrinth of the Lost*. He lives in Nottingham, UK.

YOUR NEXT READ

EPHRAEL STERN: THE HERETIC SAINT
by David Annandale

After centuries of strife guided by the Emperor's holy light, Ephrael Stern finds herself forsaken when the Great Rift dawns and the light is extinguished. When a mysterious stranger offers new hope, the Daemonifuge is thrown into battle once more…

For these stories and more, go to blacklibrary.com, games-workshop.com, Games Workshop and Warhammer stores, all good book stores or visit one of the thousands of independent retailers worldwide, which can be found at games-workshop.com/storefinder

An extract from
Ephrael Stern: The Heretic Saint
by David Annandale

Ephrael Stern soared over a breaking landscape. Tremors shattered the crust, gathering strength as if in anger at her arrival. The abominations knew she was coming for them, and at their command the volcanic chain had erupted. Crevasses opened, swallowing vaults and mausoleums; a wall of lava raced outward, transforming the surface of Parastas, creating a plateau miles high, burying all trace of the monuments that had been there. It pained her to think of the destruction this struggle was bringing to the sacred memorials of the Imperium. It was only small consolation that they had been tainted by the worldwide sweep of corruption she had found on her arrival.

Even amongst this destruction, she had faith the shrine of Saint Aphrania would still be standing. It was deep behind the enemy lines, deep within the heart of the Parastas incursion. But it was on the highest peak. It was the holiest site on the desecrated shrine world. It would have resisted.

She had faith.

She had faith.

The heat from below grew, spiking until the auto-senses of her armour strobed with warning runes. Stern shaped psychic lightning into a protective shell around her, and she flew on, closer and closer to the blinding fire and the colossal roaring where once there had been mountains. She passed into the heart of the destruction. The land beneath her screamed. It was a roiling cauldron of eruptions. Enormous columns split away from the mountainsides and tumbled, turning molten, into the magma. The roar of the destruction was a fury that came in waves, yet never seemed to subside. The blood of the world boiled.

As she reached the furnace, the daemons came for her. Through burning air, they streaked her way, screaming their fury, their material forms torn and ragged. The abominations of different aspects of the Dark Gods charged together. The injuries to the materium had been so large on Parastas that daemons of every description had poured over the world like disparate swarms of insects. A plague united in their hatred of a single enemy.

A cloud of crimson-hued furies, barely sentient embodiments of wrath, came at her left, a storm within a storm. Attacking her right was a herald of Tzeentch, riding a chariot pulled by winged, howling screamers. The daemon of change, its flesh the deep pink of exposed muscle, held the reins of the chariot with one hand, while with two more arms it conjured the power of the warp, preparing to cast Stern into a sorcerous abyss.

She clenched her fists tight, the power building around her. She called on the fury of the warp, shaping it with the purity of faith. Then she turned, diving directly at the herald, unleashing her fury.

'Die, abomination,' she roared. 'In the God-Emperor's name, *die*.'

A torrent of light, blistering to the soul, blasted into the daemon. It howled in pain, and its spell exploded. Uncontrolled sorcery enveloped it and its abhorrent steeds. The chariot began to tumble, speed bleeding away, and then a geyser of lava fountained up, swallowing the abominations. They vanished in a conflagration of molten rock and blinding warp explosions.

The furies were caught by the edge of Stern's firestorm. Wings sheared away and daemons spiralled down into the eruptions below. The others swung around, the swarm trying to get at her from behind. She turned, her righteous anger far from sated. Stretching out her arms, holy light leapt from her fists and lightning crackled from her eyes as a nimbus of shattering force surrounded her, and then launched itself forward. The furies screamed, their wrath turning to uncomprehending pain, until they fell as ash, and the ash disintegrated into scarlet sparks of warp-stuff.

Stern flew on, faster now, rushing with the momentum of combat. She weaved around the largest eruptions. Her shell preserved her when she passed through the magmatic blasts she could not avoid. She streaked through a world wracked with convulsions. Nothing was solid. Mountains were sinking. This portion of Parastas had returned to the moments of the planet's shrieking birth.

This is your doing, an insidious voice whispered within her head. *You called this destruction upon this world. This is what the abominations will do to stop you.*

'This is judgement,' Stern replied out loud, her voice vibrating with power. 'Parastas has fallen. Its people turned from the Emperor. Now it pays for its apostasy.'

While all else succumbed, the Shrine of Saint Aphrania would not. That would still be standing. It had to be.

And it was.

The Mountain of Faith Eternal loomed ahead. Deep in the volcanic chain, it rumbled with tremors, but had not yet erupted. As she drew closer, she saw rockslides cascading down its flanks. The ocean of lava had risen to almost a third of its height. Wreathed in smoke and ash, it still towered over every other landmark.

On its rounded peak, the Shrine of Saint Aphrania weathered the cataclysm. It was a squat, brooding structure, its massive walls surrounding the dome that concealed the tomb and reliquary. The saint who slept within had been a visionary and a conqueror, and her monument was even more single-minded in its fortification than the Sepulchre of Iron Sleep. That monument, to the west of the volcanoes, was where Stern had been forced to establish her base, and where she had gathered the relics she had rescued from destruction. The Shrine of Saint Aphrania was ten times stronger. It was designed to hold off a siege that would never come, and protected no one but the dead.

Only the siege *had* come. The invaders clustered along its ramparts, their obscene forms seeming to dance in the hurricane winds of fire and cinder. The abominations had taken the fortress. The holy relic she sought was their hostage. And squatting astride the dome was the worst of the monsters to have come to Parastas. It was a bloated, suppurating, corpulent mass. Internal organs bulged outward from the huge lesions in its gut. It carried a gigantic, rotten, rusting bell in one hand, and a blackened axe, the blade pitted and oozing, in the other. It greeted Stern's arrival by rearing up, flames sliding off its viscous flesh, and spreading its arms in welcome.

'Come to me, thrice-born! Let the rulers of two fortresses meet! Come, and receive the gifts of a present, generous god.'

The daemon had a name, and Stern knew it. She knew it because of the seven hundred within her, the seven hundred Sisters and their knowledge. Because they had fought so long and learned so much of the Ruinous Powers before they had fallen, she knew the daemon too. This was a Great Unclean One, and his name was Thylissix, the One Who Gnaws. He was the spreader of cancers, the sower of tumours. At his presence, flesh and bone devoured themselves. But Thylissix attacked much more than the body.

'Accept the embrace of the Grandfather. He will never abandon you!'

Thylissix found special delight in the canker of the soul. He harvested the blisters of doubt, and the oozing pustules of despair. But while Stern knew this daemon, he knew her too. He attacked while there was still a distance between them, seeking to prise open her faith and set the rot loose inside. He offered her an obscene mirror, drawing connections between them, and then presenting a contrast. His god was always with him. His was the god of perpetual giving.

'You will always be worthy. You will always be rewarded.'

Thylissix shouted with welcome and joy, but Stern heard something quite different behind the daemon's words. She heard pain. She heard anger.

'You are desperate, filth!' Stern shouted back, closing in. *'You should be!'*

The tremors on the Mountain of Faith Eternal intensified. It was stirring to life in order to die. Steam blasted up from opening craters. The walls of the shrine shook and split, hurling daemons down the mountainside and into the cauldron.

Thylissix raised his great bell and swung it. A muffled yet deafening toll resounded over the volcanic chain. Each peal was louder than the eruptions, and sounded like a corpse striking lead. The bell swung, and the ash in the air turned to flies. They battered upon Stern's shield, buzzing and biting. Each insect was a fragment of doubt, and millions surrounded her. The shield blackened. The light became dirty. Heat and corrosion reached for Stern.

'Hear the call of the Grandfather! Hear the wonder of his promise!' the daemon shouted.

His bell tolled and tolled and tolled.

Stern saw nothing but the night of flies. She sensed the arc of her flight altering. Her stomach dropped. She was falling. Tumbling into the waiting, lethal embrace of the Great Unclean One.

'No,' she hissed. 'You will fall to me, abomination. I am the invader now. I am the threat, and you, Thylissix, cannot hide your fear.'

The flies could not touch her. The doubt could not touch her. She had lost the favour of the God-Emperor, but she served Him yet. She always would. He was the Father of Mankind. There could never be a capitulation to the Grandfather of Disease.

Stern summoned the light again. She felt the power of the warp surge through her body, her mind, her spirit. She moulded it with the outrage of faith, then sent it out to burn the One Who Gnaws.